BODY OF EVIDENCE

The yard was very dark; no lights were on in the house to which it was attached, the fence was high, and my eyes were still accustomed to the streetlights. But I could make out something on the ground, about thirty or forty feet away . . . and it seemed to me that across the yard there was a movement, another gate opening, and someone going through. There was nothing I could put my finger on . . . but something about that distant, moving figure sent a sudden shiver down my spine. "Hello?" I said tentatively.

There was no answer, though I heard a faint *clack* noise of the other gate shutting in the distance. "Sorry to intrude, but I heard something . . . ?"

Still no answer, but no sudden attacks from darkness either. I took a deep breath and stepped inside, walking slowly towards the object lying on the ground in front of me. Even before I reached it I had a very nasty feeling I knew what it was. I pulled out my keyring and turned on the mini-flashlight, pointing it downward.

Lying on the ground before me was a dead man.

"Oh, for crissakes," I heard myself say. "I'm on *vacation,* dammit!"

DIGITAL
KNIGHT

RYK E. SPOOR

Copyright © 2003 by Ryk E. Spoor

A Baen Books Original

Baen Publishing Enterprises
P.O. Box 1403
Riverdale, NY 10471
www.baen.com

ISBN: 0-7434-7161-X

Cover art by Gary Ruddell

First printing, October 2003

Distributed by Simon & Schuster
1230 Avenue of the Americas
New York, NY 10020

Production by Windhaven Press, Auburn, NH
Printed in the United States of America

This book is dedicated to:

Jim Baen, for giving me a chance;

My wife, Kathleen, for her constant support;

The "Butcher of Baen" for his invaluable help.

Gone in a Flash

I clicked on the JAPES icon. A second picture appeared on the RAN-7X workstation screen next to the digitized original, said original being a pretty blurry picture of two men exchanging something. At first the two pictures looked identical, as always, but then rippling changes started: colors brightening and darkening, objects becoming so sharp as to look almost animated, a dozen things at once. I controlled the process with a mouse, pointing and clicking in places that were either doing very well or very poorly. JAPES (Jason's Automatic Photo Enhancing System) was a specialized plug-in program module I'd designed, which combined many of the standard photographic enhancement techniques into a single complex operation controlled partly by me and partly by a learning expert system.

The computer-enhanced version, on the other hand, was crisp as a posed photo; except that I don't think either the Assemblyman or the coke dealer had intended a pose. Yeah, that ought to give Elias Klein another nail to put in the crooks' coffins. I glanced at my watch: eight-twenty. Time enough to enhance one more photo before Sylvie came over. I decided to do the last of Lieutenant Klein's; drug cases make me nervous, you never know what might happen.

I inserted the negative into the enlarger/digitizer, popped into the kitchen for a cream soda, sat down and picked up my book. After seventeen minutes the computer pinged; for this kind of work, I have to scan at the best possible resolution. I checked to make sure the scan went okay, then coded in the parameters and set JAPES going, then went back to *Phantoms*. Great yarn. After the automatic functions were done, I started in on what I really get paid for here at Wood's Information Service ("Need info? Knock on Wood!"): the ability to find the best "finishing touches" that make enhancement still an art rather than a science.

A faint scraping sound came from the back door, and then a faint clank. I checked the time again; nine-twenty-five, still too early; Sylvie's occult shop, the Silver Stake, always closed at precisely nine-thirty. "Lewis?" I called out.

Lewis was what social workers might call a displaced person, others called a bum, and I called a contact. Lewis sometimes did scutwork for me—as long as he was sober he was a good worker. Unfortunately when he was drunk he was a belligerent nuisance, and at six foot seven a belligerent Lewis was an ugly sight. Since it was the first Friday of the month, he was probably drunk.

But I didn't hear an answer, neither voice nor the funny ringing knock that the chains on his jacket cuffs made. Instead I heard another clank and then a muffled thud. At that point the computer pinged again, having just finished my last instructions. I checked the final version—it looked pretty good, another pose of the Assemblyman alone with his hand partly extended—then downloaded all the data onto two disks for the Lieutenant. I sealed them in an envelope with the original negatives, dropped the envelope into the safe, swung it shut, pulled the wall panel down and locked it. Then I stepped out and turned towards the backdoor, grabbing my book as I left. Just then the front doorbell rang.

It was Sylvie, of course. "Hi, Jason!" she said, bouncing through the door. "Look at these, we just got the shipment in today! Aren't they great?" She dangled some crystal and silver earrings in front of me, continuing, "They're genuine Brazil crystal and the settings were handmade; the lady who makes them says she gets her directions from an Aztec she channels—"

There was a tremendous bang from the rear and the windows shivered. "What the hell was that?" Sylvie demanded. "Sounded like a cannon!"

"I don't know," I answered. "But it wasn't a gun. Something hit the building." I thought of the photos I was enhancing. It wouldn't be the first time someone had decided to erase the evidence before I finished improving it. I yanked open the righthand drawer of the front desk, pulled out my .45, snicked the safety off.

"You're that worried, Jason?"

"Could be bad, Syl; working for cops has its drawbacks."

She nodded, her face serious now. To other people she comes across as a New Age bimbo, or a gypsy with long black hair and colored handkerchief clothes. I know better. She reached into her purse, yanked out a small .32 automatic, pulled the slide once. I heard a round chamber itself. "Ready."

I raised an eyebrow, Spocklike. "Why the gun?"

"This may be a fairly nice neighborhood, Jason, but some of the places I go aren't. And you get a lot of wierdos in the occult business." She started towards the back. "Let's go."

I cut in front of her. "You cover me."

I approached the door carefully, swinging to the hinge side. It opened inward, which could be trouble if someone slammed it open; I took the piece of pipe that I keep around and put it on the floor in the path of the door. Then I yanked the bolt and turned the handle.

I felt a slight pressure, but not anything like something trying to force the door. Sylvie had lined up opposite me. She glanced at me and I nodded. I let the door start to open, then let go and stood aside.

The metal fire door swung open and Lewis flopped down in front of us. Sylvie gasped and I grunted. Drunk like I thought. I reached out for him. That's when he finished his roll onto his back.

His eyes stared up, glassy and unseeing. There was no doubt in my mind that he was very dead.

I stepped over the body, to stand just inside the doorway. I peered up and down the alley. To the right I saw nothing but fog—God must be playing director with mood machines tonight—but to the left there was a tall, angular figure, silhouetted by a streetlamp. Pressing myself up against the doorframe in case bullets answered me, I called out, "Hey! You up there! We could use some help here!"

The figure neither answered nor came closer. He moved so fast that he just seemed to melt silently into the surrounding fog. I watched for a few seconds, but saw nothing else. I turned back to Lewis.

Fortunately, there wasn't any blood. I hate blood. "Aw Christ . . ." I muttered. I knelt and gingerly touched the body. It was cool for a spring evening, but the body was still warm. Shit. Lewis was probably dying all the time I was reading *Phantoms*.

"Jason, I have a bad feeling about this." Sylvie said quietly.

"No kidding!" I snapped. Then I grinned faintly. "Sorry, Syl. No call for sarcasm. But you're right, this is one heck of a mess."

She shook her head. "I don't mean it that way, Jason. The vibes are all wrong. There's something . . . unnatural about this."

That stopped me. Over the years I've come to rely on Sylvie's "feelings"; I don't really believe in ESP and all that crap, but she has a hell of an intuition that's saved my job and my life on occasion. "Oh. Well, we'll see about it. Now I'd better call the cops; we're going to be answering questions for a while."

Normally I might have asked her more about what she meant; but something about the way she'd said "unnatural" bothered me.

The sergeant on duty assured me that someone would be along shortly. I was just hanging up when I heard a muffled scream.

I had the gun out again and was around the corner instantly. Sylvie was kneeling over the body, one hand on Lewis' coat, the other over her mouth. "What's wrong? Jesus, Syl, you scared the daylights out of me!"

She pointed a finger. "Explain that, mister information man."

I looked.

On the side of Lewis' neck, where the coat collar had covered, were two red marks. Small red dots, right over the carotid artery.

Two puncture marks.

"So he got bit by a couple mosquitoes. Big deal. There are two very happy bugs flying high tonight."

Sylvie gave me a look she usually reserves for those who tell her that crystals are only good for radios and jewelry. "That is *not* what I meant, and you know that perfectly well. This man was obviously assaulted by a nosferatu."

"Say what? Sounds like a Mexican pastry."

"Jason, you are being deliberately obtuse. With all the darn horror novels you read, you know what nosferatu means."

I nodded and sighed. "Okay, yeah. Nosferatu. The Undead. A vampire. Gimme a break, Syl. I may read the novels but I don't live them. I think you've been reading too much Shirley MacLaine lately."

"And I think that you are doing what you always laugh at the characters in your books for doing: refusing to see the obvious."

I opened my mouth to answer, but at that moment the wail of sirens became obvious. Red and blue lights flashed at the alleyway—jeez, it must be a quiet night out there. Besides the locals, I saw two New York State Troopers; they must've been cruising the I-90 spur from Albany and heard about Lewis over the radio. I felt more comfortable as I spotted a familiar figure in the unmistakable uniform of the Morgantown PD coming forward.

Lieutenant Renee Reisman knelt and did a cursory once-over, her brown hair brushing her shoulders. "Either of you touch anything?" she asked.

I was glad it was Renee. We'd gone to school together and that made things a little easier. "I touched his face, just to check if he was still warm, which he was. Sylvie moved his collar a bit to see if he'd had his throat cut or something. Other than that, the only thing I did was open the door; he was leaning up against the door and fell in."

"Okay." She was one of the more modern types; instead of scribbling it all down in a notebook, a little voice-activated recorder was noting every word. "You're both going to have to come down and make some statements."

"I know the routine, Renee. Oh, and I know you'll need to keep the door open a while during the picture taking and all; here's the key. Lock up when you're done."

I told the sergeant we'd be taking my car; he pulled the PD cruiser out and waited while I started up Mjolnir. It was true enough that I could afford a better car than a Dodge Dart, even a silver-and-black one, but I kinda like a car that doesn't crumple from a light breeze . . . and it wasn't as though Mjolnir was exactly a factory-standard car, either. But that's not important here.

Sylvie's statement didn't take that long. Mine took a couple hours since I had to explain about Lewis and why he might choose to die somewhere in my vicinity. A few years back I'd been in the area when two drug kingpins happened to get wiped. Then Elias got me involved in another case and a potential lead fell out a closed window. I was nearby. Cops don't like it when one person keeps turning up around bodies.

It was one-thirty when we finally got out. I took a left at Chisolm Street and pulled into Denny's. Sylvie was oddly quiet the whole time. Except for ordering, she didn't say anything until we were already eating. "Jason. We have to talk."

"Okay. Shoot."

"I know that you don't believe in a lot of the Powers. But you have to admit that my predictions and senses have proven useful before."

"I can't argue with that, Syl. But those were . . . ordinary occasions. Now you're talking about the late-night horror movies suddenly doing a walk-on in real life."

She nodded. "Maybe you can't feel it, Jase, but I am a true sensitive. I felt the Powers in the air about that poor man's body. And that noise, Jason. Big as Lewis was, even he wouldn't make that kind of noise just falling against the door. Something *threw* him, Jason, threw him hard enough to shake the windows." I nodded unwillingly. "Jase, it's about time you faced the fact that there are some things that you are not going to find classified on a database somewhere, comfortably cross-indexed and referenced. But I'm not going to argue about it. Just do me a favor and check into it, okay?"

I sighed. "Okay, I'll nose around and see what I can find out. No offense, but I hope this time your feelings are haywire."

Her blue eyes looked levelly into mine. "Believe me, Jason, I hope so too."

2

I got back to WIS at 2:45. The cops were gone but one of those wide yellow tapes was around the entire area. Damn.

I went to the pay phone on the corner, dialed the station, asked for Lieutenant Reisman. I was in luck. She was still in. "Reisman here. What is it, Jason?"

"You know, I happen to live in my place of business. Do you have to block off the *entire* building?"

"Sorry," she said. "Hold on a minute."

It was actually five minutes. "Okay, here's the deal. You can go in, but only use the front entrance and stay out of that back hallway."

"But I store a lot of stuff there."

"Sorry, that's the breaks. Tell your informants to die elsewhere from now on. Anything else?"

"Yeah. This thing has Sylvie really spooked. She's

really nervous about this, and being in the business she is, it gives her weird ideas."

"So what can I do?"

"Just give me a call when the ME report comes through. If there's nothing really odd on it, it'll make things much easier."

She was quiet for a moment. "Look, Jason, medical examiner reports aren't supposed to be public knowledge, first off. But second, just what do you mean by 'odd'?"

I grinned, though she couldn't tell. "Believe me, Lieutenant, you'll know if you see it."

"Huh." She knew I was being deliberately evasive, but she knew I probably had a reason. She'd push later if events warranted. "All right, Jason, here's what I'll do. If the ME's report is what I consider normal, which includes normal assaults, heart attacks, and so on, I'll call you and tell you just that, 'normal.' If I see something I consider odd, I'll let you know."

"Thanks, Renee. I owe you one."

"You got that straight. Good night."

I went back to my building and up to my bedroom. I was drifting off to sleep when I suddenly sat bolt upright, wide awake.

The figure I had seen in the alley, backlighted by a streetlamp. I had thought it just moved away too fast to follow in the fog. But the Tamara's Tanning neon sign had been on its left, and the lit sign for WKIL radio on its right. One or the other should have flickered as it passed across them.

Both had stayed shining steadily. But that was impossible.

It was a long time before I finally got to sleep.

I got up at twelve-thirty; that yellow tape would keep away the customers who might drop by, and as a consultant I keep irregular hours anyway. I was just sitting down with my ham sandwich breakfast when the phone rang. "Wood's Information Service, Jason Wood speaking."

"This is Lieutenant Reisman, Wood. I've just read the ME report."

"And?"

"And I would like to know what your girlfriend thinks is going on here, Mr. Wood."

"Syl's not my girlfriend." Not exactly, anyway, I thought. "What did the ME find?"

"It's what he didn't find that's the problem." Renee's voice was tinged with uncertainty. "Your friend Lewis wasn't in great shape—cirrhosis, bronchitis, and so on, and various malnutrition things—but none of those killed him. He'd also suffered several bruises, someone grabbed him with great force, and after death the body was thrown into your door. But death was not due to violence of the standard sort."

"Well, what did kill him then?"

"The ME can't yet say how it happened," the Lieutenant said quietly, "but the cause of death was blood loss." She took a breath and finished.

"There wasn't a drop of blood left in his body."

I made a mental note that I owed Syl a big apology. "Not a drop, huh?"

"Well, technically speaking, that's not true. The ME told me that it's physically impossible to get *all* the blood out of a corpse. But it was as bloodless as if someone had slit his throat with a razor. The thing that's really bothering him is that the man had no wounds that account for the blood loss. He'll have the detailed autopsy done in a few days, but from what he said I doubt he's going to find anything."

"You're probably right. Well, thanks, Renee."

"Hold on just one minute, mister! You at least owe me an explanation."

"Do you really want one?"

She was silent for a minute. Then, "Yeah. Yeah, I do. Because there's one other thing that I haven't told you yet."

I waited.

After a few moments, she said, "All right, here it is. This body is not the first we've found in this condition. The others all had wounds that could explain the loss . . . but the ME told me privately that there were certain indications that made him think that they were inflicted after death."

"Okay, Lieutenant, but you are not going to like it."

"I don't like it now, Wood. Let me have it."

"Sylvie thinks we are dealing with a vampire."

There was a long silence. "Would you repeat that?"

"A vampire. As in Dracula."

Another silence. "Yeah. And damned if I don't half believe it, either. I must be getting gullible. But no way can I take this to my supervisor. He's the most closed-minded son of a bitch who ever wore blue."

I laughed. "I don't expect you to do anything about it. Just keep an eye out. I'm going to start some research of my own. If we are dealing with something paranormal, I doubt that normal approaches will work."

"God, listen to me. A cop dealing with vampires? I'll call you later, Jason. This is too weird for me to handle right now."

I cradled the receiver. I couldn't blame her for needing time to sort it all out. Hell, I was stunned that she accepted it as much as she did. Somewhere in the back of her mind she must already have decided that something was very wrong about those other deaths.

I went upstairs into my library, started pulling down books: *Dracula*, *'Salem's Lot*, *The Vampire Lestat*, *The Saint-Germain Chronicles*, and various folklore reference works I'd picked up over the years; I like checking the accuracy of legendary "facts" used in my favorite books. I reconsidered and put back *The Vampire Tapestry*; a vampire that was little more than a human with an indefinitely long lifespan wouldn't be a big problem; one bullet would stop him.

I sat down at my workstation, started keying in information from each book. I hesitated at first at including fictional information; I mean, what good will someone else's imagination do me? But then I thought of two important points. First, the prevalence of the vampire legend. In some form, it is found around the entire globe; there are vampire myths in Europe, South America, China, and in almost every other major culture past and present. I couldn't discount some kind of Jungian "collective unconscious" that these writers tapped into. Second, and more important, was the possibility that one of these writers was writing from experience.

After three hours, my neck and arms started getting really cramped. I broke for a late lunch, headed back towards the computer just as the phone rang.

"Wood's Information Ser—"

"Hello, Wood."

I knew that gravel-scraping voice, even though it usually didn't call before the night shift. "Hi, Elias. I've got your photos done."

"Anything good?"

"Let's just say that I'll be real surprised if we aren't electing a new Assemblyman soon."

He laughed, a quick explosive chortle. "With an attitude like that, I don't see you getting on jury duty, that's for sure. Listen, I'll be over to pick 'em up soon. 'Bout an hour and a half good?"

"Sure thing, Elias."

I needed a little break from bloodsucking freaks anyway. I pulled the envelope from the safe, rechecking the pictures on disk against the negatives. By the time my recheck was done, dusk and Elias were here. "Hey there, Jase," he said, ducking slightly as he entered. He really didn't have to—the doorway's seven feet high and he's six foot six—but it was a habit he had. Add a gangly frame, a sharp-edged nose, black hair, black eyes, and a slight stoop; Elias Klein always reminded me of a youthful buzzard. He came into my office to get a quick look. He liked them all, until we got to the last one.

"Nice joke, Jason."

"What do you mean, joke? It looks pretty good to me."

"Oh, sure, Assemblyman Connors looks just lovely. But without Verne Domingo to complete the picture it's nothing but a publicity shot."

I pointed to the next to last. "What about that one? They're swapping right there, what more could you ask for?"

"That's just a second-string doper, Jason! Domingo's the big man, and that is the photo that should show him."

I shrugged. "Too bad. Next time make sure he's in the picture."

"Don't give me that, Wood! I know he was in that shot, I was the one looking through the viewfinder."

I handed him the negative. "Look for yourself."

He stared at it. "What the hell?" Then he swung towards me. "Wood, you'd better not be dicking around with the evidence! I've been on this for eight fucking months, and if you're—"

"Oh, cut the tough cop act, Elias. Kojak you ain't. You know damn well that I only play jokes, I don't really mess with my clients' stuff. If I did, would the city PD be paying me ten grand a year? That negative is the one you gave me and it's in the same shape as it was when it got here."

"But that's impossible." Elias glared at the negative as though a hard stare would make the missing figure materialize. "If you look through the viewfinder of an SLR, what you see is what you get. Besides, dammit, look at your own enhancement. He's got his mouth half open, saying something, and he's about to shake hands. Then look at that angle. Do you put your hand out twenty feet from the guy you're going to shake with?"

"Nope." I was mystified now. Then a quote spun across my mind: *"This time there could be no error, for the man was close to me, and I could see him over my shoulder. But there was no reflection of him in my mirror!"*

I took the negative and stared at it again. "You're right, Elias. Mr. Domingo should have been in this picture. That leaves only one explanation."

He looked at me. "And that is . . . ?"

"That you are dealing with someone whose image doesn't appear on films."

Elias didn't like that at all, but he had to admit that I had no motive to screw around with the negatives. "So what are you suggesting? He has some kind of *Star Trek* cloaking device that wipes his image off film? I won't swallow it."

"Trust me, Elias, you don't want to know what I think. Since this negative is worthless as is, mind if I keep it? Maybe there's some kind of latent image I could bring up."

"Dammit, Jason! Tell me what is—" He broke off, having caught sight of the pile of books and papers on the desk.

He looked at them. He picked them up, examined them. Looked at me. "And Reisman said . . ." he began, then stopped. He glanced at the negative again. Back at me. A long pause. "You're right." he said finally. "I don't want to know. Keep the negative." He grabbed his hat and sunglasses, left quickly.

I went back to typing.

The phone rang again.

"Hello, Jason," said Sylvie. "What have you heard?"

"Enough. I apologize for doubting you, Sylvie. We've either got ourselves a real honest-to-God vampire here, or someone who is doing his level best to fake it. And with the technical problems of faking some of this, I'd rather believe in a vampire than in a faker." I glanced down. "And I think I've found our bloodsucker, too." I gave her a quick rundown on Klein's negative.

"But, Jason, isn't that an incredible coincidence?"

"I thought so myself, at first. But I've been thinking, and it isn't as far out as it first seems. In most legit businesses you have to do business in daylight hours at some point. Maybe a vampire *can* live in a musty coffin underground all the time, but I'll bet they sure don't want to. They want all the creature comforts they can enjoy and that means money. So they'll just naturally gravitate to the 'shady' side of commerce, pardon the pun. And with their natural advantages, it isn't surprising at all that one might be high up on the ladder."

"I hadn't thought of it that way. But drug deals happen in the day, too."

"But if you've got muscle to back you up you can get away with a lot of odd quirks. Avoiding sunlight might be possible."

"True. And, by the way, apology accepted. I've been calling around and getting my better occult acquaintances on the alert. They'll see what they can find."

"Good." Privately, I didn't expect much from Sylvie's pals. Sylvie herself might have something, but most of the people who visited the Silver Stake were your typical muddled New-Age escapists who confused

Tolkien and Shirley MacLaine with real life. "I'm work-ing on something here that might help. Stop by after you're done, okay?"

"Sure thing, Jason. Just promise me no more bod-ies, huh?"

"I make no guarantees. Bodies never consult me before arriving. See you."

"Bye."

It was eight-ten by the time I finished. Then I put WISDOM to work. Wood's Information Service Database Online Manager can analyze information using many different methods. WISDOM was instructed to examine the information on all different kinds of vampires to construct the most likely abilities that an actual vampire might be expected to possess. It took WISDOM only a few minutes to do its calcu-lations. I sat down and read. It was grim reading.

3

"What in the world are you doing?" Sylvie asked.

I put down the loading kit. "Preparing. I figure that if I'm going to deal with a vampire, I'd better have something other than conventional ammo."

She picked up a cartridge. "Silver? I thought I read somewhere that you actually couldn't make silver bullets; something about balance?"

"I heard that too, but it's a silly statement on the face of it. Lead's softer and just as heavy, and they've been making bullets from lead as long as they've been making guns." I checked the fit of another bullet. "Not that I expect those to be of much use. WISDOM only gave a twenty-five-percent chance of a vulnerability to silver. That seems more of a werewolf thing."

She examined the other kinds of ammo. "Well, I'll

say this for you, you have one heck of an assortment."
She reached into her purse, pulled out a small wooden
box. "Here, Jason."

"What's this?" I opened the box. On a slender silver chain was a crystal-headed hammer, handle
wrapped in miniature leather thongs, the head an angle-
faced box. "It's gorgeous, Syl! Thank you!"

"I remembered how much you like the Norse
pantheon—you even named your car after Thor's
hammer—and if you look real closely on the hammer
head, you'll see Mjolnir engraved there in Nordic runes."

I squinted closely at it, and I could just make out
the spiderweb-thin runic lines. "It's really beautiful,
Sylvie. But why now?"

"I was actually saving it for your birthday next
month, but with this vampire thing going on, I decided
it was best I give it to you now." She saw my puzzlement. "It's not just a piece of jewelry, Jason. I made
it especially to be a focus, a protection against evil, for
you."

"But you know I don't really believe in that stuff."

She gave a lopsided smile. "Jason Wood, how in the
world can you believe in vampires and sneer at crystals and spirits?"

"Touché." I slipped the chain over my neck. It felt
cool against my skin. The three-inch-long hammer
made a slight bulge below my collar. "This could look
a little strange. I don't wear jewelry often. I think I'll
put it on the wall. Or on Mjolnir's rearview mirror."

"No, Jason." Sylvie had her "feeling" face on again.
"Wear it. Even if you don't believe, it will make me
feel better if you keep it on you."

I wasn't about to test her accuracy after the last
time. "Okay."

"Now what else has your machine come up with?"

"Nothing good. The problem is that there are so

many versions of the vampire legend in myth and fiction that the best I can do is estimate probabilities. Problem with that is that even a low-probability thing could turn out to be real." I picked up a printout. "But I can't prepare for everything. So I've constructed a 'theoretical vampire' using all the probabilities that showed a greater than eighty-percent likelihood." I started reading. "Strength, somewhere between five and twenty times normal human, with a heavy bias towards the high end of that range; he can probably tip over a station wagon like I can a loaded shopping cart and leap small garages in a single bound. Invulnerable to ordinary weapons. What can hurt it is a nice question; only two probables showed up, sunlight and a wooden stake, although three more, running water, holy symbols, and fire, were just below the threshold. Does not show up on mirrors; after that photo I think we can take that as proven."

"Maybe he just doesn't show on film?"

"The legend started long before there was film. Stands to reason the mirror business had something behind it. Okay, where was I? Shapeshifting. This might have started as a blending of the werewolf and vampire legends, but most are pretty emphatic that at the very least the vampire can assume a noncorporeal form, like a cloud of gas. Changes those bitten into others of its kind, that's how they reproduce."

Sylvie shook her head. "No, Jason, that's silly. If getting bitten made vampires, we'd be up to our earlobes in bloodsuckers in nothing flat."

"So I simplified it. Actually, the transformation requires a full exchange of blood; the victim has to both have some of his taken and drink some of the vampire's. As an aside, if that happens, there is a fair chance that the new vampire is controlled by the old one. And speaking of age, the legends also tend to emphasize that the older the suckers get the tougher they are."

"Anything else?"

"Yep. They have a special attachment to the earth, particularly their 'home earth'—ground of the area in which they were first buried. They tend to be inactive in the daytime, and may have psychokinetic abilities. One other interesting note: many legends state that a vampire cannot enter a personal dwelling—house, apartment, whatever—without the permission of a legitimate resident therein. However, once given, the permission is damned hard to revoke." I put the printout down. "That's about it. Lower down on the list you get some really odd stuff—you should see the Chinese 'hopping vampire' subtype."

Sylvie sat in frowning thought for a few minutes. "So sunlight is the best bet?"

I waved a hand from side to side. "It's chancy. The problem is that while it's virtually certain that the vampire is somewhat vulnerable to sunlight, the degree of vulnerability is highly variable. Just about any vampire would die if you could stick it out on a beach thirty minutes from shade, but in the first twenty minutes it could do a lot of damage to anyone in the area. Several of the legends emphasize that an old and powerful vampire can even rise and walk about in daylight as long as they wear clothing that covers most of the skin and don't stay out overlong. Besides, I doubt he'd answer an invitation to a beach party."

"So what are you going to do?"

"See if I can get a handle on him somehow, so he has to come to me. And I think this negative is the key."

4

Two hours later, I wasn't so sure. "Funny, Jason . . . that picture looks the same."

"Oh, very funny, Syl." I stared at the screen, willing a faint outline to appear.

"Sorry, Jason. But this is not exactly the most exciting date I've ever been on."

"I'd have thought last night would have been all the excitement you could handle. Besides, we are not dating."

"Oh? So you kiss your male friends good night too?"

"Okay, then I won't do that any more." I pounded another set of instructions into the machine, a little harder than was really wise. Syl always rattles me when she gets on that subject.

"Oh, honestly, Jason! Don't sulk like that. I didn't mean to pressure you. It just strikes me funny."

"What strikes you funny?"

"You, Jason. You can face down an angry policeman, send crooks to jail, run a business, and you're calmly trying to track down a vampire . . . and you just fall apart whenever a woman smiles at you."

"I do not fall apart!" With dismay I watched the entire background turn a pale lavender. Hurriedly I undid my mistake. "I just . . . don't want to get involved. I don't have time. Besides, we are off the subject here." I ignored her tolerant smile.

"So what are you doing now?"

I turned back to the screen, then shrugged. "Nothing, actually. I've tried everything and it's no use. Either he simply does not show on any wavelengths or else, more likely, this film just has no sensitivity at all in any non-visible spectra. I can't bring up something that the film doesn't have on it." I slumped back, depressed. I really hate losing.

"Well, then, why not work with what has to be there?"

I looked at her. She looked serious, but there were little smile wrinkles around her eyes. "What exactly do you mean?"

"Well, this vampire's solid, isn't he? I mean, you don't shake hands with a ghost."

"Right. So?"

She pointed to the area in front of Connors. "He's standing right there somewhere. So his feet must—"

"—be on the ground there . . . and he'll be leaving *footprints*! Syl, you are a genius! And I am an idiot!" I selected the area in front of Connors that his invisible opposite should be in, started to enlarge it.

A few stages of enhancements passed. Then I smiled and sat back.

On screen, in the gravel of the pathway, were the unmistakable outlines of two shoes. A sprig of grass was caught underneath one shoe, showing an impossible half-flat, half-arched outline. "Syl, I could kiss you!"

"I'll bet you say that to all the guys." She looked pleased, though.

I saved the data and hid the disk away. "For that, I'll buy you dinner."

5

I tried to call Elias the next morning, but they told me he was back on his usual night shift. The police removed the yellow tape that day, and I found myself busy with regular customers until six-thirty; two major research literature searches for a couple of professors at RPI, a prior-art and patent survey for a local engineering firm, and a few simple source searches for a few well-heeled students who'd rather pay me than spend hours in the library. Sometimes I wonder if I'm doing people like that a service, but what the heck, they'll pay for it one way or another. At seven I locked up and called Elias again. He was in this time.

He protested at first, but eventually gave me what I asked for: Verne Domingo's phone number. As I hung up, it occurred to me that Elias had actually not fought very hard. According to regulations, it was illegal for him to hand out that information, so he had to have wanted me to get it. I remembered him looking at the books yesterday. Maybe he just didn't want to get directly caught in the weird.

I punched in the number. After a few rings, it was answered. Yes, Mr. Domingo was in. No, he could not come to the phone. No, there would be no exceptions. Would I care to leave a message?

"Yes. Tell Mr. Domingo that I have a photograph that he is not in."

The unctuous voice on the other end was puzzled. "Excuse me? Don't you mean one that he is in?"

"I mean exactly what I say. Tell him that I have a picture that he is not in. I will call back in one half hour." I hung up.

I pulled out several "blackboxes" from their hiding place behind some equipment. I knew that, if these guys were well equipped and had half a brain between them, they'd slap a lock-and-trace on my call right away. My little blackboxes, though, would send them on a merry chase around Ma Bell. I hadn't lost my old hacker's paranoia.

Precisely thirty minutes later, I called back. A different voice answered. "Verne Domingo speaking."

"Ah. You got my message."

"Yes. I'm wondering what it means."

I felt a faint tinge of uncertainty. Could I be wrong? I dismissed it, though. The photo was unmistakable evidence. He was playing it cool. I looked at an indicator; there were more than two people on this line. "Are you sure you want me to talk about it with all those others listening?"

There was a fractional pause, then a chuckle. It was a warm, rich sound. "Very good, young man. I suppose there is no harm in talking to you privately. The rest of you, off the line."

The indicator showed four people dropping off. "All right, young man . . . what should I call you?"

"Call me . . . um, John Van Helsing."

That got a real pause. "Interesting. Go on. Tell me about this picture."

"I have a photograph that could place you in a very difficult position. A photo of you involved in a felony."

"You said that I was not in the photo."

"Indeed. Your accomplice is, but even though you should undoubtedly be in the photograph, there is no trace of your image."

He chuckled again. "Obviously the photographer made a mistake."

"Not in this case, Mr. Domingo. You see, even though you do not appear, your physical presence left definite traces, which modern technology could define and discover. I think that you would find life even more difficult if this photo were publicized than if you simply went to jail."

I heard no humor in his voice now. "I despise cliches, Mr. . . . Van Helsing. But to put it bluntly, you are playing a very dangerous game. You sound like a young and perhaps impulsive person. Take my advice and stop now. I am impressed by your initiative and resources . . . not the least of which is your ability to nullify my tracer. But if you do not stop this now, I will have no choice but to stop you myself."

That response confirmed everything. If he hadn't been a vampire, he would have dismissed me as a nut.

"Sorry, Mr. Domingo. It can't be dropped. This is a matter of life and death. Several deaths. I'll be in touch."

I hung up the phone immediately.

Now I had to figure out what to do. I'd verified my guess. Domingo was the vampire, no doubt about it. Now what? I couldn't just march up to him some night and hammer a stake through his heart. Never mind the technical difficulties like bodyguards and the fact that he'd probably be less than cooperative; I'd probably be arrested for Murder One and put away. But aside from just killing him, what other choices were there? Lieutenant Reisman would believe me, and maybe Elias Klein if I pushed him. But try getting a warrant out for a murderer with no witnesses except a photo that doesn't show him and some wild-eyed guesses.

I decided to sleep on it. Sometimes the subconscious works out solutions once you stop consciously worrying at it. I had dinner, watched *Predator* on HBO, and finished reading *Phantoms* before I turned in.

I woke up suddenly. I glanced at the clock; it was 3:30. What had awakened me?

Then I heard it again. A creak of floorboards. Right outside my bedroom door.

I started to ease over towards the nightstand; I keep my gun in that drawer at night.

The bedsprings creaked.

The door slammed open, and three black figures charged in. I lunged for the nightstand, got the drawer halfway open, but one of them smacked my wrist with the butt of a small submachine gun. "Hold it there, asshole. Move and you are history."

I used to think Uzis looked silly on television, like a gun that lost its butt and stock. There was nothing funny about the ugly black snout with the nine-millimeter hole ready to make a matching hole in my head. My voice was hoarse and my heart hammered against my ribs. "Okay! Okay, I am *not* moving! What do you want?"

"It's not what we want. Mr. Domingo wants to talk to you. Now."

After a nasty frisking, I was dragged out to a large car. My captors made it clear I was to sit down and shut up. The ride was fast and silent. We pulled up in front of a very large house, fenced and guarded. The three hustled me out and into the hallway. They handed me over to a more polished butler, with a kindly admonishment that if I caused any trouble one of them would come back and castrate me.

I was brought into a library that looked like Alistair Cooke should be sitting in it for the next episode of *Masterpiece Theatre*. I sat down in one of the chairs to wait. I'm glad it was a cool night; if it had been hot I would have been buck naked and my captors had shown no inclination to let me change clothes. As it was, a red-and-blue running suit looked pretty silly.

Of course, I supposed that what I looked like was probably the least of my problems. But if I didn't think about inane topics like this, I'd probably be screaming.

I hadn't even heard the door open again, but a voice suddenly spoke to me. "Good evening, Mr. Wood. Welcome to my house."

I guess I was jumpier than I thought. I leapt out of the chair and whirled. "Jesus!" He smiled slightly as I did a double-take. "Son of a . . . you even look like a vampire!"

He did, too. Not the walking-corpse kind; he looked like a taller Frank Langella. "Fortunate casting on their part, I assure you." He smiled again, and this time I noticed pointed teeth. Two fangs. It suddenly seemed very cold here. "Sit down, please." He rang a bell; the door opened almost instantly, framing the silver-haired butler who'd guided me upstairs. "Morgan, bring a suit of clothes for my guest here." He rattled off my measurements in a lightning-fast stream. "And send up some hors d'oeuvres; I have yet to meet a young bachelor who isn't hungry at all hours."

What in hell was going on? I expected to be taken out back and shot. Now he's treating me like a visiting dignitary? This is very weird. "How in the world did you find me?" I asked once the butler left.

He shook his head, looking amused. "Mr. Wood, you are indeed a very clever man. But you are, I am afraid, not an expert in espionage or covert operations. Certainly you left no direct clues, but consider! From my conversation with you, I knew the following: you were a young man; you were in possession of a photo which, from your description, could only have been obtained from a covert surveillance camera; you were certainly not the police; you had considered possibilities that most people would dismiss offhand; you had either access to or actually possessed abilities to process the images on that film.

"In short, then, I had to look for a young man who was on close terms with the police, who worked with computer-enhancements or had access to them, who had an open mind, and, from the tone of your voice, who had had at least one death recently that he was personally concerned with. I think you will admit that the field of choices becomes very narrow."

I flushed. I had been a cocky moron. I had set myself up.

The clothes and food arrived; he directed me to a small alcove to change. I came out feeling almost human again and I was actually hungry. "So what are you going to do with me? I presume that if you intended to kill me you'd already have done so."

"I do not kill unless in self-defense, Mr. Wood. You are entirely mistaken in your impression of me. I have killed no one since I arrived here three years ago."

The last thing I expected here was denial. "Entirely mistaken? Are you saying you are not a drug dealer?"

He winced. "I dislike that term. I am a supplier of substances which your government terms illegal, yes."

"Then you've killed hundreds by proxy. That's even worse."

He glanced at me; his expression was mild, but his eyes seemed to flame momentarily. "Do not seek to judge me, young man. What your culture calls illegal is its business, but I do not acknowledge its sovereignty over me or others. I was long before the United States was even a possibility, and I will be long after it has gone. If members of your population choose my wares, that is their affair. I do not sell to children, nor do I sell to those who do. Adults make their own choices of salvation and damnation. I supply the means to make that particular choice. I live in comfort on the free choices of these people."

"Once they're addicted, it isn't much of a free choice! And some of them—many of them—turn to drugs because of their dead-end lives."

He flicked a hand in a negation, red light flashing from a ruby ring on his finger. "Mr. Wood, I did not bring you here to discuss my business affairs. But I will say that I target my wares to those who can afford them. They have both the choice and the resources to make or unmake the choice. I take no responsibility for the idiocy of others." He held up the hand as I started to answer. "No, that is enough, Mr. Wood. You are a well-meaning young man, and I would enjoy talking with you on other subjects. But this discussion is closed.

"To the point, Mr. Wood. I presume that you believe

that I killed your . . . friend, this Lewis. Would you tell me why I might do such a thing?"

Could he be that dense? "Obviously you were hungry."

He nodded. "I see. And can you think of any other reasons?"

"Lewis was one of my contacts. Maybe he knew something about you or your operation."

He began to smile, then he laughed. It was as warm and rich as the chuckle, ringing like a deep bell. "Come with me, Jason."

He led me out of the library, down a hall, and into his own chambers. He pointed at a cabinet. "Open that."

I pulled on the handles. The rosewood opened, to reveal a large refrigerator. Inside were dozens of bottles filled with red liquid.

"I can obtain blood legitimately from several sources, Jason. It can be expensive, but I have millions. I can even warm it to the proper temperature. I can eat normal food, though I derive no nourishment from it, and it gives me what a mortal would call cramps; but thus I can maintain a masquerade."

I was stunned. I had missed all this totally. How could I be so stupid? "But what if Lewis knew something? You—"

"Really, Mr. Wood, you can't think that I would personally kill him? I have thugs for that, thugs who use bullets like anyone else, or who strangle with generic wire. What earthly reason would I have to kill someone in a fashion so bizarre as to draw just this sort of attention?" He led the way back to the library. "You are a reasonable man, Jason. Unless you believe me so insane that I have lost any semblance of rationality, then you cannot believe I am responsible for these terrible killings."

I nodded. How could I argue? I should have seen

all this stuff without ever having to have it rammed down my throat. "Then what you are saying is that there is another vampire in the city?"

"I see no alternative."

"Shit!" I saw a scandalized raise of an eyebrow. "Sorry. But this puts me back to square one. Now I'll have to sort him out from a hundred and fifty thousand people in the area."

"I may be able to help you."

He sure had my attention. "How?"

He leaned back in his chair. "Normally I do not get involved in squabbles between my other brethren and you mortals. If they are stupid enough to be discovered, they deserve the fate that you weaker but numerous mortals will inevitably dispense. But in this case, this one's actions have almost led to me suffering that fate. So I will tell you something very useful." He reached out, pulled out a drawer, and dropped an envelope on the desk.

I opened it; the negative was inside. "How . . ." I began, then thought a moment. "Never mind."

Verne Domingo pointed to the photo. "That is the key, you see. Not in the way you thought, of course. It is the fact of its existence."

"How do you mean?"

"I have been well aware of my effect, or lack thereof, on photographic film for many years. Therefore, I do not permit myself to be photographed. Moreover, I am always aware of all mortals in my vicinity. If I concentrate—and I always do when outside—I know who is about me, within a large radius." He shifted his gaze to me. "The only beings I cannot sense—and thus the only beings who could photograph me without my knowledge—are my own kind."

My appetite vanished and my stomach seemed to knot. Who had taken the picture? Who liked night shifts? Who had argued with me until I realized I had a photo of a vampire? Who had handed over a phone number and practically pushed me toward Verne Domingo?

Lieutenant Elias Klein.

The dark-skinned hand came down on mine, effortlessly forced the telephone receiver back to its cradle. "No calls, Mr. Wood, please."

"I have to at least let Sylvie know I'm all right."

"You do not have to do anything of the kind."

"But—"

"Will you listen to yourself! Think, mortal, use that mind of yours! Why are you here?"

That was a silly question. "Because three thugs with Uzis dragged me out of my bedroom and brought me here."

He closed his eyes and drew a breath. "That is a simplistic answer, Mr. Wood. It is nearing dawn and I am tired. Now please think about your situation."

Okay, what did he mean? I thought about it, piecing together causes, effects, Klein . . . "I'm here because Klein wanted you to come after me; he wanted me out of the way."

Domingo opened his eyes and smiled. "Light begins to dawn. So what will happen if you call?"

"Sylvie wouldn't tell."

"Perhaps not; I lack the pleasure of the young lady's acquaintance, so I am ill-equipped to judge. However, she would very likely not show an appropriate level of worry. Why should you risk your present position when her authentic emotions can serve a better purpose?"

Finally the idea clicked. *God* I am slow sometimes. "You mean, let Klein think you got me . . . that I'm dead or removed."

"Precisely."

"But then what? I can't prove a thing against him

without coming back out, and even then I'd have to expose you, and I assume you wouldn't . . . no, you wouldn't."

Domingo drained a wineglass of red liquid; I tried not to watch, but it had a horrid fascination about it. He set the glass down and looked at me. "I shall have to help you, Mr. Wood. There are certain things—'loose ends,' as you would say—which Elias must clear up in order to secure his position. One is this negative. He must find it and destroy it; he can ill afford to let evidence of vampires remain. I am, of course, another."

"Loose ends . . . Sylvie!"

He nodded slowly. "Yes, she is certainly one. She knows far too much for him to be safe, and moreover she believes . . . and has psychic resources as well."

I started to stand, then looked at him suspiciously. "How do *you* know that Syl's . . . psychic? I didn't think you even knew her!"

Domingo chuckled slightly. "Personally I do not. However, it is in my best interests to determine what people of Talent exist in my vicinity, and it was not long at all before my people had compiled a considerable dossier on the young lady. Your own reaction, skeptic though you are, merely confirms my impression; she is one of the few who truly possesses what she claims to have."

This time I did stand, and started for the door. "Then I have to go! Her safety's more important than mine or even nailing Elias."

Without so much as a flicker, Verne Domingo suddenly stood between me and the door. "Not more important to me, young man. This Elias has dared to use me—*me*—as a pawn in his games." For a moment I saw, not a vampire of the modern world, but a man of a far more ancient time, a lord whose honor had suffered a mortal insult. "He will regret that."

"I don't give a damn about your stupid ego, Domingo! He could be going after Syl this minute!"

He spread his hands, yielding a point. "Well spoken; if I do not respect your reasons, I cannot expect you to respect mine. But he will make no move until tomorrow night; or rather, tonight, since we are well into the morning. He must have the police—probably through your young lady—discover that you have been taken. He believes me ruthless and willing to kill to protect myself, and will assume you dead. Only tonight will he search your quarters and deal with your Sylvia."

An idea occurred to me. "Is it true that vampires cannot enter a dwelling unbidden?"

He hesitated a moment. "Yes. It is true."

"Then Syl should be safe if she stays home."

"Indeed? Elias Klein, respected lieutenant of police, friend of yours, shows up on her doorstep with news of you; do you truly believe she would have him stay on the porch?"

I shook my head reluctantly. "I guess not."

"I guess not as well! No, there is only one way to handle Mr. Elias Klein, and this is the way it shall be done . . ."

6

I ejected the clip from the .45, checked it, returned it to the gun.

"Believe me, Mr. Wood. I have no reason to tamper with your weapon. Your captors were instructed to bring any weapons they might find; not to interfere with them."

I clicked the safety off. "It isn't that; it's just always wise to recheck your weapon before you might need it."

"Indeed." Verne Domingo touched my arm suddenly, and pointed.

From our concealment to one side of Tamara's Tanning, I saw the tall, angular figure of Elias Klein emerge from the Silver Stake. There was no mistaking the long black hair of the person with him. "Sylvie! He's got her!"

Domingo's hand almost crushed my bicep. "Wait! Can you not see that she is leading him? Obviously he has not yet revealed himself to her; she is probably trying to aid him. When they enter your office, then will be your time."

"My time? What about you?"

"I have done all I intend to. If you fail, then I may have to act more directly. I prefer, however, to let you finish the job at hand."

I glared at him, but he simply gazed back with expressionless eyes. "Are you sure he can't sense me?"

"Quite. Any vampire can cloak a limited number of mortals from the senses of other vampires; undoubtedly our friend Klein used that to conceal whatever partners he worked with. Mr. Klein will not notice you until he actually sees you. At that point, my protection will be gone." He glanced outward. "They have entered. Good luck, Jason Wood."

I gave his hand a quick shake. "I wouldn't say it's been fun . . . but it has been interesting."

Carefully, I started for my front door. I slipped inside and walked with great care along one side of the hallway. As I approached my office, I heard Klein's voice.

"Where else? Think, Sylvie! That negative may be the only thing keeping Jason alive now!"

Sylvie's voice trembled faintly. "I don't know, Elias— wait. He kept data disks in a safe, over there behind the wall panels."

Footsteps as they went from the upstairs towards my workstation; then a rattle as the panel was pushed open. I peeked around the corner from the den.

Sylvie was standing behind Elias, who was bent down over the small safe. "Sylvie, do you know the combination?"

"I don't know if I should tell you that."

He turned towards her; I ducked back just in time. "Sylvie, please! Domingo knows that negative is the only hard evidence we have! Without it we don't have a thing to bargain with."

She sighed. "All right. It's 31-41-59."

He snickered a bit. "Of course. Pi." I heard him turn back to the safe.

My only chance. As quietly as I could, I stepped through the door and snaked an arm around Sylvie, clapping my hand over her mouth and nose so she couldn't make a sound. Then, as Elias was swinging the safe door open, I yanked Sylvie's head towards me enough so she could see me. Her eyes widened, then narrowed when I put a finger to my lips. I could see her glance towards Klein as I let go. One nod told me she'd figured out the situation. She slowly started back out the door.

"Sylvie, it's not there! Where else—you?!" As Elias turned, he caught sight of me. I'd never seen someone's jaw literally drop before. He stood there for several seconds, just staring.

"Hello, Elias." I raised the gun.

"Wood? Wood, what the hell are you doing? How did you get away from Domingo? We were worried to death about you!" He started forward.

I gestured with the gun; he stopped. "No, I don't think you were worried at all, Elias. You were sure that after I called Domingo he'd cancel my ticket for you. Save you the trouble."

"What are you talking about?"

"Don't try it, Elias; I can see you thinking about moving. It must've been a shock to you when you came in and saw all those vampire books on my desk. You knew right then that I was closing in on you. You saw one chance to send me off on a one-way chase after the wrong guy; that negative. All you had to do was call my attention to it; you could rely on me to imagine the rest." I shook my head. "Even then, you almost blew it entirely by pointing out that SLR—Single Lens Reflex—cameras show exactly what's in the picture. You see, SLRs use *mirrors* to send that image to the viewfinder. I knew that, but with everything else I didn't think of it at the time. Anyone taking snapshots of a vampire through an SLR would've known something was funny . . . if, of course, he wasn't a vampire himself. I dunno if you even realized you'd made a mistake there, but whether you did or didn't the whole thing was fantastic control on your part; you must've noticed the books as soon as you came in, and you never gave a sign. And your shock at seeing them—only after you'd made sure I knew the significance of the photo—oh, that was perfect. But Domingo wasn't the ruthless guy you thought he was." I clicked the safety twice, so he knew it was ready to fire. "There's only one thing that puzzles me, Elias."

He dropped the pretense. "What, Jason?"

"Why? I mean, does it have to be human blood? And do you have to kill?"

His hands twitched aimlessly. "Human blood has . . . more of a kick to it, I guess. And when they die, you get this incredible rush, a feeling of such power . . ." He'd been looking at his hands. When he raised his face, my guts turned to ice. Deep in his eyes was a hellish red glow. And as he spoke, I saw lengthening fangs. "Besides," he continued, and now his voice had an edge of hysteria, "besides, they had to die. They

saw me, you see. And it wasn't as if they were anyone important."

"Not anyone . . . Elias, they were human beings!"

"You always did take the liberal view, Jason." His
face was distorting, somehow shifting before my eyes.
"I really liked you, Jason . . . But now you have to die
too." He smiled, and there was very little of the old
Elias in that deadly smile.

"Don't, Elias. I don't want to kill you."

He started forward slowly. "Let's not pretend, Jason.
You can't arrest me, and I need blood."

I backed away, trying to make myself pull the trigger. But, Jesus, Elias was my friend! "Stop, Elias! For
God's sake, you're addicted, that's what you're talking
about! There's therapy for addicts."

He laughed. "That's funny, Jason. Should I go to AA?
'Hello, my name is Elias, and I'm a vampire?'" He
shook his head. "I didn't want to kill you, but I have
no choice. Neither have you. It's a shame that you can't
do anything about it." He was barely human now, a
Hollywood vampire straight out of *Fright Night*. "Good-
bye, Jason." He rose straight off the floor, a nightmare
of fangs and talons.

My finger spasmed on the trigger.

There was a roar of thunder.

Elias was hit in mid-descent. The force of the round,
as it mushroomed within him, hurled him back over
my desk. He rose, only a scorched bullet hole in his
suit showing he'd been hit.

"So much for silver," I said as I sprinted out the
door. I almost bowled Sylvie over as she came running
back. "Go, Syl, Go!" I heard jarring footsteps behind
me, whirled and fired the second bullet.

The bullet caught him square in the chest; Elias'
scream shook the windows as white flame exploded
from the incendiary bullet.

"Wood! You bastard! That hurt!" As I backpedaled away, I could see the burns healing. "I think I'll break a few things before I kill you!" He ducked away before I could get another clear bead on him.

"Shit. Anne Rice failed me too. I should have known better than to trust a book with a punk vampire." I glanced around nervously. If I were a vampire, where would I come from next . . . ?

I whirled, in time to see Elias coming through the wall like a ghost. I leapt through the doorway to the kitchen, but Elias' hand caught me just as I reached the side door. "Gotcha!"

I tried to pull away, but I might as well have been pushing on a vault door. He bent his head toward my neck. I screamed.

Then it was Elias who screamed, a yell of utter shock and agony. I fell to the floor and rolled heavily away, looked up.

Sylvie stood there, holding a large ankh before her. "Back, Undead! By the power of Earth and Life, back!"

The incantation sounded silly; Elias obviously saw no humor in it. As he turned away, trying to get around the looped cross, I saw a black imprint on his back where the ankh had hit him. I raised the .45, fired the third bullet.

The heavy shell hit him like a sledgehammer, spinning him completely around, smashing him into the stove. He put a hand to his chest, where a red stain was beginning to spread. His expression was utter disbelief. Then he fell facedown.

"What did you hit him with?"

I looked down at the body. "A wooden bullet. Thank you, Fred Saberhagen."

"Who's he?"

"He wrote *The Holmes-Dracula File*; that's where I got the idea." I holstered the gun and started out of the

kitchen—I didn't want to look at the body while I tried
to figure out what I was going to say to the cops.

Elias' hand shot out and grabbed my ankle.

I felt myself lifted like a toy, smashed into Syl,
sending her ankh flying. Then there was a crash and
I felt slivers of glass cut me as I was hurled out of the
window. I remember thinking vaguely that I'd gotten
the genre wrong. It wasn't a mystery novel; it was
Friday the 13th, where the psycho never dies.

I landed badly, barely rolling. I heard the gun skid
out of the holster. I scrabbled after it; but then a
leather-skinned hand closed clawed fingers around it.
"You almost had me, Jason," said the thing that had
been Elias Klein. "Too bad you missed the heart. It
still might have worked, but you must've used an
awfully tough wood; most of the bullet went right on
through." He squeezed. The barrel of my gun bent.

I got up and ran.

I didn't get twenty feet.

Talons ripped my shirt; he pitched me the rest of
the way across the street and through a storefront. A
shard of glass ripped my arm, and my ankle smashed
into the edge of the window. I looked up, seeing Elias
approach me, the inverted neon letters above lending
a hellish cast to his distorted features.

Neon letters?

I scrambled away from the window, limped towards the
back of the store, grabbed the doorknob, ducked inside.

It was a tiny room with no other exit. I was trapped.
The door opened. "A dead end. How appropriate."
Elias smiled. No reluctance now, he was happy to kill.

I tried to duck past him; his hands lashed out like
whips, lifted me clear of the ground. He turned while
holding me. "Trying to get out the door?" He shoved
me through the doorway, pulled me back. "It's over,
Wood . . . and I am hungry." He bent his head again.

Suddenly the crystal hammer went warm against my chest. Elias cursed and dropped me. "*Damn* that bitch! She made that, didn't she?"

I didn't answer. I hurled myself towards the switch by the door.

Elias caught me with one hand. But I swung my body and kicked the switch up.

The tanning booth blazed to life, uncountable rows of sunlamps flooding the air with concentrated sunshine. Elias shrieked, dropped me, threw his arms across his face. "Shut it off! Oh, God, shut it off!"

I took a limping step back.

"Please, Jason, please!" Elias stumbled blindly towards me.

I swung my right fist as hard as I could.

He was off balance already. He fell backward onto the tanning bed. "Oh God oh God I'm burning alive Jason please!!"

Blisters popped across his flesh. There was a stench like burning meat. I felt my stomach convulse, turned away.

"Oh I'm sorry I'm sorry oh just help me Jason!"

"I'm sorry too, Elias," I choked out. I put my hands over my ears but I couldn't drown out the sound of frying fat.

"HELP MEEEeeeee . . ."

Slowly I uncovered my ears. Then I opened my eyes and turned around.

On the tanning pallet lay a blackened, scorched mummy, mouth gaping wide, revealing the razor-sharp fangs. One hand was frozen above the clouded eyes, clawing the air in a vain attempt to fend off the radiance, blistered skin drawn tight over the bone. As I watched, the skin began to peel away and turn to oily smoke.

I was violently sick.

7

"So what are the police going to do about this?" asked Sylvie.

It was the next evening. I was lying on my bed with my left ankle's cast propped on a pillow. "I was lucky. It was Renee Reisman who got there first. Between us and the ME we faked up a story that should hold."

"So what's the official line?"

"Klein was running a sideline of drugs and protection and was going to set Domingo up to take the fall. The victims like Lewis were connections who knew too much. When I was called in, I got suspicious. Klein decided I had to be removed too, came after me. In the fight, we ended up in the salon, where he swung his gun into one of the lights and electrocuted the shit out of himself."

Sylvie looked at me like I was crazy. "Are you nuts? No one will swallow that yarn for a second! One look at that body and any layman would know there was something fishy . . . once he stopped tossing his cookies."

"First, no one is going to see that body. Second, most of that department are hard-nosed realists. They don't want to believe in vampires and are not going to reopen the case if that is the direction the investigation will take them."

"Is that all?"

"Nope, there is one more thing." I nodded my head in the direction of the door.

Verne Domingo stepped into the room.

Sylvie's eyes widened.

"Greetings, Ms. Stake. Thank you for inviting me into your home, Jason."

I shrugged. "I figured I should return your favor."

"I am the final reason the ruse will work, Ms. Stake . . . or can I call you Sylvia?"

"Uh . . . Call me Sylvie." She looked at me. "Jason, are you sure this is safe?"

"Syl, if Mr. Domingo wants my ass, he doesn't have to do it himself."

"Exactly, Mr. Wood."

"So just exactly what are you doing to make this silly story work?"

"Vampires have many talents, Sylvie. One of them is a degree of mental control. I have exerted this ability so as to make the involved people believe the story as presented."

"You hypnotized them?"

"Something a bit more reliable, Sylvie. It is obviously in my interest to make this story work, as you put it." He bowed to me. "An excellent bit of work last night, Mr. Wood. Congratulations." With that, he simply . . . faded . . . away.

It was several seconds before we stopped staring. "Wow," Sylvie said finally.

"Yeah." I agreed. I blushed a little. "Uh, Syl . . . I didn't say thanks. You saved my life twice last night. First with that crazy stunt with the ankh, then with the hammer charm." I pulled it out and looked at it. "These things are only supposed to work with faith. I don't have much of that. Yours must have been enough for us both."

She flushed to the roots of her hair. "Don't sell yourself short, Jason. It was made for you; any strength it showed came equally from your own spirit."

We sat in silence for a few minutes.

Sylvie suddenly gave a little exclamation and snapped open her purse. "Oh, Jason, I have something to show you." She handed me a slip of paper.

"What's this?" I asked as I took it.

"It's a little ad I placed today in several of the paranormal journals. Just read it."

I looked. Then I burst out laughing.
The ad said:

Problem the authorities won't believe?
CALL US!
WOOD 'N STAKE
Vampire Hunters

Lawyers, Ghouls, and Mummies

⚓

It is an immutable law of nature in any business that *just* as you go to hang up the "Closed" sign, the phone will ring or a customer walk in. It gets to the point that you automatically hesitate for a few seconds before finally turning the lock and setting the security system, not because you've forgotten anything, but because you're giving the inevitable a chance to make its appearance less painful through preparation.

This does not fool the gods, however, so just as I stopped hesitating and turned the key, the phone rang. I gave my usual mild curse and picked up the phone. "Wood's Information Service, Jason Wood speaking."

"Ah, Mr. Wood. It is good to hear your voice again."

There was no way I could forget that deep, resonant voice with its undefinable accent. "Mr. Domingo! This is . . . a surprise."

I hadn't heard from Verne Domingo in several

weeks, ever since we'd finished the Great Vampire Coverup, and hadn't expected to ever hear from the blood-drinking gentleman again.

"No doubt. I was wondering if you would do me the honor of joining me for dinner—in the purely normal sense—sometime this week."

Well, now, there was a poser of a question. And given that he obviously had more than enough people to call around and arrange his schedule, it must be rather important to him if he was calling me personally. "Ummm," I said smoothly. "Might I ask why?"

To my surprise, he, also, hesitated for a moment. "There are several matters I would like to discuss, but at least one of them was touched on during your first visit to my home. In a sense, you might consider this a business meeting."

"I'm aware of certain elements of your business, Mr. Domingo," I said, trying not to sound overly cold despite my distaste for drug-runners. "Without meaning any undue offense, I don't think that I could be of much assistance, given certain other elements of my own." Such as wanting to stay on the right side of the law, for instance.

I was startled to hear a soft chuckle. "Would you be willing to take my word for it that you would find any business proposal I would make to be neither overly onerous nor morally reprehensible to you?"

I considered that. "As a matter of fact . . . yes, I guess I would. All other things aside, you strike me as a man who takes his word very seriously."

"Your perceptions are accurate. Can I take that to mean you will accept my invitation?"

"Now that you've gotten my curiosity up? You'd have a hard time keeping me away. I can't manage it tonight, but tomorrow night or Thursday would do."

"Excellent. Tomorrow night it is, then. I shall tell

Morgan to expect you at eight o'clock. Have you a preference for a menu?"

What the hell, I knew he wasn't hurting for money. "Since you're buying, I have a fondness for fresh lobster and shrimp."

"Noted. My chef rarely has a chance to show off; I shall let him know someone will be coming who can appreciate his work, as he has himself a preference for seafood dishes."

"Great. Um, should I bring anything with me, this being partly business?"

"For this meeting, I think just your mind will suffice. If we reach a significant agreement, then we shall go into the more formal details."

"Gotcha. Okay, see you at eight then."

"I shall be looking forward to it. Good-bye, Mr. Wood."

"Good-bye, Mr. Domingo."

I stared at the phone for several minutes afterwards. "I have a dinner date with a vampire."

9

It was, at least, somewhat more comforting to be pulling into the huge curving driveway in my own car under my own control. My prior visit had been rather informal, when several thugs in Domingo's employ had dragged me out of bed, bundled me into their car under gunpoint, and shoved me into his parlor while still in my pajamas. So this time I was not only here by choice, but I was better dressed, too.

The door opened as I reached the landing, and I saw the impeccably elegant butler/majordomo I remembered from the last visit. "Thank you . . . um, Morgan, wasn't it?"

"Indeed, sir," Morgan replied, with a small bow. "Your coat, sir? Thank you." I handed him my overcoat, which he took and handed to another servant. "If you will be good enough to follow me, sir, Master Verne is waiting for you in the dining room."

The manners in the Domingo household, I had to admit, had never given me room for complaint. I followed Morgan to an absolutely magnificent room, with an actual cut-crystal chandelier shedding a sparkling light over a huge elongated dinner table which could easily have seated fifty people. The panelling was elegant, real wood I was sure, and there were small oil paintings tastefully set along the walls.

Verne Domingo, resplendent in an archaic outfit, rose upon my entry and bowed. "Welcome to my home, Mr. Wood. Enter freely and of your own will."

I couldn't manage to keep a straight face, though I tried. After I stopped laughing, I spread my hands. "Okay, okay, enough. I see you have a sense of humor too. At least you have the looks to carry it off."

"I thank you. Please, sit down and tell me how my chef has done his work. Alas, I am unable to directly appreciate such talents any more."

It was a lobster-and-shrimp dream—seven different dishes, small enough so that I could eat something of each of them without feeling like I was going to put a large number of crustaceans to waste. As it turned out, small enough so that if I felt like a pig, and I did, I could make sure no crustacean went untouched. I sat back finally, realizing I'd overeaten and not regretting it one bit. "Magnificent, sir. I haven't eaten that well since . . . um . . . I don't think I've ever eaten that well, actually. Seven dishes, four cuisines, the spices perfect, neither over nor underdone . . . I'm going to miss this when I go home, I can tell you that."

Domingo smiled broadly, giving a view of slightly-too-long canines. "Excellent!" He glanced to the side. "Did you hear that, Hitoshi?"

A middle-aged Japanese man came in. "I did. Many thanks for your kind words, Mr. Wood."

"Jason—may I call you Jason?—this is Hitoshi Mori. He has been my chef for several decades now, but he rarely has had a chance for a personal command performance. I am sure he finds it good to know his skills have not faded."

"They certainly haven't." I glanced at Verne. "Surely your entire staff isn't vampires? I mean, Hitoshi-san must have people to cook for?"

Hitoshi bowed. "It is true that, aside from Domingo-sama, his household needs to eat. But it is also unfortunately true that a man can become too accustomed to a routine—either the chef to the tastes of the household, or the household to the work of the chef. Only one who is new can truly permit the chef to measure his skill."

"Well, you have my vote. I've eaten in top-flight restaurants that served far worse. And I'm sure that at least one—the grilled lobster with the citrus and soy sauce—was an original."

Hitoshi looked gratified. "You are correct, Mr. Wood. I am glad that my efforts met with your approval." He bowed again to Verne and me, and left.

"Okay," I said, leaning back to let my somewhat overstressed stomach relax, "Let's cut to the chase, Verne. What, exactly, did you want to talk to me about?"

For the first time, I saw Verne Domingo look . . . uncomfortable. Almost as though he was embarrassed. "As I mentioned, it has to do with a discussion we began the first time we met. You described your objections to my profession, I dismissed them.

"I have . . . reconsidered some of my statements."

I raised an eyebrow at him. "Oh? You no longer want to argue about whether drug-pushing is an acceptable profession?"

He cast a faintly annoyed glance at me, then nodded, conceding that I had the right to phrase it that way. "Philosophically, I remain of the opinion that your government is committing an act of extreme idiocy in criminalizing these substances. In terms of morals and practicality, however, I have considered your words and realized that there was far more truth to them than I was originally willing to grant.

"While ideally I sold only to those who were both wealthy and foolish, I discovered that this was in practice virtually impossible to maintain; some of my . . . products were inevitably being sold down an ever-branching hierarchy of smaller and smaller distributors, eventually to be marketed to the very unfortunates I would never have intended to ensnare. Moreover . . ."

He trailed off, then rose from his chair, walked over to a window, and looked out into the darkness.

I waited a bit. Finally, I said, "Yes?"

He took a breath—I noticed that he didn't seem to do that habitually, which was a subtle but definite clue to his nature—and seemed to force himself to continue. " . . . moreover, I found that I was not pleased with my own behavior, when I compared it with your own. I do not think my own people—those bound to me by oaths and by the power that makes them able to share my journey through time—could ever complain of their treatment at my hands, but outside of this isolated and self-contained circle, I have not been the sort of man I originally meant to be." He gripped the windowsill, tight enough that I heard faint crackling sounds and was sure that if I went there later I'd find dents the shape of fingers in the wood. "Many things happened in the past centuries which soured me, made me less than I had been in many ways. I do not think, were I to talk with my self of ages past, that he would be proud of what I have become; in truth, I think he would pity me. I have had no true friends outside of these, my people, for a very long time indeed. I was, despite my unchanging appearance, becoming a bitter, cynical old man. I had . . . and may still have . . . enemies who would have considered that a triumph and amusement." He turned to me. "I wish to try to change that. I would abandon this peddling of illegal substances, find some other venture to provide for myself and my people, and, perhaps, find a way of in some small manner rejoining humanity."

Other people might make a speech like that for effect; but the way that he spoke, I could hear pain under the restrained and dignified words. In my business, you often make a living by guessing who you can and can't trust. Verne Domingo, vampire and drug-runner, still struck me as a man whose word was inviolate and who would never say things like this unless they came from his heart. I nodded. "For what it's worth, Mr. Domingo, I agree with your philosophical position. I think people have the right to be fools, and that the criminalization of things like drugs was proven to be a failure during Prohibition. The same market forces that eliminated booze as a profitable black-market item here would pretty much eliminate the crime caused by drugs, if we just stopped making it illegal to sell them. Doesn't mean that this wouldn't create other problems, but I think the new problems would be a lot more manageable than the old ones." I studied him. "But I think you called me here for more than to basically admit you'd made mistakes— although I appreciate immensely your decision, and find

it pretty darn gratifying that you decided to tell me
this personally. So . . . what do you want from me?"

"In a sense . . . little more than you have already
given, Jason."

"Excuse me?"

"Aside from the words you have already spoken,
which eventually led to this revelation, the fact that
you have known what I am, and have nonetheless
chosen to leave me to myself—and have even trusted
me, to assist in hiding what happened here, and to
come here and speak with me, on nothing more than
my word." He was looking at me very gravely. "I have
trusted no mortal with my secret for a long time. You
have taken that trust and already repaid it.

"Yet I confess that there is another, more practical
need I have of you." He sat down again, looking slightly
less formal than he had moments earlier. "As you can
see, I live quite well; this involves the expenditure of
money, for which I would prefer to have a visible
source. It is undoubtedly true, however, that I am
hardly a man of these times, and I have no idea what
professions I could do well in."

I blinked at that. "Mr. Domingo—"

"Call me Verne, if you would."

"Okay. Verne, I'm not an employment agent or
counselor."

"This I understand, Jason. Yet it is true, is it not,
that finding jobs, or evaluating people, could be con-
strued to be something involving finding and analyzing information?"

I chuckled. "Well, yeah, I guess you could put it that
way. I could probably do a halfassed job at those kind
of things, but a professional advisor would be a lot
more effective."

"This I cannot argue with," Verne conceded. "However, to do their job to the best of their ability, such

people would need to understand many things about me—including what makes my situation unique."

I saw what he was getting at now. "In other words, they'd have to be able to understand why you were in the position you are—most likely have to know there was something weird about you, at the least, and maybe learn exactly what you are."

"Precisely. Now, I have already confessed that I have been a sour old man for far too long, but that does not mean that I have decided it would be wise to spread the secrets of my existence far and wide. In fact, I suspect that this is one area in which I must remain as careful as I have ever been."

I nodded slowly. "Can't argue that. Despite *The X-Files* and other similar shows, the world is not ready for real vampires as standard citizens. And the angry mob these days carries automatic weapons, molotov cocktails, and explosives." I dropped into my professional mode and started analyzing the problem.

"Okay, Verne, let's take this a step at a time. I find it hard to believe that you don't have scads of money stashed away somewhere—you've had centuries, and it's pretty obvious to me, just from your mannerisms, that you've been used to being in the upper crust for a long time. So I guess the first question is, why do you need a job at all?"

He looked pleased. "Indeed, you cut to the heart of the matter. I do, as you surmise, have quite considerable wealth in various locations and institutions around the world. However, this is not quite as simple to access as you might think. Until recently, you see, there was little ability to examine the flow of funds from one country to another, and thus it was relatively simple for a man such as myself to move from one place to another and bring my fortune with me, needing only a rather simple cover story to explain why I had so much."

"Gotcha. Transferring significant sums around, making formerly inactive-for-a-century accounts active, dragging in large quantities of gold or whatever, tends to draw the notice of the IRS and other agencies interested in potentially shady activities." This was an issue I hadn't really considered before, having grown up in an era where the government was already well in place with computers monitoring any significant transaction. Oh, it had become more pervasive in areas since I was born, but the basic idea that income was watched by the IRS had been taken as a given. Someone like Verne, who had been living for hundreds of years in civilizations which didn't communicate much between countries and who had at best spotty ways of tracing assets, would indeed find the new higher-tech and higher-monitoring civilizations a bit daunting, to say the least.

"As you say. In addition . . . I am accustomed to doing some form of work. I have been many things in my time, but even as a nobleman I tried to busy myself with the responsibilities such a position entailed. I would feel quite at a loss if I had nothing at all to do." He waited for me to acknowledge this second point, then continued. "Now, my former profession, while illegal, has the advantage of being paradoxically expected. When the government sees large sums of unexplained cash, it expects drugs are the source. If it finds what it expects, then it digs no farther. And if I can deny it admissible evidence and have . . . connections who pay the right people, it is unlikely to do more than try to harrass the suppliers. Supplying drugs also, as I understand you deduced, has the advantage of no set hours. If I wish to be eccentric and meet people only at night, well, this is no stranger than some of the other people involved in this business."

I rubbed my chin, thinking. "Uh-huh. You have this double problem. Not only do you have money of unknown provenance—and thus, from the point of view of any cop, probably crooked somewhere—you can't afford to have people look at you too closely because there's some aspects of your own existence that you have to keep hidden.

"So what you need is a job or profession which permits you to communicate with people exclusively, or nearly exclusively, during darkness hours, which has the potential to earn very large sums of money, and which you can at least fake having the talents for. Either that, or you need a way to get a huge sum of money here where you can use it openly and have an ironclad reason for getting that money."

"I think you have summed it up admirably, yes. I also have something of a philosophical objection to the rates of taxation applied to certain sources of income, but that's a different matter."

"And way out of my league; finding more acceptable employment is one thing, convincing the federal government that it shouldn't tax income is another." Verne smiled in acknowledgement. I went on to the next item of business.

"And what are you doing about your soon-to-be-former business associates?" At a glance from him, I hastily added, "No, no, I'm not asking if you're going to turn them in or anything. Just when and how you're going to get out of the business, so to speak."

"I have, in point of fact, already sent the relevant persons my decision. I will of course clarify my position to them if any of them desire it."

I looked at him questioningly. "You do realize that some of these people may not think of retirement as an option?"

He smiled, but this smile was colder somehow, less

the smile of a gracious host and more the bared-fang expression of a predator. "I am sure I can . . . persuade anyone who might think otherwise, Jason. Do not concern yourself with that side of the equation."

I gave an inward shiver, remembering what Elias Klein—barely a baby by Verne's standards—had been capable of. No, I didn't suppose Verne would have much trouble there.

"Okay," I said, "I guess I can give it a shot. I'll have to think about it a bit, and of course we're going to have to go into your skills and knowledge areas. I'd feel kinda silly giving you a standard questionnaire, so I'll just have to talk to you for a while on that—get a feel for what you would enjoy, what you'd hate to do, what you've already got the skills and knowledge for, and what you'd learn easily. Also, you'll have to confirm or deny the various limitations I guessed for your people, and how they apply to you, so I know what things are definite no-nos and which ones are 'well, sometimes, but only rarely,' if you know what I mean."

"I grasp your meaning, yes. Would you like to start tonight?"

I ran over my schedule in my head. "Unfortunately, no. I'd have to leave here in about another hour anyway—I have some early clients to see—and I'd like time to just let the concept percolate through my brain. How about Thursday—day after tomorrow? I know that one was clear, since I checked on it yesterday."

"Thursday will be eminently satisfactory. I shall expect you at the same time, then?"

"Fine with me." I got up and extended my hand.

He shook it with a firm but not oppressively strong grip. "You have neglected to mention your fee, Jason."

I shrugged. "This isn't a normal job—I have no idea what to charge at this point. We'll cross that bridge when we come to it. In fact, I have a better idea. When

I bring over the work-for-hire agreement, the price will be left open to your discretion. You can decide after the fact what the work was worth to you."

"Are you not concerned I might take advantage of this option?"

I shook my head. "You're a man of honor. You'd feel too guilty. In fact, I will probably come out ahead, since you're likely to charge yourself more than I would."

He laughed. "You are indeed wiser than your years would make you, Jason. Good night, then, and have a pleasant journey home."

"After that dinner, I certainly will. Thank you, Verne."

10

"All right," I said, "you *can* meet people in the daytime if necessary. Just not a good thing to do often. That's great—there are a lot of things, like signing papers, getting permits, and so on, that are close to impossible to manage if you can't get the principal to make himself available when other people are."

I was going over the notes I'd gotten that night, while Verne answered my questions and read the work-for-hire agreement. "Yes, I understand that," Verne confirmed. "I will certainly make myself available for official meetings in the daytime, but would strongly prefer such things be very few and far between. By the way, I admire your wording in this agreement—making clear that part of your job is to take into consideration my special requirements, while being so utterly generic that someone getting a look at this agreement wouldn't think anything of it."

I grinned. "Wish I could take credit for that one, but I stole most of the wording from similar agreements for people with disabilities." I stood up. "Okay, let's take a look around your house here. Sometimes what you see in a man's home gives you ideas—I'm assuming you keep at least some things around because you like them, not just for show."

"Indeed I do. Most things are for my enjoyment, or that of my people." Verne rose also and began to lead me on a tour of the house.

Verne Domingo's "house" was one of the only ones I'd ever visited that deserved the apellation "mansion." It rose a full three stories, sprawled across a huge area of land, and had at least one basement level (given my host's nature, I was not at all sure that there weren't parts of the house, above or below ground, which were being concealed). His staff numbered twelve—thirteen, if you counted Morgan. He seemed wryly amused at the coincidence of the number, and noted to me that it had been that way for at least three hundred years. "Therefore," he said, "you must forgive me for putting little stock in triskaidekaphobia."

"So none of your staff is less than three hundred years old?" I asked, trying to get my brain around the concept.

"Not precisely. What has happened is that, on the occasions I have lost a member of my household over the past few centuries, I have quickly found a replacement. This number seems to be suited to my requirements for efficiency, comfort, and security. My youngest, in fact, you have met—Hitoshi Mori is scarcely seventy-five years old, and has been in my service for forty-two years."

"Morgan, I know, can work during the day. So they aren't vampires like yourself, right?"

Verne nodded, pausing to point out the engravings which were spaced evenly around the walls of this room. "It is possible for someone such as myself to bind others to my essence—allowing them to partake of the power that makes me what I am—without giving them all the limitations of the life I follow. Naturally, they do not gain all the advantages, either."

"No blood-drinking?"

Morgan shook his head, opening the next door for us. "No, sir. We do have a preference for meat, given a choice—our metabolism, to use the modern terms, seems to use more protein and so on. We gain immortality, some additional strengths and resistances, but nothing like the powers accorded to Master Verne."

"This is my library, Jason," Verne said as we entered another large room, with tall windows that admitted moonlight in stripes across the carpet before it was banished by Morgan's finger on the switch for the overhead lights. "One of them, to be more precise. This contains those works which might be commonly consulted, or read for pleasure, and which are not so unusual or valuable as to require special treatment."

The other three walls were covered with bookshelves—long, very tall bookshelves. A runner for one of the moving book-ladders I'd seen in some bookstores ran the entire circumference of the room, aside from the one window-covered wall. Other tall shelves stood at intervals across the room, with a large central space for tables and chairs. Two people were there now, one taking notes from a large volume in front of him, the other leaning back in her chair, reading a newspaper. "Ah, Camillus, Meta, good evening."

The two had gotten swiftly to their feet upon seeing that Verne had entered. Camillus was a man of average height, slightly graying brown hair, brown eyes, and the wide shoulders and bearing of a career soldier; despite a strongly hooked nose, I was sure that Syl would have rated the tanned, square-faced Camillus highly on looks. Meta was a young lady—or, I amended, a young-looking lady—whose height matched Camillus', but whose long, inky-black hair very nearly matched her skin shade. Despite that, her eyes were a quite startling gray-blue, and her features were sharp and even, giving her a look of aristocratic elegance that made questions of beauty almost inconsequential.

"No need to rise," Verne said with a smile, "But since you are up, please say hello to Jason Wood."

"Mr. Wood." Camillus' grip was as strong as I would have expected. "Domingo's spoken of you quite a bit of late. Let me know if there's anything I can do to assist."

"Sure," I said. "What exactly do you do?"

"I'm the master-at-arms and in charge of security here," he responded.

I noted the nature of the material scattered around his side of the table and grinned. "And how do you feel about that?"

He understood exactly what I meant and grinned back. "You have me there. By all the gods, security has changed in the past century! At least in the old days the common man didn't have access to sorcery; nowadays, you can pick up one of these," he gestured at several home electronics catalogs, "and order up something with the eyes of an eagle and the hearing of a bat that will send all it sees and hears right back to you."

"Well, I noticed the security setup you have here; it's not bad for a man who seems to still be playing catch-up on the century."

He acknowledged the comment with a bow. "Mostly done on contractor recommendations. I'm not comfortable, though, with having anything in the house that I don't understand."

"Then ask me; once I've got Verne's problem out of the way, I'll be glad to bring you up to speed; I've got plenty of resources in the security area."

"I'll do that." he said, smiling. "Oh, sir," he said, looking at Verne, "Carmichael sent a pretty pissed-off message to you. I don't like the tone of it."

The two of them went off a ways to discuss Carmichael. I turned to Meta and shook her hand. "And your position here is . . . ?"

"I suppose you might call me . . . librarian? Archivist? Something of that sort." Her grip was much more gentle, though not a limp fish by any means.

"Ah, so I'm in your territory here."

She smiled. "It is of course Master Domingo's, but I have jurisdiction as he allows."

Meta and Verne let me wander the library for a few minutes; it was rather instructive, I thought, to see just what Verne thought of as "not unusual or valuable enough" to warrant being kept elsewhere. Even with my relatively limited knowledge of books, I noted several items on the shelves that probably would bring in several hundred dollars if sold.

The next hour or so of the tour passed without notable events—the other staff might be sleeping or out for the evening, but whatever the reason I didn't run into any more.

Finally, Verne led me down a wide flight of stairs into the basement, which was as high-ceilinged and opulently furnished as the downstairs but had clearly greater security. "And here is my bedroom."

"Wait a minute. I thought you said that room on the second floor was your bedroom?"

"My show bedroom—the one that visitors of most sorts will be told is my bedroom, if they have any occasion to ask or discover it. I can rest there, if necessary, but here, enclosed in the earth itself, I am better protected."

The room was very large; I was vaguely disappointed not to see a classic pedestal supporting an open, velvet-lined coffin, but instead there was a huge four-poster bed with heavy curtains about it. Several small bookshelves stood at intervals along the walls, along with some large and oddly elaborate frames for paintings, a desk and chairs, a fair-sized entertainment center, and two wardrobes. Besides the paintings there were a few other objects on the wall, most of them weapons of one kind or another. I wandered around the room, studying these things carefully. The oddity of the painting frames became clear when I realized they were double-sealed frames—museum quality, for preserving fragile materials against the ravages of time. Probably nitrogen-filled.

"So, Jason," Verne said finally, "Does anything occur to you?"

I rubbed my chin. "I'm getting something of an idea, it's just being stubborn and refusing to gel. I need just one more thing to trigger it. Unfortunately, I haven't got any idea what that one more thing is."

"Well, I have saved the part I believe you will find most entertaining for last," Verne said. "It is of course natural that I would place those things I value most in the most secure area. Here is the entry to my vault— a small museum, if you will." He led the way to another room, relatively small and undecorated, whose far wall was dominated by a no-nonsense, massive door of the sort suitable for banks and government secure areas. Verne placed his hand on a polished area near the door, then punched in a number on a keypad and turned the large handle. The door opened onto another set of stairs going down to a landing which ended in another door (also clearly strong, though nothing like the several-foot-thick monster Verne had just swung open). I paused, but they gestured me down. "Go first, Jason. I think you will find it more effective to see it without us leading the way."

I shrugged, then went down the steps. As I reached for the door handle, I saw it turn and push inward, as though grasped by an invisible hand. I felt the prickle of gooseflesh as I realized that this wasn't any cute gadgetry, but a subtle demonstration of Verne Domingo's powers, clearly for the effect. I felt myself momentarily immersed in something mystical, standing at the edge of ancient mysteries. The black door swung open, into inky darkness. Then the same unseen force switched on the lights.

I can't remember what I said; I think I may have gasped something incomprehensible. What I do know is that I stood for what seemed an eternity, staring.

In that first instant, the room seemed ablaze with the sunlight sheen of gold, the glitter of gems, the glow of inlay and paint so fresh it might have been finished only yesterday. At first I couldn't even grasp the sheer size of the vault's collection; it wasn't possible, simply wasn't even imaginable that so many artifacts and treasures could be here, beneath a mansion in upstate New York.

There were statues of animal-headed gods, resplendent in ebony and gold, bedecked with jewelled inlay. A wall filled with incised hieroglyphics provided a sufficient backdrop to set off coffers of jewelry, ceremonial urns, royal chariots. Farther down, beyond what was obviously the Egyptian collection, were carefully hung paintings, marble statues, books and scrolls in glass cases . . .

I stepped slowly forward, almost afraid that the entire fantastic scene would disappear like smoke. I reached out, very hesitantly, and touched a finger to the golden nose of a sitting dog.

"From the chambers of Ramses II," Verne said from behind me, almost making me jump. "His tomb was looted quite early, as things go; I managed to procure a large number of the artifacts, which was fortunate since otherwise they would have been melted down or defaced for valuable inlay and so on."

I just shook my head, trying to take it in. Ramses . . . II? "That's the one they associate with Moses?"

"Indeed."

I walked cautiously around this first incredible chamber, stopping at a huge sarcophagus. The golden face rang a faint bell, which was odd because there were very few Egyptian nobles I'd ever seen statues or busts of. What . . . I studied some of the symbology, not that I was an authority or even much of an amateur in the field, but because maybe something would trigger a memory. As an information expert, it's a matter of pride to get the answers yourself, even if it's by luck.

There! That disc, the rays . . .

My head snapped up and I looked at Verne in disbelief. "No. It can't be."

He inclined his own. "Can't be . . . what?"

"Ahkenaten. That's the Aten, and it's all over here. And I've seen a couple busts supposed to be of him. But I thought they found his mummy."

He smiled faintly. "I did hear that someone had found something they believed to be Akhenaten's mummy. Since this has never been out of my, or my people's, possession since shortly after finding out that the Sun-Pharoah's tomb was being looted, I must incline to doubt that what they found was indeed Akhenaten."

It was then that the idea finally crystallized. "Good God, Verne, I've got it."

He looked at me. "What is it?"

"Art, of course!" I waved my hands around at the treasures that surrounded us. "The art world can be tolerant of strange hours and stranger habits. You've already *got* stuff to sell or donate—no, wait, hear me out. You speak many languages, you certainly have various connections around the world, and, well, you appear to have taste and style which I don't have. You could deal in rare artworks, maybe be a patron to newer artists, and so on."

Verne looked thoughtful. "True. I have in fact been a student of the arts, off and on through the centuries; I could determine authenticity in many ways, not the least being firsthand experience of how many things were actually done. Even though I would not, of course, wish to reveal the source of that information, simply knowing the correct from the incorrect is something that I could justify with the proper scholarly logic."

"Yep. It's always easier to write the impeccable logical chain to prove your point if you already know where you're going."

"But selling these masterworks . . . I have kept them safe for thousands of years, Jason. Do not speak lightly of this."

"I'm not taking it lightly, not at all," I said earnestly. "Verne, these things would rock the archaeological world—and I haven't even looked in the rest of this vault; to be honest, I'm almost afraid of what I'll find. Stuff of this historical and cultural value should be out there for other people to appreciate. Hell, just the aesthetic value would justify putting it out there on the proper market. Okay, it's impolite at the least to go around breaking into someone's tomb and ripping off their stuff, but since it was done long ago, shouldn't the work of those ancient artists at least have the chance to be fully appreciated?"

Verne's expression was pained; a man listening to someone trying to tell him to give up his children wouldn't have looked much more upset. Then Morgan spoke.

"Begging your pardon, sir, but I think Master Jason is correct."

Verne just looked at him, silent but questioning.

"If you truly wish to open yourself up, as you once were, sir, I think this means not keeping everything locked away. Not just your feelings, sir, but those things of beauty which we treasure. We have guarded them long enough, sir." He gave another look that I had trouble interpreting; it seemed filled with more meaning than I could easily interpret, something from their past. "We already know of someone whose love of beauty and fear for its fate transformed him . . . in ways that I would not wish to see happen to you."

Those last words got through to Verne; he gave a momentary shiver, as of a man doused with cold water. "Yes . . . Yes, Morgan. Perhaps you are right." He turned back to me, speaking in a more normal tone. "Your idea certainly has merit, Jason. I shall consider it carefully, and discuss it with my household. I would appreciate it if you would be so kind as to examine the best ways for me to begin on such a course of action."

"Sure," I said, wondering if I'd ever quite know what was going on there. "I suppose I'll leave you to it, then."

I cast a last, incredulous glance over my shoulder at that vault of wonders, then headed up the stairs.

11

The apartment door opened in front of me, at least to the limit that the chain on it would permit. Two bright blue eyes looked somewhat up at me, framed by blue-black hair and set in a pretty, well-defined face. "Hi. Can I help you?"

"I'm Jason Wood."

"Oh, right, Dad's expecting you! Hold on, I'll get the chain off here." The door closed. I heard rattling, and "Dad! Your guest's here!"

When the door opened, I saw Sky Hashima walking towards me, wiping his hands on a towel. "Mr. Wood, please come in." He shook my hand. "This is my daughter, Star," he said, and I shook hands with the girl who had greeted me. "Star, we'll be in my studio—this probably won't take long, but please don't disturb us."

"Okay, Dad. You want anything to drink, Dad, Mr. Wood?"

I smiled at her; she obviously knew something was important about my visit. "A soda would be nice— ginger ale?"

"We've got that. Dad? Water for you?"

"For now, yes. Thank you, Star."

Sky led the way into his studio; his hair was longer than his daughter's, but despite traces of silver here and there, was otherwise just as night-dark. Their features were also similar enough; there wasn't any doubt about who her father was, and in this case that was a good thing for Star. "A very polite young lady."

Sky gave a small chuckle. "Ahh, that's because she thinks you might be a good thing for her dad. If she thought you were trouble, you'd have needed a crowbar to get inside the house."

"And when she's old enough to date, I'm sure you'll be just as protective."

"Star will be old enough to date when she's ninety. I've told her that already." We shared another chuckle at that. "I recall meeting you at that little show I did at one of the libraries, Mr. Wood, but I didn't think you were really interested in art."

"I'm not, really," I confessed. "Thanks, Star," I said, as she came in, handed us each a glass, and left. "I came to that show with Sylvie, who is interested in art and found some of your pieces quite fascinating. But I do have a few other acquaintances who have more than a passing interest in art."

"And . . . ?"

"And it so happens that one of them is looking to find people to sponsor—to be a sort of patron of the arts. I remembered you and wanted to see what kind of work you were doing, and if (a) you were serious about it, and (b) you were willing to meet with him to discuss it." I studied some of the canvases set around the studio. One thing that impressed me was Sky's versatility; I saw paintings which were, to my uneducated gaze, random blots of colors, shapes, and streaks, and others which were landscapes or scenes of such sharp realism you almost thought they were windows rather than paintings, and some in-between, which really didn't follow the accurate shapes or lines yet somehow conveyed the essence of the thing he was depicting.

Sky had an expression that was almost disbelieving; I realized that it must sound almost like that classic of Hollywood myth, working in a restaurant and being discovered by the famous director who stopped in for a cup of coffee. "You're joking."

"Not at all. Would you like to meet him, then?"

"If he's ready, I'll go right now."

I laughed. "Not *quite* that fast—I have to let him know, then he'll either set up the meeting, or have me do it. He's a bit eccentric—"

"That's almost a requirement for being a private patron these days. It used to be standard practice, back in Leonardo's day." He took a gulp from his glass and looked at me. "The answer to the first question is yes, I am serious about it. I make an okay living from my framing work, but if you look around you you must realize that the stuff I'm producing represents major investment of time and effort. I could do an awful lot of other things with the money I spend on my art, but my art's worth it to me." He smiled again. "That doesn't mean I'm at all averse to seeing my art start making money rather than taking money, however."

I grinned back. "Excellent. Now, why don't you just show me a few of your favorites here and explain to me what you're doing, so I can give my friend a capsule overview and he'll know what to expect."

Sky was only too pleased to do that, and I spent a good half-hour or more listening to him describe his intentions and techniques in several of his works. I noticed that he, like almost all artists I've ever met, mentioned all the myriad ways in which his works failed to live up to his expectations. It's always been a source of frustration that someone can produce something that's clearly amazing, and all they can think about is how it is flawed—often in ways that no one but they themselves can see. It does however seem to be an almost required characteristic for an artist, and I've heard similar things about writers.

Finally I shook hands with him again and left. "Thank you, Sky. I'll be getting back to you very soon. Nice meeting you, Star."

A short time later I pulled up into the curved driveway which was becoming increasingly familiar to me, and smiled to Morgan as he opened the door. "Good evening, sir. Master Verne is in the study."

"Morgan, do you ever get tired of playing the butler?"

He gave me a raised eyebrow and slightly miffed expression in reply. "Playing, sir? This is my place in the household, and I assure you it is precisely what I wanted. I have, with some variation in regional standards of propriety, been performing these duties for considerably longer than the Roman Empire endured, sir, and had I found the task overall onerous or distasteful, I assure you I would have asked Master Verne for a change."

People like Morgan gave the phrase "faithful retainer" an entirely new, and impressive, meaning. "Sorry. It's just that it sometimes strikes me you're too good to be true."

He smiled with a proper level of reserve. "I strive to be good at my job, sir. I feel that a gentleman such as Master Verne deserves to have a household worthy of his age and bloodline, and therefore I shall endeavor to maintain his home at a proper level of respectability."

"And you succeed admirably, old friend," Verne said as we entered. "Jason, every member of my household has chosen their lifestyle and I would never hold them to me, if any of them chose to leave. It has been a great pleasure, and immense vindication, that not one of my personal staff has ever made that choice . . . though on occasion, as of my recent descent into less-than-respectable business, they have made clear some of their personal fears and objections." He put away a book that he had been reading and gestured for me to sit down as Morgan left. "I have been taking up some considerable portion of your time, Jason. I hope I am not interfering in your personal life—your friends Sylvia and Renee, for instance, are not suffering your absence overly much?"

I laughed. "No, no. Syl's off on some kind of convention for people in her line of work and isn't coming back for something like a week from now, and I only get together with Renee once in a while. Most of my other friends, sad to say, aren't in this area—they've gone off to college, moved, and so on, so I only talk with them via phone or email. Really. So have no fear, I'm at your disposal for at least the next week or so."

"Excellent." Morgan came in with his usual sinfully tempting tray of hors d'oeuvres and snacks. "By the way, Morgan, have there been any further problems from my erstwhile business associates?"

"No, sir. They have found that it is not easy to intrude here and have apparently given up after I was forced to injure the one gentleman at the store."

"Very good. I shall send another message to Carmichael emphasizing that I will be extremely displeased if any more such incidents happen, but it does appear he has learned something about futility." He turned back to me. "And how did your meeting go?"

"I think he'd be a great choice, Verne. He's clearly serious about his work, and with my limited grasp of art I think his stuff is really, really good. If you want to meet with him, he's willing to meet any time you name."

"Then let us not keep him waiting overlong. Tomorrow evening, at about seven, let us say."

"I'll give him a call now." Suiting actions to words, I picked up a phone and called Sky Hashima. As he'd implied, he was more than willing to meet then, and assured me that he'd be able to assemble a reasonable portfolio by that time.

"I'm glad you're going to check him over yourself," I confessed. "I know just enough about art to know that I really don't know the difference between 'illustration' and 'art,' and that the latter is what you are interested in."

Verne smiled. I was, at least, getting used to seeing the fangs at various moments, although I also had to admit that they weren't *that* obvious; someone who didn't know what he was would quite probably just assume he had oddly long canines. "You may be confident, my friend, that I would still wish to see for myself even were you an expert in all things artistic.

If I will sponsor anyone, it will be because I am convinced the person deserves my support. Now that that is settled," he said, pulling out a chessboard, "would you care for a game?"

I pulled my chair up to the table. "Sure . . . if you take black and a queen handicap. You've got a few years on me."

"A *queen*? A rook."

"You're on."

12

I opened the trunk and helped Sky get out his portfolio. Innocent that I was, I thought a "portfolio" would be a notebook-sized collection of pictures—reproductions, etc. Artists, of course, do not do things that way. Reproductions are often used, but they're done as near as possible to full size as can be managed, and Sky had a lot of samples. He was trying to show a number of things about his work (most of which I could only vaguely understand) and accordingly had put together a very large collection of material.

Morgan bowed us in the door, and Verne came forward. "Mr. Hashima, it is a great pleasure to meet you."

Sky smiled back and shook his hand. "The pleasure's all mine."

I nodded at Verne. "I'll be off, then. I know you people have plenty to discuss and I won't have a clue as to what you're talking about."

"Of course, Jason. Thank you for bringing Sky over; Morgan will arrange his transport home once we are done here, so do not trouble yourself further."

I waved, said "Good luck!" to Sky, and got back into Mjolnir, turned down the driveway and headed home.

It was only when I turned the key in the office lock that something bothered me. I felt it click . . . but at the wrong time. The door had already been opened. Not having expected any trouble, I wasn't carrying, either. Then again, I supposed it was possible, though unlikely, that I'd forgotten to lock it in all the confusion. I pushed it open, letting the door swing all the way around and bump the wall to make sure no one was hiding behind it. Nothing seemed out of place. I went in and locked the door behind me.

With the lights switched on, I still didn't see anything disturbed in the office—which was what I'd be mainly concerned with. I checked the secure room at the back; nothing. That left only my living quarters upstairs. I went through the connecting door.

Something exploded against my head. I went down, almost completely unconscious, unable to see anything except vague pain-inducing blurs. Rough hands grabbed me, dragged me out the back door, threw me into a car, and then shoved something over my mouth and nose.

By then I was focused enough to fight back, but these people were stronger than me and had the advantage. Eventually I had to breathe, and whatever they'd put in it finished ringing down the curtain.

I came slowly awake, my head pounding like a pie-pan in the hands of a toddler. With difficulty I concentrated on evaluating myself. I could feel a focused ache on the side of my skull, where I'd been conked on the head. My stomach was protesting, an interesting but unpleasant combination of hunger and nausea; some hours had gone by, I figured. There was the generalized headache, of course. Chloroform? Halothane? I supposed that the specific chemical didn't matter, though it had seemed too fast for classic chloroform. I'd been in too much pain to notice the smell clearly, if there'd been one. I was sitting upright—obviously tied up in a chair or something similar, because I could feel some kind of bindings on my arms, legs, and chest.

Now, if this was a proper adventure novel or TV episode, they'd have left me my Swiss Army knife or something for me to attempt an escape by, but I could in fact feel that, while I was still dressed, there wasn't a damn thing left in my pockets except possibly some lint. Not being an escape expert or martial artist or superhero, I decided I'd gotten about all I could out of just sitting and thinking, so I slowly raised my head and opened my eyes.

The pain only increased slightly and then started to ebb. Leaving aside the niceties of being tied up with a knot on my head, I was in a rather pleasant room, large and airy, with a big picture window looking out on a driveway somewhat reminiscent of Verne's own, although this one was a wide drive that turned into a circle at the end, rather than a drive shaped like a teardrop. The landscaping was also different, more sculpted and controlled, less wild; Verne liked a more natural look, while whoever owned this clearly preferred symmetry and precision. The trees and fountains and bushes were all laid out in a smoothly rolling but still almost mathematically precise manner.

I was facing the picture window; off to my left were some cases of books—which I was fairly sure were chosen for show, rather than actual reading material, judging from what I could see—some pictures, an in-wall television screen, and some chairs and low tables. Looking off to my left, I saw a very large desk. The person behind the desk, however, made the desk look small. He was as blond as I was, but tanned, wearing a suit that had to be custom made because he was large enough to be a pro wrestler—six foot eight standing was my guess, maybe even bigger—but the suit fit him perfectly, making him look simply like a well-dressed adult in a room made for twelve-year-olds. His hair was fairly long, pulled back in a smooth ponytail, and his face had the same square, rough look that many boxers get, complete with a slightly broken nose.

He had been reading a newspaper, but when I turned my head to look at him the movement apparently caught his eye. "He's awake," he said in a deep, slightly rough voice.

I heard a couple chairs scrape back behind me, and heavy footsteps approached. Twisting my neck around, I was able to see two large men—though neither of them quite the size of the guy behind the desk—walk over. They picked up my chair and turned it to face the desk.

"Good morning," I said. "Mr. Carmichael, I'd presume?"

He didn't exactly smile, but something in his expression acknowledged my feeble sally. "That's right."

"I was afraid of that. As far as I knew, I didn't have anyone who disliked me enough to use a blackjack to introduce themselves, and I haven't been on any really nasty cases lately."

"Since you know who I am, we can get to business." He nodded, and one of the silent thugs pulled up one of the small tables with a telephone on it. "I'm going to call Domingo. You'll listen in on that extension. You say nothing—and I mean nothing—until I tell you. When I tell you, you will confirm to Domingo that I do indeed have you here, and that I'm going to have you painfully killed if he doesn't cooperate."

I nodded. There wasn't much point in arguing with him; in my current position, what was I going to do?

He did give a small smile at that. "Good. I hate people who don't cooperate. You might actually get out of this alive, if Domingo doesn't screw up." He punched in the numbers, and one goon picked up the extension and held the receiver to my hear.

"Domingo residence, Morgan speaking."

"Morgan, buddy, this is Carmichael. I need to talk to Domingo right now."

Morgan paused. I could see that it was, in fact, morning, so Verne was doubtless sleeping. "Master Verne is not available at the moment—"

"Listen up. I know for a fact he hasn't left that mansion—my people were watching yesterday. So okay, he went to bed. Get him up. Now. I'll guarantee you he'll be the one regretting it if you don't do it."

Morgan sighed. "If you insist, sir. Please hold the line."

Faint strains of classical music came on; apparently Verne or whoever ran the phone system agreed that dead air was no fun to listen to. Carmichael made a face. "'Please hold the line.' Jeez, I still can't figure this clown. He think he's in a fucking *Masterpiece Theatre* show or something?"

I didn't say anything; I figured silence was my best policy right now.

Several minutes later, the music cut off and Verne's voice spoke. "Mr. Carmichael."

"Verne! Good to hear you, buddy. Look, if you want to cut out of the business personally, I want you to know, that's okay with me, so long as you aren't going to rat. But your leaving like this is causing me a problem, and I'm not okay with that."

"What you are 'okay' with, Mr. Carmichael, is not really much of my concern."

Carmichael gave a nasty laugh. "I think I got an argument about why it is, Verne old buddy. Take a listen and then tell me." He nodded at me.

"Hello, Verne," I said. I at least managed to sound casual.

There was silence for a moment, then, "Jason? Is that you?"

"I'm afraid so. Mr. Carmichael made me an offer I couldn't refuse and invited me to visit him. He's instructed me to tell you that if you don't go along with what he wants, he's going to have me killed. Painfully."

I could envision the offended shock on the other end. "Carmichael. What do you want?"

The nasty laugh again, combined with a nastier grin. "I thought you might want to ask about that now. I want your contacts, Verne. You had some seriously smooth pipelines to bring stuff in from various places. No matter how hard I tried, never could quite figure out who was doing it, and you never lost a fucking shipment. I admire that, really. That's art. But I was depending on those pipelines, and suddenly you cut me off? Where the fuck do you get off thinking you can just tell me to go screw? What is that shit? You wanna go play with your English butler in teatime land, fuck, I don't care, but without a replacement I'm eating into my reserves and I ain't got supply for my customers to last more than a couple more weeks. And I ain't going to go for a supplier that's gonna cost me more or give me lower quality. So, if you ain't doing the supply end, I'll take your place. You just hand me your contacts, whoever ran the pipelines, and I'll do it from there. Your friend here goes home, we all end up happy. Get stupid with me and I'll send him to you in pieces."

Verne's voice, when it finally answered, seemed as calm as usual; but, now that I was familiar with it, I detected a hint of iron anger I'd never heard before. "Mr. Carmichael, my . . . contacts would be useless to you. When I stopped, they stopped. They no longer trade in the same merchandise."

"Well, baby, that sounds just too bad. You'd better tell 'em to start trading in it again, and give me the names double-quick. I ain't got too much time, so my patience is totally gone." He pointed at the other thug, who stepped up and kicked me hard in the shin.

I know I screamed or shouted something in pain, then cursed. I hadn't been ready to try to stay quiet at that.

"Hear that? That wasn't much, Domingo. Right now he's just got a couple bruises."

"I will need some time."

"You never needed much, buddy, so don't you even think about stalling me. I'll give you to midnight tonight, Domingo, to start coming through. Either you start the supply back up yourself, or you hand me the people who were doing the job for you, or I'll finish your friend here off."

There were a few moments of silence. "Domingo, do you hear me? I need an answer, buddy, or do I have to make your friend uncomfortable again?"

"I hear you," Verne answered. "I will have something for you before midnight, Carmichael. But if you harm Jason again, you will be exceedingly sorry. That I promise you."

"Not another touch, Domingo, unless you try something cute. His safety's all in your hands. I'll call you later tonight. Be ready." He hung up, and so did the thug holding the receiver.

"You did that good, Mr. Wood," Carmichael said. "Now, boys, you can untie him, take him to the bathroom if he needs to go, and we'll get him some food. You're not going to do anything stupid, are you?" he asked me.

"Nope," I said honestly. "I don't know exactly where we are, and I'm sure you've got lots more where these guys come from."

"Great. Y'know, I grabbed another guy once, few years ago, thought he was a fuckin' action hero. Busted up a few of my guys, tried to get out, ended up shot. Nice to see not everyone's that stupid."

Privately, I wondered. Verne was an honorable guy; he'd probably see it as his obligation to get me out of this, but it would really suck if a bastard like Carmichael got access to his drugs again.

But no point in worrying now. Using the bathroom sounded good, and now that my stomach was settling, so did food. I figured I'd just try to be a good Boy Scout and Be Prepared.

<h1 style="text-align:center">13</h1>

"Ten o'clock," Carmichael said. "Jeez, will you look at that shit come down!"

Even as worried as I was, I had to admit it was an impressive storm. Gusts of gale-force winds battered the house, blue-white lightning shattered the night, torrents of rain came down so heavily that they obscured our sight of the front gate, even with all the lights of the estate on. An occasional rattling spatter showed that there was some hail as well.

"Man, did the weatherman ever screw up this one. Forecast said clear and calm all night. Boy, that put the crimp in some party plans, I can tell you." Carmichael picked up the phone and dialed. "Yo, Morgan, put Verne on the line." He listened and his brows came together. "What do you mean, 'not available at the moment'? Listen, you just tell him he's got two fucking hours . . . Yeah, well, he damn well better be 'planning to discuss it with me momentarily.'" He slammed the phone down. "I dunno, bud, maybe Domingo doesn't give a shit about you."

I glanced outside. Could it be . . . ? "I wouldn't bet on that if I were you."

He looked out speculatively. "He couldn't be *that* dumb, could he?" I heard him mutter. Then he pushed a button on his desk—looked like one of several, probably security—and said "Hey, Jay, look, I know it's a dog's night out, but pass the word to the boys— Domingo and his gang might try something on us tonight. Yeah, yeah, I know, they'd be morons to try, especially in this crap, but people do dumb things sometimes."

He leaned back. "If he does try, I'll make sure he gets to see you shot, you do know that, right?"

I looked back at him. A faint hope was rising, along with the shriek of the suddenly redoubled wind. "Yeah, I guess you will."

The intercom buzzed. "Mr. Carmichael, Jimmy and Double-T don't answer."

His relaxed demeanor vanished. "What? Which post were they on?"

"Number one—the private road entrance."

"The line down?"

"No sir, it's ringing, they just aren't answering."

He glared at me, then flicked his gaze to the window, as did I. So we were both watching when it happened.

The huge gates were barely visible, distorted shapes through the wind-lashed storm; but even with that, there was no way to miss it when the twin iron barriers suddenly blew inward, torn from their hinges by some immense force.

"What the fuck—" Carmichael stared.

Slowly, emerging from the howling maelstrom, a single human figure became visible. Dressed in black, some kind of cloak or cape streaming from its shoulders, it walked forward through the storm, seeming almost untouched by the tempest. I felt a chill of awe start down my spine, gooseflesh sprang out across my arms.

Battling their way through the gale, six men half-ran, half-staggered up to defensive positions. Strobo-scopic flashes of light, accompanied by faint rattling noises, showed they were trying to cut the intruder down with a hail of bullets. Even in that storm, there was no way that six men with fully automatic weap-onry could possibly miss their target, especially when it continued walking towards them, unhurried, no attempts to dodge or shield itself, just a measured pace towards the mansion's front doors.

The figure twitched as gunfire hit, slowed its pace for a moment, was staggered backwards as all six con-centrated their fire, a hail of bullets that could have stopped a bull elephant in its tracks. But the figure didn't go down. I heard an incredulous curse from Carmichael.

The figure raised one arm, and the three men on that side were suddenly slapped aside, sent spinning through the air as though hit by a runaway train. The other arm lifted, the other three men flew away like rag dolls. The intruder came forward, into the light at the stairway that led up to the front door, and now there was no mistaking it. Verne Domingo had come calling.

He glanced up, seemed to see us, even though the sheeting rain and flashing lightning would have made that impossible. The winds curled down, tore one of the trees up by the roots, and the massive bole smashed into the picture window, showering both of us with fragments of glass.

I felt Carmichael's immense arm wrap around me and a gun press into my temple. Verne came into view, walking slowly up the tree that now formed a ramp to our room. He stopped just outside of the window. "Put the gun down, Carmichael," he said, softly.

"You . . . whatever the hell you're doing, you just fucking cut it out, or you can scrape up Wood's brains with a spatula!" Carmichael shouted.

I wondered why the heck Verne wasn't doing something more. Then it clicked for me. "Come on inside, Verne," I said. "We were just talking about you."

With my invitation, I saw a deadly cold smile cross his face, one that showed sharper, whiter teeth than I'd seen before. "Why, thank you, Jason. I do believe I shall."

The two thugs charged Verne; with a single backhanded blow he sent both of them tumbling across the floor, fetching up unconscious against the back wall.

Carmichael's hand spasmed on the gun.

Nothing happened. I felt, rather than saw, him straining to pull a trigger that had become as immovable as a mountain. Verne continued towards me. "Put my friend down now, Carmichael," he said, in that same dangerously soft tone.

Carmichael, completely unnerved, tried to break my neck. But he found that his arms wouldn't cooperate. I squirmed, managed to extricate myself from his frozen grip, and backed away.

Now Verne allowed Carmichael to move. Deprived of me for a hostage, the huge man grabbed up the solid mahogany chair and swung it with all his might.

Made of wood, the chair was one of the few weapons he could've chosen that might have been able to hurt Verne. But to make it work, he also had to hit the ancient vampire, and Verne was quite aware of what he was doing.

One of the aristocratic hands came up, caught the chair and stopped it as easily as if it had been a pillow swung by a child, and the other whipped out and grasped Carmichael by the neck, lifting him from the ground with utterly negligible effort.

"You utter fool. Were you not warned to leave me and mine alone? I would have ignored you, Carmichael. I would have allowed you to live out your squalid little life without interference, if only you had the sense to let go. Now what shall I do? If I release you, doubtless you shall try something even more foolish, will you not?

Purple in the face, Carmichael struggled with that grip, finding it as immovable as though cast in iron. He shook his head desperately.

"Oh? And should I trust you? The world would be better off with you dead. Certainly for daring to strike in such a cowardly fashion I should have you killed."

"No, Verne."

He looked at me. "You would have me spare him?"

"Sure. Killing him will force the cops to investigate. You haven't killed anyone yet, have you?"

He shook his head. "No. Battered, unconscious, and so on, but none of his people are dead, as of now."

"Then leave it. I think he's got the point. It's not like he'd be believed if he told this one, and he can't afford the cops to come in anyway; even if they tied something to you, they'd also get stuff on him."

Verne gave an elaborate shrug, done as smoothly as though he was not actually holding three hundred pounds of drug lord in one hand. "As you will, then. I, also, prefer not to kill, even such scum as this." He let Carmichael drop. "But remember this well, Carmichael. I never wish to hear your name again. I do not ever want to know you exist again. If you, or anyone in your control or working for you in any way, interferes with my life or that of my friends again, I shall kill you . . . in such a manner that you will wish that you had killed yourself first. Believe me. I shall not warn you a third time. This is your final chance."

Carmichael was ashen. "I gotcha. I won't. You won't ever hear from me again, Domingo, I promise."

"Good." Verne turned to me. "My apologies, Jason.

It never even occurred to me that you might be in danger. Let me get you home."

Outside, the storm was already fading away, as though it had never been.

14

"How did you find me?"

Verne and I were comfortably seated in his study. He smiled slightly. "I have always known roughly where Carmichael lived, just as he always knew where I lived. Once I arrived in the general area, it was simple to sense your presence and follow it."

"Thanks."

"No need to thank me, Jason. It was my fault entirely that you were involved. I should have realized that once he found my household impenetrable, he would look for anyone outside that was connected to me."

"Maybe you should, but so should I. Heck, you hadn't *had* anyone 'outside' connected to you for so long that I'm not surprised you sorta forgot."

"For far too long, but I thank you for your understanding."

"You think he'll keep his hands off from now on?"

Verne gave that cold smile again. "Oh, yes, I assure you. I was not concerned with the niceties of civilized behavior at that point, Jason. I made sure that he was, shall we say, thinking very clearly. He knows precisely what would happen to him if he ever crosses me again. And as you pointed out, the authorities won't believe him even if he tells his story, nor would it do him much good if they did."

"So how did your interview with Sky go?"

"Excellently well," he replied, offering me a refill

on the champagne, which I declined. "Your casual evaluation was, as far as it went, accurate. Mr. Hashima is a true artist, a dedicated one, and highly talented in several ways. I will have no qualms about supporting him fully. He is naturally a bit cautious—I do seem to him to be a bit too good to be true—but I am sure that we shall get past this minor difficulty."

I sipped, appreciating the unique taste that a real champagne offers. "And the antiquities?"

Verne grinned, a warm smile that lit the room. "As usual, you and Morgan are right. I shall be donating, or selling, many of the items in question to people who will both appreciate them and be willing to place them on proper display. Some discreet inquiries have already elicited several interested responses, and I expect several archaeologists to visit in a few weeks in order to authenticate, insofar as is possible, the artifacts and prepare a preliminary assessment. I have already decided to send Akhenaten, at least, directly to Egypt. Let the Sun Pharoah return to his home." He raised his own red-glinting glass in salute. "My thanks, Jason, again. You have indeed found something that I shall enjoy doing, something which will contribute to the world as well. And you have given me your friendship, which I value perhaps even more."

I managed, I think, to keep from blushing, although I do tend to do that when praised extravagantly. "It was my pleasure, really. Well, aside from being kidnapped, but that wasn't completely in your control. I just hope he has bad dreams about you whenever he goes to sleep."

"I assure you, your hope will be more than adequately fulfilled, Jason," Verne said, with the expression of someone with a small secret.

"Why?"

"As I implied, I was quite capable of hearing his

thoughts when I extorted certain promises from him, and discovered one quite serendipitous fact." He paused for me to urge him to finish, and then said, "Many people are afraid of various things, real and otherwise.

"It turns out that Mr. Carmichael's greatest and most secret fear . . . is vampires."

I laughed out loud. "Well, I'll drink to that!"

Photo Finish

15

When I can't talk and can't act and can't work . . . I drive. I cruised down the various highways—the Northway, then part of the Thruway, 787, back to I-90—the windows wide open and the wind roaring at sixty-five. Even so, I barely felt any cooler; for sheer miserable muggy heat, it's hard to beat the worst summer days of Albany, New York, and its environs, which unfortunately includes Morgantown.

How long I was out there driving I wasn't sure. For a while I just tried to follow the moon as it rose slowly, round and white. It was the flashing red lights that finally drew my attention back down to earth.

No, they weren't chasing me—I wasn't speeding; there were two police cars up ahead and flares in the road. I slowed and started to go around them; then I saw a familiar, slender figure standing at one car. I pulled up just ahead of the squad car. "What's up, Renee?" I asked.

She jumped and her hand twitched towards her gun. "Jesus! I didn't even hear you come up."

That was weird in itself. "Must be something pretty heavy if you didn't notice Mjolnir pulling in."

She gestured. "Take a look if you want. Just don't go beyond the tape. We're still working here."

I went down the steep, grassy embankment carefully, finally pulling out my penlight to pick my way down. Despite the moon it was pitchy dark, and the high, jagged pines blocked out what feeble light there was; at least it was cooler under the trees. The slope leveled out, and the light from the crime scene started brightening. The police had set up several portable floods and the area was almost bright as day. I stopped just at the tape.

At first it just looked like someone had stood near the middle of the clearing and spun around while holding a can of red-brown paint. Then one of the investigators moved to one side.

A body was sprawled, spread-eagled in the center of the clearing. The green eyes stared sightlessly upward and the mouth hung open in a frozen scream. His throat had been torn out. The charcoal-gray suit was flung wide open, the white shirt now soaked in red-brown clotting blood where his gut was ripped open. My stomach gave a sudden twist as my gaze reached his waist.

Something had torn his legs, still in the pant legs, off at the hip; then that something had stripped every ounce of meat off the bones and laid the bones carefully back, to gleam whitely where the legs had been.

I got my stomach under control. A few months ago I might have lost it, but since then I'd watched a vampire fry under a hundred sunlamps; that's about as gross as it gets.

Still, it was an ugly sight, and I felt pretty shaky as I climbed back up the hill. "Jesus Christ, Renee! What kind of a sicko does things like that?"

She shook her head. "That's what we'd like to know."

"Who was he?" I asked.

"ID found on him says he's a Gerald Brandeis of Albany, New York. ID also says he's Morgan Steinbeck of Hartford, Connecticut. His last ID says he's Hamilton Fredericks of Washington, DC; also says he's a Fed."

That got my attention. "Fed? What kind of Fed?"

She glanced hard at me. I made a zipped-lips motion. I may not be with the police, but they make a lot of use of my agency and I've done them a lot of favors. Renee in particular knew she could trust me. She nodded. "Okay, but make sure you keep it zipped. His ID says he's NSA, Special Division. Occupation is just 'Special Agent.' His Hartford ID makes him an insurance investigator for Aetna; the one for Brandeis gives him IRS status."

I whistled. "One heavy hitter, that's for sure. Was he carrying, and if so did he get off any shots?"

"Answer is yes to both." She pointed inside her squad car. I glanced in, could just make out a Beretta 9mm. "Smell indicates it was fired just recently and we found three shell casings. With all the blood around we haven't been able to tell if he hit anything offhand. We're trying to find the bullets, but in that sandy-soiled forest chances of getting all three is slim."

A blue-flashing vehicle pulled up; the medical examiner's office. He got out and nodded to me, turned to Renee. "Your people done?"

"With the body, yeah. But ask the other officers to direct you, we're nowhere near finished with the site yet and we don't want anything here messed up." The ME gestured and he and his assistants started down the hill.

"How'd you get on to this?" I asked Renee.

She looked uncomfortable. "Someone called us."

I could tell there was something bothering her. "Someone who found the body?"

She shook her head.

"Then what? Come on, Renee."

She shrugged. "The station got a call from someone at 7:40 P.M. who claimed to have left a body at this location. The operator said it sounded male, but kind of deep and strange. He didn't stay on long enough to trace."

"That is weird. I'd assume he didn't give a name."

"You'd assume wrong." Her face was grim. "He gave a name, all right.

"The name was Vlad Dracul."

16

Red liquid swirled warmly in the crystal glass, throwing off crimson highlights. Verne Domingo sipped. I swallowed some of my ginger ale, noticing how little I was affected these days by the knowledge that Verne was drinking blood.

"Why doesn't it clot?" I asked idly.

"Heparin, my friend. A standard anticoagulant."

"Doesn't that give you any problems?"

His warm chuckle rolled out. "Not in the least, Jason. Nor does anything else within the blood. Disease and toxins cannot harm me. It does change the taste somewhat, and on occasion I do need some fresh blood; but that, too, can be arranged. Enough of these pleasantries, Jason. Tell me what is bothering you."

"An awful lot of things, really. This has been the kind of day that makes me think I should have just slept on to tomorrow." I put the glass down and fiddled with my keys. "I really don't want to bother you, either. I guess any problems I have would seem pretty insignificant to you anyway."

"Perhaps not, my friend." He took another sip. "I am

many centuries old, that is true, and such a perspective makes many mortal concerns seem at best amusing conceits. But the affairs of the heart, and the concerns of a friend, these things are eternal. Those . . . immortals who lose sight of their basic humanity become as was your friend Elias Klein."

Klein had been a damn good cop who also turned out to be a vampire; he'd tried to frame Verne Domingo for the killings Elias was responsible for, and when I'd gotten too close to the truth he'd gotten me to go after Domingo. Fortunately for me, though Domingo was indeed a drug runner, he also had a code of honor and knew what the real score was. With his help I'd finally figured out that Elias was behind it all. Elias almost killed me before I trapped him in a tanning booth.

He put the glass down. "Truly, Jason. I am interested. It is a rare thing for me, remember, to again think of, and take part in, the ordinary things of humanity."

That much was true. "Well, first, I had to give a speech to a bunch of high school kids on information science. That wouldn't have been so bad except that one of them had seen that 'Paranormal Investigators' ad that Sylvie put in the psychic journals. I had my fill of Ghostbuster and Buffy jokes long ago."

"Understandable. Go on."

"Then I get back and Sylvie wants to talk to me." I hesitated.

He smiled. He probably meant it to comfort me, but the kindly effect was slightly offset by the sight of his fangs. "I can guess, my friend. The *affaire d'amour*, eh? And you are, I have noticed, a bit uncomfortable with the subject."

I stared carefully at my drink. "That obvious, huh?"

"Quite." He raised his glass and drank. "A word of

advice, if you will take it? Women are indeed different from men in many ways; but both like things that are certain and predictable. If you do not intend a romantic involvement with the young lady, then comport yourself accordingly. I know you, my young friend. You are attracted to her, but at the same time I can sense that you are, to put it bluntly, petrified at the thought of such an involvement. When she demands a decision, she is not telling you to either become involved with her or she will leave; she is telling you to treat her as either lover or simple friend, not something of each. It may be easy for you to behave as your impulses lead; it is hard on her."

I stared harder at my glass. That was a cutting analysis. I hate having to see myself like that. But he was right. "Sylvie . . . she's different from everyone else. It's strange, really. You intimidate me a lot less than she does."

Verne laughed. "Now that *is* odd, my friend. I agree, most certainly, that the lady is different. She has a Power which is rare, rarer even than you or she realize, especially in this day and age. But for a man who has dueled one of the Undead and emerged the victor, a talented young lady should hardly be a great threat." His smile softened. "It seems to me that, just perhaps, the reason is that she is more precious to you than any others because of this talent—she sees within the souls of those about her, and thus you know she accepts what you are more fully than anyone else living could. To a bachelor such as yourself, she is indeed a grave threat."

I couldn't restrain a nervous laugh of my own. "I couldn't be that cliched, could I?"

The old vampire smiled again. "I am afraid, my friend, that we are all too often the cliches of our times. I am only unusual because I have outlived all those who would recognize me. Yet, in your own fiction, I have found myself being stereotyped once more." He finished the glass of blood and set it down. "Was there anything else, Jason? Though I will admit that ridicule followed by friendship troubles is quite enough to make a bad day, I suspect something worse would be needed to make you come here."

I nodded. "You could say that." In a few sentences I outlined the horror in the clearing. "So you see I had to come here."

He raised an eyebrow as he finished his glass. "I don't quite see that you had to come here."

"Reisman may be thinking psycho right now, but that's because your little hypnotism job, or whatever you call it, keeps her from remembering that there's a local vampire who could do that to someone a heckuva lot easier than an ordinary nut. And since the guy was a Fed . . . I had to find out from you if you did have him killed."

His lips tightened. "You offend me, Jason. Once before you suspected me of being a murderer, but then I had been well framed for the part. Now you know me, and yet you would think I would kill someone in such a grotesque way?"

"Look, I'm sorry, Verne. But it's a question I have to ask because Reisman *can't* ask it. I don't believe it. But Elias knew you were a drug-runner, and though we conveniently made that disappear when we did the great vampire coverup, Renee Reisman could easily find it out again, and then she would be up here grilling you. Even though you've changed your profession since, the fact that you were ever involved in that kind of thing won't look good." He sat back slowly, and I relaxed a bit. Pissing a vampire off isn't the way to ensure a long life—what he'd done to Carmichael's estate had shown that all too well. "I did have another couple of reasons. I thought you might know something, maybe about another vampire that for some ungodly reason decided to move here."

He shook his head, hesitated a moment, then spoke. "As you know, vampires are one of the few sorts of beings that I cannot sense automatically. Unless your hypothetical newcomer were to introduce himself. I'm afraid that I would have no better idea than you of his presence. Besides that, it stretches the bounds of reason to suppose that three vampires would be found in such close proximity." He chuckled slightly. "We are a rare race; were the environmentalists aware of us, I would not be surprised to find us on an endangered species list. I am still somewhat puzzled by Klein's presence; he obviously became a vampire relatively recently, yet his maker seemed unconcerned with either Klein's behavior or survival."

I raised an eyebrow. "You mean his maker might have objected to what he did?"

Verne nodded. "As a general rule, they try not to make waves, so to speak, for other beings that live in the twilight world between your civilization's 'reality' and the lands of myth. And, not to sound overly egotistical, I am an extremely well-known member of that group. I would have expected his maker to be extremely concerned about annoying me by involving me in the manner Klein did. And, indeed, if I discover who was responsible for making him and leaving him uncontrolled, I will . . . have a talk with that person."

"We never did find out how or why Klein became a vampire; couldn't this killing be due to whoever Klein's maker was?"

Verne rubbed his chin thoughtfully. "It is possible, of course. But a vampire who had decided on such a bizarre method of killing . . . I find it difficult to believe such a nosferatu would waste so much blood.

But you said 'a couple' of other reasons. What was the other?"

"The murderer apparently phoned headquarters . . . and he gave his name as Vlad Dracul."

I would never have believed it was possible, but the blood drained straight out of Verne's face, leaving him literally white as paper. "*Vlad Dracul* . . . that is not possible. It *must* not be possible." His voice was a whisper. I felt gooseflesh rising on my arms; Verne sounded *afraid*.

I didn't even want to imagine what could scare him. "Of course it's impossible. Vlad Tepes, the Dracula of legend, died a long, long time ago." Another thought occurred to me. "Unless . . . given the initials . . . you were him."

He made a cutting gesture with his hand, his ruby ring flashing like a warning. He stepped to the window; for several minutes he stared out at the moonlit landscape. "I'd rather not discuss this now, Jason. I must make some inquiries." He turned back to me. "I'm sorry to cut this short, but you'll have to leave now."

One look was enough to convince me not to argue. "Okay, Verne. Can you just tell me one thing?"

"Perhaps."

"Is it another vampire? Is that what you think?"

A very faint, eerie smile crossed his face. My skin prickled anew. "A vampire? Oh, no, not a vampire."

That smile stayed with me all the way home.

17

The door opened. "Jason!" Sylvie said, looking surprised.

"Hi, Syl. Can I come in?"

"Sure. Watch out for the books on the floor, I'm rearranging the library."

I stepped in. I noticed again the odd, warm smell of her house; the dusty, comfortable scent of old books blended with a faint tinge of kitchen spices and old-fashioned perfume, a smell that didn't fit someone as young and gorgeous as Syl—except that, somehow, it did fit, because it was Sylvie's house. Sylvie stepped ahead of me and carefully lifted a stack of books off a large chair.

"I suppose I should apologize, Jason. I was pretty hard on you."

"No, Syl, you were right." I sat down; she took the arm of the couch right next to me. "I've been trying to have it both ways and it doesn't work. I can't flirt with you half the time and then expect you to act just like a friend the other half. You can't just switch your behavior to match whatever my mood is, and even if you could it's wrong for me to expect you to."

"I know, Jason," she said gently. She put her hand on my shoulder. "I'm the person you've practically told your life story to, remember? I'm only a little surprised that you've understood yourself so quickly."

"It wasn't me, really. Someone who has better perception than I do held a mirror up to my face."

She shuddered slightly. "It was Domingo, wasn't it? You'd have named anyone else."

"Yeah. Syl, why are you so bothered by him?"

She stared at me, wide-eyed. "Why am I bothered by him? He's a *vampire*! The question should be why you have anything to do with him! I'm gone for a week or so, and when I get back I find you've gone from turning up your nose at the drug-runner to being his best buddy! For that matter," she frowned, "why does he have anything to do with you? I still don't understand why he let us remember. It sure would have been simpler for him to make *all* of us forget."

"I've gotten to know him since. He's *lonely*, Syl! Just think about it for a minute. Here you are, immortal, for most purposes invulnerable, with all these super-human powers, and at the same time you don't dare mention it to anyone! I think he got to the point that, when he realized that I wasn't all that scared of him, he just couldn't make himself do it. He needs some-one he can talk to, someone who knows what he is and still will treat him like a person.

"Also, that's smugg*led* drugs, not smuggles. Those stories aren't just for show—he really has become an art and artifact expert." I hadn't gone over the entire story before with Syl, and didn't want to muddy the waters right now.

Syl's face was serious now. She's very empathic; I could see that she understood. "But why did he leave me with my memory?"

I grinned wryly. "Because I told him that if he even thought about messing with your mind I would ham-mer a spruce through him! He knew I meant it, too. I could barely accept him mind-twisting acquaintan-ces like the coroner; no way would I let him mess with my friends."

"You let him do it to Reisman."

"Nope. Renee told him to do it. She said that she would be better off not knowing, and it would help her carry conviction in the story we cooked up."

Syl shook her head. "It won't work, Jason. You're telling me you threatened him off? He could have had you dumped in a river anytime."

"I know. He respected my loyalty, I think. Besides, I still have the original evidence against him, plus Elias' old files. Then, later on, well, we became friends." I looked at her. "I also think he hoped you would visit him. He speaks very highly of you."

She looked surprised at that, then thoughtful. "Jason,

why were you there yesterday evening? I know it wasn't just to talk about your love life."

"You're right." I gave her the whole story along with everything Verne had said. Just as I finished, the phone rang. It was Lieutenant Reisman. She was calling from a pay phone, so I took the number and called her back. "What's up, Renee?"

"Remember our Federal friend? Well, his business associates showed up. We've been told to butt out; national security and all that."

"Well, we could have predicted that. SOP."

Renee snorted. "Bullshit, Wood. Usually the Feds cooperate with the locals; they don't want to piss us off. When they go into a total stonewall like this, they're not kidding around."

"So why call me?"

"Because I know you, Wood. You dropped into the middle of it and you never give up on anything. I haven't told them you're in the picture. No one else on the site really saw you except the ME, and he's so close-mouthed he wouldn't say if he saw his own mother at her funeral. I'm just warning you about what kind of trouble you could be in if you keep poking into this."

"What about you?"

There was a pause, then an explosive, short laugh. "Yeah, you know me too."

"Can you get me the ME report?"

She thought for a moment. "I'll have to figure out some way to weasel it out of him without alerting the Feds, but yeah, I think I can. So what are you going to do for me?"

"My job. Get you information." I smiled slowly. "Don't you think it might help if we can find out why they're so worried?"

She hesitated. "It sure would. But I don't want to know how you get it."

"Right. Look, why don't you come over for dinner tomorrow, if you're not too busy? I should have something by then, and hopefully they won't try to listen in. We can set up some way to talk safely then."

"Okay. And, Jason," her tone shifted, "be careful. This is dangerous stuff we're playing with."

"I know. Bye."

I looked up at Syl. One glance froze me. She had that deep-eyed, deadly serious look again. Her "feeling" look. I trust those feelings with my life. "What is it, Syl?"

"It's bad, Jason. Very bad." She shivered. "More people are going to die before this is over."

18

I got back to my house, opened the door, and went to the kitchen. A few minutes later, sandwich and soda next to me, I booted up my terminal program. I needed to contact "Manuel Garcia O'Kelly Davis." Manuel was actually a fairly high-placed military intelligence analyst. I thought he was Air Force, but there was no way to be sure. I sent him a secured e-mail, asking for a conference. He agreed, and we set up the doubly secured relay, with me supplying a few bells and whistles that would make anyone trying to trace either one of us end up chasing their own tails through Ma Bell's systems. As per our long-established habits, neither of us used the other's real name; to him, I was "Mentor of Arisia," and he remained "Manuel."

>>Hello, Mentor. What's up?<<
>>Got a problem. You have time?<<
>>Two hours enough?<<
>>Should be.<<

I filled him in on the situation, leaving out the gory details and concentrating on the NSA factors.

>>Can you find out what their angle is?<<

>>Christ. You don't ask for much, do you. Look, I can check into it, but you'd do better to just drop out, you know?<<

>>I can't. It'd nag at me forever.<<

>>I know the feeling. :) Just remember, anything I tell you, I didn't tell you. Right?<<

>>Right.<<

I signed off, then finally got on to one of the underground boards; one run by a pirate and hacker that I knew pretty well.

>>Hello, Demon? You there?<<

>>Readin' you loud and clear, Mentor old buddy. You slumming?<<

>>Looking for info, as usual. You still keep up on the doings of the rich and infamous?<<

>>Best I can, you can bet on it.<<

The Demon was a damn good hacker and very well informed. He kept an eye on criminal doings not merely on the Net, but throughout the world. He viewed his piracy as a matter of free information distribution; since I make my living by distributing information and getting paid for that service, I found myself simultaneously agreeing and disagreeing with him. Nonetheless, we got along pretty well since the Demon absolutely *hated* the real Darksiders—people who destroyed other's work. To his mind, copying information was one thing. Destroying or corrupting it was another thing entirely.

>>Demon, what's going on now that might be bothering the Feds?<<

>>You talking big or little?<<

>>Big, but not like countries going to war; NSA stuff.<<

>>Hold on. Lemme think.<<

I waited.

>>Okay, there are about three things I can think of; but lemme ask, did something happen in your area?<<

>>Yes, that's how I got interested.<<

>>Got you. That only leaves one. NSA and the other agencies have been checking your general area trying to locate a real nasty Darksider who calls himself Gorthaur. He's a real sleaze. None of the respectable hackers will deal with him, but no one's really got the guts to tell him to kiss off. There are a lot of ugly rumors about him. Or her, no one's really sure either way. Gorthaur's been heavy into espionage and industrial spying and sabotage. A real prize.<<

>>He ever sign on your board?<<

>>He did until I found out who he was. Far as I know, I'm the only one to tell him what I thought of him. I told him that he'd better not log back on 'cause if I ever got anything on him I'd turn him over to the cops so fast it'd make his chips spin.<<

>>Bet he didn't like that.<<

>>He told me that it wasn't healthy to get in his way. I told him to save the threats for the kiddies.<<

I frowned at that.

>>Look, Demon, if it turns out this Gorthaur is part of what I'm involved in, you'd better take his warning seriously. There's already one corpse and the place is crawling with NSA.<<

>>I'll be careful then.<<

I got off and sat back. Then I shut the system down and got up, turned around. A tall, angular, dark figure loomed over me, scarcely a foot away.

"Holy SHIT!" I jumped back, tripped over the chair, dropped my glass, fell. My head smacked into the edge of the table and I flopped to the floor and just lay there as the red mist cleared.

"My apologies, Jason. Let me help you up." Verne Domingo pulled me to my feet as though I were a doll.

I pushed him away; he let go. "Christ! What in *hell* did you think you were doing? You scared me into next week!" I rubbed the already growing lump on my skull.

"I have said I was sorry. I did not wish to call you via phone; the government has ears, after all. And coming obviously in person would call just as much attention. I had only just materialized when you turned, and I had no chance to warn you."

"Okay, Okay. Sorry I yelled." I started for the kitchen, went towards the freezer.

"Sit, Jason. I will take care of that." He took the handtowel from the countertop, rinsed it, dumped several ice cubes into it. Then he folded the towel into a bundle and squeezed. I heard splintering noises as the ice was crushed. "There. Put that on the swelling."

I did. The cold helped, even when it started to ache. "What'd you have to see me for?"

"To explain, my friend." He stood with his back to the refrigerator, stiff and somehow sad. "The story you told me last night . . . it had very disturbing elements in it, very disturbing indeed. I had to check them before I could believe what my heart knew was the truth. Now I must tell you what is happening here, and for you to understand, you must hear a little history.

"Vampires are among the most powerful of what you would call the supernatural races, but we are not the only such; most have either long since died out or else found some way to leave this world that is no longer congenial to them, but a few, either through preference or necessity, still live on. My people are, on the whole, cautious not to arouse the awareness of you mortals, and this suits us. Bound as we are to the world in which we are born, we cannot leave, and so we live as best we can without doing that which could rouse you who now rule it to pursue us.

"There was another race, however, which was not so circumspect. They did not reproduce as we do, by converting mortals; they reproduced themselves as do most races, and this is perhaps why they had less sympathy for your people. But more likely they lacked sympathy because it was not in their nature; for they preyed on us as well." He looked at me steadily. "Your people call them werewolves."

I blinked. "Oh, no. Not again."

"I am afraid so. You have stumbled into the realm of the paranormal once more."

Vaguely I had the feeling that there was something missing—something Verne was avoiding telling me. But it wasn't central; the main points, I was sure, were the real thing. But something else wasn't quite . . . right. Well, maybe he'd clear that up later. I grimaced. "What was that line from *Die Hard* 2? 'How can the same shit happen to the same guy twice?' Look, how could werewolves prey on you? I mean, you guys are awfully hard to kill and once you die, well, you go to dust, at least the older ones. Klein took several days. Not much to eat there. Besides, couldn't you just turn around and eat them?"

"We are not as invulnerable as you think." He hesitated. "The truth is that it is not merely wood which can harm us. Wood harms us because it was once living. Any object composed of living or formerly living matter can harm us. Thus the werewolves could kill us with their formidable natural weaponry. As for the feeding . . . your writers have often glimpsed the truth. They did indeed consume flesh; but more, they fed on the raw emotions. Fear and despair, terror and rage, these things strengthened them; and when their victim finally died, they fed, directly, on the life force, the soul if you will, as it passed from the body. Nor could we return the favor. Their blood-scent was enticing, true; but any attempt to drain them only succeeded in slaying both parties. We immortals were a rare delicacy to them, and they hunted us with great enthusiasm.

"That threat accomplished what none of our talking had managed before; we united against the lycanthropes, and waged a long and bitter war. In the end we destroyed them. I myself confronted the last, and greatest, of the breed, and I slew him with great pleasure. He had been terrorizing the city of London while using a name which he knew would taunt me."

"Vlad Dracul."

He nodded.

"And now you wonder if you really killed him at all."

"No." He sat slowly. "I do not wonder at all. I know now that I did *not* kill him; that somehow he survived what I had believed were mortal wounds."

"You'd better tell me everything about these things. Especially how to kill them."

"Silver is the only way. I do not know in what manner, but the metal somehow disrupts their internal balance. Both teeth and claws, in their lupine form, are of some crystalline substance of great toughness. Their strength is immense, their cunning formidable, and their ability to shift shape, though confined to a wolflike predator on the one hand, is unlimited in the human range; they can be anyone at all. They do not fear night or day, nor does the phase of the moon have any effect upon them. They also have a talent similar to my own to charm and cloud other minds. They do not have my people's ability to dematerialize, but they can prevent us from using it if they get a hold on us."

"Ugh. Tell me, do they become stronger with age like you vampires?"

"I am afraid so."

"And this one was the biggest, oldest, baddest of the werewolves when you fought him?"

"Quite. I was not alone, however."

"Not alone? You mean you couldn't handle him by yourself?" The thought was terrifying. I knew how strong Klein had been, how hard he was to kill, and since then I'd seen what Verne was capable of; trying to imagine something powerful enough to beat a vampire as ancient as Verne . . .

He showed his fangs in a humorless grin. "I will admit that we never found out. I had two companions . . ." He hesitated again before continuing, " . . . both of them . . . leaders of their own clans or families of vampires. Though normally enemies, we had realized that these creatures were more of a threat to us all than any of us. We ambushed him, all striking at once with the silver knives I had designed, and threw the body in the Thames. He never had a chance to strike back."

"Marvelous." I shook my head. "Well, at least you've eased my mind on one thing."

"That being . . . ?"

"I hate coincidences. I don't believe in them. Now I know why he's ended up here." I looked across the table. "He's been tracking you. And he's going to kill you if he can."

Verne Domingo nodded slowly.

19

"Okay, Jason, what've you got?"

That was Renee, straight to the point. "A whole lot.

But first, come here; there's someone I want you to meet."

She followed me to the living room. Verne rose from the red chair, bowed as I introduced them. "Renee Reisman, Verne Domingo."

She didn't shake hands. "Jason, we've had our eye on this man for some time. I'd like to know just what his connection is with you."

"I shall explain, my lady," Verne said. "Look at me," he continued in a low but commanding voice.

Reflexively she shot a glance into his eyes—and froze.

He stepped closer, touched her temple gently with his right hand. He gazed intensely at her for several seconds. "Remember," he said.

Renee's eyes widened. A choked scream burst from her lips, and she staggered back, sagged, pale and shaking, onto my couch. "Oh dear God . . ." She closed her eyes, massaged her temples, and took several ragged breaths. Finally she raised her head. "I . . . I remember now. But until now, it was like those memories didn't even exist." She stared at Verne, still shaking.

"My sincerest apologies, Renee—may I call you Renee? Those memories were still there; merely locked away, as you requested. But Jason has convinced me that we need your aid, and we both knew that you must have your full memory to help us."

The old Renee was reasserting herself, albeit slowly. "That bad, huh?" She raised an eyebrow at me. "I'd assume that his being here means that he isn't our killer."

"You're right."

She turned back to Verne. "Okay, Domingo. Now that my brain is back, this had better be real good. Because," she shivered again, "I don't think that I'll be able to go through that again. Having my memory switched on and off like a light . . ."

Verne smiled, the gentlest expression I'd ever seen

him use; his fangs didn't show. "Milady, you showed courage far greater than mine to undergo that treatment once; neither of us either desired or expected that you would once more ask to forget."

"Damn straight." She ran her fingers through her hair, took a deep breath, and crossed her legs. "All right, let's have it."

20

I logged on and checked; I had a secured e-mail waiting. I pulled it up onscreen.

The message decoded just as though Manuel had sent it . . . but it wasn't from Mannie at all. That was so close to impossible that for a moment I couldn't do anything except gape. Then I reread the signature at the bottom, and understood.

Mentor (or should I say, Jason?): I'm sorry to tell you that Manuel has gotten himself into a bit of trouble by poking his nose into this. He doesn't have nearly the clearance necessary. He's being debriefed right now, but I'd suggest you not contact him for a while; not only is he more than slightly peeved at you, but any more contact from the outside might be taken seriously amiss by his superiors.

Since he emphatically assured me that you're too stubborn to be frightened off, and because we happen to be kindred spirits in a way, I'll give you what information I can. But let me warn you: this is dangerous. You and everyone you know could get killed if you play these games. So give serious consideration to just dropping it.

"Vlad Dracul" is apparently another alias being used by an independent operator called "Gorthaur." Gorthaur plays no favorites; he's been bypassing security and penetrating installations on five continents. Very rarely does he take direct credit for his actions except for those which he perpetrates on the Net—that's where he gets his name.

What tells us that Gorthaur's involved is the sheer perfection of his work. In every case, Gorthaur penetrates the installation in the guise of a high-clearance individual who is well known to the personnel. Fingerprints, retinals, passwords, everything checks out perfectly. These individuals vary in age, height, weight, and even sex to such a degree that we are utterly unable to imagine how one person can be doing all of these impersonations. Yet other subtle indicators tell us that it is just one person. So far, three agents have been killed in particularly savage ways while trying to locate Gorthaur. The one found in Morgantown thought he had found a hot trail. Apparently he had. Gorthaur exhibits psychopathic strength and savagery, and has killed several other people who apparently offended him at one point or another. Our best psych profile makes him out to be a complete sociopath with a megalomanic complex, but there are enough anomalies that we can't even begin to classify him. He's unique.

Watch your back. If he can disguise himself this well, he could be anyone.

The JAMMER

The Jammer; hacker legend, thief, one of the few
completely nonviolent criminals to make the ten-
most-wanted list, and probably the only one who
never had a picture to go with the wanted poster.
No one knew anything about him—even the "him"
was in question. He'd disappeared a couple of years
ago, and everyone had thought he'd retired, having
made far more money than he'd ever need. Now it
was clear that he'd been caught and recruited. But
someone with his talents couldn't be forced to work,
so they must have shown him something so important that he chose to work for them rather than
against them.

I erased the message and sat back, sweating. Who
knew what this werewolf wanted, really? Vengeance
against Verne Domingo I knew about, but that would
hardly drive him to go breaking into top secret vaults
in other countries. He had to have some other, larger
agenda. And how in the name of God could you catch
something that could change sex, fingerprints, and
genetics at will?

There wasn't any way, I realized. The only chance
to catch Gorthaur was to get him to come to us, and
only one thing was keeping him here: Verne Domingo.
Once he settled with Verne, he'd vanish forever.

I logged off that one, got on to the Demon's board.
He didn't respond to my query; probably at dinner,
which was where I should be. Then I noticed one of
my status tags:

Email: Waiting: 0 Old: 3

The last time I'd been on, there'd only been two old messages. I called up the last one:

```
>>From System Operator DEMON<<
   Okay, if it's that important we can meet
in person. Be here at six; we'll have din-
ner. I don't like it, Mentor; this had better
be worth it.
   THE DEMON
      (___)
     \* */
      \#/
```

What the hell? I hadn't written him in mail at all lately! Who . . . ?

Suddenly it hit me. If even the Jammer couldn't catch this guy . . . I shut the computer off and sprinted for Mjolnir. I had a sickening feeling I was too late.

21

I slammed the brakes on and skidded into place in front of the Demon's house. I was out the door before the engine finished dying out, my S&W 10mm out and ready. I rang the bell. No answer. I tried the door.

The door swung open quietly at my touch; it was already unlatched. The hallway was dim and silent. "Yo! Demon!" I called.

No answer.

My heart was hammering too damn fast; I'd swear it was audible a hundred feet away. I stepped slowly into the house. In the faint light I could see the hall-way and the stairs going to the second floor, and two entryways; I knew that one led to his living room, the one on the left, and past that was the den where his computer was. I took my coat off slowly and threw it through the entry. It hit the rug; nothing else moved. I dove into the living room, rolled as I hit, came up with my back to the far corner, gun up.

Nothing. Just furniture.

A faint creaking noise came from ahead of me. I stood stock- still, listening. The wind outside moaned. The creak came again. It was emanating from the den. The den door was ajar; I could see the white glow of his monitor screen leaking from the room.

I went forward one step at a time, trying to watch all directions at once; my ears would have pricked up if they could. The only sounds I heard were the whistle of the wind and that faint, periodic creaking.

I reached the door. Taking a deep, shaky breath, I flung the door wide.

A horrid red-splotched face swung toward me; I almost fired, then stopped and lowered the gun. "Jesus Christ . . ." I muttered.

Jerome Sumner, aka the Demon, hung head-down from one of the big beams of his old house. The rope that was tied around his ankles creaked as he swung slowly in the wind from the open window. His eyes stared blankly at me; his mouth was jammed open with a crumpled floppy disk. The place was filled with the faint metallic scent of the blood on his face, his clothes, the floor. I glanced away, saw his computer.

It was covered with spatters of blood; lying on top of the keyboard was a shapeless dark object. I moved closer.

It was the Demon's tongue. I swallowed bile, looked at the screen.

The BBS was off; instead there was a banner-making program on. Four giant words blazed on the screen:

He Talked Too Much

I was still staring a few minutes later when the NSA arrived.

22

I looked up as the cell door opened. Renee entered. She walked over and took my hand without a word. After a moment, she said, "You okay?"

"I guess," I said finally. "Am I getting out of here?"

"Fucked if I know," Renee said. "Jason, what were you doing over at Jerome Sumner's?"

"Bending over and getting screwed by the bastard who killed him." The fury overwhelmed me for a moment; I slammed my fist into the wall, then nursed my bruised hand. "I was set up perfectly. He was killed by this 'Vlad' guy you're looking for, and I'm supposed to take the fall."

She might have been in uniform, but she was here as a friend. Her hand on my shoulder told me that. "You won't. No one who knows you will believe it."

"But the NSA doesn't know me. How does the evidence look?"

Renee Reisman screwed up her face. "Not good. You were found there. Your fingerprints were all over the place, including on the keyboard . . . on just the keys necessary to put up that banner."

Jesus Christ. Of course they were. The bastard was imitating *me*! "But the way he was killed—I don't even think I *could* do that, even if I wanted to."

She shook her head. "You know the answer to that. Besides, you're a smart guy, Jase. Always were. Prosecution wouldn't have any problem convincing people that you could figure out how to do it." She hugged me suddenly. "I just came to let you know I'm with you. I could pull strings and get myself here. Sylvie's pulling for you too."

I hugged her back, feeling suddenly scared. If the NSA followed the evidence . . . and Gorthaur was as good at this as he seemed to be . . . I could end up put away for life. "Thanks, Renee. I mean it."

"We should get together more often. Not in a jail cell, either." She smiled faintly, and for a moment she looked like the same girl I'd first met in junior high. "You aren't going to jail. I promise you."

"Exceeding our authority a bit, Lieutenant?" a precise voice said from the doorway.

We both jumped slightly. The woman who entered was in her mid to late thirties, sharp-featured, with red hair and a tall, athletic frame. She was followed by a sandy-haired, somewhat younger man carrying a brown paper sack and a briefcase. The woman continued, "Fortunately, I don't like to make liars out of my professional associates. You aren't going to jail, Mr. Wood. Jeri Winthrope, Special Agent, at your service; this is my assistant and second pair of hands, Agent Steve Dellarocca." She extended her hand.

I shook it, then waited while Steve put down the stuff he was carrying and shook his, too. "Thanks. Glad to meet you. These have been the longest hours I've ever spent waiting anywhere."

"Couldn't be helped, I'm afraid. We didn't think you were the responsible party, but the evidence didn't look good. We had to check everything out thoroughly." She looked at Renee. "I'll have to talk to Mr. Wood alone now, Lieutenant Reisman."

Renee nodded. I gave her a smile and said, "Thanks, Renee."

"Don't mention it." The door closed behind her.

"Me, too, Jeri?" asked Steve.

"For now," Jeri said. "I want you to keep tabs on the rest of the operation."

"Gotcha. You know where to find me."

I became aware of the aroma of Chinese food coming from the bag Dellarocca had brought with him.

"Hope you like pork lo mein." Jeri said. "I thought you'd be hungry, and lord knows I never get a chance to eat in this job."

"Thanks." I started unpacking the food. "How did you people get there so fast, anyway? I only ended up there out of sheer luck."

"We got a call. Person said he heard screams from that house and saw a car pulling out fast."

"You got a call? That sounds more like police business."

She nodded. "We're manning the police phones. Mostly we just pass the stuff on, but it gives us the chance to keep sensitive material to ourselves."

"But what made that call sensitive?"

"The address. Your friend Jerome, the Demon, was on our little list of people who were potential targets of Gorthaur."

So she wasn't going to pretend I didn't know what was going on. That made it easier. "Why did he go after the Demon?"

"Several reasons. The major one is that Gorthaur hates to be laughed at or threatened; he's an utter psycho when it comes to insults. The Demon had thrown Gorthaur off his board and threatened him with exposure."

Nodding, I started to dig into the pork lo mein. Poor Demon. An image of him hanging head-down flashed in my mind; I put my fork down quickly; all of a sudden I wasn't hungry. "Okay; you seem to assume Gorthaur did him in. So what in the evidence keeps me from being Gorthaur?"

Winthrope gave a snort I interpreted as a chuckle. "Gorthaur may be able to do a lot of things we don't understand, but he's not omnipotent or omniscient. He's good at planting evidence, but apparently he either doesn't understand or neglected to remember what modern technology can do. Despite the caller's description matching your car, we were able to determine that your vehicle hadn't been there previously. We could tell how long it had been standing there—not long at all. Also, if you were calm enough to put up the banner program, you were very unlikely to have forgotten anything . . . and thus you'd never have come back." She smiled. "Interesting car, by the way. In your profession I suppose the electronic gadgetry should be expected, but I don't recall ever seeing an armored Dodge Dart before. Made us wonder if you were in our line of work for real, except that most of the other work seemed homemade rather than professional."

I grinned back. "Picked it up at one of those seized-property auctions; I think it belonged to a mid-level drug-runner. It was the silver-and-black color that caught my attention. That and the fact that I'd been shot at twice recently made an armored car sound like a good investment."

"I can understand that." She finished off an egg roll, then sat back. "Okay, let's get working. Everything here's being recorded, of course. We've got some questions for you and I hope you'll cooperate."

"Hey, I want this twit caught as much as you do. Maybe more; he killed my friend and tried to get me sent up."

"Right." She pulled out a laptop computer from a case slung over her shoulder, and opened it up. "First, tell me how you got into this and what you know so far."

I told the whole story, leaving out certain small points—like vampires and werewolves—starting with my arriving on the scene in the woods, and finishing up with finding Jerome dead. "That's about it."

"I don't suppose you'd like to tell me who your

contact was that spilled the beans on Gorthaur and his particularly annoying technique?"

"Don't even think about it. Confidentiality is a large part of my business. If the police can't trust me to keep my mouth shut, they wouldn't hire me. Nor would a lot of other people."

"Thought not." She glanced at a few papers. "Okay, Mr. Wood, now let's have the whole story, shall we?"

Oh-oh. "What do you mean?"

"Give me some credit for brains, please. Interrogation is my business. I've been doing this for sixteen years now, and I assure you I know when I'm not getting everything. So far you haven't lied to me once . . . but I know damn well that you're hiding something. So let's try specific questions and answers, shall we?"

"Go ahead," I said, trying to look confused. "I'll tell you what I can."

"First, tell me: just what was your part in the death of Elias Klein."

What the hell had put her on that track? "He was trying to kill me and accidentally electrocuted himself; you can look that up in the records."

"Funny thing about those records," Winthrope said with a nasty smile. "I find the entire thing written up as you describe it . . . but the coroner's report is about as vague as I've ever seen. In fact, our analysis department gives a ninety-percent certainty that the report was totally fabricated."

Oh shit. "I'm not the coroner; you'd have to ask him."

"Oh, I intend to. But let's go on. What was Elias Klein working on before his unfortunate demise?"

"I'm not exactly sure. Sometimes I wasn't kept up on everything he did."

"Now, that's very odd, Mr. Wood, since he appears by this receipt to have used your services just days prior to his death. What is also very odd indeed is that Klein's files for his last investigation are not to be found."

Damn, damn, damn! Renee must've forgotten the accounting office files. Either that or, more likely, some of the stuff had been misfiled and was found and properly filed some months later.

"And finally, it is very interesting that neither of Mr. Klein's partners can give a detailed account of his investigations. However, we are fortunate in that the wife of one recalled a name that her husband had mentioned during the time in question: Verne Domingo."

That tore it. The great vampire coverup was full of more holes than a colander. "Okay, Ms. Winthrope. I'd like to tell you a story. But I can't do it without permission—it affects a lot more people than just me, and like I said, confidentiality is my business."

She studied me a moment. "Sure. Here, use mine. I'll be sitting right here, of course."

I grimaced. "Naturally." I took her cell phone and punched in Verne's number.

"Domingo residence, Morgan speaking."

"Hey, Morgan, this is Jason. I have to talk to Verne."

"Of course sir." A few moments went by, and then that well-known deep voice came on the line. "Jason! I heard you were arrested! Are you all right?"

"Physically I'm fine, but we have a serious issue. I'm being interrogated by an NSA agent named Jeri Winthrope, and she's been asking some really pretty pointed questions. In particular, she's been looking into the past history of certain people, and she wants the truth about Elias Klein."

Verne was silent for a few moments. "You do not believe you can, as you would put it, 'scam' her?"

"I wouldn't want to try. I tried tapdancing around the whole subject and she yanked my chain but good.

They've found some remaining files and gotten a few comments that give them you as a lead."

I could sense the consternation on the other end. Finally he sighed. "Jason, I trust you. I have to, in this instance, for you have had it in your power to bring me down for months now, had you wished, and instead you have proven to be a friend. Tell her what you must. I will prepare my household to move, if things become impossible."

"I don't want you to—"

"I know. But also, if you do not tell her the truth—about myself and about what is behind this entire series of murders—we may be condemning her to death. Do as you must."

I swallowed. "Thanks, Verne. Maybe it won't come to that. Bye."

I turned back to the agent. "Okay, Ms. Winthrope, you win. I'll tell you everything. But I'm not going to argue it out with you. If you don't believe what I tell you, it's going to be your loss, not mine."

23

"What was her reaction?"

"About what you'd expect." Verne raised an eyebrow. "Well, she didn't believe me, that's for sure. But she also wasn't comfortable not believing, either; the stuff Gorthaur's been up to has already got them spooked."

"And she let you go rather than have you examined by a specialist? Isn't that a bit odd?

"Not really. She'd already admitted she knew I hadn't killed Jerome, and she wanted to trace me and find out who I met with and who I knew."

"How do you know that, Jason?" asked Syl; her high boots with shining metal inlay rapped loudly on the wood as she crossed the floor with the coffeepot for herself and Renee.

"Simple." I held up a small, silvery object that looked like a fat button. "She'd stuck this inside Mjolnir's front bumper." I dropped a few other tiny gadgets of varying color on the kitchen table where we were all seated. "And these were planted around the house."

Verne reached out and picked one up, examining it carefully. "Monitoring devices? How very rude. I presume you have deactivated them?"

"No."

They all stared at me. "Why in the world not?"

"Because I've already told Winthrope everything we know, so I don't have a thing to hide from her, and if I shut these off she could just put in some more that I'd never find. Right, Winthrope?" I said, addressing my words to the audio bug I'd removed from the business phone. "Besides, if Gorthaur tries to nail me, he'll be doing it on prime-time with the NSA watching. That should make the bastard think twice."

"Perhaps," conceded Verne. "But perhaps not. Have you not realized the most important part of your latest adventure?"

I thought for a moment. "I guess not. What is it?"

"Our opponent was able to imitate you perfectly. While his powers are vast, they still do have certain limitations. In order to imitate anyone, he must at least have seen them at close range. That means that you have been close to him in the past few days."

That made my skin prickle. "How close?"

Verne considered. "I would say no more than five feet. Werewolves can assume any form they can visualize, but to pick up on details as explicit as fingerprints would require them to be close enough for their aura to interact with yours."

"And the Demon's death shows he's aware of your involvement," Renee added.

I frowned. "So who . . . no, that question won't work either. He doesn't have to be a single person. He could have been a hacker watching the local boards and that's how he got on to me; then all he had to do was be someone on the street bumping into me, or even a customer."

The doorbell rang. I went to the door, looked out the peephole. "Agent Winthrope? Come in. I've been expecting you."

"I rather thought so," she said, her assistant Steve following her in. "Since you made it clear you wanted us to hear things, it seemed a waste of comfortable seating to hang around in a van trying to listen that way." She glanced at Renee. "I thought we told you to stay out of this, along with the entire police department. Oh, never mind. I've been known to ignore orders on occasion myself."

With two more people my house was too crowded; we all moved next door to Sylvie's shop, which had a big conference-room style table in one room; Syl rented the room to various groups, usually psychic types for seances.

"So all of you people are in on this clusterfuck? What in hell happened to security, Lieutenant Reisman?" Winthrope demanded, the faint smile taking some of the edge off her question.

"Wood showed up before you classified the operation, ma'am," she answered. "And the only way to get him to drop anything is to put him in jail, or shoot him."

"Not practical solutions as a general rule, I'll admit." she said. "Okay. I know why *you're* in on this, Domingo. I'm not sure I believe in it, but I know why. And I see why Jason had to brief Ms. Stake—"

"Sylvia, or Syl, please," she broke in. "You understand why."

"Hm. Yes." She shifted in her chair, glancing around

at the dark-panelled walls. "The important question is, how many others know about all this?"

Verne spoke first. "I assure you that I, at least, have told no one else. It would be a generally futile effort, and I need no advice on this subject."

Renee gave Winthrope a look. "I'd like to continue a career. If I mentioned this to anyone else my only career'd be inside padded walls."

"I've consulted with the Wizard—you remember him, don't you, Jason?—on how to deal with werewolves," Sylvie said.

"Really? And what did he say?" Winthrope asked. Her assistant Steve looked uncomfortable, probably either bored or wondering if he was trapped in a room of lunatics.

Syl made a face. "Not much. He said that most spirits can be controlled only if you know their origin, that is, what religious or spiritual discipline they belong to; otherwise you're limited to whatever their classic weaknesses are."

Verne agreed. "It is true. Vampires who believe in the Christian faith can perhaps be turned away by crosses and faith, or bound by a daemonic pentacle; but an enlightened nosferatu cares little for such things. There are certain mystical methods which work on all such . . . but even those are of no use against a Great Wolf. Silver, and silver alone, will suffice."

"Just what did you tell this Wizard character?"

"Actually not that much; I didn't want to get him involved, so I just asked about werewolves."

"And you, Mr. Wood?"

I shrugged. "No one outside of this room knows any of the weird stuff. A couple of the BBS users know I'm poking around in a classified investigation, but no more."

Steve smiled suddenly. "Thanks. That's all we needed to know."

His teeth glinted sharply as he lunged.

Winthrope moved faster than anyone I'd ever seen, even Elias Klein. Her hand blurred and came up holding a 9mm automatic. Before she could fire, though, the werewolf's hand grabbed her arm and pitched her like a horseshoe straight into Verne Domingo. "Steve" was no longer human at all, but a shaggy, lupine nightmare with crystal-sharp claws and razor fangs. If the monster hadn't been delayed by its quick attack on the agent, it would have got us all in the momentary paralysis of shock. Chairs crashed to the floor as we all rolled, sprang, or ducked away from the huge, monstrous thing that had appeared in the place of Steve Dellarocca.

Verne caught Winthrope, set her aside. "You must be a fool, Virigar. Though this mortal was not prepared for you, the rest of us have expected to deal with your sort. And our prior duel seems to have rendered you less than what you were. Against us you stand little chance."

It smiled, showing glittering rows of crystal teeth. "Not so. My name is Shirrith. I am honored that you mistake me for the Great King, yet I am but His servant. And we are not unprepared ourselves." It gave an eerie howl.

In a shower of glass, two more werewolves crashed in through the large windows. One sank claws into Verne's shoulder, but Verne smashed it aside with a tremendous backhand blow that sent it back through the wall into the night. Verne shoved Winthrope towards me. "Run!" he shouted. His face showed shock and, chillingly, the same fear I'd seen before.

Shirrith began to dash after us, but Verne Domingo dove across the room and caught him. The third werewolf almost reached Renee, but she had her gun out and pumped three shots into him. The .357

magnum slugs drove the creature back enough for her to jump out and slam the door between the conference room and the Silver Stake's main floor. The werewolf tore the door off its hinges and threw it at us. The impact knocked me and Renee down, sending my 10mm with its silver bullets skittering out of my hand. The creature lashed out, caught Sylvie, and bent its muzzle towards her throat.

Silver inlay flashed as the toe of her right boot slammed into the werewolf's groin. Its eyes bulged; a ludicrously tiny whine escaped its lips, and it staggered back a step. As it folded in pain, Sylvie grabbed a large silver candlestick from a shelf and clobbered the werewolf over the head; it crumpled to the floor.

A tremendous crash shook the building as the battle in the conference room escalated. The second werewolf came flying out of the broken doorway; it rolled and came up, slashing at Sylvie. She swung the candlestick but it just glanced off the thing's arm; the claws left long trails of crimson across her dress. I had the pistol now; before the creature could lunge again, I put three shots into it. The wolflike face snapped back, glaring at me in astonishment. Then it sagged and fell.

"Syl! Jesus, are you okay?" I ran to her. Blood was soaking her dress, spreading quickly.

"I'm fine," she said weakly. "Help Verne!"

I hesitated, looking around. Renee had hit her head when the door got us; she was still dazed. Winthrope was just backed up against the wall, staring at the two bodies and repeating, "Oh shit . . . oh shit . . ." She cradled her right arm, which hung limply; Shirrith's grip had crushed it like a paper cup.

Another crash echoed through the Silver Stake. I heard Verne cursing in some Central European tongue. With one more agonized look at Sylvie, I charged back into the conference room.

I had the gun ready; then I stopped. "Son of a bitch!"

Verne Domingo looked back at me . . . Twice.

Two Vernes were locked together, straining against each other. They were identical, down to the tears on their clothing. The damn thing could even emulate clothing? That really sucks. There was simply no way to tell them apart; their curses sounded the same, and both were calling each other "Shirrith." One was faking . . . but which?

I could have kicked myself. How stupid can you get? I raised the gun and fired twice.

The one on the left twitched as the bullet hit; the one on the right screamed and tore itself away from the real Verne Domingo, its disguise fading away. It dove for the window, but as it did it presented a perfect target. I aimed and fired.

There was a *clack* as the gun jammed. "You *bugger*!" I cleared the jam, but it was too late. Shirrith was long gone.

Verne gazed out the broken window, then turned away.

I shoved past Winthrope, who was coming in muttering apologies, ran to Syl. "How're you doing, Syl?"

She tried to smile; she failed miserably. "Not so good."

Blood was pooling on the floor.

"Verne, call the hospital, quick! Get an ambulance!"

24

"Jason, you need your rest. It's been twenty-seven hours. Go to bed."

I was too tired to jump at the sudden voice from a formerly empty space. "Verne, I've got work to do.

I'm going to find that bastard and silver him like a goddam mirror. I don't have time to sleep. You heard what Winthrope told me."

"About her assistant being found dead? Yes."

"Then don't talk to me about sleep. Every hour I sleep could get someone else killed." I rubbed my throbbing forehead. "Besides, every time I close my eyes, I see Syl getting slashed by that other werewolf." Fury took over. "That *other* werewolf, dammit!" I shouted at Verne, feeling my eyes sting. "You said there was only one, the last one, and all of a sudden it's *The Howling III* around here!"

Suddenly Verne looked tired himself, tired and very, very old. "I know, my friend. It was my arrogance and stupidity that lead to that mistake. I should have realized that to exterminate an intelligent race is well-nigh impossible; these are not passenger pigeons or dodos. Virigar must have survived and sought out the few that remained, perhaps only a single female, and for the past century they have increased their numbers, awaiting the time of revenge."

My anger evaporated. "Damn. Sorry, Verne. I shouldn't have taken it out on you. We *all* should have realized that where there was one there might be more." I wiped my eyes, half-noticing how damp they were. "It's just that Syl . . . Syl of all of us should have been the last to be hurt. She saved Renee and me—did you know that?"

He bowed his head. "I had not known. But I would have expected no less from her."

"She did. Then the last one got her. Now . . ."

"She will make it, Jason. I give you my word on that. Sylvia will not die for my mistakes." His dark eyes held mine, lent his words conviction.

"Thanks," I said, and meant it. "I hope you're right."

"I have never broken my word yet."

"Why didn't you go after him, Shirrith, when he ran?"

"Because . . ." He hesitated, staring down at his hands. "Because, I am ashamed to admit, my past century of soft existence has made me slow and not as adept in combat as I was in years past. I must remedy that. And because it would have done no good. He would never have led me to Virigar, unless that was his plan . . . in which case I would be dead." He sighed, and glanced at the odd tubular object on my workbench. "Since you will not rest, perhaps you can explain what you are doing?"

"Sure." I picked the tube up, showing the lens at one end with the eyepiece on the other. "This viewer fits onto this little headband, like this."

"I see that, yes. But what function does this device perform?"

"Well, it . . ." I broke off, thinking for a minute. "How well versed are you in the sciences?"

He made a modest gesture. "I am sufficiently educated that I consider myself a well-read layman."

"Good enough. Then you know that visible light is just one small part of the electromagnetic spectrum, right?" He nodded. "Well, I thought for a long time about how to find a hiding werewolf. Normal methods can't work. Their physical imitation seems to be so perfect that they may even be duplicating the DNA of the subject. But if that was true, then they must be more than merely material beings—you follow me?"

He thought for a moment, then nodded again. "I believe so. You are saying that if they were purely physical beings, once they assumed a perfect duplicate form, they would then become that person . . . and lose all their special powers."

"You've got it. So if they aren't just matter, that leaves some additional energy component. A werewolf has to be surrounded, permeated, with a special energy field." I locked the viewer into the holder, checked the fit. "That's where this comes in. That field has to radiate somehow, in some wavelengths outside the visible."

He raised an eyebrow. "I see. But what wavelengths? And would psychic powers, or mystic ones if you prefer, radiate in such mundane ways?"

"At some point I'd think they would," I answered, clipping on a power lead. "If these fields interact with matter, matter will produce certain emissions. As to what wavelengths, I'm betting on infrared. In the end, all energy decays to waste heat, you see. But I've also added an ultraviolet switch to this viewer, and these two little gadgets cover other areas—magnetic fields and radio waves, respectively."

He smiled. "I am impressed, Jason. I had thought you were only proficient with your computers and databases; I had no idea you were adept with the technical devices as well."

"Any real hacker has to have some skill with a soldering iron and circuitry," I answered. "But I just happen to like gadgets. The Edmund Scientific catalog is some of my favorite bedtime reading. Heck, most people think I named my car Mjolnir just because I'm weird. Actually, I've put thousands of dollars into gadgetizing the hell out of it. Mjolnir doesn't fly and if you drive it into water it just stalls like any other car, but it's got some optional features that even Lee Iacocca never thought of installing." The phone rang; I grabbed it fast.

"Hello? Doctor Millson?" I said.

"No." The voice was deep and resonant in a peculiar way; it sounded like a man in a tin closet. "We met earlier, though you did not realize it at the time. I am Virigar, Mr. Wood."

Adrenaline stabbed my chest with icy slivers. "What do you want?"

"To deliver an ultimatum, Mr. Wood. You know why I am here. I presume that you care for the young lady, Sylvia? If you wish her to survive the night, you will do one of two things: either you kill Verne Domingo for me . . . or you deliver him to me, that I might kill him myself. Do this, and my people—who even now walk that hospital's corridors—shall spare the lady's life."

"You bastard." I barely recognized my own voice. "If I'd known—"

"Yes, well, we all have things we'd have done differently 'if only,' do we not, Mr. Wood? You are worthy prey; it makes the chase and the kill sweeter. But for Domingo I will let you and your mortal friends live. Bring him, or the ruby ring he wears, to the old warehouse on Lovell Avenue within the next six hours. Any trickery or failure on your part, and the lady shall die . . . painfully." The line went dead.

I put the phone down slowly and looked up. Verne looked grimly back at me.

"I heard it all, my friend," he said softly.

25

"Why the hell not?"

I gestured at the ornate gold ring. "Why not, Verne? If he's going to be satisfied with the ring, just *give* it to him! Then we hit him later."

Verne rubbed the ring gently, turning it about his finger and making the ruby send out sparks of crimson. "The reason he would be satisfied with the ring, Jason, is because he knows that I will never remove this ring. *Never*. I gave my word many, many years ago, to one who meant more than life itself to me, that I would wear her ring until the final death claimed me." He looked up; his eyes were black ice, cold and hard.

"I value my honor, Jason. Nothing, not even God himself, shall compel me to break my word."

"That's asinine, Verne! We're talking Sylvie's life here, and you're worried about honor! Whoever your lady was, I'm sure she'd understand!"

"You are probably right," Verne said, his eyes unchanged. "But I cannot decide on the basis of what might be. She and she alone could release me from my vow, and she cannot, unless she be born again and regain that which she was. I do not expect you to understand; honor is not valued here as it was when I was young."

"Where is the honor in letting a friend die?" I hurled the question at him.

He closed his eyes, drew one of his rare deep breaths. "There is none in that, my friend. I have no intention to let Sylvia be killed; did I not also give my word that she would not die?" He opened one of my drawers, looked inside.

"Then you are going to give me the ring," I said, relieved.

"No," he said, taking something out of the drawer and handing it to me. "You will take it from me."

I looked down. In my hand was a clip for my automatic; one loaded with wooden bullets; a vampire special.

It took a minute for that to sink in. Then I threw the clip against the wall so hard it left a dent. "Christ, no! Kill you?"

"It seems the only way. I would rather die by your hand than his, and only my death will satisfy him; else Sylvia dies."

"Look," I said, glancing back at the pistol clip, "Maybe if . . . well, I could shoot your finger off, I guess."

He made the dismissing gesture I'd come to know

so well. "Impossible. It matters not how the ring leaves my possession, my word will still have been broken if it leaves my possession with my connivance and I yet live."

I couldn't believe this. "You want to die?"

"Of course not, Jason! I have spent many centuries trying to ensure my safety. But I will not break my word to her whose ring I wear, nor shall I break my word to you. That leaves me little choice."

"Bullshit! " I couldn't really understand this; how the hell could anyone take promises *that* seriously? But I could see he was deadly serious. "You only made that promise to make me feel better. Forget it, okay? I release you from that obligation. Whatever the formula is. You know as well as I do that Virigar has no intention of letting *any* of us go. For all I know, he's got a hit squad waiting outside."

He relaxed slightly. "I thank you, my friend. Yes, I also doubt Virigar's benign intent; but I had to make the offer. None of you would be imperiled were I not here . . . and were you not my friends."

"Bullshit," I said again. "Maybe we wouldn't be on today's hit list, but we'd sure as hell be on tomorrow's menu." I looked at him again. "Is this the same Verne Domingo who sent me out to take on Elias Klein with nothing more than a mental shield and moral support?"

For the first time I saw his features soften, and his smile for once held nothing unsettling. "No, my friend. For you are my friend now. I have had no true friends since . . . well, since before your country was born. In the past few months, you have shown me what a precious thing I was missing. More; you have given back to me the faith I lost, oh . . . when I lost my family. That, Jason, is a debt I shall be long in repaying."

I couldn't think of anything to say; I guess I didn't need to.

As quickly as it had come, Verne's gentle expression faded and his face returned to its usual aristocratic detachment. "We are agreed that Virigar's offer is without honor; thus we cannot follow that course of action. So what do you suggest?"

I stared at the ring again. "Well, even if he isn't trustworthy, if I *did* deliver the ring it might give us *some* advantage."

"I have already explained to you that I cannot—"

"I know that." I said, cutting off his protest, "I'm not saying take it off."

"Then just what do you mean?"

"For guys rich as you, jewelers make housecalls. Surely one could make a duplicate in a few hours?"

That stopped him. He looked very thoughtful for several minutes, but then shook his head. "I'm afraid it would never work. The time element aside—and we would be cutting it extremely close—you are underestimating Virigar. He would undoubtedly check the authenticity of the ring; I would not be surprised if he were himself an expert in jewelry. Moreover, we have no way of ascertaining if he has watchers about our residences; a visiting jeweler would tell him all he needed to know." He shrugged. "In any case, it is irrelevant. He would know that ring in an instant, for it is more than mere jewelry."

"Seriously, Verne, could he really spare that many to watch us? I mean, we killed one and injured another; how many more could there be?"

He gave me a look reserved for idiots. "You are the expert in mathematics, my friend. Calculate how many descendants a single pair could have in one hundred years, assuming a twenty-year maturity age."

I winced. "Sorry, so I'm slow. That'd be eighty from the original pair alone that'd be full-grown."

"That, of course," Verne admitted, "assumes that they

maintain normal human birthrates and take no 'breaks,' so to speak, from parenting. In reality this will not be the case, but even so, I would be surprised if there were less than a hundred or so all told."

A hundred! Christ! I didn't even have that many silver bullets! "Outnumbered and outgunned . . ." Suddenly one of my favorite, if crazy, quotes came to mind: "It's you and me against the world . . . When do we *attack*?"

I put the viewer's headband on, fitted the straps, then took it off and packed it carefully in a foam-lined bag. "We're both targets as it is; the only chance we have is to attack. Get him off-balance, surprise the shit out of him. I've got to hope that one of the gadgets I've got can spot the buggers; I'm going to get to the hospital and protect Syl."

"And I . . . ?"

I grinned nastily, remembering what Verne had done to a drug-lord's estate and his thugs. I pulled out another drawer, and handed him the rings inside. "All silver rings; I got them because I liked the looks but I just never wear any of them. You are going to put those on and go down and beat Virigar's door in. Any werewolf that jumps at you then, just give him a left hook and keep going."

He put the rings on slowly. "I cannot enter a dwelling without permission of the residents, you remember."

"I didn't say enter; I said beat his door in . . . and his walls, and everything else. We have to disorganize him."

Now he smiled coldly, the fangs lending it the right predatory look. "Precisely so. Shall we . . . ?"

"After you."

We left by the back door; Mjolnir was parked in that alley.

I got into the car, locked the doors, and nodded to Verne; he faded into a cloud of mist, and then disappeared. I still stared at that; I don't think I'll ever get used to vampires. I started the engine, put Mjolnir in gear, began to pull out of the alley.

With a shuddering *thump* a shaggy, glittering-fanged nightmare landed on the car's hood. Then the car jolted to a stop; in my mirror I could see a werewolf that had grabbed the rear bumper and lifted the wheels clear of the ground. I swear my heart stopped for a second; then it gave a huge leap and tried to pound its way out of my chest. I yanked the gun out and pointed it at the one on the hood; the glass was bulletproof but hopefully it didn't know that.

It didn't; the werewolf rolled off the hood and to the side. I shoved the pistol into the gunport the previous owner had thoughtfully installed and fired twice. Neither shot hit it, but the werewolf decided that retreat was a good idea. I hit the hidden release and part of the dashboard flopped out and locked, revealing the small control panel. As the one in back began to yank harder on the bumper, trying to tip the car over, I pressed the second button.

Mjolnir's engine revs rose to a thundering shriek as the nitro supercharger kicked in; blue flame shot two feet from the tailpipe, and what I'd hoped for happened; the werewolf yipped in startlement and pain, and dropped the bumper.

I mashed the pedal to the floor; the V8-318 engine spun the wheels, throwing rubber smoke in the things' faces, and Mjolnir hurtled onto the street. By the time I passed Denny's I was doing fifty. A glance in the rearview almost made me lose control; three hairy killers were in hot pursuit, and they were closing in!

I searched the panel for any other tricks I might play, wishing I had James Bond's armamentarium . . . or even Maxwell Smart's. I triggered the rear spotlight, blinding them momentarily and gaining me maybe a hundred feet before they recovered.

Mjolnir shuddered as I hit a series of potholes at sixty-two miles an hour. I wrenched the wheel around, skidded onto the interstate entrance ramp. Behind me, I could see my pursuers catching up fast. On the straightaway I hammered the gas again, watched the speedometer climb towards triple digits. I heard myself talking: "That's right, come on, come on you little bastards, let's see how fast you really are!"

At seventy-five they started to fall back; the largest made a final desperate dive and hooked onto the rear bumper. I tried to bounce it off by running off and on the shoulder, but the creature just snarled and held on tighter. It started to claw its way up the back.

If Mjolnir had been an ordinary car, those crystal claws would've torn straight through and the thing would've climbed right into my lap. Instead, its talons made long gouges in the armor but failed to get any real purchase as I swerved the car back and forth. The werewolf scrabbled desperately at the trunk, but there was nothing for it to grab; with an indignant glare it pitched off the rear bumper and somersaulted to a defeated halt. I gave it a salute with my middle finger as it disappeared in the darkness. Then I turned down an off-ramp and headed Mjolnir towards St. Michael's Hospital.

26

The hospital was quiet; at three-thirty only the emergency crews were around. I parked, checked my gun, and put the viewer on. I looked weird but that didn't worry me; the only thing I was worried about was that the werewolves would be able to hide from anything technology could think up. I didn't believe that . . . but what if I was wrong?

I went in through the side entrance; I got some strange looks but no one got the courage to ask me just what I was doing before I was past them. I've often noticed that if you look like you know where you're going and why, people just don't ask questions. And once you get past them, they're too embarrassed by their hesitation to go after you.

I got to the fifth floor, where the ICU was set up. Outside sat a familiar figure.

Renee raised her head, looked, and looked again, a startled expression on her face. Then she smiled. "Hello, Wood. I thought you'd be home getting some shuteye."

"I thought the same about you. Why are you here?"

"Winthrope and I both agreed she should have some kind of watch over her. I took this shift." Renee glanced inside; Sylvie was sleeping. Renee turned back to me. "What the hell is that on your head?"

"An idea that doesn't seem to be working out." I'd looked at everyone I'd passed through it, and even glanced at the patients. I could tell when someone had a fever, but if there were any werewolves around the viewer didn't seem to be able to spot them. I looked at the magnetic indicator and the radio meter; none showed anything helpful; hell, with the MRI unit in this building neither one would be likely to pick up anything.

"Well, it's been quiet as hell here. You might as well go home. I'll call you if there's any change." She gave my shoulder a tentative pat.

I noticed a movement behind her.

Sylvie's eyes had opened suddenly. Her head turned weakly towards me; her eyes widened, and it felt like icewater was running down my spine as I saw her face: her "feeling" face.

I nodded my head sharply; the viewer dropped down, and I looked through it.

Renee Reisman's face sparkled in infra-red, a network of tiny sparks and lines rippling across it.

Everything seemed to freeze. I had never looked at anyone through the viewer at this range; it could be just what moving muscle looked like close up. If I was wrong, I'd be killing a police lieutenant and a friend.

But if I was right . . .

It only seemed to take a long time; my body made the decision even as I glanced down. The 10mm fired twice before I was quite sure what I should do.

Renee staggered back, shock written on every line of her face, and I realized I'd made a horrible mistake; it wasn't a werewolf at all! I started forward . . . just as claws and fangs sprouted like deadly weeds from her twisting form. But the werewolf was dead even as it lunged for me; only one claw caught me, leaving a thin red trail across my left cheek.

Screams and shouts echoed through the hospital. Three figures appeared around the corner. When they saw my gun out, they dodged back. "Who are you?" one called out. "What do you want? This is a hospital, for Christ's sake!"

"I'm not here to hurt anyone," I said, realizing how utterly asinine that sounded coming from a man holding a pistol in front of the ICU. "I'm just trying to protect my friend in here." I could just imagine their thoughts: a homicidal paranoid is holding ICU patients as hostages.

"Look," one said very quietly, reasonably, "I'm going to just step around the corner, okay? I just want to talk with you, is that all right?"

I heard another voice mutter something in a heated

undertone; it sounded like "Are you nuts? Don't do it!"

"Sure." I said. "Just do it slowly."

A young orderly, my age or a little younger, eased carefully around the corner. He had his hands raised. "See, I'm not going to hurt you."

"I know what you're thinking, but I'm really not crazy." I gestured to the body. "Just look at that; you'll see what I'm up against."

He walked forward slowly, hands over his head.

As he got closer, the viewer image slowly started to sparkle.

"Hold it right there. You're one of them."

The expression of sudden terror, the pleading look, they were perfect. I had another attack of doubt.

The claws almost took my head off before I fired. The werewolf howled in agony and died quickly. I saw two pairs of eyes staring widely in shock as the creature that had been playing their friend expired. "Fucking *Nightmare on Elm Street*, man! What is going down here?"

"Werewolves," I answered, "and if you're smart you'll get out of the hospital."

"I'm history," one said, "But I've gotta go through where you are."

"If you aren't one of them, go ahead. Otherwise you'll be number one with a bullet."

He had more guts than I would have. He just walked out, crossed the hallway to the nearer door, and started down the stairs. Once his friend had gotten across safely, the other one walked across with his hands up, then bolted down the stairs.

Just then I heard the hall window shatter. A tall blond man, rather like a young Robert Redford, dropped lithely into the hall from outside. He straightened and looked at me. "You are most extraordinarily

annoying, Mr. Wood. I have been considering how best
to kill you." The deep, strangely resonant voice was
chillingly familiar.

I raised the pistol, centered it on his jacket. "Virigar,
I presume."

He bowed. "At your service."

If Virigar was here . . . God, had he already killed
Verne? "What are you doing here? I thought—"

"Yes, you thought I would be at the warehouse." For
a moment the good-humored mask dropped. My blood
seemed to freeze at the sheer malevolence in his face;
had he attacked then, I couldn't have moved a muscle
to stop him. Then he regained control. "In point of
fact I was; then that thrice-damned vampire began his
attack and I knew precisely what you had planned. I,
also, believe in keeping my word, so I came to make
sure the young lady was killed." He glanced around at
the two bodies. "A wise choice, it would seem."

He inclined his head. "You have been lucky and
resourceful so far. I look forward to tasting your soul;
it should be a strong and, ah, heady vintage. Then I
will finish with Domingo. Your interference has been
really quite intolerable."

"Aren't you overlooking something?" I asked.

"Such as . . . ?"

"The fact that I'm going to blow you away in the
next two steps?"

He laughed. "I doubt you could hit me. I am not
one of these younglings."

I wasn't going to dick around with him. Before he
could react, I put three shots in the bulls-eye where
most people keep their hearts.

His eyes flew wide; he stared at me, then down at
the three neat holes in his suit. He sank to his knees,
muttered something like "Impressive aim . . ." and then
his eyes rolled and he fell.

I waited a few minutes, keeping the gun on him; he didn't move. I went forward a few feet just to check.

Something hit my hand so hard it went numb, picked me up and hurled me down the hallway. I fetched up against the far wall, disoriented. When I focused my eyes again, I saw Virigar standing there with my gun dangling from his hand. Grinning pleasantly, he shrugged off his coat, revealing the bulletproof vest beneath.

"I should have blown your head off." I shook my hand, trying to get feeling back into it.

He nodded cheerfully. "Yes indeed, but I depended both on legend and training. The legend of three silver bullets to the heart for a Great Werewolf, and the fact that most people are taught to shoot for the body rather than the smaller target of the head." He tossed the gun aside. "Your friend Renee lasted for a few minutes, Mr. Wood. Let us see how well you do."

He began to change. I froze. I had seen another werewolf change . . . but this was not another werewolf.

This was Virigar.

This was no transformation like a morphing, but more; a manifestation of the truth behind the facade. The air seemed to thicken and condense, becoming black-brown shaggy fur. The eyes blazed with ravenous malevolence, flickering between blood-red and poison yellow. The head reared up, seven feet, eight, nine towering, hideous feet above the floor, the marble sheeting cracking and spitting powder from the energies that crackled about Virigar like black lightning. It drew a breath and roared, a shrieking, bellowing, rumbling impossible sound that shattered every window on the floor and deafened me. The head wasn't really wolflike . . . wasn't like anything that had ever lived. Dominating it was the terrible mouth, opening to a cavernous diameter, unhinging like a snake's, wide enough to sever a man in one bite, armed with impossibly long, sparkling diamond fangs like an array of razor-sharp knives . . .

For a moment all thought fled; all I had was terror. I ran.

Virigar let me get some distance ahead before he began following; I remembered what Verne had told me, that they fed on fear; obviously Virigar wanted a square meal. I ran down the steps, taking them two, three at a time . . . but I could hear his clawed footsteps closing in on me.

I remembered a trick I'd first read about in the Stainless Steel Rat series. If I could do it I might gain a few seconds.

I jumped as I reached the next flight of stairs and hit them sideways, one foot raised above and behind the other, both slightly tilted. My ankles protested as the stairs hammered by underneath me like a giant washboard; I hit the landing, spun, and repeated it, then banged out the doorway, sprinted down the hall, ignoring the ache in my feet. It worked!

My heart jumped in panic as Virigar smashed out of the stairwell fifty feet behind me, the metal fire door tearing from its hinges and embedding itself in the opposite wall. Nurses and orderlies scattered before us, screaming. Oh, the bastard must be gorging himself now.

Somewhere in the distance I thought I heard gunshots. Too far away to make any difference now, though . . .

Around the corner, trying to find another stairwell. Oh, Christ, I'd found the pediatric wing!

A young girl with dark hair in two ponytails blinked bright blue eyes at me in surprise as I raced past her wheelchair, her attention to her late-night sundae momentarily distracted. With horror I recognized her: Star Hashima, daughter of the artist Verne was a prospective patron to. Virigar skidded around the corner after me, growling in a grotesquely cheerful way. I faltered momentarily, realizing that the monster was already trailing blood; he wouldn't hesitate to kill again.

Her face paled, but at the same time I could swear there was almost an *interested* expression on her face as she saw the huge thing bearing down on her. Then Star calmly and accurately pitched her sundae into the King Wolf's face.

The laughter in its growl transformed instantly into startled rage and agony; blinded, Virigar stumbled and cannonballed into a wall, smashing a hole halfway through and clawing at its face. Star spun her chair around and rolled into one of the rooms, slamming the door behind her.

Virigar roared again, shaking the floor. "*Bitch!* I'll have your *soul* for that!"

I ran, praying this was the right decision. Would Virigar waste the time taking care of Star right now, or would he chase me first because of what I knew? And what in the name of God had that girl *done*? As I half ran, half fell down the back stairs, I suddenly remembered a faint sparkle from the ice-cream bowl. Silver-coated decorations.

No, Virigar couldn't afford to waste his time now. If I got out to Mjolnir, I could draw him off, outrun him probably, and then too many people would know too much. I shoved open a door, ran out.

Oh no. I'd come down one floor too many. This was the basement! Ammonia and other chemical smells from the labs filled the air. Above me I heard the stairwell door smashed open.

I ran.

Technicians and maintenance gaped at me. Signs flashed by, Hematology, Micro Lab, Urinalysis, Radiology . . .

At Radiology I scrambled to a halt, dove inside. A last-chance plan was forming. Behind me screams sounded as Virigar charged after me.

I shoved the technician there aside. "Get the hell out of here!"

Hearing the screams, and the approaching snarls, the tech didn't argue; he split. I ducked into the next room, grabbing a bucket that stood nearby, slammed and locked the door. I worked fast.

Heavy breathing suddenly sounded from the other side of the door. "Dear me, Jason; you seem to have cornered yourself."

I didn't have to fake terror; I knew my chances were hanging on a thread.

The door seemed to disappear, ripped to splinters. "It's over, Mr. Wood!" Virigar leapt for me.

That leap almost finished me; but the door had slowed him just enough. With all the strength in my arms, I slung the contents of the pail straight into Virigar's open mouth. The sharp-smelling liquid splashed down the monster's throat, over his face, across his body, soaking the fur. Even as that pailful struck, I was plunging the bucket into the tank for a second load.

Virigar bellowed, a ragged-sounding gurgling noise of equal parts incredulity and agony. He was still moving too fast to stop; one shaggy arm brushed me as I leapt aside and he smashed into the tank itself, tripping and going to his knees, one arm plunging into the liquid. The metal bent, but then tore as he scrabbled blindly at the thing he'd run into, disgorging its remaining contents in a wave across his thighs and lower legs. Momentarily behind him, I doused him with my second pailful, soaking him from head to toe.

The Werewolf King's second scream was a steam-whistle shriek that seemed to pierce my head, but lacked the awesome force of the roar that had shivered hospital windows to splinters. Foul vapors like smoke were pouring from him, obscuring the hideous bubbling, dissolving effects the liquid was causing. The monstrous form staggered past me, mewling and screaming; incredibly, I felt the earth itself heave as it wailed wetly, and a flash of yellow-green light followed. Lamplight poured through a ragged gap in the far wall and was momentary eclipsed by the horrific silhouette of something half-eaten away as Virigar clawed his way to the outside . . . and disappeared into the night.

Cautiously, a patch of light approached. The flashlight ranged across me, then went to the tank, broken into pieces and leaving its sharp-smelling contents flowing harmlessly across the floor. The light showed me the way out, its beam illuminating the wall just enough to show the sign painted there:

X-Ray: Developer, Fixer, Silver Recovery

27

Winthrope waved me past the yellow barricade. I pulled up a hundred fifty feet farther on. I got out, went around and helped Sylvie out into the wheelchair. She still looked pale and weak, but it was good to see her moving at all. She smiled at me, then looked up and gave a little gasp. "Vernc did that?"

I felt as awed as she looked. The hundred-foot-long, three-story warehouse was nothing more than a pile of charred boards and twisted steel, still smoking after several days. The last rays of the setting sun covered it with a cast of blood. From the tangled mass of wreckage, two I-beams jutted up, corroded fangs, mute testimony to the power of an ancient vampire's fury.

"You still haven't heard from him, have you?"

"No. It's hard to believe, but . . . there were dozens of them in there. Winthrope's still finding bodies. They must've gotten him somehow, maybe by sheer numbers." I felt stinging in my eyes, blinked it away. "And Renee . . ." This time I couldn't blink away the tears. Syl said nothing, just held my hand.

It was hard to believe I'd never see her again. But Renee had been found in her house, her body sitting in a chair and her head on the table in front of her.

"I'm so sorry." Syl said finally. "All I remembered was looking over, seeing her, and knowing it wasn't really her at all. What about Star?"

"I got to see her the next day. She made me promise not to say anything to anyone about her helping me; her dad was already throwing a fit that she'd even been in the hospital when it happened. She thinks her father is the greatest thing in the world, and doesn't want to worry him. I just hope she'll be all right; that was quick thinking on her part, but I don't believe any kid that age could see that monster coming at her and not at least get some nightmares out of it."

Syl started to say something, but suddenly choked off; her hand gripped my arm painfully. I turned fast.

A man was standing next to Syl. He looked at me.

I knew that face, with the dark eyebrows, crooked grin, streaky-blond hair, and green eyes. I should know it; it looked at me every day in my mirror.

I went for my gun, found to my surprise that it wasn't there. The man before me smiled, his face shifting to the Robert Redford lookalike I remembered all too well. He held up his hand, my gun sitting in it. "Good evening, Mr. Wood. I believe we have some unfinished business."

"Never mind the dramatics," I choked out, hoping he'd prolong them, "Finish your business, then. Nothing much I can do."

"Dear me. No respect for tradition? I must congratulate you; I haven't been hurt that badly in centuries; even our mutual acquaintance, Verne, failed to injure me as grievously. Why, I'm genuinely weakened. A clever, clever improvisation, Mr. Wood. I'm minded to let you live for a while."

I blinked. "Umm . . . thanks. But why?"

The urbane smile shifted to a psychotic snarl. "So you will suffer all the more while everything you value is destroyed before your very eyes!"

I read his intention in his eyes, leapt hopelessly for his arm; he tossed me aside like a doll. His hand came up and the fingers lengthened, changed to diamond-glittering blades. Sylvie stared upward, immobile with terror.

Something smashed into Virigar, an impact that flung him a hundred feet to smack with an echoing *clang* into one of the two standing girders. The girder bent nearly double.

Virigar snarled something in an unknown tongue. "Who dares . . ."

"I dare, Virigar. Will you try me, now that I am prepared?"

Between us stood a tall figure, with a streaming black cloak, seeming to have materialized from the gathering shadows of night. "*Verne!*" I heard Sylvie gasp.

Virigar began to snarl, wrenching himself from the beam's grip. Then he stopped, straightened, and laughed. "Very well! Far be it from me to argue points with Destiny." He bowed to Verne, who made no motion to acknowledge it. "You have won a battle against me, Mr. Wood. And your friend here has surprised me. This game is yours. Your souls are still mine, and shall be claimed in time. But for now, I shall leave you. One day, I shall return. But no other of my people shall touch you, for that which is claimed for the King is death for any other who would dare to take it." He turned and began to stride off.

"Freeze! Hold it right there!" Jeri Winthrope had the Werewolf King in her gunsights, and I had no doubt that this time it was loaded with silver bullets. Even with the cast on her arm, I was sure she wouldn't miss.

Virigar turned his head slightly. He ignored Jeri entirely, looking at Verne. "My patience is being tried. Tell the child to put her weapon away now."

"Do it," Verne said.

Jeri glanced at him, startled. "But—"

"*Do it!*" Verne's voice was filled with a mixture of loathing, fury, and a touch of fear.

Slowly Winthrope lowered her gun. Virigar smiled, though the expression was barely visible. "Wiser than you look. Until later." He turned a corner around a large chunk of warehouse.

"Why?" Jeri demanded after a moment of silence. "I had him right there!"

Verne glared at her. "Think you that something as ancient as he didn't know of your approach? I heard you as soon as you turned from your post. Your bullet would never have found its mark, and he would have killed us all. Even the fact that he spared us was a whim. Something to *amuse* him," Verne spat the word out as though he could barely tolerate the taste, "until he has an artistic way to destroy us."

"I thought," I said, "he spared us because he wasn't sure he could win against us."

Verne shook his head. "If he appeared here, he was ready. Perhaps I could have defeated him." I noticed that he didn't say "we." "But I believe he left because . . ." Verne seemed to be searching for the proper way to describe something. " . . . because he had lost the game as he himself put it. This battle, even your injuring him, was to him nothing more than a game. The object was vengeance against me, and then against you once you became an impediment of note. But we managed to meet some . . . some standard he set for his opposition. You injured him; I reappeared from the dead. He is as immortal as I, and older; he must find his own amusement where he can. But where I find mine in the elegance of art, in friendship, in more ordinary games, he finds his in the dance of destruction and death, in evil versus good." Verne shuddered, a movement so uncharacteristic of him that it sent chills down my spine. "Perhaps I could have defeated him," he repeated softly. "But I very much wish never to find out."

Jeri shrugged. "Not my problem now. Okay. We'll talk later." She walked off.

I grasped Verne's hand, realizing how much it would have meant to lose him. "Jesus, it's good to see you. We thought you were dead!"

"Hardly, my friend." He looked even stronger, more assured and powerful than he had ever been. "Though not for want of trying on their part, I assure you. How does it feel to have changed the world?"

Sylvie spoke up. "Verne, pardon me, but I don't understand why any of them died in there. I thought—"

"That only silver could harm them? Quite so, my lady." He gazed at the wreckage. "Once I knew the werewolves had returned, I laid in a supply of diverse forms of silver—although I must confess," he bowed slightly to me, "it never occurred to me that *preparations*—compounds—of silver would be efficacious as well. Part of my armament was a large supply of silver dust. I hurled this into the warehouse from several different points with sufficient force so as to disperse it throughout the interior rather like a gas."

I winced at the mental picture. "Instant asthma attack. Ugh."

"Precisely. In addition, since nearly all surfaces then had silver upon them, even falling beams became capable of causing harm."

"That still doesn't explain where you've been the past few days."

"Ah, yes." He looked somewhat embarrassed. "Well, in the end the battle degenerated so that I was reduced to physical confrontation. By the time the last of them came for me, I found myself without silver of any kind. Your rings, I am afraid, were not meant for combat. They . . . ah . . . came apart. So when the last one attacked, I was unarmed against her great natural weaponry. I was thus forced to a course of action whose results I could not foresee."

"Well?" I said when he hesitated.

He coughed and examined the ruby ring studiously. "I . . . drained her."

"You mean you bit her? But you said that was fatal!"

He nodded. "Other vampires had tried it; they had all died along with their intended prey. I found out why." He shook his head slowly. "The power was . . . incredible. No younger nosferatu could have survived it."

I thought about that for a moment. "Then in a way you, also, drain souls?"

"Yes and no. There is a linking and exchange, usually, of energies. However, in the case of something like combat, it can become a direct drain, and against a werewolf or something of similar nature, it must be. As it was, my body fell into what you would call a coma for several days as my system adjusted. I was fortunate; we were underground in one of these abandoned buildings' basements; had that not been the case, I would have faced the irony of dying in sunshine on the morning of my triumph. But survive I did, and I find that I am stronger for it." He smiled, the predatory grin of the hunter. "It is fitting that their attempt to destroy me would only strengthen me; it is . . . justice."

We nodded, then Sylvie spoke. "What did you mean when you said Jason had changed the world?"

"Is it not obvious, my lady?" He gestured at the lights of the city, silhouetted against the darkening sky. "For centuries humanity has wondered if there were others out there, beyond the sky; but always they were secure in their science and civilization, knowing that here, at least, they ruled supreme. The Others—vampires, werewolves, and so on—hid themselves away, not to be found by the scientists who sought to chart the limits of reality, and so became known as legend, myth, tales to frighten children and nothing more. On this world, at least, humanity knew that it was the sole and total ruler of all they could survey.

"But now they know that is not true; that other beings walk among them. And this is not one of their stories, a book to be read and then closed, to disappear with the morning light." Verne shot a glance at me. "You recall, my friend, how you spoke about the horror stories, the Kings and Straubs and Koontzes?"

I thought for a moment, then I remembered the conversation he meant. "I think I see."

"Yes. You were disturbed by their stories showing such titanic struggles, and yet no subsequent stories ever referred to them; as though such power could ever be concealed. But this is the true world. The genie cannot be replaced in the bottle. Even your government has realized the futility of a cover-up. Winthrope speaks on the news of these events to an incredulous nation, and scientists gather to study that which is left. The world changes; we have changed it. For good or ill, the world shall never be the same."

He fell quiet, and we gazed upward; watching as the stars began to spread—like silver dust—across the sky.

Viewed in a Harsh Light

28

"I must thank you, Jason," Verne said, surveying the mound of equipment assembled in his dining room. "The advice of an expert is always appreciated."

Verne had decided to fully enter the coming twenty-first century, adding telecommunications and computers to his formidable range of resources. I grinned. "No thanks needed. Advising someone on what to buy is always fun, especially when you know that the person in question doesn't have a limited budget." One of the workmen looked at me with a question in his eyes. "Oh, yeah. Verne, how many places are you going to want to be able to plug in a PC? I mean to the phone lines." Extra phone jacks were a good idea; cable didn't yet run out to Verne's house, so at the moment that was his only option, and even when it did I didn't think it was a bad thing to have extra hookups for the phones.

"Ah, yes. I would say . . . Hmm. Morgan?"

"Yes, sir?"

"Are any of the staff likely to need such access?"

Morgan smiled slightly. "I would say most of them, sir." While Verne was modernizing, he was still not quite grasping how much of a change it was going to bring to his household.

Verne sighed theatrically. "Very well, then." He turned to the workman. "You might as well rewire the entire house, first, second, and third floors, and put two phone jacks in every bedroom and study, as well as one here in the living room," he pointed, "and another three in my office, marked there."

Ed Sommer, the head worker, smiled broadly, obviously thinking of the money involved, and glanced at the plans. "We'll write up a work order. What about the basement?"

"No need for anything there."

"Gotcha."

Sommer cut the work order quickly—I'd recommended his company because of their efficiency, despite the fact that they were the new kids on the block—Verne signed it, and we left the rest of the work in Morgan's hands. "Coming, Verne? Syl's out of town on a convention and I'm up for a game of chess if you're interested."

He hesitated, the light glinting off the ruby ring he never removed. "Perhaps tomorrow, Jason. All these strangers in the house are upsetting."

"Then get away from them for a while. Morgan can handle things here. Besides, how could anything upset *you*?" This was partly a reference to his vampire nature—I'd kinda expect a man who's umpteen thousands of years old to be comfortable everywhere—but also to his constant old-world calm approach, which was rarely disturbed by anything except major disasters.

"You may be right. Very well, Jason, let us go."

The night was still fairly young as we got into my

new Infiniti. Verne nodded appreciatively. "Moving a bit up in the world, my friend?"

"The only advantage of being attacked by ancient werewolves is that the interview fees alone become impressive. And the publicity for WIS has made sure I've got more work than I can handle, even if I do have to turn down about a thousand screwballs a day wanting me to investigate their alien abduction cases. Not to mention that the government groups involved in the 'Morgantown Incident' investigation would rather use me as a researcher than an outsider." I gave a slightly sad smile. "And age finally caught up with old Mjolnir."

"He served you well. Have you named this one yet?"

"Nope. I was thinking of Hugin or Munin—it's black and shiny like raven feathers." We pulled out of his driveway and onto the main road into town. We drove for a couple minutes in silence.

"I was not deliberately changing the subject," Verne said finally. "I understand how you would find it hard to imagine me being disturbed by anything. I was thinking on how to answer you."

I was momentarily confused, then remembered my earlier comment. It was sometimes disconcerting talking to Verne; his long life made time compress from his point of view, so that a conversation that seemed quite distant to me was still extremely recent for him, and he sometimes forgot that the rest of us didn't have his manner of thinking.

"You have to remember that one with my . . . peculiarities rarely can have an actual long-lasting home." Verne continued. "So instead, one attempts to bring one's life *with* one in each move. Rather like a hermit crab, we move from one shell to another, none of them actually being our own, yet being for that time a place of safety. Anything that enters your house, then, may be encroaching on all those things you bring with you—both physical and spiritual. Work-men and such are things beyond my direct control, especially in a society such as this one."

"Are you afraid they'll find out about you?"

Verne shrugged, then smiled slightly, his large dark eyes twinkling momentarily in the lights of a passing car. "Not really. Besides the fact that Morgan would be unlikely to miss anyone trying to enter the basement, the basement itself contains little of value for those seeking the unusual; the entrance to the vault and my true sanctum sanctorum is hidden very carefully indeed, and it's quite difficult to open even if found. And my personal refrigerator in my upstairs room is secured very carefully, as you know well." Verne referred to the fact that I'd installed the security there myself. "No, Jason. It is simply that my home is the last fading remnant of my own world, even if all that remains there is my memory and a few truly ancient relics. The mass entry of so many people of this world . . . somehow it once more reminds me how alone I am."

I pulled into my new garage, built after werewolves nearly whacked me on the way to my car, and shut off the engine. "I understand. But now you're reaching out to this world, Verne. You're not alone. If something in your house concerns you, come to mine. I mean it; you were willing to die to protect me and Syl."

"And you revived my spirit, Jason. I had let myself die in a sense a long time ago; only now am I becoming what I once was."

The kitchen was warm and well-lighted—I like leaving those lights on—and the aroma of baking Ten Spice Chicken filled the room. I was slightly embarrassed by Verne's words, but at the same time I knew he meant them. Our first meeting had struck a long-dead chord in him; during our apocalyptic confrontation with Virigar I'd discovered just how much he valued friendship . . . and how much I valued him. "I'd offer you some, but it's not quite to your taste."

"Indeed, though I assure you I appreciate both the thought and the scent; I may be unable to eat ordinary food without pain, but my sense of smell is undiminished. . . . You still have some of my stock here?"

"Yep." I reached into the fridge and pitched him a bottle which he caught easily. "I never thought I'd get to the point that I wouldn't notice a bottle of blood in the fridge any more than I would a can of beer." Yanking on a potholder, I reached into the oven and pulled out the chicken, coated in honey with a touch of Inner Beauty and worcestershire sauce and garlic, cilantro, pepper, cardamom, cumin, red pepper, oregano, basil, turmeric, and a pinch of saffron. I put that on the stovetop, pulled out two baked potatoes (crunchy the way I like 'em) and set the microwave to heat up the formerly frozen vegetables I'd put in there before leaving for Verne's. By the time I had my place set, my water glass filled, and the chicken and potatoes on the plate, the veggies were done and I sat down to eat. Verne had poured his scarlet meal into the crystal glass reserved for him and he sat across from me, dressed as usual in the manner one expected a genteel vampire to dress: evening clothes, immaculately pressed, with a sharp contrast between the midnight black of his hair and jacket and the blinding white of his teeth and shirt.

"I haven't asked you lately—how's the art business going?"

Verne smiled. "Very well indeed. Expect an invitation from our friend Mr. Hashima in the mail soon, in fact; he will be having an exhibition in New York in a month or so."

"Great!" I said. "I'm looking forward to it. I was a bit concerned, to be honest—it seemed that he was hemming and hawing about doing anything with you for a while."

Verne nodded, momentarily pensive. "True. There were some oddities, some reluctance which I do not entirely understand . . . but it is none of our business, really. What is important is that he and I are now enjoying working together." He leaned back. "In other related areas, I'm sure you saw the news about Akhenaten being returned to Egypt, but thus far the archaeological world is keeping the other treasures quiet while they're examining them. Most of the truly unique artworks are already elsewhere, and I confess to feeling quite some relief. As their custodian, it was something of a strain, I came to realize, to have to be concerned about their preservation along with my own whenever I was forced to move."

"You can't tell me you've emptied that vault?" I asked in surprise.

He laughed. "Hardly, my friend. There are pieces there I keep for beauty's sake alone, others for historical value, ones which are personally important, and so on. And even of those I would consider selling or donating there remain quite some number; it would be unwise for me to either flood the market, or to risk eliminating one of my major reserves of wealth in case some disaster occurs."

I couldn't argue that. "But let's hope there aren't any more disasters. I've had enough of 'em."

"To that I can wholeheartedly agree."

We finished dinner and went to my living room, where I set up the chessboard. Playing chess was fun, but for us it was more an excuse for staying and talking. Neither Verne nor I tended to feel comfortable "just talking"; we had to be *doing* something.

"So," I said after we began, "what did you mean about 'letting yourself die' a while back?"

Verne took a deep breath and moved his pawn. As I considered that position, he answered. "Perhaps the first thing I need to do to answer you is to clarify something. I am not a vampire."

"Huh?"

"Or perhaps I should say, not a vampire in any ordinary sense of the term. True, I drink blood and have a number of supernatural abilities and weaknesses. But these are not the result of being infected by a vampire of any sort. To me, my abilities were a blessing, a gift, not a curse. I am not driven by those impulses that other, more 'normal' vampires must follow."

"So why didn't you tell me this before?" I decided to continue with the standard opening strategy. Getting fancy with Verne usually resulted in my getting roundly trounced in fifteen or twenty moves. "It does explain a few things—I remember thinking that you seemed to hesitate at times when talking about vampires. But why dance around the subject?"

Verne smiled. "It was much easier to just go with the obvious assumptions, Jason. And by doing so, I minimized the chance of anything being learned that I wished kept secret. And it was *much* simpler. The word 'vampire' can be applied to any one of several sorts of beings, not merely one." His smile faded. "Your friend Elias . . . he was of a type which, typically, go mad as they gain their power, until they have grown used to it. They were made in mockery of what I am."

"And what is that?"

He hesitated, not even seeming to see the board. When he finally answered, his voice was softer, and touched with a faint musical accent unlike any I had ever heard. "A remnant of the greatest days of this world, my friend. In the ending of that time, I was wounded unto death; but I refused to die. I would *not* die, for there were those who needed me and I would not betray them by failing to reach them, even if that failure was through death itself.

"Perhaps there was something different about me even then, or it was something about the difference between the world that was and the world that is now, for certainly I cannot have been the only man to ever attempt to hold Death at bay with pure will; because I did not die. I rose and staggered onward, to find that my solitary triumph had been in vain." I heard echoes of pain and rage in his voice, tears he'd shed long ago still bringing a phantom stinging to the eye, a hoarseness to his words.

"Of those who had been my charges, none remained; and all was ruins. But in the moment I would have despaired . . . *She* came." He moved again.

I could hear the capital letter in "She" when he spoke. "*She?*"

"The Lady Herself." The accent was stronger now, and I was certain I'd never heard anything quite like it. Not even really close to it. The accent was of a language whose very echoes were gone from this world. Then it was as though a door suddenly closed in his mind, for he glanced up suddenly. When he spoke again, the accent was gone, replaced by the faint trace of Central European I was used to. "I'm sorry, Jason. No more."

"Too painful?"

He looked at me narrowly, his eyes unfathomable. "Too dangerous."

"To you?"

"No. To you."

29

The man sitting across from me was small. Oriental, handsome (at least that's what Syl told me later; I'm not much of a judge), average-length hair just a bit shaggy. He was dressed in fairly casual style, but that wasn't much indication of his job or resources; people come to WIS in different guises than their coworkers usually see.

"Okay, Mr., um, Xiang—that right?—okay, what can I help you with?"

Tai Lee Xiang shifted uncomfortably in his chair, obviously ill at ease. "I'm trying to locate someone."

Locate someone? That didn't sound particularly promising. There's some kinds of work I might do once in a while, but don't consider worth much. Finding old girlfriends, enemies, and so on was one of those. "What kind of a someone?"

"My father."

Okay, that was more interesting, maybe. "Your father? Okay. How'd you come to not know where he is? A family argument?"

He squirmed again, then stood up, pacing in the short distance available. "It's . . . hard to explain. I didn't have any argument with him. It's . . . I've just not seen him in a long time." His voice was heavily accented—Vietnamese, if what he told me was right—but the word "long" was clearly emphasized.

"What do you need to find him for? Just a family reunion?"

"Why do you need to know?" he countered, slightly annoyed.

"I don't necessarily *need* to know, as long as there's nothing illegal involved, but any information can sometimes help." I had to put in that clause about "illegal" somewhere—it wasn't at all unusual for people to try to use Wood's Information Service to get info they had no business getting.

He frowned at me, then shrugged. "I am new in this country, and he is my only living relative, aside from my children."

"Fair enough." This actually sounded interesting. Finding a man can be a relatively easy thing, or almost impossible, depending on how much information you had to go on. "I'll need everything you can possibly tell me about your father. The more I know, the easier it will be to find him."

He looked somewhat embarrassed and uncomfortable again. "I . . . I can't tell you too much. I have . . . memory trouble."

"Amnesia?" I was surprised by this little twist.

"Um, yes, I think that's what they called it. I remember some things well, not other things."

Interesting case. "Okay. Can I ask why you chose WIS for this job?"

"I saw the reports on the werewolves . . ." he began. I already knew the rest; the "Morgantown Incident" was a great piece of advertisement. I was wrong.

" . . . and of all the investigators out there, only you seemed the sort to be ready to search for someone . . . unusual."

I raised an eyebrow. "Are you telling me there's something out of the ordinary about your father?"

"Yes."

"Tell me."

Tai Lee looked at me. "I can't tell you any more unless you agree to do the job. You . . . feel like an honorable man to me, which means if you agree to do the job, you won't talk about it to other people if I don't want you to."

He had me pegged right. I thought a moment. "Nothing illegal involved in this job?"

"I know of nothing that would be illegal in finding my father, no."

"Very well, then. I agree. I'll find your father, if it's at all possible."

His nervous fidgeting quieted almost instantly; he relaxed visibly. "Thank you."

"So what can you tell me about your father? Skip the description for now—I've got a computer program we'll use later to construct the best picture. Tell me any facts his appearance wouldn't tell me."

"That is where my memory is weak. I can only tell you five things about Father."

"Shoot."

"Excuse me?"

"That means, go ahead, let me have them."

"First, he was not my natural father. I was adopted. He was not of Oriental blood, but I think Westerner instead."

Well, that weakened one approach. Obviously there'd be no link in appearance between father and son, and not necessarily one of immigration, either. "Next?"

"Father was a priest. Priest of . . . um . . . nature? I'm not sure the term . . . ?"

That was interesting. "You mean of the earth itself? Not Shinto or something of that nature?"

"Yes. The world's spirit?"

"Our word for that is generally 'Gaia.'"

"Yes! That is it." He nodded, apparently recognizing the word. "Father also had a ring that he wore, which he would never remove."

"Kind of ring?"

"A big, wide, heavy gold ring, with a very large red stone—I think a ruby—set in it."

I blinked for a moment. "O . . . kay."

"Something wrong?"

"No, nothing. Go on."

He hesitated. "This is the . . . weird part."

"I'm ready."

"No, I mean, really strange. Please believe me when I tell you this is not a joke?"

I studied him carefully. "I believe you're not playing

a joke on me. You seem too serious to be able to joke about it at all."

"Thank you." He had tensed up again; my assurance made him relax. "All right . . . my father didn't eat; instead, he drank blood."

I stopped dead in mid-keystroke. *No. This was ridiculous. What were the odds? But* drinking blood? *A red-stone ring that never came off?*

Tai could tell something had happened to me. "Mr. Wood?"

"What was the fifth thing?"

"What?"

"That's four facts about your father. What's the fifth?"

"His name . . . the name he was using then. His name was V'ierna Dhomienkha a Atla'a Alandar."

It was impossible. But it had *to be.* I stood up. "Excuse me for a minute; I'm going to check something."

"What? Mr. Wood, what is it?"

"I'll be back in a moment."

I stepped into the back office, grabbed the phone off the hook, and dialed Verne's number.

"Domingo Residence, Morgan speaking."

"Morgan, this is Jason. I need to speak with Verne."

Morgan's voice was puzzled. "But, Jason, you know that Master Verne is never awake at this time. Why, it's barely two o' clock."

"Then wake him. I know he *can* move about in the day, if he wants. This is important!"

There was a long pause—even longer to me, sitting on the other end doing nothing. But finally I heard the familiar voice pick up at the other end. "Jason? What is the emergency?" Tired though he was, what I heard most in his voice was worry. "It isn't the Wolf, is it?"

Jesus, I should have realized that was the first thing he'd think of. "No, no. Nothing that bad. Maybe not bad, really, at all. I have a guy here looking for his father."

His tone was slightly nettled. "And how does this concern me?"

"Because of what he told me about his father: that he wore a ruby-colored crystal in a gold-setting ring that he never took off, and that he drank blood."

There was dead silence on the other end for several moments. "Interesting coincidence to say the least, Jason. But I have no children."

"He said he wasn't a natural child of this man— adopted. He also said that his father was some kind of priest of nature, and he gave his father's name. I'm not sure quite how to spell it, but it sounded awfully like yours . . ."

In a whisper almost inaudible, I heard, "V'ierna Dhomienkha a Atla'a Alandar i Sh'ekatha . . ."

"Holy shit," I heard my own whisper. I still couldn't believe it.

"That name? He spoke *that* name? But . . . that is impossible." Verne's voice was at the edge of anger, laughter, or tears, I couldn't tell which, and hearing that strain in his voice was more upsetting than I'd imagined. "I am on my way, sun or no sun."

I hung up and stepped back out into the office. Tai Lee Xiang looked up at me. "Mr. Wood?"

"If what you've told me is accurate, Mr. Xiang . . . I think I've located him already."

As his jaw dropped, a chill wind blew through the closed office, and from my back room stepped Verne Domingo, dark eyes fixed on my visitor.

There was no recognition in Verne's eyes, but there was no doubt about Tai Lee's reaction. He leapt to his feet, eyes wide. "Father!"

Verne fixed him with a cold glare. "Who are you? Who, that you know that name unspoken for generations unnumbered, that you would claim to be son to me?" That alien accent was back and emphasized by his anger.

There was no mistaking the shocked, wounded look in Tai Lee Xiang's eyes. "Father? Don't you recognize me? The boy in the temple?"

Verne's mouth opened for a bitter retort, but at the last words his mouth slowly closed. He stared at the young man intensely, as though he would burn a hole through him by gaze alone. I felt a faint power stir in the room. Then Verne's face went even paler than usual, and he stepped forward, reaching out slowly to touch the Oriental's face. "The scent is wrong . . . but the soul. I know that soul. Is it really you, Raiakafan?"

Tai jerked as Verne spoke the name, as though slapped in the face, then nodded. "Y . . . yes. Yes. That was my name."

For the first time since I'd known him, Verne seemed too overcome to speak. He simply stepped forward, around the desk, and stared straight into the young man's eyes. "Even with what I feel . . . I must have proof. For you disappeared . . ."

Tai—Raiakafan?—studied me, and suddenly I had a completely different impression of him. The uncertain, nervous young man was gone; instead I was seeing a black, polished-stone gaze as cold as black ice. I found myself stepping backward involuntarily; only once before had I gotten an impression of such total lethality, and that had been when I had stood in a hospital hallway and watched Virigar himself assume his true form. That feeling carried the utter conviction that Tai was not merely trained in the arts of killing, but a killer to his very core. "In front of him?" he asked coldly.

I could see that Verne was slightly surprised by the tone, but not apparently by the question. "It may be necessary later . . . but you are quite correct. We shall speak in private. But I would appreciate it if you moderate your tone of address to one who is not only my friend, but the one who has reunited us."

The cold gaze softened abruptly, replaced by an apologetic look. "I'm sorry, Father. You are right. Mr. Wood, forgive me. It has been a difficult time for me. But I am very grateful . . . and amazed."

I shrugged. "Don't mention it. Not as much a coincidence as I thought at first; anyone who was Verne's friend would have been around during the last dust-up. The only *real* coincidence was that one of those friends happened to be an info specialist. No," I said as I saw him reaching for a wallet, "no charge. Not only is Verne a friend, I hardly had to do any work on this one."

"Still, I thank you, Jason," Verne said.

His hand on Tai's arm, Verne and the mysterious visitor disappeared into thin air. I jumped a bit at that, but my mind was distracted by the fact that I'd seen a new and different sparkle in Verne's eyes as they vanished.

Vampire tears are just like ours.

30

"Guess who!"

Two soft hands covered my eyes in time with the words. To my credit, I managed to keep from jumping, though she probably knew how much she'd startled me anyway.

"Madame Blavatsky?"

She giggled. "Nope."

"Nostradamus?"

"Do I feel like I have a beard? Try again!"

"Then it must be the great Medium of the Mohawk Valley herself, Sylvia Stake!"

The hands came away as I turned around. "You guessed!"

"No one else has a key to this place, and Verne's voice is two octaves lower and his hands five sizes bigger."

Sylvie was looking good this evening, in one of her gypsyish outfits, black hair currently styled in tight ringlet-like curls pulled back by several colorful scarves, a low-cut dress with a long skirt, and a big over-the-shoulder bag that was handwoven with enough different colors to supply a dozen rainbows. "Oh, is *that* the only difference?" she said, leaning forward.

Sylvie makes me nervous. I don't know why; she's not the only woman or girl I've ever dated, and I never got this nervous around them or anyone else for that matter. Because she always saw it, Syl assumed it was all women who made me nervous. And she always enjoyed flustering me. Leaning forward in *that* dress was just another such approach. "C'mon, Syl, cut it out. I can't take the games today."

She switched gears immediately. "Sorry, Jason. I noticed you seemed tense, but I thought it might be just work and the fact I'd been away so long."

"It's not like I fall apart when you go away, you know."

"Then what's bothering you?"

I turned back to the computer screen. "Sorta business, sorta personal."

"Verne." It was a statement, not a question.

"How did you know?"

"Just a feeling."

At least part of what made Syl tough to be around was that she was able to sense things. Until vampires and werewolves showed up, Syl was the only truly paranormal thing I'd ever encountered, and I'd denied even that until the night one of her New Age crystal trinkets had kept a vampire from crushing my throat. She was also the only person either I or Verne had met who could at times see through a werewolf's disguise. According to Verne, in fact, that should be impossible . . . but Sylvie had managed to warn me with a glance just in time to keep me from being sliced to ribbons by a werewolf disguised as my friend Renee. "You know, it's tough to hide anything from you. A guy came in the other day, asking me to find his father, who he'd been separated from for years. It turned out that his father is Verne."

"Well, that's wonderful . . . isn't it?"

"I dunno." I pointed at the screen. "Verne didn't recognize his face at all, just said something about recognizing his 'soul,' and then the two of them went off to talk together. Verne seems convinced that he's bona fide, but I have to wonder. Even if he *is* the real McCoy, that doesn't mean he couldn't have something nasty up his sleeve."

"Jason, it's not like you to be this paranoid."

I told her about that cold gaze. "That just started me thinking, though. I wouldn't go around worrying if that was all it was. But because of that, I decided to just run a background check on this guy, and I didn't like what came up."

Syl looked at the screen. It showed a front-page story from a Vietnamese paper of several months ago, accompanied by two pictures. One showed a Vietnamese in a business suit in one of those typical "ID Photo" poses; the other showed a blond-haired, sharp-featured young man with a cold, angry expression.

"If you color that hair black," I said, hitting the command as I spoke, "that guy's a twin for our 'Tai Lee Xiang.'"

"What does the story say?"

"Says that the unnamed subject—the blond guy—

here killed the man in the picture while escaping from a maximum-security hospital for the criminally insane. Doctor Ping Xi, the dead man, was a very important man, apparently." I hit a few more controls, and another newspaper headline appeared. "A couple days later, they claim he killed off a colonel in their army, and he's been hunted ever since. International warrants, the whole nine yards."

"You don't really think even a madman would be a threat to Verne, do you?"

I chuckled slightly in spite of myself. If I glanced out the righthand window, I was able to just make out one of the two girders left standing from the warehouse that Verne had single-handedly demolished while killing Virigar's brood of werewolves. "It does sound a little silly, doesn't it? But this guy isn't an ordinary killer. According to the files I've been able to worm out, this colonel was practically torn apart." I felt a spike of ice suddenly form in my chest as I spoke those words, and remembered a particular clearing in the woods.

Sylvie paled suddenly. "You don't think . . ."

" . . . Yes, I do think. We'd better get over there."

Neither of us had to explain the hideous thought that had occurred to us. Werewolves. Shapeshifters whose guises were perfect, impenetrable, even down to the molecular level. Beings who could be anyone and fool even an ancient vampire like Verne. If Virigar, their King, knew something about Verne's background . . . how very easy to have one of his people change into some form with a good background story. If Verne knew no way to tell a werewolf from a real man, that meant that they were even capable of imitating souls.

Pausing only to grab a couple pieces of equipment, we headed for the car at a dead run.

31

"Good evening, Master Jason." Morgan said, opening the door.

"Evening, Morgan." I answered, glancing around. There were still lots of pieces of clutter around from the work that was being done on the house. "Verne around?"

"He and Master Kafan are in the library at the moment, sir."

I opened my mouth to ask who "Master Kafan" was, then remembered Verne calling Tai Lee Xiang "Raiakafan." "Thanks, Morgan."

"Your coats, sir, Lady Sylvia?"

Though impatient, I didn't show any sign of our concern. Neither did Syl; we both knew that if it *was* a werewolf, any hint that we suspected it could be fatal.

The library was much neater than the other areas. I remembered that Verne pushed the contractors to finish that room first and to clean it up each day; he valued the library more than just about any other room, except naturally whatever room it was that he slept in during the day. Verne and Tai were sitting together, bent over what looked like an atlas, with other books scattered about the table. Both looked up as we entered.

"Jason!" Verne rose. "I did not expect you. And Lady Sylvie." He took her hand and bowed deeply over it.

I felt slightly jealous as Syl developed a slight blush and thanked Verne for his courtesy. She used to be scared stiff of Verne, but that seemed to be a thing of the past now.

Tai nodded to me and stood up at a gesture from Verne. "Tai, please meet my good friend Sylvia Stake," Verne said.

We'd hoped for a setup like this. As he reached out,

his attention focused on Syl, I pulled my hand out of my pocket and flung what was in my hand at him.

Neither of us saw everything that happened; from Syl's point of view Tai suddenly seemed to disappear. I, on the other hand, saw a blur move toward me and felt myself lifted into the air and slammed into a wall so hard that breath left me with an explosive *whoosh* and red haze fogged my vision. I struggled feebly, trying to force some air back into my lungs.

The pressure on my windpipe vanished suddenly as my attacker was yanked backwards. "Raiakafan! Jason! What is the meaning of this?" Verne demanded.

"I saw him move quickly; the characteristics of his motion strongly implied an attack." Tai's voice was level, cold, and flat, almost like a machine rather than a living being. "I therefore moved to neutralize him."

"No one 'neutralizes' a member of my household or my friends." Verne stated flatly. "As to Jason's action, I am sure he will explain himself . . . immediately." The last word carried a considerable coldness with it.

"Urrg . . ." I gurgled, then managed to gasp, pulling precious air back into my system. "Sorry . . . Verne." I studied Tai carefully. Yes . . . I could see traces of the stuff. It had definitely hit him. Hell, he'd charged straight into it. Obviously he didn't realize what kind of an attack it had been, if it had actually been an attack. "In a way, Tai was correct. Under the right circumstances, what I was doing would have been an attack. A lethal one."

Verne's eyes narrowed, fortunately showing more puzzlement than anger; we'd been through enough that he knew that I'd never do anything like this without damned good reason. "And just what circumstances would that have been?"

Syl answered. "If Tai had been a werewolf, he'd be dead now."

Tai blinked, brushing away the silver dust I'd thrown in his face.

Verne's expression softened in comprehension. "Ahh. Of course. You could hardly be blamed for such a suspicion, Jason. Without knowing the extent of my senses, you had no way of knowing that I *knew* this was the real Raiakafan, no matter what his outward seeming. And he has confirmed it in other ways since then."

"According to what you told me," I said, "a werewolf could foil even your senses."

"True," Verne admitted. "But there are other things that mere duplication of the soul and body cannot achieve, such as the memories that would have to be derived from . . . well, from someone supposedly dead a very, very long time ago. You still seem unsure, Jason. Please, tell me what troubles you."

Without a word, I pulled out a printed copy of the pictures and articles I'd located and handed it to Verne, who read them in silence, then studied the picture and Tai carefully. Finally he handed them back.

"As we expected, Raiakafan," he said. "I am of the opinion that we must tell them everything."

That dead-black gaze returned; I saw Syl shrink back from it and it took some effort not to do so myself. "Are we sure?"

Verne waited until the strange young man was looking at him, and then answered. "Jason has risked his life to protect me. He has rekindled the Faith that was lost. And the Lady Sylvia is his best companion, a Mistress of Crystal, and born with the Sight. If I cannot trust them, then I cannot trust you, and if you cannot trust them, then I am not who you believe." His words were very strange, half-explanation, half-ritual, spoken in a measured, formal manner that sent a shiver up my spine; that alien accent had returned again.

Tai studied me again, less ice in that gaze than before. Finally he nodded. "As you wish, Father."

Verne relaxed, and so did we. The last thing any of us wanted was a real conflict. Whatever was going on here, it was obvious that Raiakafan—Tai—whatever his name was had some real problems in his life, and they might be coming after Verne too.

"Morgan!" Verne called. "Send in refreshments for everyone." He turned to us. "Make yourselves comfortable, Jason, Lady Sylvie. This will be a long and difficult story, but a necessary one, for I see no other way around it but that I—that both Raiakafan and I—will need your help to solve the difficulties that face us." Morgan came in, bearing a tray of drinks, and went out to return a moment later with two trays of hors d'oeuvres. Verne took a sip of his usual and frowned faintly. "How to begin, though . . . ?"

"How about using the White King's approach?" I suggested. "Start at the beginning. Go on to the end. And then stop."

Syl and Verne chuckled at that; Kafan (I'd decided to use Verne's name for him) just looked puzzled. Verne smiled sadly, his eyes distant. "Ahh. The beginning. But it's always hard to mark the beginning, is it not? For whatever beginning you choose, there is always a cause that predates it. But it is true that for most great things there is a point at which you can say, 'Here. At this point, all that went before was different.' Perhaps I should start there . . ."

"No, Father! It is too dangerous—for them."

Verne sighed. "It would be too dangerous not to tell them, Raiakafan. Jason works best with maximum information. But you are correct, as well." He turned to us. "Before I proceed . . . Jason, Sylvia, I must impress upon you these facts.

"First, that much of what I am going to tell you contradicts that which is supposedly scientific fact.

"Second, that these contradictions—though they be on a titanic, global scale—were nonetheless *designed*; that it was intended by certain parties that the information I possess would never again be known to a living soul. My own existence is due as much to blind luck as it is to my own skill and power.

"Third, once you have been told these things, you become a potential target for the forces that would keep these things secret . . . and so will anyone to whom you reveal these things. And the forces behind this are of such magnitude as to give even Virigar pause, so powerful that the mightiest nations of this world are as nothing to them." He gazed solemnly at us. "So think carefully; do you still wish to involve yourselves in these matters? I will think no less of you either way, I assure you. But once I speak, there is no going back. Ever. Even my ability to hide memories will not save you; they will never believe a memory completely gone when they can ensure it by killing the one with the memory."

Verne's deadly serious warning made me hesitate. He had only been this concerned when Virigar had come, and at that time there was no doubt that all the Great Wolf's forces were directed towards him. Now, he was speaking of forces that didn't even know he existed and yet were so fearsome as to warrant the most frightening warning he could give me. Not a reassuring thought.

Syl replied first. "I want to hear the truth, Verne. I believe we were meant to hear it. If not, I would not be here."

I nodded. "I didn't think I'd be able to make friends with a vampire and not get into trouble sometimes. Might as well know what's really going on. Seriously,

Verne . . . if you have troubles on that scale, you're going to need all the help you can get someday."

Kafan studied us for a moment, and then smiled very slightly. "They are strong friends, Father."

"They are indeed." Verne leaned back in his red-cushioned chair. Light the color of blood flashed from his ring as he folded his hands. "Then, my friends, I start . . . or no. Raiakafan, would you begin? For what I must tell them is not only the more dangerous part, but the one that is less immediate. Your story is immediate. Mine is important to explain why even your story is insufficient."

Kafan nodded. Turning to us, he began.

32

He looked around and smiled, satisfied. Despite his oddities, the village accepted him. His children were growing up strong and healthy. His wife took care of them all. In a country torn by civil war all too often, this village had managed to keep itself isolated and secure. Untouched by the strange devices of the outside world, unimportant in the maneuverings of whatever politicians or dictators might rule one part of the land or another, it looked much the same as it would have two hundred years ago.

He shivered, suddenly, as though chilled, despite the bright sunlight streaming down on him. The village and his home seemed to him now like a veneer, a fragile layer of paint laid over something of unspeakable horror. But he knew that the real horror was what lay in his past. He had escaped that, hadn't he? Years gone by now . . . he must be safe, forgotten. Thought dead and lost forever. Surely they would have come for him long ago had they known . . . wouldn't they?

The wail of a child demanding attention came from within the house, that sound that in a parent could simultaneously bring frustration, warmth, and concern. But he could hear something else in it, as could any who knew what to listen for: the sound of the past. It was the reason he could never, ever be sure they were not watching and waiting, though with his utmost skill and caution he had stalked the dense mountain forests and found not a single trace of intrusion. Genshi, his sister, and two brothers were reason enough for them to wait.

Kay put a hand on his shoulder. "Tai . . . you aren't thinking about *that* again, are you?"

Tai turned and gazed at his wife. Several inches taller than he, willowy, with skin the color of heartwood, she was the only proof (aside from himself and his children) that there *was* an "outside world" different from the one the village knew. Kay was a strange woman by anyone's standards—which was fortunate, because no other woman could possibly have accepted what he was, let alone married him while knowing the truth. He still thought her coming to this village had been more than coincidence; it had felt like destiny. She had belonged to some organization she called "Peace Corps." The aircraft carrying her and a number of other workers for this group had crashed in the mountains; Kay had become separated from the other survivors in a storm and wandered for a long time in the wilderness. Had she not been trained in survival, she would have died. Instead, when Tai found her, she was using a stream as a mirror, cutting her hair in a ruler-straight line as though working in a beauty salon. Her civilized, calm, utterly *human* demeanor even in the midst of what to her was complete wilderness ensnared Tai instantly. He had brought her to the village and helped her recover from her ordeal; by the time she was recovered, she didn't want to leave. She had no relatives or real friends elsewhere; here she felt that she belonged.

"What else?" he answered finally. "I can't help it, Kay. You weren't a part of it; little Tai is too young to remember it. Only Seb remembers. Seb and me."

"We've been over this again and again, Tai. They've had all the time in the world to find you. If they wanted you back and thought you were alive, they'd have gotten you long ago. They had no reason in the world to believe you'd be able to survive out here and fit in; you'd either have died on your own or been killed by a frenzied mob from their point of view. Stop worrying. Maybe someone caught up with them and they don't even exist any more."

Oh, all the gods of all the world, let that be true. Please let that be true, he thought.

"Maybe," he said aloud.

He followed her inside, feeling better. Kay had been sent to him from the skies above; surely that was a sign in itself.

The children were all inside—the two youngest, Genshi and Kei, on one side of the table, the two others, Seb and little Tai, opposite them. Not for the first time, it struck Tai as a strange coincidence that even though the older children had a different mother, all four were much darker-skinned than their father. Tai and Genshi, in particular, looked very similar . . . if you ignored the *difference* that Genshi, unlike his older siblings, could not hide. Kei had been born without it, looking very much like a copy of her mother.

Kay began serving the food, beginning with Tai and ending with the toddlers. As they began to eat, Seb suddenly stiffened. "Father—"

A single sound; the sound of a metal catch being released.

The coldness returned, became a lump of ice in his

gut. "I heard, Seb. Kay, get down. Everyone, on the floor, now!"

He moved stealthily towards the side door, caught a faint scent and heard movement. Then a voice boomed out, impossibly loud.

"Attention! This house is surrounded. Surrender quietly and none of you will be harmed!"

"Go away!" he shouted hopelessly. "I don't want to go back! Leave us alone!"

The unfamiliar voice was replaced by the oily, ingratiating tones of the Colonel. "Now, now, let's not be that way . . . Tai, is it? There's been an enormous amount of investment involved in you and your children. You can't expect us to just throw it all away. If you'll come back quietly, I promise you that you can even keep your whole family with you. Just cooperate and you can find yourself living quite a lavish life."

"I like the life I have here!" He saw that Seb and Tai had crawled over and pulled up the floorboards to get at the weapons. He nodded. Good boys. Kay was pale, tears running down her face.

"Sorry I was wrong," she whispered.

"It's all right." he said, knowing nothing was going to be "all right" again. "You made us feel better while it lasted. I love you."

"I love you."

The Colonel spoke again, no longer trying to be friendly. This time his voice was precisely reflective of what he was: a military commander of ruthless and amoral determination, efficient and pitiless. "All right, Alpha. Give up. You are all surrounded. There is no way you can escape. The less trouble you give us, the less pain your children and your wife suffer. We know very well that you don't give a shit about pain for yourself, but how about your family? Surrender immediately, or all of them go the the labs along with you!"

"With all respect, Colonel, you and your ancestors were all sheep-fucking perverts. Shove your offer up your ass!"

The Colonel didn't respond verbally; suddenly a volley of canisters flew through the leaf-shuttered windows and began hissing yellow vapor.

Kay knew what that was as well as he did; holding her breath she dove out the largest windows with the infants, who immediately began screaming. Tai was too busy to worry about that; they had to win. And there was only one way to do that.

He dove out the window nearest the Colonel's booming voice. A soldier tried to strike him as he went out, but Tai was too fast. Seb and little Tai followed momentarily; the soldier blocked Seb's escape. Tai continued on, nodding to himself as he heard the man scream and then the sound of a head being separated from a body.

There was no more need for subtlety here. Concealment was useless. As the men ahead raised their weapons, he *changed*.

Horror froze them. Though they must have been warned, there's an infinite difference between being told of something impossible and seeing it coming for you, savage and hungry, in real life. His claws ripped the armor off the first soldier, sent him staggering back. He was the lucky one. The other two fell dead, one fountaining blood from the throat, the other with a broken neck. He tore through their ranks, closing on the Colonel. If he could just reach the man . . .

Several small explosions erupted through the clearing; he caught an odd odor, tried to hold his breath; droplets of something dotted his skin. Tai found himself slowing down, tried desperately to force himself forward. As his vision began to fade into blackness, the last thing he saw was the sardonic smile of the Colonel, only twenty feet away.

Tai blinked his way back to consciousness slowly. He wished he hadn't. The sterile white walls . . . the thick one-way glass wall . . . the ordinary-looking door that was locked and armored like a vault . . .

He was back at the Project.

He'd barely come to that bleak conclusion when the wall screen lit up. The Colonel looked back at him. The figure next to him sent shivers up Tai's spine, causing his light fur to ruffle. Ping Xi. Doctor Ping Xi. The Colonel might give the money and the facilities, but it was this man, with his narrow eyes, white hair, long pianist's hands, and cold, calculating brilliance who ruled the Project.

"Congratulations, Alpha," the Colonel said. "A fine group of youngsters. Dr. Xi was just telling me how useful they're going to be."

With difficulty he choked his rage back. Once he started fighting, even verbally, it was impossible to stop, and intelligence went out the window. "Leave them alone. I'll cooperate. Just leave my family out of this."

The Colonel shook his head. "I gave you the chance for that, but you insisted on the hard way. Now that you're caught, of course you'll try singing a different tune. I'm afraid not."

"At least let Kay go!" he said, fighting to keep the killing fury under control. "She's not one of us!"

This time it was Ping Xi who answered. "Impossible. The most important questions here will be what the results are of the cross-breeding. This would be impossible without having both of the parents available for study. It is particularly interesting that the children represent a dichotomous birth in both ways—fraternal twins of different sex and one showing all the Project characteristics and the other not. It will take a great deal of study to determine just what caused such a fascinatingly clear division of genetic expression."

It was no use. With an inarticulate roar of anger he launched himself at the wall screen. Bouncing off it as he always did. As if from a great distance, he heard the Colonel remark calmly, "Just as usual. Some things never change, eh?"

He fought them after that. But he wondered, if he had been fully human, if he would have. Why bother? For years they'd been watching him. Waiting. The patience itself was frightening, not at all what he had thought was the norm for military and governments. As though they had all the time in the world. But fighting was a part of him.

And once more they drugged him. Days melted into weeks of sluggish thought and dulled senses, only sharpening when, for some test or another, they needed him unimpaired. Sometimes he thought he could sense Seb or little Tai or even Genshi, but he never saw them.

Time passed. Where had he come from? He wasn't sure. Had the labs really made him? It was all he really knew . . . and yet . . . and yet . . .

In the depths of one of his rages, something snapped. A memory . . .

Tall twoleg thing. My territory! Kill!

Pain! Hit me! Where? How? Fast twoleg!

Brightsharp metal! Cut! No. No cut! Hit! Why no cut?

Claw twoleg! Miss? Bite twoleg! Miss? Miss? How miss?

Pain! Hit again! Twoleg growl! Leap! Not hit ground???

Twoleg hold up! Stop in air! Twoleg too fast!

*°Idea° Twoleg holding me . . . can't get away! Claw!
???MISS??? PAIN! Blackness. . . . Death coming . . .
Wake up. Not-dead? Twoleg here!
Twoleg . . . Twoleg stronger. Twoleg still not kill.
Not able kill Twoleg? Twoleg not kill?
Stop. Wait . . .*

Tai's eyes snapped open, but he wasn't really seeing anything in the room with him. Just the final scene
from that frighteningly disjointed, animalistic memory.
A face. Dark-skinned, human, a face sharp-edged, with
the look of the hawk. Clothing that would be strange
in any place he had ever heard of. And eyes . . . eyes
the color of stormclouds and steel, huge gray eyes filled
with calm certainty.

That is a real memory, he thought. *Impossible
though it is, that is real.*

At night, when he slept, the drugs loosened their
hold. He dreamed . . .

*Standing in a strange pose, the Master nodded. Tai
launched himself at the tall, angular figure, claws
outstretched. The Master moved the slightest bit, and
Tai's claws caught nothing but air. Again. And again.
No matter how fast, no matter what direction or technique he tried, he could never touch the strange man,
let alone harm him. Finally he stopped and waited,
wishing he could express what he felt to the figure
before him. The figure made sounds . . . he stopped and
thought. Those sounds . . . were they . . . were they a
way to . . . tell other people things?*

*As he thought that, the Master's sounds fell into
recognizable patterns. Though it would be a while
before he understood words, the sounds remained:* "Well
done, little one. You have learned the concept of practice and of when to stop practicing. When you begin
to speak, then truly your training can start."

More days passed. More dreams. Pain. Tests. Most

of the dreams faded before waking, but one, finally, remained.

Revelation.

He stood in the center of his room. Drugs fogged his thoughts, made thinking an almost impossible effort. So much easier to just lie down, relax, do nothing. Anger burned away the fog, but replaced it with the smoke of fury. No, anger was no good now. They knew anything that he could do when driven by rage. Only discipline, only by the power of his mind, could he hope to surprise them.

The Master studied him as he practiced. "There is a Power in the soul, little one. The mind and the body are one, and yet each has its own strengths and weaknesses. One trained sufficiently in both can never be defeated, or so it is said. You have a special strength, a power that enough training will bring to its peak. That path I can show you how to begin."

He brought his arms up and parallel, in the stance that his Master had taught. He looked in the one-way mirror, and then closed his eyes, focusing on himself. Tai visualized himself in every detail, every hair, the way the faint air currents in the room moved the clothing he wore in infinitesimal patterns. The fog began to recede from his mind, pushed back by the extremity of what he was doing, by the focus in his soul. He trembled, forcing his body to obey. He needed more. A way out. But panic and fear would do him no good. He remembered the last dream, the last lesson of the Master:

"When your body betrays you, it must be disciplined by the spirit, by the mind. Only the mind matters. Think upon water, little one. Water. It is all but the smallest part of what you are. All but the veriest fraction of the world. And all but indestructible, infinitely adaptable, nothing you can grasp in your hand, yet able to become

*something irresistible, unstoppable, infinitely fast like
a flood, infinitely slow like a glacier, yielding to the
smallest object, yet able to wear down the mountains
themselves; in fact, all but the very essence of life itself.
You have learned the Hand Center. You have seen the
Wind Vision. You have found in yourself the High Center. Now, take into yourself the Water Vision."*

He thought of water. A droplet, condensing in a
cloud. The droplet, a single thought. Droplets coalescing, becoming a raindrop; the raindrop, a single idea.
The rain falling, becoming a puddle, a thousand
puddles, a downpour; a day in the life of a man or a
woman, a thousand thousand thousand thoughts moving
as one. The downpour, still made of a trillion trillion
droplets, pouring into rivers, the rivers into a mighty
ocean that covered the world; the ocean, a man. Infinite
in complexity, yet united in the substance of the soul.

Tai didn't really understand what it was he was
doing. It was an art, a technique, a skill taught to him
so long ago that only the dreams showed him some
of the teaching. Yet in his bones he understood it. He
would not fail the Master, even now.

The ocean was his soul. How, then, could anything
withstand it? How could a drug, however potent, have
any effect when diluted unnumbered times in the
waters of his mind? It could not. And so it did not.

Tai felt his mind clearing. Yet just by noticing that,
he trembled at the edge of losing this transcendent
moment. He knew he might not reach this point again;
it required the desperation and, perhaps, the paradox
of the drugged calmness to reach it this time.

But the very instability was the key. Like the shaken
ocean, his soul gathered into a roiling wave. He spun
and gathered the force of the oceans into his movements, a fluid lunge at a wall of armored, tempered
glass that could withstand explosive shells.

But what is anything next to the power of a tsunami? What use armor plate against the relentless pressure of a glacier?

The wall bulged outward like cheap cardboard, bulged and then shattered into a billion fragments that glittered in the laboratory lights like diamonds. In that moment, he saw the shocked faces of the scientists in the lab, and the calmness evaporated. Berserker fury took him.

Breathing hard, Tai slowly came back to sanity. Blood was splattered on him from head to toe; he chose not to look at what he had left behind him. In front of him was a door, and behind that door . . .

"FATHER!"

He hugged Seb and Tai fiercely for a moment, then pulled away. "Go. The way out is clear. Run."

"But what about you?" Seb asked, fighting to keep from crying.

Tai shook his head. "I have to go after Genshi, Kei, and Kay. But I won't have you staying here any longer. Go. And keep going. As far away from here as you can get, to another country if you can. Don't look back. I will find you. If it takes a year or a dozen years, I'll find you. Just make sure that you're safe."

Seb looked torn, but then looked at little Tai and realized what his father meant. It was his time to be a protector. "Yes, Father."

He watched until the two were out of sight. Then he loped down the corridor. Turning the corner, he backpedaled to a halt.

Dr. Ping Xi was there, holding a black box. "Tsk. Are you forgetting something, Alpha?"

"I AM NOT ALPHA!" Loathing and fear held him where he was. Dr. Xi was the only thing he could remember that frightened him.

"Do you think I left everything to chance? The coded transmissions this sends out will detonate a small implant in your brain. A hideous waste, one I would rather avoid. But your children will serve well enough in the lab. You have become, as the Colonel would say, a far too expensive luxury."

The black box seemed to pull his gaze towards it like an evil magnet. One button, and he would cease to exist. He didn't doubt Dr. Xi. Dr. Xi never bothered to lie, it wasn't in his nature.

But was it better to live in the grip of the Project?

That thought decided him. He would win either way. But his children . . .

He had to succeed. He remembered his Master's movements. He had to combine his own speed with the Master's inhuman accuracy. And only one chance to get it right.

He let his shoulders sag, as though realizing he was hopelessly trapped. Then he lunged forward, leaping across the forty feet separating them like a missile.

He saw Xi's eyes widen, and knew in that instant that he was too late; the bastard had more than enough time to press the button.

But he saw the finger hesitate; perhaps, in the end, it was just a little too hard for the doctor to destroy his greatest work. And then he was on Dr. Ping Xi, and his blood tasted like freedom.

33

I rubbed my temples, trying to take this all in. "Okay, let's see if I have this straight. You are some kind of genetic experiment? And this wanted-poster stuff about you is all lies made up by the Evil Government Conspiracy?"

If Kafan had been a cat, his fur would have bristled; as it was, he did a pretty good imitation by glaring at me. "I don't like your tone of voice."

"Gently, Raiakafan." Verne said sternly. "The story is not one to be accepted easily. Jason has a mind that is open . . . but not so open that he is utterly credulous."

Kafan snorted, but turned back to me. "It's not the government, except a few key people. At least that is the impression I got. The group that . . . made . . . me is a self-contained organization. There were some references to a prior group that they belonged to, but I never really heard much. Educating me was not what they were interested in." He stood up again, as he had many times during his story, and paced a circle around the room like a caged lion. "Why do you find this so hard to believe? I haven't been here that long, but I know that genetic engineering *is* part of your civilization, while magic is not, but you accept Verne . . ."

"That's why," I answered. "First, I've seen Verne and other things like him in action. I don't ignore things that I actually see. But I know a fair amount about genetic engineering, at least for a layman, and I *do* know that we haven't got *close* to the level of technology we'd need to make something like you claim to be. And other elements—this 'super martial arts' or whatever it is you say got you out of their holding cells . . ." I chuckled, then looked apologetic. " . . . sorry. But that kind of stuff comes out of video games and bad Hong Kong flicks. Accepting it as 'real' just isn't easy."

Kafan shrugged helplessly. "I can't help what you believe. I know what I am."

"What happened after you killed Dr. Xi?" Sylvie asked.

Kafan's gaze dropped to the floor. He stood still for

a moment, and just the slow sagging of his shoulders told us more than we really wanted to know. "I failed.

"I found where they were keeping Gen, Kei, and Kay. And I got in. But by then the Colonel had organized a counterattack. I was separated from them . . . I had Gen, but Kay and our daughter . . ."

Syl put her hand on his shoulder; he turned his back on her, but didn't pull away; his back shook for a moment with silent sobs. Then he turned back. "They were back in *their* hands."

"And the Colonel?"

The iron-cold expression returned. "I tracked him all the way to Greece, where he had a secondary headquarters. But he'd tricked me. Even as I killed him, he laughed at me. I'd come all the way across the continent and all the time Kay and Kei were still there, in another part of the lab complex!"

I winced; Sylvie just looked sympathetic. "So what brought you here?"

"In my travels across the continent . . . I started remembering other things of my past. The few things I told you, Mr. Wood. And I thought that America was the best place to begin looking, especially once I saw the news about the werewolves and realized that there was someone here who was able to deal with such things."

"So can you prove this story of yours?" I asked.

Kafan narrowed his eyes, then smiled—an expression that held very little humor. "I think so." He turned and looked out the door, towards the entrance hall where the stairs ran up to the second floor. "Gen? Genshi! Come in now, Gen."

There was a scuffling noise with little scratching sounds, like a dog startled up and starting to run on a wooden floor, followed by a thump and a high-pitched grunt. Then a small head peeked around the edge of the doorway, followed by an equally small body crawling along on all fours.

The little boy had a mane of tousled blond hair, bright green eyes . . . and a coating of honey-colored fur on his face. His hands were clawed, as were his feet, and canine teeth that were much too long and sharp showed when he gave us a little smile and giggle, and crawled faster towards his father. His long, fur-covered tail wagged in time to his determined crawl.

"Genshi! Walk, don't crawl."

Genshi pouted slightly at his father, apparently thinking that crawling was more fun, but pushed himself up onto two legs and ran over to Kafan, jumping into his arms and babbling something in what I presumed was a toddler's version of Vietnamese. Kafan replied and hugged him, then looked at us.

Sylvie was smiling. I was just speechless. "Can I see him, Kafan?" Sylvie asked.

Kafan frowned a moment, but relented. "All right. But be careful. He's very, very strong and those claws are sharp." He said something in a warning tone to Genshi, who blinked solemnly and nodded.

Sylvie picked up the little furry boy, who blinked at her and then suddenly wrapped his arms around her neck and hugged her. Syl broke into a delighted grin. "What a little darling you are. Now, now, don't dig those claws in . . . there's a good boy . . ." she continued in the usual limited conversation adults have with babies.

I finally found my voice. "All right. Can't argue with the evidence there. I find it hard to believe, though, that you were the only product of their research. They couldn't have built a whole complex around you alone."

Kafan's smile was cold as ice. "They didn't. When I went to kill him, I found that the Colonel was no more human than I am. Some kind of monster."

"Shit." I didn't elaborate out loud, but to me it was

obvious; if Kafan was telling the truth, these people were not only far ahead of anyone I'd ever heard of, but they were also crazier than anyone I'd ever heard of. Trying out experimental genetic modifications on yourself? Jesus! I thought for a moment. "But . . . something's funny about your story. If you were a lab product, what's this about Verne being your father, or your being trained by this whoever-he-was?"

"That," said Verne, "is indeed the question. For there is no doubt, Jason, that I did, indeed, have a foster son named Raiakafan Ularion—Thornhair Fallenstar as he would be called in English—and there is no doubt in my mind that, changed though he may be, this is indeed the Raiakafan I raised from the time he was a small boy. Yet I knew Raiakafan for many years indeed; he could never have been the subject of genetic experiments. Yet here he is, and there is much evidence that these people he speaks of exist.

"These two things, seeming impossible, tell me that vast powers are on the move, and grave matters afoot. For this reason, I must tell you of the ancient days.

"I must speak . . . of Atla'a Alandar."

34

The Sh'ekatha, or Highest Speaker, gazed in bemused wonder at the tiny figure before him. Beneath the tangled mass of hair, filled with sticks and briar thorns, two serious, emerald-green eyes regarded him. Across the back was strapped a gigantic (for such a small traveller) sword, three feet long with a blade over five inches wide. A bright golden tail twitched proudly behind the boy, who was dressed raggedly in skins.

Yet . . . yet there was something special about this boy, more so than merely his strange race. The way he stood . . . and that sword. Surely . . . surely it was workmanship of the old days.

"Yes, boy? What do you wish?"

The boy studied him. "You are . . . in command here?" he said in a halting, unsure fashion. The voice was rough, like a suppressed growl, but just as high-pitched as any child's.

V'ierna smiled slightly. "I am the Sh'ekatha. I am the highest in authority that you may speak with at this time, yes."

The boy frowned, obviously trying to decide if that met with whatever requirements he might have. Then his brow unfurrowed and he nodded. "My Master sent me here to you."

V'ierna understood what he meant; he had been being taught by a Master of some craft, and now this Master wished the Temple to continue and expand his education. "But there is no certainty that there will be an opening here, young one. We select only a certain number of willing youngsters, and then only when there is proper room for them."

The boy shook his head. "You have to take me. You have to teach me. That is what he said." He blinked as though remembering something. "Oh, I was supposed to show you this." He reached over his back and unsheathed the monstrous blade. Holding it with entirely too much ease for such a tiny boy, he extended the weapon to the Sh'ekatha.

Puzzled, V'ierna studied the weapon. Old workmanship, yes, and very good. But that didn't . . .

It was then that he saw the symbol etched at the very base of the sword: Seven Towers between two Parallel Blades.

His head snapped up involuntarily. He scrutinized the child more carefully now. Yes . . . now that he knew what to look for . . .

He gave the blade back. "Have you a name, young one?"

"Master said that you would give me one."

"Did he, now?" V'ierna contemplated the scruffy figure before him. Certainly of no race born of this world. He smiled. "Then your name is Raiakafan." He reached out and gently pulled a briar free of its tangled nest. "Raiakafan Ularion." He turned. "Follow me, Raiakafan. Your Master was correct. There is indeed a place for you."

"It has never been done!"

V'ierna shook his head. "In the ancient days, there were no such distinctions made, milady. None of these separations of du*y or of privilege. I am not at all sure that the comfort brought about by such clear divisions is worth the price paid in inflexibility. Be that as it may," he raised a hand to forestall the First Guardian's retort, "in this case, it *will* be so. The Lady Herself has so decreed it. If Raiakafan can pass the requirements, he is to be trained for the Guardianship."

Melenae closed her mouth, arguments dying on her lips. If the Lady decreed it and the Sh'ekatha concurred, there was nothing more to be said. "As the Founder decrees, so will it be," she said woodenly, and turned to leave.

"Melenae."

She looked back. "Yes, Sh'ekatha?"

"I will not tolerate any manipulation of the testing. If he is held to either a higher or lower standard than any other trainee, I will be *most* displeased. And so will the Lady."

Her mouth tightened, but she nodded. "Understood."

V'ierna watched her leave. He sighed, and began walking in the opposite direction, down the corridor that was open only to himself, the corridor that led to the Heart. How long had it been? Three thousand years? Four? Ten, perhaps? Long enough for mortal memory to fade, and fade, and cultures to change even when one who founded them tried to retain that which had been lost. Even the name of the city was, to them, little more than a name. To him, it was so much more; Atla'a Alandar; *Atlantaea Alandarion* it had been, "Star of Atlantaea's Memory." But he was one man. Highest Speaker, yes. Blessed in his own way, noted in ritual and in action. But even his longevity was nothing more than a faded echo of the Eternal King, and he had no Eternal Queen, save the Lady Herself.

He emerged into the Heart. The Mirror of the Sky glinted as a wind ruffled the sacred pool's surface. V'ierna knelt by the Heartstone and closed his eyes.

Time changes all things, V'ierna.

I know that, Lady. As always, he felt warmed merely by the silent voice within his mind. Her limitless compassion and energy seemed to lighten the world merely by existing. *But is it so necessary that I see loss as well as change? Have we not lost enough already? Atlantaea—*

—was as near perfect as a society of humanity shall ever be, V'ierna. But that very perfection was its destruction. If your people are ever to attain such heights again, they must work themselves through all the difficulties, all the perils and hatreds and disputes, that are part of growing up. You are all part of nature; I am loving, but a stern teacher as well. Even to my most favored I am not without requirements or price, as you know well.

V'ierna knew. *I understand, Lady.*

He could see her now, night-dark hair ensnaring the heavens in a warm blanket, her face the hardness of the mountains and softness of the fields, beautiful and terrifying and comforting all at once. *And Raiakafan? What is his place in this?*

She smiled. *He has a higher destiny than he knows. His people are filled with violence, a race of savage killers; yet by being born here—his mother landing here, on this world, and giving birth to a child—it was permitted that I touch upon him. He is a part of me, a part of the Earth for all time. He will become my Guardian, as you are my Speaker, and Seirgei my Priest. . . .*

It will not be easy.

The arguments of the Guardians will be overcome by his ability. Jealousy cannot be helped. Evil will come of it. But no choices worth making come easily. The Power fades, my love; those who destroyed Atlantaea bent all their power to sealing it away, and Zarathan, our sister world, now lies beyond our reach. Without something truly extraordinary, even I shall fade from the world, and then . . . her phantom face looked forlornly into the distance *. . . then only a miracle will restore that which was gone. And you will have to provide that miracle.*

V'ierna's heart seemed to freeze within him. This was the first time the Lady had spoken so clearly about the possibility of her own death. *I? What can I possibly do? If you go, Lady, will I, too, not pass from this world? For I am nothing but a man blessed by your powers.*

Her smile seemed to light the world again, driving away the ice in his heart by the certainty of her love and concern. *V'ierna, to the one who held to me beyond death itself I have given all that I can. You are tied to this world more strongly than I, and by the Ring that symbolizes the Blood of Life, you carry my blessing. You are a part of Earth's life, and so long as this world lives, so shall you, though the quality of that life*

*may well change. Through you, some part of me will
survive though all other magic be sealed away from
the world by the actions of the ones who destroyed
Atlantaea. If the worst comes to pass, still will there
be you, to find the path to miracle that will bring the
Spirit of the Earth back and let Eonae, the Lady, be
reborn.*

He stood, feeling her presence fade. But he felt
more ready now. The Lady was right; he could do no
more for these people than he had already done; to
force them into a mold of his own vision would deprive
them of the full understanding of the reasons behind
that mold. Better a return to barbarism than the iron
dictatorship he would have to create.

35

"I wonder if I would have thought that," Verne
concluded, "had I known what would come to pass."

For the second time that night, I was speechless.
After battling vampires and werewolves, I'd thought I
was ready for anything. Even Kafan's story was,
well . . . *modern*. Elias Klein had been a thoroughly
twentieth-century vampire. Virigar, the Werewolf King,
was at home in this world of computers and automo-
biles. Kafan's mad scientist and secret labs were just
a part of the more paranoid tabloid headlines.

But this was like opening the door to my house and
finding Gandalf and Conan the Barbarian in a fight to
the finish with Cthulhu and Morgan le Fay.

Syl, of course, was in her element. Lost civilizations,
Eonae the Earth Goddess, magic, no problem. "So what
happened?"

"Raiakafan, naturally, was perfect for a Guardian—
one of the warriors whose job it was to protect the

Temple and the priests and lead the defense of the city. The fact that he wasn't a woman caused great opposition, but even his worst enemies had to admit that in pure fighting spirit and skill, he had no real equal. He had difficulty with the more diplomatic and intellectual demands of the position, but he was by no means stupid and managed to pass those requirements as well. In the end, not only did he become the High Guardian, but he married Kaylarea, daughter to the High Priest Seirgei. Kaylarea, in her turn, became the High Priestess, chosen vessel of the Lady, so that in truth one could say that Raiakafan married the Lady Herself."

I could see Kafan blinking. Obviously much of this was as much news to him, with his foggy memory, as it was to us.

Verne looked off into the distance, seeing something in his distant past. He looked slightly more pale and worn than usual—probably because of all this stress. "Then came the Demons. The same ones, I thought, who had destroyed Atlantaea so long ago. In the fighting, Kaylarea was killed, Raiakafan and his children Sev'erantean and Taiminashi disappeared, and Atla'a Alandar was devastated. Five years later, just as we were finishing the reconstruction, the Curse fell upon us."

"Curse?"

Verne nodded. "An enemy of mine finally devised a . . . punishment suitable enough, he thought, for my daring to oppose him long ago. The curse he placed upon my people was what produced the race of vampires such as Elias Klein. It was a mockery of the Blessing of Eonae; I drink blood to remind me intimately of the ties between all living things; I partake on occasion of the life force, freely given, of others because that life-energy is what separates the world of matter from that of spirit; I am, or was in the beginning, harmed by the Sun because I am tied wholly to the Earth and other powers are excluded from me; only when I grew into my strength could I face the power from which other life drew its strength. And only things living or formerly living can harm me, because only life may touch that which draws upon its very essence. All these aspects and more were twisted and mocked in the Curse. My people . . ." He closed his eyes and clenched his jaw for some moments before he continued. "My people, for the most part, destroyed themselves in the madness of the Curse; the few who 'survived' were twisted by the magic into becoming something else. The Curse sustains itself by life-energy, so even when virtually all magic disappeared, it continued, though its sufferers were weakened. And, in the end, I myself became so embittered that for a very long time I very nearly became the same as those made in my twisted image. A diabolical and, yes, most fitting vengeance."

I shook my head and finally looked up. "Okay, so let me see if I get *this* story straight. You were the high Priest . . . er, Speaker for Eonae, what we'd call Gaia. The spirit of the Earth itself. And Eonae talked to you, for real. That's where you get your power. And Kafan here was a little boy who trained to become palace guard. *How* long ago?"

"Approximately five hundred thousand years."

I gagged. "*What*? Half a *million* years?! Are you completely out of your mind, Verne? There weren't even *people* back then, at least not human beings like we know today!"

"I told you," Verne said calmly. "Much of what science knows about that era is wrong. Not because your scientists are stupid or are, as so many foolish cultists would have it, looking in the wrong places or 'covering up' the truth. No, the truth is far, far more

frightening, Jason. Your scientists are looking at falsified evidence. The geological record . . . the traces of
the greatest civilization ever to exist . . . all of them
erased, and rewritten, rewritten so as to make it as
though they never existed at all, to expunge from all
memory the knowledge of what was."

I tried to imagine a power capable of such a thing;
to wipe out every trace of a civilization, to remove fossil
traces of one sort, replacing them with another . . . I
couldn't do it. "Impossible. Verne, you've flipped your
vampiric lid."

"If only it were so simple. Do you understand now,
Jason? Why even after all this time I must be terribly, terribly careful not to reveal the truth to any save
those who absolutely must know it? Power such as that
is beyond simple comprehension. Although much of
that power would now be useless here, with magic
closed off from this world, still there remains the
potential for unimaginable destruction."

I searched Verne's face, desperately hoping for some
trace of uncertainty, insanity, self-delusion. Even a
lunatic vampire was preferable to believing this. But
there was no trace of any of those; just a grim and
haunted certainty that this was truth, truth known by
one who had lived through it. Like a delayed blow,
another fact slammed into me; that meant that *Verne*
was that old, older not just than any civilization we knew
of, but older than the very species *Homo sapiens* should
ever have been. Old enough to have seen the mammoths
come and go, to have watched glaciers flow down from
the north to invade the southern plains and retreat again,
like frozen waves on a beach. And becoming more powerful with each passing year . . . and yet still terrified of
the powers that had destroyed the world he knew.

I shook my head and leaned back. "This . . . this is
awfully hard to take in, Verne."

"I understand. Do you understand why it is necessary to tell these things to you?"

I rubbed my jaw. "Not completely. I see the connection—that is, that you've got two separate histories here for the same man, both incompatible with each other. But why it's necessary that I be made aware of more than one of these histories . . . no, I'm not quite clear on that."

"Neither am I," Kafan said.

Verne sighed. "Because we need you immediately for something having to do with the first, and because the very existence of the second means that anyone involved in this may have to face the legacy of that past. Jason, think on what I've told you. Five hundred millennia ago, my adopted son and his two children vanished from the face of the Earth. All my powers and those of the Lady could not tell us where they had gone, or why. Kafan's people are long-lived, but they age. Yet Raiakafan is scarce older than when he disappeared. His presence here is utterly impossible, as is this other life. Somehow he was returned here. But if my son can return, I cannot help but worry that this means that the enemies against which he guarded us have returned as well. So I cannot, in good conscience, bring you into this without making you aware of what dangers you may face."

"It's simpler than that," I said after a pause. "If these people were willing to wipe out entire civilizations, surely they're the kind that prefer to be 'safe than sorry'; because I know you, they'd likely kill me anyway, just to be sure."

"Indeed." Verne nodded. "And to be honest . . . my friends . . . I lost my faith—in myself, in the Lady—long ago. In great part, you, Jason, allowed me to start accepting myself again. In the past between that of the Sh'ekatha and the time we met, I did things which repel me, which were the very antithesis of what I am.

Yet . . . yet her blessing was never truly withdrawn from me, though it could well have been. Her last Speaker survives still . . . And that which was lost may be regained now, as she wished. But I will need friends. And those friends must know that which they may face."

"I'm warning you: I'm not religious, and despite all this paranormal wierdness going on around me, I don't believe in gods of any kind."

Verne smiled. "Raiakafan claims the same thing, these days. Yet it does not matter if you believe in the gods; it only matters to those who *do* believe . . . and whether the gods believe in themselves." He sat back, the light emphasizing the vampiric pallor that lay beneath his naturally darker skin. Despite his smile, I could see how tired he looked. It was pretty clear that no matter how cheering this resurrection of his son had been, he'd been under an awful strain.

"Okay, Verne," I said. I glanced up at the time— damn. There went any chance of opening the shop at a reasonable time. Oh, well . . . cosmic revelations don't happen every day. "If I have any questions on this . . . I'll think of them later. What can I do for you?"

"A simple question with a simple answer. Two answers, actually. First, Raiakafan needs an identity— a safe one. While I of course have my own contacts which provide such things for me, I'd rather that our identities not share that kind of tie; that is, if either of us is found out, I'd rather that it didn't necessarily bring the other one down with the first."

"Faking ID isn't exactly in the WIS rules . . . but you're right, I know people who can arrange it. Jeri might, too. And the second thing?"

Kafan answered. "Find my children. Find Seb and Tai. And Kay and Kei."

I smiled slightly. "So we're back to the thing you originally wanted to hire me for; to find someone. At least *this* is something I'm ready to deal with. Since we're obviously not going to be going to sleep at a reasonable hour anyway, why not come down to WIS right now and we'll get full descriptions set up in the machine so I can start searches?"

"Father?"

"If you want to, Raiakafan, go ahead. Jason wouldn't offer if he didn't mean it."

Kafan looked at me. "You are sure you don't need to sleep first?"

I snorted. "I probably *should* sleep, but after all this? I don't think I'll be ready to go to bed until tomorrow night. Come on; the sooner we locate your kids and get you settled in, the more *all* of us will sleep."

36

I frowned at the faces on my screen. One was definitely nonhuman; Tai as he'd be if he changed. Seb's inhumanity was less obvious, though it was still there in subtle ways. The other two were how the children looked in their human guise. This was my first look at the pictures with a really clear head; after going over the details with Kafan several times, I'd wandered around my house sort of in a daze before finally going to bed. I hadn't opened WIS today; it was evening now, and I was finally able to take a look at things and think about them.

This search wasn't going to be routine. Assuming the truth of Kafan's story, and seeing his furry child I really couldn't doubt it, I wasn't the only person looking for them. I also had to be very careful with the searches so I didn't tip off anyone else. The last thing we wanted was to alert the government agencies that they had a genetic experiment living in Morgantown.

For that reason I'd decided not to involve Jeri Winthrope in this. She'd ended up taking a job as a police liaison here, though it was pretty certain that her *real* employers were still in Washington somewhere. I couldn't ask her for phony ID without a lot of questions I didn't want to answer. She'd be poking around asking things soon enough anyway, since she tried to keep an eye on Verne.

Well, might as well run it through the simple stuff. I booted up photo-comparison programs and then set a search running with various parameters to locate pictures of children from that general geographic area who were within the correct age range, and then to compare those with the two pictures on screen. I hadn't written this program alone—I'd contracted three or four parts of it out—but as far as I knew it was one of the most advanced of its kind in the world. As a programmer I'm only so-so, but I'm damned good at pattern logic problems, and that was the kind of thing information retrieval and photo comparison relied on. I didn't expect much out of this first run; after all, it would be virtually impossible for them to be anywhere visible to the public without a good searcher finding them quick. But it would be stupid of me to pass up any chance. My search parameters might be different than the opposition's, or I might have access to pictures they didn't.

I leaned back and sorted through my mail. Bills . . . damn NiMo bill got higher every month. This bulky one . . . oh, the pictures from the State Police they wanted me to look at. This . . . the invoices from Ed Sommer on the work he was doing for Verne; Verne wanted me to look over them and make sure everything was okay. I wondered for a moment how he'd managed to hide Tai and Kafan from them, even though a lot of the work had already been done by then. I glanced over the invoices . . . damn, even with all the money I was making these days I couldn't pay this without selling everything I owned. Complete rewiring, lights . . . the works. I marked a couple of borderline entries—I didn't know if all these things were needed, but if they were all installed we wouldn't gripe, so I scribbled "tell Verne check if installed" on them and put it away.

The next letter brought a grin. Mom and Dad had written again. I opened the envelope and scanned the contents. Dad had gone to a jeweler's convention—he made jewelry as a sort of hobby—and was working on some new stuff. He was about to retire from the college (Professor of Chemistry). Mom had retired from teaching a couple years ago and we had a continuing exchange of ideas going; I was going to have to read *that* section in more detail later, since there was no way to just dash off a reply to anything Mom wrote; she was too deep for that. They'd also included a Dilbert cartoon they thought I'd appreciate. I'd have to write back soon. It was sometimes a little difficult to write these days, though; I mean, they obviously knew about Virigar, but I was still trying to keep a lid on Verne. But Mom was an *awfully* sharp cookie and she'd know if I was hiding something.

The rest of the stuff was junk mail, which I consigned to the permanent circular file. I stretched, went to the kitchen and reheated some of the taco meat I'd made earlier that week. Fortified with a couple tacos sprinkled with onions, cheese, lettuce, and homemade salsa, I sat down at my second terminal and started downloading my e-mail. One got flagged immediately— it came from a remote drop which was a remote drop for a remote drop for . . . well, you get the picture. Only one person used that route: the Jammer.

Probably the best hacker/cracker in the world, the

Jammer had taken a sort of brotherly interest in protecting my butt when Virigar first showed up. Since then, we'd had occasional correspondence. Once I'd started thinking about false ID, he'd been at the top of my mind. However, the way he'd disappeared a while back had indicated to me that, like Slippery Jim DiGriz, he'd gotten "recruited" by some bigger agency a while back. So I'd had to tiptoe around the subject to see what his reaction was.

TO:(Jason Wood)wisdom@wis.com
FROM:(The Jammer)
SUBJECT:RE: Old days

You're not bad yourself, JW. I particularly liked the triple-loop trick you set up to make people trying to track this down follow the message in circles. But you really need to relax. Trust me, there isn't anyone on the planet who can trace or decode a message I want kept secret except God himself, and even He'd have to do some serious work first.

It was hard to decide if I should laugh or growl at that. The problem with the Jammer was that he had an ego the size of the entire solar system. I was tempted to write back something like "If you're that good, who was it that caught you?" but impulses like that are just stupid; if stroking his ego got good results, why should it bother me? I laughed. At least he had a sense of humor, which was more than a lot of geeks.

What you're asking is if I still do some non-legit work? Normally no, but for you . . . as long as it's not aiding and

abetting a real crime, no problem. I've been
itching for an excuse to hack something on
my own lately anyway. My, um, friends
don't like to let me out to play very often
except "on duty." Not that that isn't chal-
lenging work in itself, but . . . Doing an
analysis of your prior inquiries, I'll bet you
need an ID.

I blinked. Thinking about it, and glancing through
my messages again . . . yeah, I suppose you might be
able to get that . . . but it took a pattern sense as good
or better than mine to do it dead cold. Maybe I
shouldn't call it "ego."

If it's one for yourself, I've got everything I need already; if it's for someone
else, I need all the info you can give me—
blood type, fingerprints, photos, the works.
The more I can work with, the more I can
give you. Drop me a line and let me know.

The JAMMER

Not bad. One major problem probably solved. I
glanced over at the comparison program, sorting
through picture after picture . . . no hits. I didn't expect
any. Picking up the phone, I called Verne. As usual,
Morgan answered and called Verne to the phone.
"Hello, Jason."

"Got a couple marks on those invoices—you just
have to make sure he installed all the stuff he says he
installed. I'll come over and do that now, if you like.
I've got the machines running on something that
doesn't need my presence. I'm going to stop by the
mini-mart for a couple things, then I'll be right over."

"By all means. Thank you, Jason."

The mini-mart wasn't too busy as I walked in the door. I noted the security camera with its odd bulbous attachment. Nothing brought home the profound changes that were happening more than this prosaic addition: that attachment was, with slight changes, basically the same as the headpiece I'd worn while searching out werewolves in the hospital hallways. That reminded me . . . I had to call back that lawyer in New York.

I grabbed the few items I was looking for and headed back out.

There were unaccustomed faint lines of concern on Morgan's usually impassive, English-butler face. I saw the reason immediately. "Verne!"

Nothing essential had changed in him; he still had the dark, wide eyes that could hold you with a magnetic presence, the distant and aristocratic stance. But beneath the dusky olive color natural to his skin, his paleness had become something beyond mere vampiric pallor; he seemed washed out, diminished, as though being slowly leached of his color and his strength. The way he stood was unnaturally stiff. And in his dark hair I thought I saw a few strands of white and gray. "Jesus. Verne, you look like shit."

A tired smile crossed his face. "As usual, your diplomacy is staggering, Jason. You are not the first to inform me of this. And your face said all that needed to be said."

"What's wrong?"

Verne shrugged. "I am not sure. There have been a few, a very few, cases in which I felt similarly, aside from the one time I was forced to cross desert plains with little to no shelter—that was infinitely worse. I suspect all the changes in my life, from finding

Raiakafan to simply trying to become more human again have made me overwork. For if I lie down to rest, and my mind does not enter the proper state, I do not gain the proper amount of rest; those of my sort do not sleep in truth, any more than the Earth sleeps, but there is a difference between activity and rest even so."

I couldn't keep the concern from my voice. "I hope that's all it is. Look, just take it easy. Anyone would be a little punchy after all this stuff's happened, but you're the only one who can take care of you. I mean, what would I do if you collapsed, call 911 and tell the paramedics I have a sick vampire here?"

"Indeed." Verne straightened with a visible effort. "But let me see these invoices . . . Ah, I see. I believe those sockets were installed, but let us check."

We went through the huge mansion, checking off the items. Personally, I'd rather have seen Verne go to bed, but his tone and manner indicated that, weak or not, he wasn't about to listen to me or any other mortal doing a mother hen imitation.

From that, I figured he was a lot more worried than he let on. In his room, we stopped and he grabbed a bottle of AB+, draining the entire thing without even letting it warm. This made him visibly less pale, but something about it struck me as vaguely false, like the temporarily alert feeling you might get from amphetamines or a lot of coffee. Still, he moved more easily and the gray strands were no longer visible in his hair. Maybe he just hadn't been eating right. Was there such a thing as vitamin deficiency for a vampire . . . nature priest, whatever?

"Very good, Jason," Verne said finally. "All seems to be in order. I will pay these invoices, then. Thank you for checking them."

"No problem. Where's Kafan?"

"Sleeping. He tends to keep to Gen's schedule, and we don't want Gen to become habitually nocturnal."

"Well, say hi for me. I don't know how long this search is going to take me, but I've already started on it. Might as well get home and try to get *my* schedule back on track."

"An excellent idea. I will see you later, then."

I stopped and turned in the doorway. "Verne, take care of yourself, okay?"

"Of course, Jason."

I drove back to my house slowly. If Verne was really sick, I didn't see how anyone could do anything. Presumably he and Morgan knew more about that than anyone else. Maybe Kafan, I suppose. Would there have *been* anything like first aid for Verne's kind, or was that like thinking of stocking bandages for God?

I really should have started work on those State Police photos, but my heart just wasn't in it tonight. I put in *Casablanca* and let it run while I ate a very late-night snack. Finally, as Rick and Louis walked off through the rain, I headed upstairs to get to bed; I wasn't that tired, but if I didn't get back on track . . . I glanced over at the search station. It had stopped comparisons finally. I reached out to shut it off, when the message on the screen hit me with delayed impact:

Matches: 10

Ten matches? I hadn't even expected *one*! Bedtime forgotten, I sat down at the keyboard and had it call up the ten matching pictures.

As they appeared onscreen, I heard myself say "Oh, shit."

I'd had a vague feeling that the boys' faces were familiar, but I'd put it down to having seen their father and talked over their appearance for hours. But as soon as the photos with their headlines appeared, I remembered all too well where I'd seen them:

Senator MacLain adopts two Viet children.

37

Verne and Kafan stared at the reprinted articles, while Sylvie peeked over their shoulders. "*H'alate*," muttered Verne. "This is most inconvenient."

"Maybe not quite as bad as it seems." I said. Verne had looked like Death warmed over when he came in, but that might have been the yellow street lights. He seemed to look a little better, here in the office, than he had yesterday. I hoped that meant he was taking it easy. "With that kind of high profile, yeah, it's certain that your enemies know where the kids are. But the good thing is that the high profile also makes it virtually impossible to just kidnap the kids. Doing a snatch-and-grab on some random runaway is one thing; kidnapping the children of a senator of the United States—especially one like Paula MacLain, who's one of the most outspoken and uncompromising people I've ever seen—is very, very different."

"True," Verne said. "But it will be difficult to convince the lady to return her children to their father when that father is wanted across the globe. Giving him a new identity would work for ordinary situations, but you can be sure that if we ask her to hand over her children to us that she will have us investigated to the full extent of her powers, which are quite considerable. She would most certainly discover your internationally known identity, Kafan, and might find out some rather unwelcome facts about myself as well."

Syl nodded. "And . . . didn't she have a son before?

One about Tai's age? He got killed somehow. She's going to hold on to those kids like grim death."

I winced. I'd forgotten about that—it had happened about ten years ago, a little before I really started reading anything about politics, since in high school things like that seem pretty unimportant. But now that Syl mentioned it, I remembered; a plane crash, killed her husband and son, and it had something to do with her job so she might even have blamed herself somehow. "We'll have to think about this."

"What is there to think about?" Kafan demanded. "I am their father. They belong with me."

"I'd tend to agree," I said, "but the rest of the world knows you as a psycho killer, wanted by an international task force. Not exactly the kind of parent people want for children, you know."

"Then we'll tell her the truth."

"Which truth? The one about genetic experiments? Kafan, that'd be a quick way to end up in yet another lab. The one about ancient civilizations that can't have existed by all we know today? *That* would be a good way to get us *all* locked up. No, I'm sure there's an angle here, but I'm going to have to work on it. At least relax some; we know where they are, and they're being treated very well. They're not suffering, and it's for damn sure this organization won't dare touch them as long as they're in the Senator's custody."

Kafan's lips tightened, showing faint hints of fangs underneath, until he got his temper under control. Then he seemed to shrink back, depressed even though the news was at least partly good. "You are correct. I cannot fight this whole world if I wish to live here." He brooded for a moment, then asked, "What about Kay and Kei?"

I shook my head. "Sorry. Nothing yet. If they were captured again as you said, I'm not going to turn up anything quickly, even if they did move them. Most likely they're still in the lab compound you mentioned, if they managed to keep it hidden this long. You can't tell us where it is?"

"No." The short, blunt monosyllable carried a world of frustration. "Showing me where I was on a map was never something they had in mind. And I just ran when I escaped. I had no time to mark bearings. Oh, put me back in the general area and I'll find it, that I promise you, but I can't show you where it is."

"Too bad. But if we're going to even *think* about finding some way to go back and get them, we absolutely *have* to find out where the compound is, and to be honest a whole lot more about it, too." This was getting more and more difficult. I wasn't James Bond, and I didn't know anyone who qualified for the part, either. Jeri Winthrope was about as close as I got, and I sure didn't like the idea of involving her in this— both because of the problems it could cause for us and the problems it'd cause for her. That was ignoring the possibly cosmic threat hanging over anyone who got too close to this mess. "Guess I'll have to work on that too."

Verne, still pale but looking definitely better than he had yesterday, sat up. "Jason, at this point I insist on paying you. This may require a great deal of your time and resources, and perhaps more than you can easily afford."

I opened my mouth to protest, then shut it. It grated on me to charge a friend for something so important to them, but Verne was right. If I followed this thing to its logical conclusion, I might end up having to do everything from pay out bribes to mastermind and equip a commando raid! I shook my head at that; I didn't think I knew anyone who even *knew* anyone who could do that. Oh well, one thing at a time. "Thanks,

Verne. You're right. This is going to get expensive no matter how I slice it."

Taking out his checkbook, Verne wrote quickly and tore out the paper. I gagged at the amount. "Verne—"

"Don't protest, Jason. Better to be overpaid than underpaid. You have no idea how little such a sum means to me, nor how highly I value your services."

I nodded. "Okay." I gestured at the pile of newspaper copies. "Take those if you want. I'd better get back to work. Besides this snafu, I've also got three other regular jobs on the burner."

Sylvie remained behind after Verne, Kafan, and Gen had left. "Verne isn't well, Jason."

"Tell me something I don't know." I said. "He looks better than he did yesterday, though."

She frowned, a distant and unfortunately familiar look on her face. "Maybe . . . but I have a bad feeling about that."

I sighed. "Syl, sweetheart, maybe you can do something. It's for sure that I've got enough to do here. I'm no vampire medic. He regards you very highly and talks about your being a 'Mistress of Crystal,' whatever that means. Maybe you can do something."

Her expression lightened. "Why, thank you, Jason! For calling me 'sweetheart,' that is."

I blushed; I could feel the heat on my cheeks. "So maybe it wasn't ever a secret. Syl, you're the only woman that makes me still feel like I'm fourteen, clumsy, and tongue-tied. Maybe that's a good thing." She started to say something—I could tell it would be another of the kinds of things that embarrassed me more—and then stopped. "Thanks. I don't need to blush more than once a day."

She smiled, a very gentle smile. "It doesn't hurt your looks at all, you know. And that clumsy approach of yours helps me keep thinking *I'm* still in my teens too, so I'd say it's a good thing."

I smiled back, still nervous. "I guess you make me nervous because you're the only woman I'm serious about."

"Are you?"

I swallowed. "I've been in love with you for years, Syl. Just not ready to admit it."

You can insert your own experience of a first happy kiss here; I'm pretty sure they're all the same to the lucky people involved. Time stops, or passes, but it certainly doesn't behave the same, and the rest of the world doesn't exist. Oh, I'd kissed Syl before, quick pecks or something, and I'd certainly kissed a girl or two once I got out of my geek stage, but there just wasn't any comparison at all. I'd been waiting to do this since I met her, and from her response, she'd been waiting just as long.

When lack of air finally signaled the end of eternity, I pulled back from her for a moment, looking into those deep blue eyes. "Whew."

"So what was it you were so afraid of, Jason?"

"This. I like having control over my own life, and there's no control over this."

That smile again. "Do you want to change your mind?"

"Don't you even *think* about it. After all the courage I had to work up there to mention that four-letter word 'love,' you're not getting a chance to get away." I wanted to spend the rest of the night—maybe the rest of the week—continuing what we'd started, but I couldn't ignore business, either.

Especially when business also involved a friend. "Syl, can we make a date for tomorrow night? Right now I'd better keep working—I've already lost a couple days as it is. And do you think you can do anything for Verne?"

She grinned. "Not jealous of him any more?"

"What?!"

"I can sense things, you know that. And I could see your little pout every time Verne put on the charm and I smiled back at him."

I gave a sour look. "Well, he does have a kind of overwhelming presence, not to mention that perfect sense of style."

"Jealous, like I said. Don't worry, Jason. I knew you were the one for me as soon as I saw you. I had a feeling about it."

Now that *really* made me wince. "I don't believe in destiny."

"Then call it a self-fulfilling prophecy. I'm heading over to Verne's. Maybe I can't do anything, but then again maybe I can."

"Thanks . . . Syl."

Even after she left, it took a while to start concentrating on the work at hand.

Perfume stays with you.

38

TO:{Jason Wood}wisdom@wis.com
FROM:{The Jammer}
SUBJECT:EXCUSE ME????

Did you have ANY idea what kind of mess you were trying to get me into? No, let me revise that. Do you have ANY idea what THAT kind of mess can do to me?

Dammit, Wood. This guy's an international fugitive and you want me to give him a bulletproof ID? What are you mixed up in THIS time?

So there *were* limits to what the Jammer would take casually. Nice to know, but I wish he'd stayed in his omnipotent mode for a while longer.

Look, I know enough about you to know that you know perfectly well who this guy is, at least on the public-international level. So, since I also know you're not into helping criminals every day of the week, I'll assume you know something I don't know, hard as that is to believe, that makes this guy worth helping. Okay. But for this little bit of work, I'm charging. Not money, naturally. You'll make available a writable CD-ROM on a dial-in line, at 2:15 Tuesday evening. When it's finished writing the data that gets sent to it, you'll take the disk—without reading it, and believe you me I'll know—and deliver it to some secure locale of your choosing. In a separate letter, you tell me the location. Once that's done, I'll deliver your IDs.

Oh, man. What was I getting myself into? He could be downloading anything from recipes to Top Secret documents into the drive, and I had no doubt at all that if I made a single attempt to read the contents that he *would* find out; he was that good.

But then again, what was I asking him to do? Make a set of ID for a known international criminal. And if my guesses were right, he might well be working for one of the organizations that was supposed to track Kafan down. No, the Jammer had the right to ask something like this; I was asking him to put his ass on the line for me, so he was asking me to stick my own neck out.

I typed out a very short reply,
      Terms accepted
and sent it off.

A week into my work and I wasn't really any closer to figuring out how to approach Senator MacLain without opening about a dozen cans of worms that were better left closed. On the other hand, I was starting, I thought, to close in on the location of this mysterious Project. The break had come a few days ago, when a search program had highlighted the Organization for Scientific Research; a check showed that not only had the OSR always been heavily involved in biological research, but it had previously had a couple branches in the far East—one in or very near Vietnam. During the '70s, those labs had been discontinued. A bit of digging on my part, however, showed that the discontinuance had actually been a transfer of ownership to interested parties, probably in the Viet government. Details on the site were vague—the OSR files from the '70s were hard to access, since it had been a UN venture to begin with, and now that it had separated from the UN and become a private corporation it was possible all the old records not directly relevant to operation had been purged. And stuff that old often wasn't online anywhere in any case.

It might be possible, however, to take the vague info I had and combine it with a careful modeling of the layout as Kafan remembered it and see if a pattern-recognition program could come up with anything using satellite photos of the area. Probably there were records of the installation on one of the intelligence computers—NSA, CIA, whatever—but I wasn't about to try hacking one of those. This had to be an independent operation if at all possible. With Verne's backing, we at least didn't need to worry about whether we could afford it.

That brought up the next problem. Verne. Syl had tried a number of things, but though it appeared to help some, over the next couple of days Verne went downhill again. He was visibly older.

I closed my eyes. Genetically engineered people, ancient civilizations, vampires, priests. . . . damn, it was a wonder my head didn't explode. All that stuff combined was enough to . . .

All that stuff combined?

I straightened. Reaching out, I grabbed the phone. "Verne? Sorry to disturb you, but I just thought of something."

Verne's weariness was now evident in his voice. It was still as rich, but the underlying tone lacked the measured certainty that was usually there. "And what is that, Jason?"

"Verne, you talked about how certain forces might have returned, right? Isn't it possible that what's happening to you is an attack? Maybe even carried by Kafan, not consciously, but nonetheless part of him?"

The silence on the other end was very long. Then:

"Not merely possible . . ." Verne said slowly, "but even probable. Nothing like this has ever happened to me, in all these thousands of years. Can it be coincidence that it happens now, of all times? Most unlikely. My brain must be affected as well, if I did not think of this myself."

"Is there a way to find out?"

"Most likely," Verne said. "With Sylvie's help, Morgan and I should be able to determine if any mystical forces other than my own are operant here."

"What about biological? You did say that living things could affect you."

Verne hesitated a moment, considering. His voice, given hope, was stronger now. "I do not believe any disease, howsoever virulent, could affect me without some small mystical component. This was one of the Lady's blessings, and it is not within the power of ordinary science to gainsay that, even in this era. My metabolism differs so greatly from that of anything else on this world that I doubt it would even be recognized as living by most tests. No, if this is an attack, it must be a magical one. Thank you, Jason."

"No problem. Will you need me for anything?"

"No, my friend. You have given all that was necessary. We will endeavor to make this as short as possible, that your lady be not unduly inconvenienced."

"Is it that obvious to everyone?"

Verne's laugh was the first genuinely cheerful thing I had heard from him in a week. "Jason, such things are always obvious. And welcome, I assure you. You have finally accepted that which was always in your heart."

"Don't you start. I may have been slow and dumb, but I don't have to be reminded every day."

He chuckled. "Good night, Jason."

39

I stared down at the disk in my hand. The fact that it contained possibly treasonous information made it seem as heavy as lead. But it wasn't the worst of the things I had to deal with. My date with Sylvie last night, our third "real" date, had been bittersweet at best. We were happy to be together finally, but another fact overshadowed our enjoyment: despite three days of careful work, Syl, Verne, Morgan, and their few other trusted contacts had turned up precisely nothing. My "brilliant idea" was a washout, and Verne was worse than ever. Once in a while he seemed to improve slightly for a few hours, but it always came back. No mystical influences alien to the house. No mental controls on Kafan that they could find. Nothing.

I sighed. Syl wasn't coming over today—the Silver Stake had three shipments that needed to be classified, and she didn't want to be faced with Verne right now anyway.

Putting the CD into a protective case, I put the case into my backpack. Time to send it off on a delivery.

As I opened the front door, I saw a package lying on the doorstep. I picked it up, noting that it had no mailing stamps, no return address, nothing.

Belatedly it occurred to me that being in this business I might expect to start getting mail bombs soon. Well, if it was a bomb, it certainly wasn't movement activated. I hefted it a couple of times; light, not much more than paper in here, if anything. There could still be enough plastique in it to do serious damage, though; it didn't take much high explosive to do a number on you.

I shrugged. Not likely to be a bomb; what the hell. I ripped it open.

No explosions. Looking inside, I saw another envelope and a sheet of paper. It was a note:

Jason, you have the god-damned devil's luck. Here are the IDs. Destroy the disk. Since I know you're too damn curious for your own good, I'll tell you that somehow whatever you're up to got the attention of one of my bosses and they caught me. Instead of shutting us down, he told me to make the IDs. Must be personal—he told me not to even mention this to the other members of our, um, group. So this one's free. But I'd worry, if I were you. If even HE thinks you're involved in something

important enough to let you off a felony
charge without so much as a warning,
you're playing with nukes, not fire.

Jammer

I stared at the package, then opened the envelope.
Birth certificate . . . passport . . . driver's license . . . Jesus,
even documents showing he was proficient in wood-
working and construction (about the only salable skills
I could find) and a Black Belt certification from
Budoukai Tai Kwan Do in California. I looked closer.
That was a genuine passport, seal and all.

Who *were* these people? And what the hell had I
gotten myself into *now*?

40

"Senator MacLain?"

The voice on the other end was as distinctive over
the phone as it was in public address or on television:
precise, educated, a pleasant yet cool voice that carried both authority and intelligence—it reminded me
somehow of Katharine Hepburn. "This is Paula
MacLain. Mr. Jason Wood?"

"Yes, ma'am. I don't know if you know who I am—"

"Young man, if I didn't, I wouldn't be speaking to
you." There was a tinge of humor that took any sting
out of the words. "In any case, a senator for New York
who wasn't aware of everything having to do with
Morgantown, in these days, would be a sad example
of a legislator, don't you agree?"

"I certainly do, Senator. And I certainly didn't mean
to imply—"

"Don't concern yourself with my feelings, Mr. Wood.

I know when offense is meant and when it isn't. Now that you and I have finally managed to connect, let's waste no more time. What can I do for you? You were intriguingly uninformative to my staff."

I took a deep breath. I'd decided to go for the most honest route I could, while trying to tapdance around the more dangerous areas. "Senator, a few weeks ago, a man walked into my office, asking me for help in locating his family. To make a long story short, he originally comes from Vietnam. And the descriptions of his two children, and pictures made from those descriptions, match those of your adopted children in every particular."

There was a long silence on the other end; I'd expected as much, given her history. Finally, "That . . . is quite remarkable, Mr. Wood. Am I to presume that you would like to find a way to confirm that they are, or are not, your client's children? And that he would subsequently want to obtain custody of them, if they are indeed his children?" Her voice was carefully controlled, but not perfectly so; she wasn't taking this as calmly as she'd like me to think.

"Basically correct, Senator. But we also don't wish to distress the children overly much, either by giving them false hopes or by forcing them to leave a stable home. What I was hoping was that we could permit someone you trusted to take a sample for genetic comparison and do a paternity test on them."

Senator MacLain was known for her quick decisions. "That much I will certainly do. But I must warn you and your client, Mr. Wood: I will never relinquish custody of my children unless I am absolutely certain that they will be happy and well cared for, regardless of who is the blood parent. I love them both very much."

I nodded, though she couldn't see it. "Senator . . .

Ms. MacLain . . . we expected no less, and to be honest if you felt any differently you wouldn't be a fit mother for them. It's not going to be easy either way, but I assure you, I feel the same way. I'll make that clear to my client."

"I appreciate that, Mr. Wood. And I appreciate, now, the trouble you went to to keep this all confidential. Let me see . . ." I heard the sounds of tapping on a computer keyboard, "Ah. If you would be so kind as to have the sample sent to Dr. Julian Gray, 101 Main, Carmel, New York, he will see to the comparisons. I have no trouble with your obtaining the samples for him; falsifying genetic evidence would seem a bit beyond anyone's capacities at the present time."

"Indeed. Thank you very much for your time, Senator. Good-bye."

Maybe not beyond *anyone's* capacities, I thought as I hung up the phone, but certainly beyond mine.

The invoice for the State Police job finished printing, and I tore it off and stuffed it into the package along with all the originals and enhanced versions. Sealing it up, I affixed the prewritten label and dumped it into my outbox.

So much for the simple part of my current life.

It had taken a couple of days to install my newest machine, a Lumiere Industries' TERA-5. Without Verne's money, I'd still be looking at the catalog entries and drooling and thinking "maybe next decade." Now that it was up and running, I'd given it the biggest assignment I had: sorting through all the recent satellite data that I'd been able to find, beg, borrow, or . . . acquire, and look for various indications of hidden installations. So far it had given me at least twenty positives, none of which turned out to look at all promising. I was starting to wonder if there was a bug in some section of the program; some of the positives it was giving me were pretty far outside of the parameters of the installation as described by Kafan. There was one that might be a hidden POW camp—I'd forwarded that to one of the MIA-POW groups I knew about. Never thought those things really existed any more, but maybe there was more than hearsay behind all the rumors.

The TERA-5 was still chugging away at the job, meter by detailed meter on the map, but this was going to take a while even for the fastest commercially available general-purpose machine ever made. A specifically designed machine for map-comparison searching would be far faster, but not only would it be lots more expensive, but it'd be next to useless for anything else; there's always a catch somewhere. I preferred to wait a little longer and have a use for the machine later on as well. My only consolation was that I could bet that only an intelligence agency had better equipment and programs for the job.

Of course, with the situation with Verne, I didn't know what good this was going to do. Without Verne, we'd be pretty much stuck even if I did know where the installation was. I looked sadly down at the thick document lying on my desk. Verne's will. Morgan as executor, Kafan and his family as major heirs, and, maybe not so surprisingly, me and Sylvie figuring prominently in it as well. This aside from numerous bequests to his efficient and often nearly invisible staff. The sight of it told me more than I needed to know. Verne knew his time was up.

My friend was dying. It hit me harder than anything all of a sudden. I collapsed into my chair, angry and sad and frustrated all at once. He'd been the gateway through which a whole world of wonder opened up for me, and he'd said I'd helped him regain his faith. It wasn't *fair* that it end like this, him wasting away to nothing for no reason.

And there was nothing I could do. Yesterday night he'd shown us all the secrets of his house . . . "just in case," he said . . . but we knew there was no doubt in his mind. The place he called the Heart, built out of habit and tradition, only recently having been used by him for the purposes that it had existed . . . once more to become an unused cave when he died. All his papers and books and even tablets, here and elsewhere.

He'd found his lost son, I'd found his son's children, and for what? He wouldn't live long enough to see them reunited, he'd barely lived long enough to be sure it was his son. Dammit! I slapped at the wall switch, killing the lights as I turned to leave.

Then I froze.

I remembered what I'd said to Verne months ago, when Virigar first showed: "I don't like coincidences. I don't believe in them."

What if my idea was still basically true?

There was just one possibility. I switched on the lights again, spun the chair back around and switched the terminal back on. It was a crazy idea . . . but no crazier than anything else! Just a few things to check, and I'd know.

It took several hours—the data was hard to find— but then my screen lit up with a few critical pieces of information. I grabbed my gun, spare clips, a small toolbox, and a large flashlight and sprinted out the door.

41

Morgan opened the door, startled as I pushed past him without so much as a "hello." "Master Jason . . . ?"

I looked around, shrugged, jogged into the living room and climbed up on a chair. Verne was in that room, staring at me curiously out of hollow eyes set in a leathery, lined face and framed by pure white hair. "J . . . Jason," he said slowly, as I mumbled a curse to myself and dragged the chair over a bit, "what . . . are you doing?"

"Maybe making a fool of myself."

I reached up and unscrewed one of the bulbs from the fixture and pulled the fixture itself towards me. Everything looked normal . . .

The other lights on the fixture went out. Morgan stood near the switch. "Perhaps, if you are intending on tinkering with the lighting, you may wish the electricity off, sir."

"Thanks, Morgan." I said absently. Pulling out a small screwdriver, I unfastened the interior baseplate of the fixture.

There. Underneath the base. I didn't know what it was . . . but in essence, I did. "Morgan, you said it. Kill the electricity—*all* the electricity in the house! *Now!*"

"Sir . . . ?" Morgan only hesitated for a moment, then hurried off towards the basement and the main breakers. I switched on the flashlight; a moment later the house was plunged into darkness.

"What . . . what is going on, Jason?" Verne asked.

"I was right all along, Verne," I said. Morgan entered; he had a much larger portable light. "You might even want to shut off that light, Morgan. Go with candles, unless you bought that light in the last few days." I turned back to Verne. "It wasn't magic. It was technology that was killing you. Every one of your lights, and maybe even some other devices, is fitted with a gadget that turns ordinary light into the kind of light that hurts you. In the short term, it can't damage you, but with enough exposure . . ."

" . . . yes." Verne said slowly. "It . . . it becomes like a slow cancer, eating away at me. But even in the day, when I sleep in darkness?"

"Probably a device in those rooms does the same thing. If, as I suspect, it's not just one wavelength of light but a combination of them, it probably can't do enough in darkness to continue *hurting* you during the day, but it could slow your recovery so that you'd always be getting damaged more than you were healing during your rest. Especially if the really critical wavelengths are combinations of ultraviolet and infrared."

"How did you know?"

"There were a lot of clues, but the biggest one—that didn't register until almost too late—was that the few times you were *outside* of your house you actually started to look a tiny bit better. But when you and Sylvie couldn't find anything, I was stumped . . . until I remembered that coincidence is damn unlikely."

We both thought for a moment. "I must confess, Jason, that I don't quite understand." Verne said finally. His voice was slightly steadier already, testament to the tremendous recuperative powers that were his, and I started to relax slightly. It looked like I might be right. No, I *knew* I was.

"Take both your stories. Let's say that they're both true. Well, to kill you, someone would have to know what you are, exactly. Maybe one of your old enemies, right? Who else would know precisely how you could be killed subtly, without alerting everyone for miles around? But this happened just as Kafan showed up, so that's not coincidence either.

"So what if the lab Raiakafan escaped from was being run *by the same people* who were *your* enemies, Verne?"

"Impossible," Verne breathed. "After all this time . . ."

"But it would explain everything. And there's evidence for it. Raiakafan himself—if your enemies didn't have a hand in this, how else? You survived all these years, they certainly could have. And another thing, one that's bothered us both for quite a while: Klein. Where the hell did he come from? Only another vampire—of the kind made by one of your enemies, note—could create him. And what did he do? He *set you up*, that's what—tried to get you killed off! Somebody knew where you were, and what you were! Somebody who knew that converting Klein would give them a weapon to entrap you, and they damn near succeeded. If Virigar hadn't shown up, I suspect there would have been another attack on your life." I took another breath, continued, "And look at the timing. Klein showed up sporting a new set of fangs, if my calendar's right, a few weeks after Kafan whacked the good doctor. *They knew who Kafan really was, and they knew where he was coming.*"

"Very good, Mr. Wood."

I knew that voice. "And Ed Sommer's business started about the same time. Funny thing, that, Ed. Digging into your background produced some fascinating blanks."

Ed was holding a large-caliber gun—.44, I guessed—pointed at us. While ordinary bullets wouldn't hurt Verne and probably not Morgan, either, none of us expected that he would be using ordinary bullets. For me, of course, the point was moot; if you fired a wad of gum at the speed of a bullet it'd still probably kill me. "I've gotta hand it to you, Jason. If we hadn't been watching the house constantly the past couple of days, you might have blown the whole thing. We wanted him," he nodded at Verne, "to go unconscious before we actually moved."

"How very convenient for you that I happened to decide on remodeling at just the right time." Verne tried to deliver the lines in his usual measured and iron-sure way, but his weakening had gone far past the point that a mere effort of will would banish it.

"Convenient, but hardly necessary. Morgan, down on the floor. Once we'd tested to make sure that our precautions rendered us invisible to your casual inspection, the installation could have been made at any time. More dangerous and risky, but no major enterprise is without risk. And after we began remodeling, the whole house was wired in more than one way." He smiled. "We learned a great deal recently. It does bother me about Kafan's new identity. Why anyone would take that much interest in this case is a matter for concern. But not for you." Ed shifted his aim directly to Morgan and, to my horror, began to squeeze the trigger.

Weakened and sick Verne might have been, but when it came to the life of his friend and oldest retainer all his supernal speed must have come back. There was movement, a blur that fogged the darkened air between Ed and Morgan for a split second; then Ed Sommer was hurled backwards into the front stairwell with an impact that shook the house. The gun vanished somewhere in the darkness.

Then the lights came on. There must have been more of Ed's people in the house. Caught in the light again, I could see Verne sag slightly.

From the ruined wood there came a curse, but that wasn't the voice of a human being. A monstrous figure tore its way out of the wreckage, a hideous cross between man, lizard, and insect. Humanoid in form, scaled and clawed and with patches of spiked, glistening armor from which hung the tattered remains of Ed's clothing. "A good final effort, Sh'ekatha," the Ed-thing hissed. "But foredoomed to failure."

While it was focused on Verne, I had time to draw my own gun. Its gaze shifted towards me just as I got a bead on it.

BlamBlamBlamBlamBlamBlamBlamBlamBlamBlam!
I emptied a full ten rounds into the monstrosity. The

impacts staggered it, battering at critical areas until it toppled backwards. "Run!" I shouted. Verne and Morgan were already moving, and I ejected the clip and slammed in a fresh one as I sprinted after them. A single glance had sufficed to show me that the bullets hadn't done any notable damage. "Just *once* I'd like to find something I can shoot and *kill*, like any normal person!"

Verne staggered down the basement steps, to be caught by something indescribable that tried to rip him apart; Morgan intervened, shoving the interloper through a nearby wall with unexpected strength. "Keep going, sir!" he said over his shoulder as he kept his attention on his adversary. Distantly we could hear other things smashing; the rest of the household must be under attack now as well!

"Damn you, Jason!" I heard a distant voice roar as we pried open the door to the Heart. "This was supposed to be a subtle operation!" Massive feet thundered down the stairs behind us.

The door swung open; I shoved Verne through and stepped through, pulling the door shut as a huge shadow rushed towards me. Just before it reached us, though, the door swung shut and I twisted the lock. The impact on the other side shook rock dust from the tunnel ceiling.

"It will not stop him for long, Jason," Verne forced out.

"A little time's better than none."

I'd seen the Heart only once before, as a sort of postscript to Verne's story; here, as before, things seemed quieter; like a summer forest in midafternoon, lazy, sleepy, silent. In the center of the large cavern, a perfectly circular pool of pure water shimmered in the light, blue as the vault of heaven. At the far side, a squat obelisk of black obsidian. The Mirror of the Sky and the Heartstone. Hanging on that far wall was some kind of sheath or casing.

I became aware I was gasping for breath, realizing only then that Verne hadn't really been running; that I'd been dragging him along instead. Even here, in the place most sacred to him, he had no strength any more. Technology was winning the battle.

A rending, shattering sound echoed down the corridor as I dragged Verne to the pool's far side and dropped him to rest against the obelisk. Slow, measured footfalls clicked down the tunnel. The snake-headed monster that had called itself "Ed Sommer" entered the room, smiling at me. "Too bad about you, Jason. You just happened to be in the wrong place at the wrong time."

I didn't say anything; I couldn't afford to waste my breath.

"Tired?" it asked cheerfully as it continued towards me. "Well, it will be over soon enough."

As long as he was moving slowly, with full control, I didn't have a chance. "At least I know you're not going to survive me by much, Ed or whatever your name is."

The slit-pupilled eyes narrowed. "What do you mean?"

"I mean that I found the location of your laboratory tonight. My TERA-5 got lucky and matched patterns. And if I don't send the 'no-go' code within a couple of weeks, the system I stored the info in will dump the location and all the info I have on the lab's operations into every intelligence agency and scientific forum on the planet. It'll be a lot easier to pry the kid and the mother away from a bunch of squabbling agencies than from one group of demonic crossbreeds with a unified purpose."

The lie worked; it fit perfectly with what they knew of my capabilities, and if I *had* found the location, was precisely what I would've done if I had no other choices. The giant figure charged forward. "I'll have that code out of you if I have to rip it out of your heart!"

Jesus he was fast! Fast as Klein! But with him charging, everything changed. I jumped up onto the Heartstone and lunged to meet the Ed-thing just as he leapt towards us across the Mirror of the Sky.

The impact stunned me, and I felt at least three armored spikes go deep into my arms, but I held on. My momentum had mostly canceled his, and the two of us plummeted directly into the deceptively deep pool below.

A detonation of leaf-green light nearly blinded me as the entire pool lit up like an emerald spotlight; surges of energy whipped through me and I came close to blacking out. Boiling water fountained up and I was flung outward to strike with numbing force on the altar, shocked, parboiled, and aching. Electrical arcs danced around the edge of the water, then spat outwards, shattering the lightbulbs across half the room. A roar of agony echoed from the depths of the Mirror of the Sky. Then the boiling subsided, the eerie green light faded away. Blinking away spots, I looked down. A few pieces of spiky armor, bubbling and dissolving away like Easter Egg dye pellets, were all that remained.

"One more guess confirmed." My voice, not surprisingly, shook. I reached down and retrieved my gun from where I'd dropped it near the Heartstone.

Verne gave a very weak chuckle. "If they were my enemies, they would be the very antithesis of the power I wielded. Yes?"

"I hoped so."

Another voice spoke from the entranceway. "And you were quite correct."

I felt my jaw go slack as I looked across. "Oh . . . oh shit. You're dead."

In the bright lights that remained, the Colonel, resplendent in his uniform, walked towards us. "As is oft-quoted, reports of my death were greatly exaggerated. Kafan, poor boy, didn't realize precisely what I was, so he only damaged my body. As you learned," and suddenly, without any visible pause, he was there, taking the gun from my hand with irresistable force, "ordinary weapons are rather useless against us. Tearing out my throat was an inconvenience, easily remedied. But it seemed more convenient to appear to die and hope he'd lead us to the other two children, rather than just keep fighting him." Despite all my struggles, he picked me up and tied me up with rope he had slung over his shoulder. A casual kick from him sent Verne sprawling. "Now we can fix things. Pity about Ed, though. Rather promising in some ways, but a trifle dense. If only I'd been a moment sooner . . . good bluff, boy. But your mind is a bit transparent." He set me down on the Heartstone and groped under his uniform. "Now where . . . ah, there it is." His hand came back into view, holding a long, sharp, crystalline knife. He smiled.

I couldn't maintain my usual facade of confidence here. I swallowed, tried to speak, found that my throat had gone completely dry.

"Don't bother trying to speak. You see, a ritual sacrifice on this stone will negate its very nature, ending the power of this shrine, which is quite painful to me, and in his weakened condition it should also destroy the priest. So you, by virtue of your very bad fortune, shall be the one through which we cleanse the world of the last trace of Eonae and her nauseating priests."

"So why are you bothering to tell me?" I managed to get out. "Just a melodramatic villain with a long-winded streak?"

He laughed at that, a cheerful sound all the more macabre because it was so unforced and honest. "Why, not at all; a purely practical reason, I assure you. You see, fear, despair, and the anticipation of death are part of what strengthens the ritual. They are antidotes to life and endurance and all the other things that this shrine represents. The more I allow you to muse upon your end, the more you see your friends weakened and destroyed, the stronger my final sacrifice will be. If it were just a matter of killing you, I'd have had you shot from behind weeks ago." The blade rested on my Adam's apple, pricking my skin coldly. He drew a line down my throat. I felt a warm trickle of blood start. "And your little seer friend, the girl . . . she, also, has a part to play in this."

"She'll see you for what you are, and get away."

"I think not. We had her caught earlier this evening, actually. I was anticipating the priest's incapacitation this morning." He raised the knife, brought it towards my right wrist.

A blurred motion swept past me, taking the Colonel away in that instant. A confused set of motions later, the Colonel and the blur separated and stopped.

The Colonel regarded Kafan with tight-lipped amusement. "I must confess I didn't expect you quite yet."

Kafan answered in Vietnamese; the two squared off. "What do you hope to accomplish, boy?" the Colonel asked. "You failed the last time. What is the point of fighting me again?"

I began wiggling my hand towards my Swiss Army knife. If I could just get it out . . .

"This time you're not coming back," Kafan growled. He and the Colonel exchanged a blinding flurry of blows and blocks, neither of them touching the other.

"Really?" the Colonel said. He swept Kafan's feet

out from under him and hammered the smaller man's face with his elbow. Kafan barely evaded the next strike and rolled up, throwing a punch at the Colonel that left a dent in the wall. They circled each other, Kafan spitting out a mouthful of blood as the Colonel's grin widened, the teeth sharpening. "And why is that?"

"Because now I know what I am."

The Colonel hesitated fractionally. Not quite as much as Kafan obviously hoped for, but even so Kafan's instantaneous lunge nearly decapitated him. As it was, the Colonel's preternatural speed pulled his head aside barely in time, Kafan's claws scoring his cheek with five parallel scratches. "Feh! Kr'lm akh! What difference is that, boy? So you were meant to be a Guardian! Without the Goddess behind your power, what are you but a simple thug, one whose blows are nothing more than stinging sand?" I'd hoped his words were boasting, but seeing how those five cuts were already closing up, even as he spoke, I realized that the Colonel was only speaking the truth.

Kafan returned the Colonel's grin, with interest, his form fully changed into a tailed, fanged humanoid. He straightened slightly and brought his arms into a strange, formal stance. "I don't need the Goddess behind my power. All I need are two words, given to me by the Master who taught me."

The Colonel seemed to tense.

"*Tor.*"

At that word, the Colonel stepped back.

Not fast enough. Two slashing movements of Kafan's hands, too fast to follow, ripped aside blocking arms as though the Colonel hadn't even tried, and a third strike against the uniformed chest sent him flying into the wall with a combined sound of shattering stone and breaking bone.

While the Colonel slowly rose, bones forcing

themselves back to their proper positions and healing in moments, Raiakafan sprinted to the section of the wall nearest me. "And *Shevazherana*," he said. He pulled the sheath from the wall and drew the immense, squat-bladed sword from it.

The Colonel's eyes widened. His form began to shift and he leapt away, towards the exit.

Raiakafan stood there, impossibly having crossed the room in the blink of an eye. "No escape for you, monster. For my father—*this!*"

The first slash took off the changing form's right arm. It screeched and tried to stumble backwards. It ran into something, spun around to find itself facing . . . Raiakafan again. "For my children—*this!*"

The other arm flew off in a fountain of red-black blood. Screeching in terror, not a trace of humanity left on its bony, angular form, the thing flapped feeble wings and flew upwards, away from the implacable hunter. A hunter who disappeared from view while both the monster and I stared at him

And once more the creature that had been the Colonel rebounded from something that had appeared in its path. Falling along with the stunned demon, Raiakafan shoved it downwards so it landed prone on the grassy floor of the cavern. "And for my wife."

The great sword came down once more. In a flash of black light, a flicker of shadow that momentarily erased all illumination, the thing dispersed.

A pile of noisome dust sifted away from Kafan's sword, dust that slowly evaporated and turned into a smell of death and decay . . . and faded away to nothing.

"Get up, Father," Kafan said, helping Verne up. "It's over now."

I staggered wearily to my feet, feeling the warm trickle of blood down my arms. "No. Not yet. They've got Sylvie!"

Kafan cursed in that ancient tongue. "But where?"

"Only one guess. If she isn't being held in a van or car nearby, she's got to be at Ed's place. At least, I hope so. Because without the Colonel to tell us, it'll be a long hard search if that's not where she is." And I couldn't afford to think about that.

"Is it not . . . possible that he was bluffing?" Verne said weakly.

"Do you think he was?"

Verne didn't answer; his expression was enough.

"Neither did I. He wouldn't bluff that way. He was smart enough to set things up ahead of time."

Kafan looked at me. "You're not in any condition to fight."

"Don't even *think* about keeping me out of this. Who else are we going to call?"

Somehow we got to the top of the stairs. Morgan, with his usual imperturbable expression denying the very existence of his torn clothing and bloodied form, smiled slightly as we emerged. "I'm glad to see you're all still alive."

"Can you drive, Morgan?"

Morgan raised an eyebrow. "Certainly, Master Jason. I presume there is some urgency?"

"If any of these monsters are left, they've got Syl."

Morgan snatched the keys from my hand and half-dragged me along. Verne was moving somewhat easier, but it was plain that neither of us was up to a fight with a half-dead Chihuahua, let alone a group of demonic assassins. The fact that neither Morgan or Kafan said anything told us that they knew that we'd never allow ourselves to be left behind.

The drive across town was excruciatingly slow. It seemed that every block was ten times longer than it had ever been when I drove along it before. We entered Morgantown's main district, crossed through, and continued. Though only fifteen minutes had passed, I felt as though precious days were passing. Syl. How *could* we have left her unguarded?!

Ed Sommer's house was lit up like a full-blown party was going on inside. The fence around it looked normal, but I could tell it was stronger than it appeared . . . and electrified, too. A contractor like Ed wouldn't have had trouble installing all sorts of bad news for intruders.

"Hang on, gentlemen," Morgan said.

"What are you doing?" I asked.

"Going through the gate, of course," he said calmly, as the engine on Verne's limousine roared and we were pressed back by acceleration. "Without being in suitable combat condition, our best chance is . . ."

With a rending crash, the limo shuddered but tore through the gateway.

" . . . total surprise and uncompromising speed. Prepare to attack."

We dove out of the limo, expecting a counterattack momentarily. The front door of the house popped open. Arms screaming in pain, I still managed to bring the gun up, sighted on the target—

—and dropped the gun immediately. "Don't shoot! It's SYL!"

Sylvia emerged fully from the doorway, stepping gingerly over the limp body of a demonoid as she did so. As I raced up the steps and embraced her, she smiled and said, "I see you missed me."

The events caught up with me, and I nearly fainted. Syl caught me and supported me, helped me towards the car.

"We should hurry, Master Jason," Morgan said. "There may be others pursuing her."

"There aren't," Syl said with calm certainty.

42

"I must confess, Jason, that there are a few things which remain unclear to me."

Rebuilding Verne's mansion was taking some time. It had also taken a lot of fast talking to keep Jeri from poking her nose too far in; even though the mansion was relatively isolated, the battle between the half-demonic things which the Colonel had employed and Verne's household had been more than loud enough to draw a lot of attention. Now, a week later, we were meeting in the repaired living room.

Verne was back to his old, debonair self, black hair glistening sleekly in the lamplight, dark eyes as intense and deep as they ever were. "Firstly, Jason, how did all the people gain entrance without us knowing of them?"

"Since the house was bugged," I answered, reaching out for an hors d'oeuvre and wincing slightly from the pain in my arms, "Ed and the others heard me come in. Then, when I said to shut down *all* the electrical power in the house, that took out the alarm systems. Your own personal alarms—mystical ones—weakened along with you, of course. I'd presume that they had some ability to subvert magical wards as well. And of course once the shooting started, none of us would've noticed an alarm much anyways."

Verne nodded. "True enough. In my condition, I wouldn't have noticed much, nor cared, I admit. Now, second . . . Lady Sylvia."

Syl grinned from ear to ear. "It was almost worth being kidnapped by those things to see the expressions on your faces. Jason, dear, you try to take me seriously, but like so many people—men and women—you look at my gypsy facade and my crystal earrings and pendants and forget what I really am." She paused. "So did they. They really didn't search me at all; I didn't resist much except to scream and struggle a bit. Then when they had me locked away . . ." for a moment her face had a grim expression on it, one I'd never seen before; I wasn't sure I liked it. " . . . I prepared myself, and then left."

"Indeed, milady. But *how*?"

"You trust my visions. So do I. That's because I'm not a fake."

I remembered Elias Klein dropping me in agony because the touch of a rock-crystal amulet burned him. I thought about what that meant.

So did Verne. "My apologies, milady."

"No apologies needed, Verne. You saw me as I prefer to be seen; a somewhat airheaded, gentle mystic with no taste for war and a hint of the Talent. But when my friends are in danger, I'm not as gentle as I look. The truth is that they weren't ready for a real magician, even a very minor one. And that was fatal." She looked ill for a moment.

"It's okay, Syl," I said.

She looked up at me. "You're not too shocked?"

"It'll take a little readjustment, I guess. But not that much. You carry a gun. I should've known that you're smart enough not to carry something unless you were sure you could use it if you had to. So I shouldn't have been surprised that you'd be able to fight. I'm glad it still bothers you, though. As long as we're both bothered by it, we're still human."

Verne nodded solemnly. "Killing is a part of life at times. But it is when we come to accept it as a matter of course that we give up a part of our souls."

"I have one question of my own," I said. "Kafan, what were those words you said that made the Colonel back up?"

Kafan glanced at Verne, who inclined his head slightly. "Well, 'Shevazherana' is the name of that sword my Master gave me, the one Verne kept after I disappeared. It means . . . Dragontooth, Dragon Fang, something like that. The other word, 'Tor' . . . it is the name for the method of combat that I was taught. Why, exactly, it scares demons, I don't know, but it does."

Verne shrugged. "It was the technique of combat used by the Royal Family of Atlantaea and their guardians. And demons had good reason to fear that family's vengeance after the fall of Atlantaea. And the one who taught you . . . oh, there's good reason for them to fear anyone who knows that word."

All of us could see that Verne might know more, but wasn't going to speak. I decided I'd delved into more than enough unspeakable mysteries in the past few weeks. This one I'd leave alone. "I do have one other general question," I said.

"Only one? Dear me, Jason, then I must have already said far too much!" Verne said, relaxing.

I laughed. "No, seriously. You've often mentioned, offhandedly, things about 'other worlds' and how somehow magic was removed or sealed away. I guess my question is . . . where *is* the magic? And will it come back?"

He looked thoughtful. "This is not the first time I have considered that question, Jason. To put it simply, magic exists everywhere to at least some very small extent, but its focal point, if you will, is a single world. Why such a truly cosmic force should be so focused I do not know—I never studied magical theory, and the reasons behind such a phenomenon were probably only really understood by a handful of the wizards of Atlantaea. However, there was a link—a conduit, one might say—between that world and Earth. Kerlamion and his forces either severed or blocked the conduit.

If severed, it might well act as would a similar item in the real world, spraying its cargo of power out into the 'area,' if one could use such a term, of the break. Where that would be, of course, is a question far beyond my ability to answer. If it was sealed, on the other hand, the power has been building up behind the blockage. Perhaps there is some maximum which is already reached, and thus the barrier will remain unless something breaches it; or, perhaps, eventually enough pressure, so to speak, will build up and shatter even the Seal placed by the Lord of Demons."

I thought for a moment. "So, to summarize, 'I haven't a clue' is your answer."

Syl gave an unladylike snort that turned into a fit of coughing; she'd been just taking a sip of tea when I skewered Verne. As I apologized, the others finished laughing. I sat back in my chair, feeling a crinkle of paper that reminded me of something.

"Oh, Verne, I've got something for you." I handed him the check.

He stared at it. "Jason, I appreciate that you wish to repay me, but we're hardly done yet. Besides, after what I know you've spent, I know you cannot possibly afford this."

I grinned. "It sure shows that you've been too busy to keep up with events lately, or you'd have seen the news articles on it. Verne, I'm rich now."

"What?"

I opened up the paper. "Take a look. After the Morgantown Incident, werewolf paranoia showed up everywhere. And since there's only *one* known way to detect the things, lots of people started making Wood's Werewolf Sensors or whatever they wanted to call them, including the Feds. Well, a little pushing from the right lawyers and the Patent Office recognized that I'd done the design work and owned the rights to every

version of the thing being produced. In exchange for
a real generous licensing deal to allow them any number of the sensors for government use, the Fed made
sure that the private sector manufacturers coughed up
the bucks real fast. I'm probably going to have quite
a substantial income for a long time to come."

"Truly it's an ill wind that blows no good, Jason.
Even Virigar has brought something good out of his
visit. My congratulations."

"Speaking of those things, have they actually proven
to be of any use?"

"According to government sources—who naturally
don't want to be talked about—a number of, um,
'paranatural security breaches' were detected through
its use. That's one reason they're very happy to work
with me."

"So all's well, then." Verne said. "It is well done
with."

"We're not done yet," I said. "There's still the question of Senator MacLain. And of Kay and your daughter."

Kafan nodded, lips tight.

Verne smiled. "True, Jason. Yet I have confidence
that we will find a way to deal with these things. The
Lady is with me again. I have friends. I have my son.

"Faith, friends, and family, Jason. What more do any
of us need?"

Live and Let Spy

43

"Good evening, Jason," Verne said. "Is there a reason you come bearing a laptop?"

"Evening, Verne," I said, sitting down in the large, comfortable chair I usually took when visiting. "Yep. Remember, I asked you if you were free this evening. I want to pick your brain, or at least get a start on it."

He smiled, curious. "About what, in particular?"

"Well, when I first met you and ended up with Elias Klein turning into a charcoal briquette, I thought, 'Well, now, that's something to tell my grandkids,' but figured it was a fluke. Then Virigar and his litter of homicidal puppies showed up, and I thought, 'Jeez, twice in a year. But that ought to be that.'"

Verne sat down in his own chair. "I believe I see where this is going."

"So then along comes Ed Sommer, genetically engineered contractor-assassin, following your time-displaced contradictory-backgrounded long-lost son, and I get an infodump on the Secrets Man Was Not Meant

To Know," I continued. "At this point, I think I have to accept that as long as I'm involved with you, the Weird Shit of the World is going to keep coming to my door. This puts aside the fact that along the way I, personally, have gotten pretty high on the hit parade of several nasties—Ed and the Colonel's former organization, whatever's left of them, the vampire who sent Klein after you at their request, and of course the King of the Werewolves himself.

"So I figure that as long as I'm going to be in the deep end, I might as well know what else might be swimming around under me, nibbling at my toes." I plugged my laptop into the wall and powered up. "I've set up a database for the weird here, and I want you to help me fill it in, as much as possible, so when I run into something I'll have a chance to figure out what I'm dealing with."

"I cannot argue with the logic of this enterprise," Verne admitted. "Whether I would agree that I, personally, am the focal point—it could I think be argued with equal facility that you are yourself the crux—I am a firm believer in destiny. Giving you more information to work with has always served us well. Ask and I shall answer, to the best of my ability to do so."

Kafan appeared in the doorway. "Do you need my help, Mr. Wood?"

I shook my head. "I don't think so, Kafan. Verne probably knows more about the current 'State of the Weird' than you do, given that you spent most of your current life either locked in a lab or hiding in some Viet jungle. If I have to ask about things specific to you, I'll let you know. By the way, I got a message from the Senator; I'll be having a meeting with her day after tomorrow, and the three of us will have to decide how I'm going to approach it. But I'll do that tomorrow as a strategy meeting."

Kafan clearly wanted to discuss it now, but he restrained himself admirably. It had taken more than a little effort to hammer it through his head that there simply was not going to be any quick and easy way to get his children away from a United States senator. "I'll see you tomorrow, then," he said finally. "I'm going out for a while, Father. Morgan says that he and Meta will watch Genshi."

"Very well, Kafan. Enjoy yourself." Verne turned back to me as Kafan left. "So where shall we start?"

"Well, why not with you, Verne?" I asked. "Over the months I've gotten piecemeal ideas about what hurts you or helps you and so on, and you told me that your powers derive from your . . . goddess," I stumbled over the word; it was still difficult for me to casually discuss things as fact which had been myth to me a year previously, "and that Klein's type of vampire were made in mockery of what you are, but I'd like to have a unified idea of what you can and cannot do, and why, and then we can compare this to the Klein type of vampire, and move on from there."

"I have no objection." Verne settled back and steepled his fingers in thought. "As you know, the Lady Eonae blessed me with these powers. She is the essence of the living world; you can think of her as a spirit who reflects the nature of life and the magic of the soul. During the destruction of Atlantaea, I was one of her priests—high in her hierarchy, but not at the top—and at the moment the blow fell I was serving as . . . how should I put it . . . a minister or chaplain to the Royal Family. Seeing the demons unleashed, the Eternal Queen told me to go swiftly and protect her son, Prince Mikael, who had only shortly before left for the Great Temple. She did this partly out of her own kindness, I am sure, for she knew that my own wife and children were of necessity at the Great Temple as well."

Verne's voice took on that trace of an ancient accent, and his eyes seemed darker and sad as he continued. "It was while I raced down the Diamond Way that I was attacked by a mob of Demons. Individually they were no match for me at all, and as a group they should not have been able to defeat one of my rank and training. But even as I summoned the power of the Lady to oppose them, I felt it falter. For the first time in living memory, something was threatening the strength of Eonae herself, and because of that we, her chosen, were weakened, at the very moment when we so desperately needed her power." He sipped from his crystal goblet, eyes staring into the past. "Yet still had Queen Niadeea placed her command and charge upon me, and I would not fail her. With the shadow of power still mine to command and my own will and training, I managed to fight my way free of the Demons, but they had greviously injured both body and soul. I should have died there, moments after that desperate victory, but I could not—I would not—yield my life without reaching the Great Temple. I refused Death, forbade it to touch me, and swore upon all the Powers of the Two Worlds that I would still reach the Temple and see Prince Mikael's living face, even were my very heart torn from my body.

"Around me, as in a nightmare, I could hear the destruction of the city—screams of terror and pain, the snarls of Demons and monsters, the crumbling of buildings, the flare and thunderclap roar of spells and mystic weapons against the invaders. My breath seemed to give me no strength, yet I forced one foot in front of another, following the wavering path onward towards the building I must reach."

I found myself gripping the laptop tightly, knowing what was coming. There was pain in Verne's voice, a pain that literal ages had not been able to entirely erase. I hadn't intended to ask for his past story, just for something on what he could do, but I realized that this was a story he hadn't told for a long time indeed, and maybe a story that he *had* to tell.

"The steps of the Great Temple were covered in blood. The echo of the Lady's presence was fainter. I staggered up the steps, my shattered ribs grating, blood trickling down my side, vision narrowing until it seemed I walked down a black tunnel, a tiny sliver of light ahead of me revealing bodies, torn tapestries, nothing but death, death and destruction everywhere." For a moment his voice, the smooth, deep voice which almost never varied its controlled pitch, caught, wavered. "Then I saw them.

"Mithanda lay atop Nami and Suti, futilely trying to protect them to the last. The beast that had slain them turned towards me, grinning, feeding upon my horror and despair. I screamed, I know that, and swung my staff of office, caring nothing of how I died now. But the staff carried the enchantments, as did almost all weapons in those days, and the monster had seen my wounds; it had thought me unable to fight at all, and its lunge took it straight into the path of my blow. The staff shattered, but the mystic force slew the monster in that same moment.

"I could do nothing for my family now. I had to see if the Prince was safe. Surely he would have been taken to the Heart, and the Sh'ekatha defend him. I had nothing left, only the command of the Queen. Somehow I still moved, leaving them behind. Mourning would be for later." He drew a deep breath.

"But the Prince was not there. The Sh'ekatha was, but he was already near to death. The Lady was one of the Demons' greatest enemies, so one of their greatest killers had been sent to make her cult impotent. It had not been easy, not even for one of the Great

Demons, but even as I entered, Balgoltha broke the Sh'ekatha's back over the Heartstone. My cry of protest was barely even a cough, so weak was I, but still the Demonlord heard it and turned. Wounded though he was, he still laughed, and rightfully so. I was no threat to such as he—not even had I been unhurt. The Lady's power was faint, and fading. I had no more hope or help to give, and I had failed the Queen, for surely the Prince was dead or captured now. With no other course, I used the last of my strength and staggered into the Mirror of the Sky; at least I would die in a place where no Demon might touch my soul."

He swallowed, eyes still focused on things long gone to dust. "But the Lady is wise, and has the craft of the Earth within her. In that very instant, she drew upon the strength of the world entire, and I . . . I became the Sh'ekatha.

"Balgoltha had tried to seal the power, but even he had failed to realize how strong the Lady could be; by the time he reacted, it was too late. Here, in the center of the Great Temple, I rose from the Mirror, healed and touched by the very grace of the Lady, and he knew he was no match for me, not in that moment, not as he was. It would have pleased me to fight him, finish off at least one of the enemy, but he was no fool, and fled with a curse.

"But Atlantaea was ended, and the Demons scoured the earth. With the Lady's blessing I could hide from them, but little else could I do for long, long years. Only when they had left, confident that their work was done and only harmless savages remained, did I emerge and, taking those few things I could salvage, begin to rebuild what had been lost."

There was a long silence then. Finally, Verne shook himself and looked apologetically at me. "Dear me, Jason . . . I became rather carried away there. I had no intention of talking so long on a topic which was, at best, a side issue to the one at hand."

"It's okay. I think you needed to talk that out."

He hesitated, then nodded slowly. "You may be right, my friend.

"And though it's about half a million years too late . . . I'm sorry."

"Your sympathy is appreciated." He sipped his goblet, and then with a visible effort cast off the feeling of brooding sadness. "Enough of this. It was only after that time that I truly began to understand what I had become, and why. The powers of a Sh'ekatha, and their limitations, are all part of what it means to represent Eonae, the Lady of the World.

"Firstly, I drink blood. Blood is in many ways the essence of life; it carries all that sustains a living being, and thus I depend on it as all living things depend on each other. I am strong, a strength that represents both the unity of life and the solidity of the Earth, and a strength which grows as time does pass, just as a forest can grow from a single seed in time. Only things that are living, or that derive directly from the activity of life, can harm me as weapons. This reflects the fact that the existence of life itself is not truly dependent on the Earth's decisions, for life is a natural consequence of the world; only the turning of Life against itself, or an unnatural form of Life, can destroy life. I cannot enter a dwelling place of intelligent creatures unbidden, because the very nature of intelligence is to control nature; nature only enters a dwelling if the owner permits it, and therefore one who is the living avatar of nature may not enter without permission either. I can change my form, since life is itself mutable, and nature exists in many guises; yet the forms I can assume are constrained, because in nature the rules constrain the ways in which life evolves. Sunlight harms us because it is the source of energy for all other forms of life, but the Sh'ekatha draws his strength from the Earth itself; he is reminded, by this separation, that he is different from all other things that live because he, alone of all things, is tied to the Spirit of the World directly and can do no harm to her without feeling it rebound upon him, nor can anything long harm the world without harming him. He can no longer turn to the Sun for strength and light, but must find it within himself. I can influence the world, especially the elements of air and water, through the action of my will—although this power does not come to a Sh'ekatha immediately, but grows over time just as the physical strength. This power derives from the fact that life itself can affect and transform the world, and is in fact an expression, by its very existence, of the power of spirit over matter. Similarly, as that which lives can affect me, I can affect it to some extent, and thus I have some power over minds. As I represent the Earth itself, and life in all its guises, no mirror or image made by unthinking machines can capture my essence; a picture of myself can only be created by the power of a thinking mind that sees me with its soul as well as by crude light. As I am living, I can also reproduce, though in a way unique to myself; I can place some of my power in another who is willing, and let that power grow; my life force acts as a seed and symbiote, creating a new and stronger life, but one with some ties to both myself and to the original creature." He sat back and finished his glass of blood. "I believe that covers everything. If I recall anything else, I shall inform you."

I typed the data in, asking questions of him occasionally since I had to clarify certain points—he'd reeled that stuff off awfully fast. Finally I finished up. "Okay. How about those vampires like Klein? Is there a specific logic in the parody of your powers?"

Verne's mouth tightened momentarily. "Oh, yes. Their creator was a magician of vast power, one who in essence was attempting himself to become a demon and perhaps something even greater in darkness. I was one of his major adversaries after the Fall of Atlantaea, because I attempted to establish a new civilization based on the old and had the power to do so. He intended to create his own empire, or so I believe, in order to use the strength of the human race to further his personal quest. In any case, I became a perennial thorn in his side; he could not corrupt the world or its spirit so long as I lived. Eventually he came up with this curse, which was all too effective.

"The victims of the curse, the vampires, are parodies in all ways. Rather than a purification and extension of the true spirit, they are warped powers, turned against themselves to produce an abomination. They drink blood to represent their ties to destruction—spilling blood rather than accepting it freely. Their strength is the strength of self-hate and destruction, life turned upon itself. They shift shape to forms of nightmare because terror is their object." He gave a wintry smile. "I suspect their inability to enter a dwelling unbidden, besides being necessary in an overall parody, was also there for a purely practical reason; why permit your own quite mad and vicious creations to be able to enter your own home without permission? For they were all mad, at least for a time; just as becoming the Sh'ekatha cleanses the mind and spirit and gives you clarity and peace, at least in the beginning, so this dark mirrored version first turns the mind against itself and tests your will to live."

Verne went on, detailing the vampiric abilities and weaknesses and their relationship to his own. After that, things got more complicated, as we started discussing other "powers" in the world, what they were like, and how they did what they did.

After a while, I glanced at my watch. "Holy sheep! Verne, it's three in the morning!"

He smiled. "So you want to make an early night of it, eh?"

I grinned back, probably looking a bit dazed. "I probably should have. I had no idea how big a project this was going to become."

"Remember, Jason, many of these things either do not exist any more, in all probability, or at the least are vanishingly rare. If you wanted to do a comprehensive catalog of the entirety of the paranormal, you would never finish in an ordinary human lifetime; however, the number of such things that can even function on Earth as it is today is so small that I believe we can probably finish your little database in a few months of once or twice a week discussion."

"Well, that makes me feel some better. I think. But I'll let you know later. Tomorrow evening remind Kafan we will be going over what I'll be doing in my meeting with the Senator. "

"I shall. Get some sleep, Jason."

"Preferably *after* I get home, of course," I said, glancing at my car.

He chuckled and held open the door as I left.

44

I shook the Senator's hand. She had a strong grip, and looked as dignified in person as in her publicity shots; I was pretty sure that her "stern schoolteacher" image worked in her favor not only at the polls, but on the Senate floor. "Senator, good to meet you."

"A pleasure, Mr. Wood." She was unaccompanied—

something which showed considerable trust on her part, or at least faith that her intelligence gathering people wouldn't miss something dangerous. "Now, I don't have an unlimited amount of time here, so let's not spend too much time on formalities; you call me Paula and I'll call you Jason and we'll just call things as we see them, all right?"

I nodded. "Fine by me, Paula."

"I'll start," she said. "As you know, I have received the test results for paternity, and they clearly demonstrate that your client is the biological parent of my children. If it comes to court, I won't even bother arguing with that.

"However," she continued, "investigating your client's background has turned up some . . . confusing information. Without wasting each other's time going into the details, my investigators are of the opinion that some, or all, of his background was falsified, although they do inform me that his credentials, if forged, must have been faked by one of the very best intelligence services. My investigators also find Mr. Verne Domingo's background somewhat disquieting. I don't think I need point out that if this is indeed true, I would be extremely unlikely to agree to have my children taken away, even for short periods of time, by a man whose real name and background I don't even know."

She had good investigators. I'd expected as much, but they were damn good to ferret out some of that stuff. I'd been pretty sure of the general thrust of what they'd find, though, and because of that I'd made my decisions about how to approach her. Convincing Verne and, especially, Kafan to go along with those had taken five hours of sometimes acrimonious debate last night. "You know, I pretty much thought you'd be saying something along those lines," I said finally. "I've discussed the situation with my client, and he's given me permission to tell you certain things, but before I do, I'd like to lead up to it in my own way. The situation is much more complex than you currently understand, and I'd like to give you the big picture."

She gave me a formal nod.

I stood up and went over to a small glass case at one end of the room, opening it with a key code. Reaching in, I picked up one of the objects inside and brought it over. "Do you know what this is? Careful— it's extremely sharp."

The Senator examined the long, slender, sparkling thing—slightly curved, razor-sharp along the inside edge, coming to a needle-fine point at one end and about half an inch across at the opposite end. At first she seemed a bit puzzled, but then she glanced up suddenly. "Why, this must be . . ." she stumbled a bit over the next word, "a werewolf claw?"

"That's correct," I said. "I want you to think about what you're holding there, ma'am. That's nine and a half inches of diamond blade. The thing it came from had five of those on each hand, five on each foot, and stood taller than this room's roof if it straightened up. It could run as fast as a car given a straight distance to accelerate, was strong enough to tip a car over on its own, and had a mouth full of teeth just like those claws—a mouth that could open up wide enough to cut a man in half.

"And it could look just like you or me, or anyone else on Earth."

Senator MacLain gave a small shiver. She had a good imagination, I suspected. "I see. I do indeed, Mr. Wood. I assure you, that's one of the things that most impressed me about you—that you survived being chased by something like that."

"More luck than anything else, Senator, believe me."

She gave a refined, Katherine Hepburn–like sniff of

doubt. "Jason, to quote a movie that my older son enjoys and that you are no doubt well acquainted with, 'In my experience, there's no such thing as luck.' Rather, I see people who are competent as making their own luck through making the right choices in bad moments."

With a small laugh I ceded her point. "Okay, yes, I'm pretty good at thinking on my feet. But there's a few other points that some investigators have brought up which are relevant here—and yes, I'll be connecting it to your children in a few moments."

She looked thoughtful. "Oh. Quite so. As I recall, one of the unresolved problems, even after the briefing, was exactly who had assisted you. Some of my colleagues were under the impression that it was some special task force of our own—and from reading the transcripts, I think it's *very* clear that this was in fact the impression that the testimony was intended to give. I always felt that there was more being hidden than told, however. Are you saying that my impression is correct?"

Boy, she was a sharp one. Winthrope and her unknown employers had done a bang-up job on giving out the story without revealing anything they didn't absolutely have to, and the wording they'd used would have fooled almost anyone into thinking they'd been told all they needed to know. Senator Paula MacLain, however, was not just anyone. "Your impression is bang-on, Paula." I said. "I had help, but it wasn't anything official."

She waited.

"The second question that some people have asked—and quite reasonably so—is basically 'well, if werewolves exist, does that mean there's other things like them out there?' The answer to that is 'damn straight.'"

She had certainly seen where I had to be going with this, but her expression gave no sign of what her reaction was. She sat, waiting to see what I was going to put in front of her to evaluate.

"The werewolves are just one of at least half a dozen or more types of beings we'd call 'mythical' or 'supernatural,' even though those words aren't accurate any more; after all, it's not mythical if you can actually prove it's there, and if they're part of the way the world works, are they really supernatural?" I shrugged. "Anyway, the Wolves are in some ways the nastiest of all of these things, near as I can tell, and they've got their own enemies. In point of fact, the reason they all came here to Morgantown was that they were hunting down one of their old adversaries, who was living in Morgantown under the name of Verne Domingo."

Now her gaze was riveted on my face. Other than its intensity, there still wasn't any sign of what she was really thinking.

I took a deep breath. "Verne Domingo is, himself, one of these other types of beings; the best, really quick way I can think of to describe what he is would be to say he's a vampire, but that's not accurate. It would give you some basic idea of his characteristics, though. Verne has . . . connections throughout the paranatural world. In a sense, he's one of its most respected citizens. While he certainly doesn't know everything about all of them, virtually every one of the beings that lives this kind of double life knows about him, even if they don't know precisely where he is.

"Now, where this hooks up with Tai Lee Xiang is that Verne knew Tai Lee's family, years ago." Verne, Kafan, and I had decided that this "take" on the history would be the closest match to allow us to tell what we had to without bringing up certain contradictions which had led to other facts which none of us wanted to talk about. "They saw him as an ally and protector. Verne left for parts unknown and eventually they lost track of the ways to contact him. But the tradition of the protector was still passed down through the family line, along with the unique characteristics that separated this protector from the common man.

"So when Tai Lee Xiang found himself in trouble that he didn't dare bring to the authorities, and in fact was being hunted by the authorities for killing a man who had held him and his family prisoner for years, he came to me to find this legendary protector. By that time, he'd reached the end of his resources and was willing to try anything to find his family or stop the people who were after him. With the publicity of the Wolf incidents, my name seemed the best possible choice; I knew there were Weird Things out there, and if anyone would be both willing to listen to his story and able to find someone from some pretty strange hints, it would be me." I grinned. "As it turned out, he was even luckier than he thought; I'd already met Verne, of course, so once he gave me the list of odd characteristics, I could just turn around and phone his family protector."

She'd sat quietly throughout the whole story, gazing at me intensely as though I was on trial and she was the judge evaluating my testimony—which, now that I thought of it, was a fair assessment of the situation. Finally she leaned back slowly. "That is quite an impressive story, Jason. I would expect that much of this would be information your friend Mr. Domingo prefers to keep secret, since no mention of him has ever been made in connection to prior events in Morgantown. Why was it necessary that you tell me so much?"

"Glad to see you are as quick on the pickup as your reputation makes you, ma'am." I said. "Because Tai wasn't held in an ordinary location at all. He, and his children, were the subjects of genetic experimentation. Just by being involved in their lives, you're putting yourself in danger, because the people who did this want their 'subjects' back. Your being a senator has no doubt balked them and caused considerable concern in their ranks, but it will most certainly not have stopped them. Eventually they'll come for the kids.

"So you have to know the truth about them—not just because it's your right to know about anything that might be endangering you and your family, but also because we just don't know what the ultimate results of the genetic tampering that was done to them will be. You might come home tomorrow to find one of them suffering from some disability or condition which simply isn't even recognizable by medical science."

To my surprise, Paula MacLain didn't burst into a flurry of questions, and she didn't attempt to argue about what was going on. She looked a tiny bit more pale, and after an inquiring glance at me she lit a long cigarette and drew a slightly shaky breath. A few moments later, she dropped her gaze and considered the half-smoked cigarette. "Usually I take my time on these." She looked back up. "Jason, I appreciate your candor."

I'm sure my startlement showed on my face. "Most people would have said something else, and 'candor' wouldn't be even close to the meaning, either."

"Oh, it's a preposterous story, young man." she said. "Yet I'm old enough to know that sometimes life *is* preposterous. However, that isn't why I accept that most, if not all, of your story is true."

Taking another drag from the cigarette, she continued. "I've been on many different committees over the years. I've seen a great deal of material handed around marked 'Top Secret' and heard all the 'in the interests of national security' speeches. And so I've been familiar with the sort of reports I get from my own investigators whenever someone else has been nosing around my life.

"After I adopted Jackie and Tai, I started getting faint hints that *someone* was interested in my life again. The hints were terribly subtle, though, and whenever I hired someone to poke back, so to speak, they found nothing concrete. Just recently—about the time you first contacted me, in fact—these little hints became more frequent, and my best people came to the conclusion that whoever it was had to be top-level intelligence, and that there might be more than one group of them, all sniffing around my family. I tried using my own connections to find out what was going on, but got nothing.

"At one point, Jackie became aware that I thought someone might be spying on us. That night, he tried to leave, taking his little brother with him. When I got him back, he tried to insist that he had to, but he simply wouldn't tell me why. But he's been worried ever since, and I've gotten the extremely strong impression from him that he is more worried about my safety than his own."

I nodded. "That would fit."

"It certainly would. Now, while I happen to believe you are telling me the truth, or as much of it as you think safe, I'd appreciate a bit more in the way of solid evidence. I've come here without any fiddling lawyers or bodyguards so that we could be honest and say what we want, and so I hope we can get this all out of the way."

I glanced at the clock. "How much time do you have, Paula?"

She smiled. "A bit more than I might have implied at the beginning. Start out with the other side under pressure, that's always been my motto. If you can manage to feed me, I daresay I can stay for the rest of the evening if necessary."

Smiling back, I said, "I suppose I could manage that as we get around to dinnertime." I switched on the air filter—while I don't particularly mind smoke, some clients and friends do, and I always seem to forget at first. "Assuming that what I said is true, what would your position be with respect to Tai Lee Xiang? I'm sure you know he's already started a quite respectable carpentry and woodcarving business, so he's not a shiftless layabout, so to speak."

"My position isn't markedly changed, Jason," she answered. "I don't care what dangers come with them, they're my children now, and anyone—mad scientists or otherwise—who tries to take them from me will, I assure you, lose their hands if they touch either Tai or Jackie. Their true father is another story, naturally. I have noticed genuine sadness in the boys on the few occasions they've mentioned their father, so I know that he must have been at least able to inspire affection. This of course isn't sufficient to prove that he was, or could currently be, a good father to them, only that he wasn't such a monster or disciplinarian as to lose the love of his children. If I can be confident that he will be good for the children . . ." her face worked for a moment, " . . . well, Jason, we will work something out, I promise you. I lost my family once, you know."

I nodded.

"Then understand—I know what that feels like. If I know that Tai Lee Xiang is a good man, then I will not cause him the same kind of pain. He will see his children again. To do anything else would make me the monster, and while the thought of letting them leave me—perhaps for months at a time—hurts far more than you could imagine, I would rather bear that pain than think that I was taking another person's family away." She was back under control again, at what cost I really didn't know. "I hope that makes my position clear enough."

"Perfectly clear. And I thank you, Paula. I'm sure we will be able to work something out." I glanced at my watch. "I think I can give you some more solid evidence, but not until later today."

Seeming somewhat relieved to get away from what was a very emotional topic, she accepted a temporary shift away from the business conversation, and took up some of the time quizzing me about the Morgantown Incident—getting my version of the story, rather than the trimmed, edited, and perhaps not entirely accurate version the press releases had contained. By the time we were done with that, it was getting towards evening.

"Well, Senator," I said, "If your reputation can survive the scandal of being seen out in a restaurant with a younger man, I think it's time to get you the food I promised."

She laughed. "Mr. Wood, my reputation doesn't need protecting. And having seen pictures of the young lady you're currently dating, I suspect no one would believe any scandal about us anyway."

"I didn't know my love life was so, um, public."

"It isn't, really, but as I said, I had people investigating. You being one of the principals in this matter, there was a fair amount of digging into your background as well."

I wasn't sure I liked that, but on the other hand it wasn't anything surprising. I shrugged and offered my arm. "In that case, Paula, shall we?"

45

"Senator MacLain, welcome," Morgan said, bowing both of us inside. "Master Verne is just this way."

Verne and Kafan—rather, I reminded myself, Tai Lee—rose as she entered. "Senator, what a pleasure," Verne said, quite sincerely. "Allow me to present my foster son, Tai Lee Xiang."

The two studied each other. Tai's face was, if anything, more coldly controlled than MacLain's—not surprising, since he knew that if it came to a dragged-out legal fight for custody, this woman was virtually certain to beat him hands-down. "Senator," he said, bowing formally.

"Mr. Xiang." She extended her hand, which Tai took after a moment. "I will say the same to both of you as I said to Mr. Wood; let's not waste time on formalities. Call me Paula, and I'll call you Tai and Verne, and let's see if we can at least begin to reach some solution to this problem."

"An eminently sensible suggestion," Verne approved. "Very well, Paula. Where would you like to begin? I presume that Jason has already told you a great deal."

She managed a small smile at that. "You might say that, yes. Let us start with you, Verne. Jason tells me you are no longer associated with any of your drug-dealing contacts. Is this indeed true? For you must understand that any—absolutely any—association with drug-dealing is absolute poison to any political career. If the father of my children is found to be living in the same home as someone of that sort . . ." She trailed off, having made her point clear without needing to belabor it.

Verne sighed. "To be utterly frank, the answer is yes and no. No longer do I, or any associate of mine, have any connection with people who deal in illegal substances. However, some of the 'contacts' which I use now for other purposes are the same contacts used during my days as a supplier of such substances. They simply have shifted their, how shall I put it, inventory and supply lines."

She seemed a bit nonplussed. "You mean that the same people who used to ship, or arrange the shipping of, large amounts of cocaine and so on are the ones doing other, non-drug-related work for you now? They simply dropped such a lucrative trade?"

"Quite so."

"You will pardon me if I find that a bit hard to believe," she said. "Most people who were involved in such a business find that the money is quite tempting and continue in it no matter what."

Verne's expression was slightly amused. "In the majority of ordinary cases, I have no doubt you are correct, Paula. However, there is little ordinary in my case. My 'contacts' are not ordinary people, in any sense of the term, and have helped with matters of supply and demand, off and on for an extremely long time now. It is, in fact, their business, in which they take great pride, to be able to drop one line of supply and within days or weeks have developed another pipeline of supply for an entirely different line of materials which is, in quality and efficiency, quite the equal of the one they dropped."

Paula opened her mouth, closed it, seemed to think for a moment, then spoke. "Hm. When you say 'an extremely long time,' Verne, am I correct in interpreting that to mean something long to a man of your nature, not merely long in terms I am used to thinking in?"

"That would be correct, Paula. For instance, many of the principals involved helped me in obtaining some of the materials which recently went on display in Cairo. I received these materials shortly after they had been removed from their proper resting place, due to the fact that my suppliers knew of my interest—very long-standing—in preserving materials of historic and cultural value when I could."

Those "materials," I recalled, included the mummy of Akhenaten, the Sun King. I had guessed at something of the sort, but it was still mind-boggling to imagine some group of people who acted essentially as general-purpose suppliers and had endured since at least the middle period of the Egyptian dynasties.

Something similar was probably going through Paula's mind at this point, but her demeanor didn't change. "I must presume, then, that they are experienced at being circumspect about their activities?"

"If you are asking if they are likely to ever be connected with myself, especially in a drug-related context, I would say it is extremely unlikely. It happened once, very long ago, and those were special circumstances. In other words, you do not need to worry about these connections of mine becoming an embarrassment to you."

Paula nodded, looked at Tai. "And yours?"

Tai shrugged. "Mr. Wood only made the connection between the murderer the Viet were hunting and me because he had reasons to think something peculiar was going on, and because he's very good at what he does. The IDs that were supplied to me, Mr. Wood assures me, are pretty much unimpeachable. So I don't think any evidence will come to light unless I make a nuisance of myself somewhere and make someone really start digging."

Paula laughed suddenly. "I see! If, for instance, there was a loud, public custody battle I might cause the very kind of uproar I want to avoid."

Tai nodded.

"All right," she said, "I've had my opening shots; either of you gentlemen wish to return fire?"

"I want to know about my children. How are they? Are they safe, really?"

Paula's face softened very slightly. "Jackie—Seb, to you—and Tai are perfectly safe. They're wonderful children. Jackie always tries to do whatever he can around the house, even though he doesn't really need to, and he's so good in his studies. Tai, well, he's a bit of a scamp, but he never means any harm. As far as them being safe, I would think they're as safe in a senator's house as they're likely to get."

Until now, Tai had been in a taut posture—like a cat with its back up. But as Paula talked about the children, I saw him relax. There was no single specific change I could point to, but overall he just seemed to settle back. Something seemed to have reassured him, far beyond anything her words could have done.

"They'd be much safer here," he said, but the confrontational edge was gone from his voice. It was just a statement of fact.

Paula raised an eyebrow. "You are so sure of that?"

"I would be here," he said. "And so would Father. I know your military and your security. They aren't bad. But they could not guard a home half as well as we could."

I could see Paula wanted to debate that, but she had as good an intuition as mine, and knew that Tai was telling the flat truth, at least as he saw it. "Do you concur with his, pardon the expression, extravagant assessment of his abilities, Verne?" she asked finally.

"Better, I think, that you ask Jason," Verne replied. "He has more extensive knowledge than I of modern security, and has personally witnessed my abilities and those of Tai Lee."

In response to her questioning glance, I grinned. "Beyond doubt. Paula, you must realize how difficult it would be to just 'get out' of the drug business,

especially if there were highly placed people relying
on you. Verne was able to provide them with a convincing argument to leave him utterly alone. By himself. Tai can take care of himself and those around him
equally well."

"I see."

Morgan came in, carrying two trays of the sinful
snacks he seemed to always be pushing on visitors. It
was a good thing I didn't spend more time here, or
I'd start to become a far bigger man than I'd ever
expected. Like Elvis. "No thanks, Morgan—I really
have to cut down."

"I'll have some," Tai said, hungry as usual.

Paula took a sampler plate and accepted a glass of
wine. "Now, I was hoping for some direct physical
evidence of the more unusual claims Jason has made.
He said you would be providing such evidence?"

Verne couldn't quite restrain a smile. "I think we
could arrange that, yes. I believe the same evidence
that convinced Jason should suffice, eh, Tai?"

Tai smiled. "Why not." He swallowed another bite,
then went to the stairwell. "Genshi? GENSHI! I know
you're up there trying to listen in! Come down!"

That familiar clattering-patter of clawed feet immediately sped down the stairs. Genshi, now used to
seeing people come and go, wasn't nearly as shy as he
had been the night Sylvie and I met him; he toddled
up to Paula, who was staring wide-eyed down at him,
and smiled, wagging his golden tail.

"This is my youngest son, Genshi," Tai said. "My son
Tai, named after me, can change to a very similar form,
but was trained to avoid it. Seb's transformation is
considerably less extreme, though still very easy to
notice."

Genshi suddenly held his arms up, and Paula, clearly
a mother to the core despite her often-demanding

profession, responded by picking him up. Genshi snuggled into her as though at home. "Nice lady!" he said.

She looked almost ready to go teary-eyed, but held back. "Well, he's certainly a little charmer."

Tai laughed. "He knows how to use the cute look, yep."

"Will you be requiring a demonstration of my abilities as well, Paula?" Verne inquired.

She glanced over to him, still mostly focused on the tailed little boy. "Um . . . not really necessary, I suppose. It would be silly of me to doubt the rest of the story with the evidence right here for another part."

"Will you people be needing me any more?" I asked. "Seems that we've gotten over the potential shooting war, and I'd like to get home if it's possible."

Paula looked at Verne. "If you can provide me with transportation back to my hotel . . . ?"

"But of course. Go on, Jason. I have a feeling that we have started on a resolution to our problems."

I headed out the door, relaxing finally. Judging by the way things were going, it might be time to start feeling sorry for the late Colonel and his pals; Paula MacLain, Kafan, and Verne were going to be a very dangerous team.

46

"How is it?"

I needn't have asked; the blissful expression on Syl's face told me that the food was everything she'd imagined. "God, Jason, the chef must be a wizard!"

The New York restaurant was famous for its Southwestern-grill menu, and I'd brought Syl down with me when I came to the city because I knew her fondness for New York, shopping, and grilled TexMex cooking. She'd gotten in plenty of shopping while I took care of business, and was now temporarily lost to me as she immersed herself in the delights of cilantro, cumin, and cayenne.

This was ideal for my purposes, since it put her Talent at a definite disadvantage.

"Oops," I said, bending over to pick up what I dropped. Then I went to one knee, opening the little box as I did so, and held it so that her gaze fell upon it just as she finished swallowing and opened her eyes.

"Sylvia Rowena Stake," I said, sounding far more calm than I felt, "would you marry me?"

For once—maybe the only time I ever would—I had completely surprised her. Not with the question, I'm sure, since both of us knew it would eventually happen, but she hadn't had a clue that today would be the day. Why I was nervous, I didn't know—it wasn't like I could imagine her saying "no" any more than I could imagine asking anyone else to marry me. Maybe it was just that old fear of commitment making its last stand.

Her eyes got wider and wider until suddenly tears started rolling down her cheeks; she closed them and flung her arms around my neck. "Oh, *yes*, Jason, of course I will!"

The entire restaurant seemed to erupt into clapping, and camera flashes popped across the crowd. We both blushed, but neither of us could stop grinning as I slipped the glittering diamond ring on Sylvie's finger.

The rest of the dinner was taken up by wedding plans. Now that the CryWolf devices were rolling in the money for me, I could afford anything, so I told her that; whatever kind of wedding she wanted, from a quick Justice of the Peace to an all-out extravaganza that would empty any six bank accounts, it was all fine with me. "Just keep me from having to spend too much of my own time on it," I said, honestly. "I don't do the big fancy stuff well."

She patted my cheek affectionately. "Jason, darling, don't worry. The wedding's still more for the girls than the guys, even in these enlightened times. You just have to show up and look respectable, and I don't need to worry about you on those scores. The problem will be finding an appropriate person to perform the wedding. I'd ask Verne, he's a priest, but somehow my parents would probably balk at the idea. They're still rather Catholic, you know."

"Yeah, I do." I'd met Syl's parents for the first time relatively recently. They couldn't complain about me as a potential son-in-law, and had done their best to make me feel welcome, but it was also pretty clear that they didn't quite know what to make either of my profession, which seemed somewhat arcane and peculiar to people who weren't computer-savvy, or their own daughter, who had departed the normal world quite some years ago. They often wore the bemused expressions of birds who, after sitting on an egg for months, had watched it hatch into a flying turtle. They loved their daughter dearly, but her religion and business were so utterly beyond the pale for them that they simply didn't know how to deal with it all. My family had raised me so innocent of religion that any religion was roughly equal to me, but this also made it somewhat awkward when you were dealing with a family that joined hands to say grace, quite seriously, at every meal. Never having encountered that ritual before, I was taken a bit aback the first time. Now I saw it as an interesting and possibly heartening custom, but it was a clear departure from what I was used to—either in my own experience, or in Sylvie's breezy approach to life, the universe, and everything.

She was certainly right that having Verne, a priest

of an unknown (in this age) nature deity, perform the ceremony would lead to antacid moments for her parents. Much better to find a flexible Catholic priest and write vows that reflected our real commitment. "I'm sure we can find someone who'll fit the bill."

"I'm not worried," she said, taking another bite. "Mmmm. Since I knew we were going to be married, therefore we obviously *will* find someone."

I looked at her. "This destiny thing could become very annoying."

She gave a roguish grin. "And it's only just starting, Jasie."

47

I yawned, glancing at my watch as I went to my front door. Jeez. Another 3 A.M. morning after talking to Verne. At least I was getting a load of data, data which hopefully I wouldn't ever actually use. Oh, damn. I had to check on the tuxedo—I'd forgotten my appointment. Have to reschedule, and soon—I wanted the tux done long, long before the wedding, and the day was approaching like a runaway train.

I unlocked the door and stopped just short of crossing the threshold. Maybe I was catching intuition from Syl, or something else, but somehow I just knew my house wasn't empty. The last time this had happened had been when Carmichael's thugs had grabbed me. Since then I'd added a few tricks, however. After making sure no one was in immediate view, I nudged the wood above the doorway in just the right way, and a small liquid-crystal screen popped into view, cycling views of the various rooms from a CryWolf-fitted set of lowlight cameras, with a running status of the systems showing me what was going on, or not, in each room.

Nothing showed up in any view. Were I in an ordinary line of work, that would've been enough to satisfy my paranoia, but vampires didn't show on videotape, film, or anything else; while they had to be invited in, it wouldn't be hard to have an accomplice do that for them and then have the accomplice leave. That's why I studied the status carefully. The motion detectors were a bit different; they didn't actually try to produce images—and thus shouldn't be covered by the magical prohibition against mechanical devices "seeing" a vampire—but just detected air movement within a given volume. None of the detectors showed anything out of the ordinary since I'd closed up shop, so I shrugged. I was getting jumpy.

So I think I could be excused for jumping backwards with a shout of "what the *fuck*!?" when I entered my living room to find a man sitting in one of the chairs, waiting for me.

"Sit down, Mr. Wood." he said. He was older than me—forty-five to fifty, I'd guess, with a tanned, lined complexion. His eyes were hard, cold blue, measuring me up like I was a piece of fabric waiting to be cut to fit. His hair was brown, sprinkled with gray. Standing, he was probably average height I'd guess. His voice . . . level, slightly rough, and direct, reminding me of Clint Eastwood; in fact, there was a vaguely Dirty Harry look about him overall.

I started to reach for my gun, and found that I was suddenly looking down the barrel of what appeared to be a small cannon. After what seemed an eternity, my brain calmed down enough to recognize it as a .44—probably an AutoMag. Somewhat old-fashioned, but quite capable of blowing a pretty large hole through me. I couldn't believe the speed. This guy hadn't had anything in his hands just the moment before, and I hadn't even really seen him move. The only person I'd ever seen move that fast was Tai Lee Xiang.

"Don't think about it," he said. "I'm not here to hurt you. But I don't like people pointing guns at me either."

"Hey, it's cool," I answered, sitting down slowly. "Clearly I am not going to be much of a threat to you. Now who the hell are you and what are you doing in my house? And how the hell are you sitting here without my security systems showing you?"

"Um, that would be my doing, actually," said another, much younger voice.

Emerging from my bedroom, where he'd evidently gone to hide during my entrance, was a much younger man—in fact, I figured him for a couple years younger than me. He was slender, very tall, and very blond, and wore a grin from ear to ear that somehow carried a faint air of apology even while it screamed out "I'm *soooo* good at this!"

Something clicked in my head. No picture had ever been printed, but to do what someone had just done to my security system . . . "The Jammer."

His grin grew even wider and he gave an extravagant bow. "In the flesh!"

I looked across my coffee table at the other man. "Which would make you . . . the guy who strongarmed the Jammer into not blackmailing me."

The weathered face acknowledged that with a hint of a smile. "Mr. Locke was forcibly employed by my organization, and when necessary we rein him in." He put the gun away. "Mr. Wood, as time goes on it appears that you continue to become more involved in things that impinge upon some of my organization's most sensitive operations. I would try to recruit you, but your operations here actually serve other purposes for us while they're kept separate. It has, however, become necessary for us to meet, and for both of us to get to know the other well enough so that we can, when necessary, cooperate and not work at cross purposes. The secrecy of my organization at least equals that of our opposition—some of whom you have already encountered."

I knew that Virigar himself had been a thorn in their side, but he seemed to be referring to something larger—organization-wise, anyway—and that didn't leave me many choices in possibilities. "Whoever sent over Ed Sommer and pals."

He nodded.

It clicked then. "Winthrope! She's not NSA or any of the regular organizations, she's with you!" I'd always had a nagging doubt about Jeri—which is why even in my thoughts I'd generally avoided tagging her real employers with a particular set of letters—because she'd seemed a bit too open and flexible over certain things.

"Told you he already had it down," the Jammer said.

The older man shrugged. "If he wasn't that quick, he would've been dead already. Yes, Mr. Wood, Jeri is employed by us."

"So you know pretty much everything."

"Everything you've told her or that she's seen," he said, correcting me. "I am quite certain there's material you have never told her."

"Okay." I got up. "C'mon downstairs. I want some coffee; I've been up all day and was going to go to bed."

They followed without comment, though the older guy accepted a cup while the Jammer went for a Mountain Dew. I turned to the older man finally. "If we're going to 'get to know each other' well enough, then let's stop tapdancing. Who are you people?"

"My name is James Achernar," he answered after a moment. "My particular task force is codenamed Project Pantheon, and is part of ISIS."

"ISIS?" I repeated. "The name's very, very vaguely familiar . . ."

"The International Security Investigation Section," the Jammer put in.

Now I remembered. It was an attempt (an abortive one, I had thought) to create a sort of multinational intelligence and espionage network for the United Nations, quite some years ago. Supposedly it was going to recruit operatives from many different nations and use them to gather information to prevent international disputes, resolve conflicts, and in general be a truth-checking organization with enough teeth to allow the UN to (at least on occasion) be able to tell who was really trying to hoodwink them and who wasn't. There'd been some discussion, preliminary appropriations and so on, but I had been certain that ISIS had gone the way of many a good idea whose time will never come. "Now that's interesting. I thought ISIS never really happened."

Achernar gave a small, very cold smile. "We prefer it that way. It nearly didn't, in point of fact, but a number of countries—at the time, the US and USSR foremost—recognized that despite various competing agendas we also needed some kind of independent group that would try its best to defuse problems that could be caused by smaller countries, terrorist organizations, and even large corporations. The result was an intelligence organization operating out of a non-profit front sponsored by the UN, whose full scope of powers and operations wasn't realized by anyone save the people who made it. All participating countries supplied authentic intelligence materials for their contributions—such as genuine IDs and so on—and were given certain controls to prevent their own contributions being used against them.

"Pantheon is a subdivision of ISIS, established

shortly thereafter to deal with the most extreme and unusual intelligence situations."

"The X-files," I said.

He gave a wry smile. "Not precisely, although of late it has started to seem that way. We do have other problems that we deal with."

I studied him. "All right. Now, you said something to the effect that I seemed to be making a habit of getting involved in your stuff. Once obviously isn't a pattern, and I'd think even twice wouldn't make it certain, but I'm not able to find more than one or two possibles in my history. The recent conflict that involved me and Verne against that group from Vietnam appears to be one, and I suppose Virigar counts as another, since as Gorthaur he was busily chipping away at everyone in the intelligence agencies, but where's the 'habit' coming from?"

He gazed at me expressionlessly. Finally, he said, "I will not give you details at this time, but I will say that even from your first encounter with Verne Domingo you began to enter our business. And now that you've connected Jackie MacLain to his old family—"

"I should've known; your people are the ones hanging around Paula MacLain."

"Not just us," the Jammer said. "Them, too. The other side. Once you contacted her and someone started the paternity test, somehow they got alerted. Up 'til now the kids had gotten away with it—the baddies had lost track of them. Not any more."

"So who are they, then?"

Achernar and the Jammer exchanged glances. "At this point, you're better off not knowing," Achernar said, with the Jammer giving a reluctant nod. "I know you will find these kind of answers very unsatisfactory, but in the main it's true."

I sighed. "Look, if you're not here to give me info,

just what *do* you want from me? And why all the futzing around instead of just setting up a meeting?"

He acknowledged my frustration with another faint smile. "To answer your second question, Pantheon doesn't really exist, so to speak. Currently, as far as any official sources are concerned, I am at a psychological convention attending various seminars, and tomorrow morning I will be presenting a paper of my latest research, no doubt to considerable controversy . . . though somewhat less direct mockery, thanks in part to your own Morgantown Incident making people more open-minded."

"Seminars . . . You're Dr. J. T. Achernar!"

His movement was the seated equivalent of a bow. "Correct."

"Now I start to understand. Your name was one of the more prominent ones I came across when doing paranormal research."

"I had good reasons for being willing to be open-minded myself," he said. "My research has provided few unambiguous results, of course, but as you may now suspect—"

"—part of that is deliberate." I finished. "If you made the wrong things public, it could get very dangerous for a lot of people."

He nodded. "As for what I wanted to accomplish by coming here . . . by letting you know exactly who was behind Jeri, I would like to make it easier for you to understand if we start sending hints in your direction. We may ask for help, through her, or you might get a request for an interview—perhaps even with Dr. Achernar—or in some other manner either request your assistance, or offer some subtle assistance of our own. But we have to avoid being visible. This is a shadow war, Mr. Wood. The world at large does not know of these kind of things—even after the werewolves. Many forces exist, some you would not believe, and many of them are in their own way quite willing to trigger a holocaust if they feel that their operations are threatened or about to be revealed."

Privately I had to hide a smile. I'm sure Achernar meant every word he said, but the truth was that after Verne's revelations, not only would I be able to believe just about anything, but I probably knew stuff that made everything Pantheon knew put together look like small change. "Well, I'm always willing to help. And I'm already kinda in your debt after the little assist you gave me with the IDs for Tai Lee Xiang."

Achernar nodded. "That was our intent, although as I said that connected to one of our own operations. Let me put it this way: I'd have arranged the same thing for him myself, whether you requested it or not, if I'd become involved. So don't feel it was a tremendous favor; you just gave us a chance to do something for the enemy of an old enemy."

I studied him narrowly. "And you're just going to leave him and his kids alone? Not, um, 'recruit' them at some later time?"

"No government, and no agency—not even ISIS and Pantheon—can be trusted with them," Achernar answered.

"He's telling it straight," the Jammer put in. "Part of my job at Pantheon is to arrange for certain kinds of data to just plain disappear."

"I find it *extremely* hard to believe," I said, "that even the UN, in its best days, would like the idea that its own agents would be taking it upon themselves to decide what data should and shouldn't be reported up the chain of command."

"They wouldn't," Achernar said bluntly. "But my immediate superior created Pantheon specifically to be able to make such decisions. No, there isn't anything like that in the written files, but our meetings always at least touch on how much of what we learn is going to stay hidden in our own heads and how much will be reported up. Yes, we could all be arrested for treason or something similar if the truth somehow came out. Fortunately, our opposition generally wants the truth hidden even more than we do, so for the most part the only people who might ever be in a position to blow the whistle on us have a vested interest in not doing so."

I shuddered. "Mr. Achernar, no offense, but I can only hope to God that you'll never get a mole in your organization."

"We do our best. It may happen one day, but at the moment we have no better alternative; someone must deal with the problems we do, and at least thus far we have proven to be sufficient to the tasks at hand. Of course, your work with the Wolves eliminated the one actual threat of such infiltration we've ever had."

I had to admit that I'd missed that point. Virigar's poking through intelligence files actually made more sense now; he had, almost certainly, encountered something indicating Pantheon's existence and was trying to find out what various governments might know or guess. After his existence had been blown wide open and the CryWolf gadgets put on the market, he and his furry friends had to back out of that business, at least for a while.

"So in that sense you owe me at least as much as I owe you," I said finally.

"I'd agree with that," Achernar said. "In any case, I'd like you to memorize this number." He handed me a card with a phone number on it. I concentrated and committed it to memory by a few mnemonic tricks, handed it back. "If it ever becomes necessary for you to contact us directly, rather than through Jeri—she's

unavailable, got herself killed, you're too far away—
that will get in touch with me. But do not use it barring
a true emergency."

"I won't. Obviously you already know how to contact me. Are you planning on trying to reach similar
arrangements with Verne?"

That got a short laugh. "No, I don't think so. Mr.
Domingo has his own game that he's been playing for
a lot longer than any of us. If he needs our services,
he'll ask for them, and there isn't anyone on earth that
can demand his help." He looked at me. "Except his
friends, of course, and I'm afraid that in my business
you can rarely take the time to make friends."

There wasn't much to say to that, so I finished
drinking my coffee. "Anything else? No offense, but
I'm exhausted."

"Not at the moment. Our apologies for disrupting
your schedule. With luck, you'll hear very little from
us." He got up. "Oh, there is one more thing."

I glanced up.

"Congratulations."

I couldn't help but laugh. "My god, is there *anyone* who doesn't know I'm getting married?"

48

"Jason, Sylvie, please meet Father Jonathan Turner,"
Verne said.

I shook hands with the cheerful-faced priest. He
looked to be a mere twenty-five, hair dark and curly,
wearing the traditional uniform of his profession.
"Pleased to meet you, Father."

"It's a genuine pleasure, Mr. Wood." Father Turner's
rolling, English voice carried the warm, comforting
tones that the very best priests usually have—a kind

of voice that makes you willing to believe that God does speak through them sometimes. I'm not religious myself, but I recognize the dedication a real priest has to have. "And Miss . . . Sylvia." he went on, avoiding by himself the name pitfall that most people—including me—fell into when first meeting her. "Verne has told me a great deal about both of you. I understand you are looking for a priest who will be, shall we say, flexible in the ceremony while remaining acceptable to the more traditional elements of the wedding party?"

Sylvia smiled, obviously taking to him on first glance. "Exactly right. My mom and dad are old-style Catholic and if I don't have a Catholic wedding of *some* kind, they'll be worrying that I'm heading to Hell one way or another."

Father Turner smiled back and shook his head in a resigned way. "Not, I'm afraid, an uncommon state of affairs these days. Now, my dear, you were baptized Catholic, weren't you?"

Sylvie nodded. "Not practicing for years though."

"No matter. Would you be willing, both of you, to agree to teach any children you have in the Catholic faith?"

"How do you mean that?" I asked. "I'm basically agnostic—I'll believe in the Almighty when I see evidence for him—and you already seem to understand what Syl is."

"Let's put it cynically," he said, taking a seat across from us in Verne's living room. "As a representative of a Church that's coming under hard times, my job is to try to make it look more attractive than previous generations saw it. Sometimes you have to deal with people who are currently using the competitors' product, so to speak. Well, we don't win points with such people by insulting their choices, but on the other hand, if I'm going to perform a wedding, it's incumbent upon me to at least try to get a wedge in the door to increase our membership somehow. Yes, I generally get paid for doing the wedding, and that isn't something to be lightly brushed off, but I take my job seriously. If you'll agree to make sure that any children you have are exposed to the Catholic faith—taught the beliefs and values—I'm gaining something out of it. I'm willing to bet," he said, turning to me, "that you had almost no exposure to organized religion in your childhood. Am I right?"

I nodded. "A couple of Sunday-school attendances for reasons I can't even remember now, and some time at the Unitarian church when I was much older, but no, not much at all."

"And without you making a promise of this sort, your child or children would most likely follow a similar path—or be exposed only to Sylvia's faith or that of this decadent old bloodsucker," he said with a grin, hooking a thumb at Verne, who chuckled.

Syl and I were both startled by that; clearly Jonathan Turner knew a great deal about Verne!

"So at the very least I gain the potential of children who grow up knowing our system and aren't inherently hostile to it."

I glanced at Syl; she nodded, so I said, "I think we can agree to that. If you're not requiring us to *only* teach him in that faith, it's no problem."

"Jolly good; we should be able to get on famously." he said.

"Pardon me for asking," I said, "but just how do you come to know Verne so well?"

He was very serious all of a sudden; he looked at Verne for advice.

"It is entirely up to you, old friend," Verne said. "You know how much I trust them; let your reluctance be only personal. If you wish not to speak of

such things, do not, but they are of my family, as
though by blood."

"Quite, quite," Father Turner agreed. "It would be
a long story, and I'm not sure how to tell it without
either leaving out too much, or sounding as though I
might be boasting in one way or another. Unless you
would care to explain the essence of it yourself?"

Verne accepted the invitation, apparently feeling that
some explanation was appropriate. "Jonathan is one of
the accursed—taken by one of the vampires of Klein's
type many years ago. He has, however, managed that
which no other in my memory has done: opposed the
curse's madness with will and faith, and maintained
himself in a state of innocence. He has killed no one,
hunts no human prey, and has seemed to become
stronger because of it."

Father Turner seemed to blush slightly, though that
reaction in such a being was hard to credit.

"Is this evidence for the truth of the Faith, Father?"
Sylvie asked.

He smiled sadly. "Of course I believe so, Sylvie. Yet
I cannot deny that other priests—some at least as
devout as myself—have over the years been preyed
upon and fallen. God's will has helped preserve me,
but I have no reason for Him having saved me while
permitting others to be damned. And without such
reason, I am afraid I cannot convince others that it is
a genuine Miracle. Verne would have it that it was my
own strength; yet I don't see myself as being so much
stronger than others." He shrugged, obviously uncomfortable with the thought, and I realized that with him
there wasn't any false modesty; he sincerely doubted
he was that strong. "I had friends and others who
depended on me, and perhaps that, also, helped. Yet
the same could be said for so many others. Still, having found my mind spared and my soul unstained, I

realized that I must minister to those who had no others they dared trust. There are still some of the accursed who try, with all their will, to turn from the path the curse lays out for them, and so long as they try, I am there for them—as confidant, helper, and perhaps as an example that it can be done. This is the task Our Father has set before me, and at the least I can accept it knowing that it is a worthy goal, even if I myself am hardly equal to the burden." He took a breath and shook himself. "But enough of this. Let's talk about your wedding. I spend enough time fighting darkness, it is a positive joy to be able to work in the light."

I glanced at him. "Would that also be literally true? Because we'd like to have the ceremony during the daytime."

Jonathan nodded. "I can walk in the sunlight; the Lord has seen fit to bless me in certain ways, perhaps to help me in my mission. Our friend Verne, of course, is more than strong enough for such things."

"Goody," said Sylvie. "Then let's get down to planning the whole ceremony."

I looked around for some more snacks. This might take some time.

49

"But of course, Jason. Indeed, I would be honored. How long will it be?"

I considered. "I've put a 'price no object' priority on it, and with my various contacts smoothing the way, I figure our new house should be finished in about three months."

"Then think no more of it, my friend. All your extra possessions can remain here until that time."

That was one small load off my mind; I knew that with the moderate-sized wedding Syl planned we'd still end up with a sea of presents—it seemed that the public actually cared about what happened in my life, my fifteen minutes apparently hadn't quite come to a close, and so there were likely going to be some attempts at gatecrashing and certainly gifts from all over the place. This ignored people who wouldn't be at the wedding but that one or the other of us knew well enough that we'd be getting something from them.

"You did say something about increasing my security?" Verne prompted.

"Hm? Oh, yeah. You remember that I finally had a talk with Jeri's people?" Verne nodded. "Well, after their demonstration, I contacted them again and requested—rather strongly—that they have their, um, security specialist design and install better systems for both of us."

"That would be this 'Jammer' person?"

"Yep. They agreed that it was in both our best interests to maintain maximum security, so sometime before the wedding the Jammer will be by to help out. Put up with him; he's younger than I am, and he has that wiseass geek's attitude that I mostly outgrew, but he's the best of the best."

Verne smiled tolerantly. "Jason, I assure you that I can 'put up' with any temperament. Geniuses are often immature or asocial in many ways. For a greater degree of security, I will have no objections. I will of course emphasize, in my own way, that they are to not leave any special privileges for themselves in the systems."

I grinned. "I rather thought you might. And someone like you will probably get through his hide." I saw Kafan going by the doorway. "Hey, Kafan! Is the Senator coming to the wedding?"

He smiled. "Paula says that you'd have to lock the doors to keep her away. And she's bringing Seb—I mean, Jackie and little Tai!"

I smiled back. Legal wranglings could be murderous, and establishing truths in court almost impossible, but Paula and Tai Lee Xiang had found a way to cut through all the potential barriers; Tai Lee knew, by scent that never lied, that Paula was a devoted mother who loved children, and Paula, from long experience in judging people and promoting children's rights, could tell from Genshi that Tai was a loving parent. Once the two recognized the other as someone who genuinely cared about the well-being of their children, they were no longer adversaries, but allies who simply had a complicated problem to work out. The storybook tale of the orphans' father returning was bound to come out soon—and in point of fact Paula was laying the groundwork for the press releases already—but the stories would be of a *fait accompli*, not of a potential legal firestorm. "That's great. I'm looking forward to meeting them myself."

"Master Jason, is this list from Lady Sylvia the most accurate?" Morgan inquired as he entered, carrying a sheet of paper.

"I think so. Yeah, that's the current guest list. All the ones in red have confirmed. The few blacks are ones we expect but haven't got confirmation on." It was Morgan's concern because we were having the wedding and reception here, on Verne's extensive grounds.

"Very good, sir."

Suddenly there was a shout from down the hall, followed by a voice: "Hey! Let me go!"

Verne smiled and leaned back in his chair as Camillus entered, carrying the Jammer in a move-along hold. "Is this the young man you expected, Jason?"

I raised an eyebrow at the Jammer. I should've

expected he'd try something like this. "Caught so soon? Yes, Verne, but he's kinda disappointing me."

The Jammer flushed. "I'd like to know just how you managed to catch me at it, since I know for damn sure not one of your alarms went off."

Verne gestured, and Camillus deposited the Jammer in one of the chairs. "Mr. Locke—"

"How the hell do you—oh, Wood."

"To an extent, yes, but I have my own sources. You are Ingram Remington Locke, former resident of Long Island. I know a great deal about you, Mr. Locke."

That got the Jammer's attention; he knew that Achernar had mentioned his last name, but not his first. "Damn."

"As I was saying, Mr. Locke: you are apparently suffering under the misapprehension that my only security is technological. While you are correct in that none of my electronic security systems notified anyone of your presence, I was myself able to sense you once you entered my demesnes. I then notified Camillus of your whereabouts and the direction in which you were moving, and he was naturally then able to capture you."

The Jammer rubbed his arm and glanced at the door through which Camillus had left. "Naturally. Well, if you've got that kind of warning, I don't know if you need anything more."

"Oh, assuredly I do," Verne said. "I do have to rest, and during that time my senses are less sharp. There are also various ways to elude my senses which would not evade properly designed technological security; magic is not inherently superior to technology, merely different. I would be very pleased if you were to design a top-of-the-line security system for my home. I will not offer you money, since I am sure that is not really a major consideration for you; only the challenge of making such a large, old, rambling estate secure enough to meet your own exacting standards."

The Jammer laughed. "Okay, Dracula, you've got me pegged pretty well. My friends sent me out here to do a job, but damned if you didn't go and make it look fun to do, too. I hope you won't take this wrong, but I'm going to keep trying to get in here without you knowing."

Verne ignored the vampire witticism and nodded. "I expect no less. In fact, I would demand that you try everything at your disposal to enter this place unbidden, so that any flaws which may exist can be fixed, either with your techniques or my own."

"Then can I get up and start working?"

"By all means." As the Jammer rose, Verne said, "*However . . .*"

The Jammer froze; Verne's tone had shifted without warning, to something cold as winter ice, and his level gaze almost seemed to impale Locke. "Let me make one thing clear, Mr. Locke: your work will remain exclusive to me in this instance. You will have no 'backdoor' codes, no special privileges, and no records, after the fact, of the work. This will also be true of my friend Jason's home. I am aware of the way your sort of person thinks, and I warn you that I will not be amused if I discover anything in my or my friend's security systems that appears in the least suspicious. Is that understood?"

The Jammer was a shade paler. "Understood, sir," he answered.

"Very good, then." Verne's voice had returned to spring again. "Carry on."

I watched the Jammer leave. "It's amazing. When I was younger, I didn't really believe that crap about people with a 'force of personality' that you could actually sense. The past year or so has made me a believer. You've shaken him up pretty good."

"My sense of the matter is that he has already encountered someone with a similar force of personality, in fact." Verne commented. "Someone whom he respects and thus associates with my own exhibition in that arena. But I agree; we will not need to worry about him inserting unwanted material in our security now."

"Good. Because, lord knows, I've got enough to worry about right now . . ."

50

"Ready, Jason?"

I took a deep breath. "All set."

I walked up the sunlit aisle, lined with flowers, that ran between the rows of chairs on Verne's back lawn. I wasn't nearly as nervous as other people I'd known; the nervousness was only an echo of the proposal now. I was excited, yes, and serious.

Verne, of course, was Best Man. I saw my mom and dad, her hair still clearly blond (maybe dyed, but I'd never dare ask), Dad's a distinguished gray, both smiling broadly. Sylvie's mom sat just across the aisle from them, and was already dabbing at her eyes with a handkerchief. Why do so many people cry at weddings? Jeri Winthrope was also near the front, leaning back in a relaxed pose as she waited for the vows, having already sat through Father Turner's quick little introductory sermon; Morgan was sitting next to her, straight as a ramrod in his proper butler manner. Kafan was sitting with his three children and Paula, looking happier than I'd ever seen him. I saw Camillus and Meta a row back, along with several other members of Verne's household that I'd only glimpsed on occasion.

Then I saw Sylvie, and everything else faded. She'd chosen a traditional shimmering white for her gown, and I no longer saw the laughing gypsy princess . . . or rather, I saw the shining angel who'd hidden behind the gypsy façade.

I heard the vows, and responded, but at the same time I hardly heard them at all. Sylvie was the only one that mattered.

"You may kiss the bride," Father Turner said finally.

I lifted the veil and bent down. I don't know how long we stood there.

Then the party began. But as a favorite character of mine once said, that's a deceptively simple statement, like "I dropped the atom bomb and it went off." The reception and dinner went on for hours, and no one seemed inclined to leave early. Hitoshi had outdone himself, and even with my newfound wealth I shuddered trying to imagine the bill for this one; imported caviar was a trivial garnish, and I was quite sure that if I'd asked for a truffle I'd be handed one the same way other people might give you an apple from the fridge. Butterflied lobster, some kind of imported beef that cost twenty times what any other cut might, abalone, the list went on and on. The cake itself was a stunning edifice of the pastrymaker's art—I learned later that Verne had imported, not the cake, but the cake*maker* from Paris just for this one cake.

Finally, with most of the guests cleared out, our inner circle gathered in the living room and Sylvie and I started going through the remaining presents—those not belonging to the other guests that had attended. Most of them were exactly what you'd expect—silly knicknacks, appliances, we all know the kind of thing. But there were a few . . .

I studied the long, slender package. "Damn. Feels pretty heavy. What, a crowbar?"

Jeri smiled. "Open it and see."

I stripped the wrappings off and opened the box. "My god!"

It was a sword—katanaesque in its design, with strange upward-spiking crossguards and a hilt that could be grasped with one or two hands. There was something strange about the metal of the blade, maybe a color or a shimmer. I glanced questioningly at her. "Okay, you people seem to have found out I collect swords off and on, but I'm stumped on this one. What is it, exactly?"

"Sort of a joke," Jeri said, obviously pleased that it wasn't instantly clear to me. "Since you seem to get involved in all kinds of unearthly strange stuff, we thought an unearthly blade would be appropriate."

"Unearthly . . . ?" I stared at it. "Meteoric metal!"

"Bang on," she agreed. "There's a couple outfits that make things like this, so Achernar and the rest of us chipped in to get it."

"Well, thanks!" I hugged Jeri. "Convey my thanks to the rest of the spies."

"Will do. Hey, go help your wife over there."

Sylvie was wrestling with the wrappings on something that stood about six feet high. Finally the two of us convinced the box to open up. Sylvie gasped. "Oh, my . . ."

It was a vanity table—wood so polished that it seemed almost to shine from within, a mirror sparkling in the center, drawers so carefully fitted that they slid in and out with only a whisper of sound.

"Oh, Kafan, how beautiful!" Sylvie said, throwing her arms around Verne's foster son. "You shouldn't have!"

"Bah," said Kafan, blushing. "I don't have much

money of my own, so all I could do is make something. Jason's got matching bookcases and a dresser, but I didn't wrap those up—take up too much room."

I thanked Kafan, and while Syl hugged him again I chose another package. This one had the elegant writing on it that could only belong to Verne. Opening the small box, I found two rings, formed of gold and what appeared to be platinum and ruby, intertwined like growing vines. "What . . ."

"Gold and platinum, imperishable metals, the essence of the Earth," Verne said, "and ruby, the bloodstone, symbol of life ever-flowing." His own ruby flickered, and I thought I saw a faint answering shimmer from the twining ruby threads.

"They're amazing, Verne." Sylvie said. Her eyes became distant momentarily, and then widened. "No, Verne, you can't!"

I understood then. "We can't possibly—Verne, you took these from your true home! We couldn't take them!"

Verne shook his head. "My friends . . . my very dear friends . . . such rings were one way that couples to be married would symbolize their vows, in my own culture. In my own collection, they do nothing save gather ages of dust and memories. What better thing could I do with them, than to see the two people who brought back my very heart and rekindled the flame I thought lost wearing the last rings of the Lady? I insist."

Syl hugged him even more emphatically than she'd hugged Kafan, and I just gripped his hand. There weren't words to express this kind of thing properly, but he understood.

We went back to wading through the mass of gifts.

"Look, Jason, another blender!" Sylvie said, laughing, from the pile. "Oooh, look at this one!"

"This one" was a large box in shimmering silver-and-gold paper.

"It's heavy!" I grunted, setting it on the table. It had no card on the outside, and Morgan vaguely recalled it was among the large number sent to us via special couriers. Presumably it would have a card on the inside, as most of them did. The two of us undid the wrappings, revealing a hardboard-sheathed box held by a clasp at the top. It had an interesting symmetry of almost-invisible lines down the side, indicating that it opened in a unique fashion; when I undid the clasp, the sides fell away like the petals of a flower.

Sylvie gave a shriek and leapt back; I sucked in my breath and recoiled; I heard both Verne and Jeri gasp.

In the center of the table, the focus of the radiating sides of its box, stood a crystal sculpture of a wolf in mid-leap, facing us with savage glee. Carved on the water-clear base were the words, " 'Til Death Do You Part."

Fear washed away at that taunting, threatening phrase. I glanced around for something heavy, then reached out to heave the glittering reminder through the window.

"NO, Jason!" Verne and Sylvie both shouted.

The desperation in Verne's voice halted me, even more than the fear in Syl's. "Why the hell not?" I demanded. "The son of a bitch—and I mean that literally—wants to send me a message, I'll send him one back!"

He plucked the statue from my hands. "Please, Jason. Sit down."

My heart still pounding from the mixture of terror and fury, I did so, a little shakily. I hadn't realized just how scared I really was of Virigar until I saw the statue. "Okay, I'm sitting. Now why shouldn't I break the thing?"

Verne sighed. "Because, my friend, it would have terrible consequences. I do not argue with you what his purpose was in sending this to you, for that purpose is obvious: Fear, uncertainty, to ruin your future with thoughts of your eventual demise at his hands, and to do so on your very wedding day, yes, this is undoubtedly his purpose. Yet you also must understand that Virigar is not an ordinary adversary. He is not even what you believe him to be. He is an ancient being; evil, yes, perhaps more so than you realize, yet with a majesty and a pride that you cannot begin to comprehend. That statue was carved with his own hands, Jason. I have seen a few works like it in my years, and I cannot mistake that inhumanly perfect hand; you have been gifted with a creation the likes of which few mortals have ever even seen, and even fewer have owned. Throwing it away would be a mortal insult, one which would almost certainly require that he turn his immediate attention to your painful demise. It is, in its way, a salute as much as a turning of the screw; you are an enemy who has actually bested him, in a manner that he found artful, original, and worthy, and further one whom destiny favored sufficiently to save you even from your second confrontation. For that he has chosen to terrorize you in a manner worthy of your stature; see it that way, please, and take heart in your own success. He may threaten, but only you can fear."

Syl nodded, still so scared she didn't want to speak, but obviously seeing the truth in Verne's words.

I saw them myself. I'd faced Virigar in person. I sensed that what they said was true, and more, that the whole thing—even being beaten—was to the King Wolf nothing more than a game. If I played by his rules, I had a chance. If I didn't, I would be risking the lives of everyone associated with me. "Okay, I'm cool now. But I know what I *am* going to do with it."

I turned to Kafan. "Could you do me a favor, just once, and let me borrow your transport skills?"

Kafan nodded, confused. "On your wedding day, of course. Where are we going?"

"One second. Verne, that case over there, the one you emptied the other day—can I use it?"

"Certainly, Jason. Consider it a gift." He measured it by eye. "It will fit the statue admirably, actually."

"My house, Kafan."

He took my hand, and there was a flickering dislocation; I suddenly stood in my kitchen. "Whoa. I always wondered what teleportation felt like."

"It is less disorienting after you get used to it," he said. "Why are we . . . ?"

"Just a second. Then we can go back." I ran to the living room, got what I came for, came back. "Okay, we can pop back now."

It was still disorienting, so I presumed that it took more than a couple of times to accustom oneself to instantaneously crossing distances. After I refocused, I went to the case, in which Verne had just placed the statue, and around it placed six other sparkling objects. "I'm sure he'll find out somehow what I've done with it; let this be my message to him."

Verne smiled broadly, and Sylvie gave an emphatic nod.

The wolf still sprang, triumphantly leaping upon its cornered prey.

But surrounding it were werewolf claws.

Mirror Image

51

"Jason, you're sure about this?"

I looked over at Sylvie, who was looking through one of the Florida guidebooks. "Sure I'm sure. One of my classmates back in high school used to come here every summer with her family and found at least two."

She sighed and smiled. "Okay, Jasie. We can spend a few days in the area looking."

"Hey," I said, "It's not like we weren't planning on spending weeks at the beach anyway. Venice has a really nice beach—that's where you look for the Megalodon teeth."

Sylvie put on a mock-indignant expression. "So we'll be at the beach and all you're going to look at is fossil shark teeth?"

I reached over and grabbed while keeping my eyes on the road; her sudden giggling shriek told me I'd grabbed the area I'd intended. "Not a chance."

I glanced over at her again, quickly admiring the sight of my brand-new wife in shorts and a tight shirt—

a huge change from her habitual "Gypsy Princess" look, which ran to layered skirts, puffy tops, multicolored handkerchiefs, and acres of sparkling crystal necklaces, earrings, and bracelets, concealing details of her build from any prying eyes. I'd always thought she was pretty, although it was a lot more than that which had drawn us together and, a month or so ago, led to our marriage. It had been my immense delight to discover after the wedding that the gorgeous face was matched by the rest of her. Yes, as a matter of fact, I had *not* slept with her before marriage, not that it's any of your business. We had all our lives to make up for that lost time, after all. And I certainly intended to spend plenty of that time admiring her whenever she chose to wear something like the glittery bikini she had bought earlier today.

Venice looked much like other Florida towns—built low, no really high buildings, more recent homes and condominiums tending to follow the same vaguely Hispanic pattern while the older ones often had more individuality. It was, however, smaller than many others we'd visited, and as such was less built up and felt somewhat looser.

I chose one of the nearby hotels that had beachfront—with my current finances, I at least didn't need to worry about how much I spent on my honeymoon—and parked in a lot that was surprisingly empty of cars, only a green Ford, an orange Saturn, and a couple dully colored Hondas taking up spaces. Once more expending the effort that put the "lug" into "luggage," Syl and I dragged our stuff into the lobby.

"Reservations?" the big, cheerful-looking man behind the desk asked.

"Actually, no; I was hoping you had some openings."

"As a matter of fact, we do!" he said, grinning. "Y'all are in luck; had a small convention in here over the weekend, and as usual when they left it gave us a small hole to fill. Just the two of you? Newlyweds, I'll bet?"

"Yep," I said, answering both questions with one word. "How'd you guess?"

He chuckled. "Guess? My friend, after fifteen years in the business, there ain't no such thing. See two people walkin' in like that, draggin' a hunnert pounds o' junk without so much as a groan or a gripe, an' still tryin' to stay as close together as they know how, you know they just got hitched." He went to his computer, and glanced at another monitor near it. I knew, from its location, the glance he gave it, and the odd camera unobtrusively pointed right at the check-in desk, that it was a standard CryWolf system ($250 retail, $350 with monitor). "How many days you folks plannin' on stayin' here?"

"Two or three. Say three."

"That'd be two nights, then." A few taps on the keyboard, then, "Cash or charge?"

"Charge. Here."

I handed him my card. He turned around to his credit validation scanner, slid the card through, and sent the query through the lines which would determine whether or not my plastic was worth anything.

Had I been in a different line of business, or not been looking straight at his back, I might have missed it. But as the little credit gadget's screen lit up, I saw him stiffen, like a man opening his eyes to discover a scorpion sitting on his stomach. It was just a moment, but I was sure I'd seen it. "Anything wrong?"

He was just a hair slow in answering, and the first few words lacked the breezy, relaxed tone of our earlier conversation. "No. Not at all." His voice came back to normal. "Sorry, got distracted there, remembering something I gotta do—one of the rooms needs work and I plumb forgot. Not yours, don't worry 'bout that."

He turned back, the credit slip in his hand, and gave me back the card. I signed, he did the ritual of glancing at the card and my signature, accepted that the scrawls looked similar enough, and handed me back the yellow copy. "Okay, Mr. Wood, you're all set. Here's two keys, I've given y'all one of our ocean-side rooms, that'd be number 240. Just take the elevator there—here, lemme help you with that." He hefted our bags onto a rolling cart. "There ya go. It'll be the second door to the right after y'all get off the elevator. All the rooms got cable, air conditioning, plus the doors have the new CryWolf peephole gadgets so's you can make sure any visitor is who they say they are. Pool's open from ten to ten, and we own the beach out front there. Lifeguard's around from 10 A.M. to 8 P.M. on the beach—after that y'all are on your own. Thanks for coming, have yourselves a great time, and if y'all need anything just call down to the desk here. My name's Vic."

"Thanks, Vic, we will," Syl said.

We wheeled our luggage to the room and got it settled into the right places. While we did so, I mentioned my little observation to Sylvie.

Syl frowned. "Hmm. I didn't see it myself, but I know how good your observation skills are. Still, Jason, I didn't feel any hostility from him. I don't feel there's any immediate danger."

"Good enough for me. Let's get down to the beach."

52

"This really is a pretty little town," Syl said as we walked down one of the sand-strewn sidewalks in flipflops, looking very appropriately like tourists. She glanced around at the palm trees whose sunset shadows stretched towards the other side of the street.

"It certainly is that," I agreed. "Though not nearly as pretty as you." I luxuriated in walking on a solid surface after having spent the afternoon either sifting gravelly sand for fossil shark's teeth or chasing after a certain black-haired enchantress in a bikini.

"Are you flirting with me?"

"As usual, of course." We kissed. "Hey, how about I pick *you* out something pretty?" I said, as we were just then passing a jewelry shop.

Syl grinned. "What girl could refuse? Even if you do have questionable taste in gems."

"I make up for it by my taste in girls."

She gave me a nudge in the ribs as we entered Marie's Jewelry Box. "That had better be gir*l*, singular, Mr. Wood."

Even ignoring the clearly visible CryWolf camera pointing at the door, the store itself was a not-so-subtle reminder of the changes Morgantown had wrought. In the old days—barely a year distant—silver had been the most popular metal for affordable but adequate jewelry. Now there were considerably fewer silver pieces on display even in large jewelry stores, and those which remained were far more expensive, some of them even designed with an eye towards defense as much as for beauty. Silver had eclipsed gold in terms of price per ounce for a while, and even after the immediate hysteria had subsided silver's price remained far, far higher than it had been before the werewolves had made their debut.

I noted even fewer silver pieces in this store than usual—only two, in the back and not well displayed. The majority were gold and platinum. Syl and I spent quite a while looking around, comparing, arguing gently on occasion, before we finally settled on a very nice platinum-and-gold bracelet with multicolored stones making a spectrum around it.

"A lovely choice," the owner Marie said, smiling—not surprisingly, since it was also one of her most expensive pieces. "Can I wrap that for you?"

I shook my head. "No," I said, slipping it onto Sylvie's wrist and kissing her hand, "I think we've got a perfectly good way to carry it, thanks."

Smiling, Marie took my proffered credit card. Her smile momentarily seemed to freeze on her face as she glanced at it. She glanced back at me, eyes wide. "J . . . Jason *Wood*? As in . . . *the* Jason Wood?"

I sighed. I might not be at the level of a movie-star celebrity, but I was already resigned to the fact that I was no longer a completely private individual either. "Yes, I'm *the* Jason Wood."

She smiled—for a moment I thought it looked a bit forced, but if so it relaxed. "Well, then, welcome. Lord, what a change *you* brought down on us, eh?"

"Heh." I acknowledged the (unfortunately all too familiar) mildly amusing sally. "Not entirely my doing."

"Of course not," she agreed, and turned to run the card through. "Changed my own business enough, though—on that I can guarantee you. Hardly any silver jewelry any more, and the silver *dust* business—well, I'm sure you know all about that."

I nodded, noticing that the almost standard-issue box for silver dust packets was present but tagged "out of stock." She noticed my gaze as she handed me the slip to sign. "Oh, my suppliers ran short on everything silver this month. I'm expecting a resupply in next week, if you were needing any . . . ?"

"No, no," I said, passing her the white copy. "We won't be here more than a couple days, just driving around."

"Well, thank you very much for your patronage,

Mr. Wood—and congratulations. I hope you will both be very happy together."

"Thank you," Syl replied. "So far, so good!" She giggled as we left, jangling her new bracelet against the others she already had on.

But her face grew serious after a few more paces. "Jason?"

"Hmm?" I pulled my mind from the distraction of certain parts of Sylvie's anatomy. "What?"

"She seemed friendly enough and all, but I could have sworn . . . when she first saw your name I thought I sensed fear—almost panic."

I blinked. "Why the heck would she be afraid of me?"

Syl shrugged. "I don't know. It was a momentary impression—a flash, you know—and then everything seemed perfectly normal. Just thought I should mention it."

"Great," I grunted. "Guess I'd better check our supplies tonight. Just in case."

"Really, it's probably nothing; I don't have a bad feeling about her or anything. Let's get dinner."

It was full dark when we finally left the Cactus Steakhouse (yes, I love seafood as much as anyone, but this vacation had been awfully seafood heavy and both of us decided on a change). The stars glittered overhead, at least those which could overcome the town lighting, as we walked back towards our hotel. "Oooh, that was good," I said finally.

"It had better have been, seeing as you ate so much," Syl replied indulgently. "Jason, just because we're married I don't want you trying to settle in and grow a potbelly."

"Hey! I always eat a lot. And we were doing a lot of exercise this afternoon."

She was about to reply when something caught

our ears. A . . . grunt? A cough? A slight gasp or something? I couldn't quite place it, except it sounded somehow terrified. It was coming over the fence of a nearby yard. I glanced at Syl, to feel my stomach knot; her "feeling" face was on, that frighteningly intense gaze that focused on nothing, yet seemed to see beyond anything. "Be careful, Jason!" she hissed, knowing my actions even before I'd decided.

I nodded and gestured for her to stay where she was, near the fence, while I moved forward a bit to the gate set in the fence. Cautiously I pushed; it was open and swung easily. I wished I had my trusty 10mm on hand, and wondered if I was going to be one of the cats that curiosity killed.

The yard was very dark; no lights were on in the house to which it was attached, the fence was high, and my eyes were still accustomed to the streetlights. But I could make out something on the ground, about thirty or forty feet away . . . and it seemed to me that across the yard there was a movement, another gate opening, and someone going through. There was nothing I could put my finger on . . . but something about that distant, moving figure sent a sudden shiver down my spine. "Hello?" I said tentatively.

There was no answer, though I heard a faint *clack* noise of the other gate shutting in the distance. "Sorry to intrude, but I heard something . . . ?"

Still no answer, but no sudden attacks from darkness either. I took a deep breath and stepped inside, walking slowly towards the object lying on the ground in front of me. Even before I reached it I had a very nasty feeling I knew what it was. I pulled out my keyring and turned on the mini-flashlight, pointing it downward.

Lying on the ground before me was a dead man.

"Oh, for crissakes," I heard myself say. "I'm on *vacation*, dammit!"

53

"Well, isn't this just peachy," I said, finally stripping off the clothes that had become steadily more uncomfortable during our police interviews. "Why couldn't I have chosen somewhere else?"

As the people who found the deceased—apparently the *very* recently deceased—Jerry Mansfield, the police had not only needed to talk to us, but to issue the standard request to remain in the area.

Syl managed a sympathetic smile, though she couldn't have been feeling any more comfortable— probably less. "Jase, darling, I think we have to face the fact; it's your karma. You attract these kind of things. If we went somewhere else, that's where we'd find the trouble. Even before you met up with Verne, the cases you got involved with had some odd features."

I admitted that this was something I couldn't argue, loath though I was to admit that there was anything to Sylvie's "karma" theory. "Maybe this one will be resolved quickly . . ." I started, as I turned on the shower. I caught her narrowed gaze, sighed. " . . . or maybe not," I said. "That feeling wasn't just death?"

"It was very, *very* bad, Jason. I haven't felt anything like that since . . . since I saw Renee and knew she was going to kill you."

Renee's name sent a pang through me, despite the year that had gone by. I missed her hardcase-cop façade and quiet friendship. "Did you see his face?"

Syl nodded. "Horror."

"Well, it could have been a rictus of pain, but I agree, Syl. The first thing to come to mind when I looked at him was that he died in terror. Eyes wide open." I frowned. "Looked over the body quickly, and without touching or moving him I couldn't find any traces of injuries, either. No vampire bites, no slashes, and so on."

"A werewolf doesn't have to cut you," Sylvie reminded me.

"True," I said, stepping into the shower and letting the hot water start blasting the sand out of my bod, "but according to Verne they do have to get awfully close to you in order to suck the life out of you without physical contact. You didn't look at the area nearby, did you?"

I could just make out Syl shaking her head through the mist-fogged shower door. "Not really—we didn't want to muddle things up with more tracks."

"There was silver dust scattered over a wide arc in front of him—some of it was even on his clothes. If it had been a Wolf, I'd have expected it to either be dead next to him, or at least to have made a rather loud protest about the stuff. They never were very subtle once they got hurt. But if I actually did see the killer leaving, he or she left dead silently, smooth and without great hurry either."

"But," Syl pointed out, and it was a mark of both my worry and tiredness that observing her silhouette undressing only slightly distracted me, "the fact that there was silver at all is a pretty damning clue."

I didn't answer immediately, but lathered my hair and washed. "I dunno, Sylvie. It just doesn't quite click for me. Sure, the Wolves can kill without the slashes, if we take Verne's word for it—and I don't doubt him— but still . . . I've never actually heard of them doing it that way. And even less would they do it if the victim started showering the area with silver." I chewed it over in my mind as I ran soap over the rest of me.

"Actually, I think you're right, Jason," Sylvie said. "It didn't really feel like a Wolf to me either. But if it wasn't, why the silver?"

I'd come up with a tentative answer. "Well, if you know Wolves shapeshift, and you know someone or something is trying to kill you without touching you—and he was sure scared about something—wouldn't you think 'werewolf!' right away, no matter what the thing looked like?"

"Oh." I heard the faint sounds of Sylvie brushing her teeth. "You're right, Jason, that makes sense! Confronted by the unknown, you'll try whatever weapons you have available that might work."

"Now the real question is," I said, getting out and towelling off, "why the heck I'm spending my time trying to figure it out. Let the damn cops deal with it."

She kissed me and stepped into the shower herself. "Because you know perfectly well that they're not going to deal with this one. It's ours. Wood 'n Stake ride again."

I snorted. "Bah. I'm probably making a mountain out of a molehill. The autopsy will come back saying he died of a heart attack, and the silver dust will be glitter or something from a kid's birthday party."

Syl's outline against the glass shivered. "I hope so, Jason . . . but I don't think it's going to be that way."

When I pulled out the 10mm and loaded it, she knew I felt the same way.

54

Sheriff Carl Baker was a big, tired-looking man with thinning hair combed over the top of his head and a white-sprinkled mustache that also seemed to droop tiredly. "Sorry to have ta drag you back here, Mr. Wood." he said.

"It's okay," I said. "I know what it's like when you're doing an investigation."

"Guess y' do, at that. Anyways, to be honest we're kinda at a loss. Jerry may not have been the friendliest guy in town, but he sure weren't the nastiest, an' I don't have a clue about who would've killed him."

"Are you sure he was killed?"

Baker's moon-round face twisted in a sour grimace. "Ain't sure of anything, right now. Coroner says that so far as he's concerned, Jerry should've been gettin' up off the damn slab before the autopsy. Not a thing wrong with him—heart in great shape, brain jus' fine, everything jus' fine—'ceptin' of course that he happens to be dead." He grunted and handed me a file. "Ain't procedure, but you've got yourself a rep in more than one way—I checked out what the cops up North had to say about you. Anything in there give you an idea?"

"Well, I'll see . . ." I opened the file, started reading. Sheriff Baker, relieved of the responsibility of talking to me for the moment, went into the outer office for a while.

Baker wasn't exaggerating; while I'm no doctor, I know how to read ME reports, and this one was clearly frustrated. Jerry Mansfield, twenty-nine, had apparently been a health nut. He was in perfect shape—not too fat, not too thin, prior medical records showed wonderful cholesterol and blood pressure measurements, and so on and so forth. The coroner really truly had no idea why this man had been dead. There weren't any marks on his body anywhere, no foreign substances on his skin aside from a bit of dirt and silver dust. The latter had been found on his clothes, most heavily concentrated on the hands, head/neck area, and . . .

Wait one minute. I thought back to last night. No, there had been the regular sea breeze, but there was no way a significant amount of that would have been getting into the high-fenced yard, and even if it had, the direction was wrong. What the hell . . .

I flipped back to another section of the report, looking for something. It wasn't there.

"Sheriff . . ." I called.

Baker stuck his head back in. "Found something?"

"Can you have the coroner check for something specific?"

"Sure. What do you need?"

I looked back down at the report. "I want to know if Jerry Mansfield had any silver dust in his lungs. Your ME may be doing an autopsy on a former werewolf."

"That's ridiculous!" Baker burst out. "Jerry couldn't *possibly* have been a werewolf!"

I raised a skeptical eyebrow. "Oh?"

Baker looked nonplussed for a moment. "Well . . . look, he shopped with everyone else, didn't he? Everyone's got those things you designed—hell, there's one right over my door here. Stands to reason the man couldn't've been anything other than one of us."

I had to admit there was something to that. Unless a Wolf had replaced Jerry Mansfield very, very recently, it was hard to imagine how he could maintain the masquerade in a place like this one, which as a tourist area had apparently made it quite a point to have everything covered from the Wolf perspective. "Well, have him check it, anyway."

Baker shrugged. "I asked ya to look, I suppose I oughtta go along with it. You got any particular reason for this here idea?"

I pointed at the photos of the body and the description. "There was silver dust all over the area in front

of Mansfield, but if you look at the way it's distributed,
it wasn't *Mansfield* doing the throwing; someone threw
silver dust *at* Mansfield. He's got it on his hands where
it would be if he tried to shield himself, but mostly
on his head and other areas where it would have been
if someone tried to throw it at him. Now, I don't know
about you, but the only good reason I can think of to
throw a hundred bucks worth of silver dust over someone is if you think they're a werewolf."

Baker looked at the photos and swore mildly. "God-
damn. Now that y' point it out, it's plain as day."

"The clincher, of course," I finished, "is that
Mansfield didn't *have* silver dust on him. No pouch
or dispenser or anything like it. So it *had* to be the
other person or persons who did."

While Baker went to call the ME, I continued studying the report. Footprints and track results were very
disappointing. While they could, with difficulty, make
out my prints and some of Jerry Mansfield's, there were
hardly any readable tracks elsewhere; one investigator
said it appeared that something had been swept heavily
across the area leading from the body to the other gate,
which opened up into a well-paved side street which
would take no tracks. If that was the case, it obviously
was a murder of some kind—someone had erased the
tracks. I studied the pictures for a few moments more,
then put them back.

Baker hung up. "Okay, he'll take a look an' get back
to me soon. I hope you're wrong, to be honest. I mean,
Jerry was a friend. Not real close, but enough that it'd
kinda shake me to find out he wasn't anything like he
seemed."

"Not to mention the can of other worms it'd open
if it did turn out he was one."

"Noticed that, did ya?" Baker grimaced again. "Oh,
yeah. What do I do if he was a damn Wolf? Ain't no

laws dealing with this. The man paid his taxes an' didn't cause no trouble, so on that account I oughtta treat it like any murder, but if he was really one o' these shapeshiftin' killers . . . no thanks, there's a headache I just don't need."

"Well, Sheriff, I did what I could. Sorry if it causes you more trouble."

He waved it off. "Nah, believe me, I'd rather have the answer than not. I'll let you know what the coroner says."

"Thanks. I'm afraid that aside from that one offbeat suggestion, I can't see anything else to give you. If I think if anything, I'll call." We shook hands.

55

A few minutes later I was letting myself back into the hotel room. Syl came out of the bathroom, gave me a hug and kiss which took a few moments in itself, and then asked, "How'd it go?"

"The sheriff was actually more interested in getting my professional advice than in raking me over the coals." I answered. "Handed me the ME report, which did tell me one interesting thing; the silver dust wasn't Mansfield's. It belonged to whoever or whatever presumably killed him."

Sylvie stared. "You know that doesn't make any sense."

"Unless Mansfield was a Wolf, and as the Sheriff pointed out, that'd be hard to manage in a town that's as Wolf-wired as this one is. Or unless . . ." I trailed off. "Doesn't quite work, dammit."

"What?"

"Well, obviously whoever threw silver dust at Mansfield at least thought he was a Wolf. And it struck me that we do know one supernatural type of creature that kills Werewolves whenever it can get away with it."

Syl's face showed enlightenment. "Vampires, of course! Verne told us about that secret war they had."

I nodded. "Problem is that there weren't even puncture marks on this guy. Werewolves can kill without touching people, according to Verne, but he never said vampires could." I turned to the phone. "I'll call Morgan and see if this kind of thing rings a bell for him."

As I reached for the handset, there was a knock at the door. "Who the heck . . . ?"

I went to the door and looked through the peephole. A well-dressed man of about my own age, black-haired and brown-eyed, stood there, waiting expectantly. "Yes? Who is it?" I called through the door.

"Sorry to disturb you—but you *are* Jason Wood, correct?" he answered in a tenor voice. "My name's Karl Weimar, sir. I know it's rather irregular, but I know something about Jerry Mansfield that you might like to know—but I'm not sure I want to go to the cops just now."

I closed my eyes for a moment, sighed. No rest for the suckers. "Oh, all right, hold on." I unbolted the door and slid the chain off, turning as I did so.

Syl's eyes were wide, mirroring an inner vision of disaster.

I dove away from the door, drawing the 10mm as I did so. At the same moment the door slammed open so hard it almost tore from its hinges, and the dapper young man lunged through, shapeshifting into an all-too-familiar towering mass of black-brown fur, glittering claws, diamond teeth, and glowing soulless eyes.

But Syl's unspoken warning had been enough. I had moved and was not where "Karl Weimar" expected me.

It skidded to a halt, talons ripping great gouges in the carpet, and turned on me, to find itself staring down the barrel of my gun.

"Believe you me, this thing's loaded with silver. And if it weren't for two things, I'd blow you straight to hell right now."

It snarled. "And those two are . . . ?" it asked in the unearthly deep timbre of its kind.

As I glanced at Sylvie, I amended my comment. "Three things, actually. The first one being that I'm curious about what brought you here to kill me. The second being that, from what Virigar told me, not one of you would dare touch me or Sylvie, since he'd marked us for his own—and you sure as hell are not the King. The third being that my wife thinks I shouldn't shoot you right now, for some reason of her own." I had no idea what the reason was, but Syl had communicated that I was doing the right thing in talking, so I wasn't about to argue.

For the first time I saw an expression other than savage hunger or fury on a werewolf's face. It looked positively taken aback. "You think that even the King's ban would hold on one who'd already broken it and begun hunting His people?"

"What?" I must've looked even more confused. "Hunting you? Sure, I'd expect that you guys would defend yourselves if I was going around shooting, and I'd presume even Virigar himself wouldn't argue about that. But I haven't been hunting any of you. Do I look crazy? Do you furballs think I *like* having clawed monsters chasing me around?"

"You killed Mansfield, thinking he was one of us," it retorted sullenly.

"*I* killed . . . ? Do you Wolves smoke some of the same stuff we do, or what? I just found the goddamn body! If he wasn't a Wolf, and thus dead from sucking silver, I haven't a goddamn idea what the hell killed him. You think I can kill people—Wolf or otherwise—by waving my f . . . friggin' hand?"

It stared at me a moment, eyes flickering like evil lamps, then abruptly reverted to its human form. "Well, *scheiss,*" said Karl Weimar. "Now I'm just as confused as you are."

"I doubt that." I said.

He reached into his pocket, pulled out several bills (in the back of my mind, I noted that the fact that in Wolf mode he had no clothes, let alone a wallet, raised interesting questions as to the authenticity of the cash), and dropped them on the table. "For the damage. My apologies." Weimar turned and walked towards the door.

"Hey, you bastard, you can't just pop in, scare the crap out of people, and pop out without a little explanation!" I shouted after him, ignoring the obvious fact that he was doing just that.

I closed the door, which scraped a bit from being loosened, and collapsed into an armchair. "*Jesus* that was close."

Syl nodded and came to me, and we hugged and got over an attack of serious shakes.

Suddenly I stood up, almost dumping Syl on the floor. "Jason, what . . . ?"

"The peephole!" I answered, digging into my larger travel bag for my kit.

"What about . . . oh, my God."

"Exactly." I said grimly. "If my CryWolf gadgets don't work, it means they've figured out a way to hide from them . . . and all the people buying them are no safer than the poor bastards who bought shark repellent and thought it would keep sharks away."

But when I started checking on the door, the results were even more disquieting.

The external shell was a CryWolf sensor, or a good replica of the usual enclosure, complete with the logo . . . but the interior was nothing but an ordinary peephole lens. There wasn't even a power lead going to it.

"That son of a bitch," I heard myself growl.

"Who? That Wolf, Karl?"

"No," I said, standing up and wrenching open the door, "Our 'cheerful host,' Vic. He's ripping off everyone in the hotel—putting fake sensors on the doors to make 'em feel comfortable, but not spending the money for the sensors themselves. Well, he's about to get a little talking-to."

Vic was at the desk; the lobby was deserted, this being a nice afternoon—too early for evening check-ins, everyone at the beach, and the season being slow. He looked up, started to smile a greeting, then stopped at the look on my face. "What's wrong, Mr. Wood?"

"I was attacked in my room just now. By a werewolf."

Vic looked horrified. "But . . ."

I tossed the dummy sensor on the desk. "And don't even try to tell me it's impossible. Give me one good reason I shouldn't call about a dozen lawyers down on your ass right now."

Vic's gaze barely flickered to the sensor; the fact of my being attacked seemed to have overwhelmed him. "But they couldn't have gotten in here . . . ?" he said, looking pathetically frightened.

Then I remembered my prior brush with death at Verne's house and how Verne had nearly died. Vic probably didn't install his own stuff any more than Verne did. "Then you got screwed by your contractors, Vic. If the one in my room's a dummy, I'll bet all of them are."

His expression went from shocked disbelief to fury.

"All of them? Jesus H. Christ, sir, I'll be looking into this, you can bet on it." He frowned. "What can I do in the meantime . . . Please, don't mention this to the other guests . . . ?" he made the request a question.

I nodded. "Okay. I don't want to ruin your business, but get it fixed fast. Don't worry about my room—I have my own CryWolf gadgets, of course."

"But you don't have to . . ." he began, then realized that of course I had to do this myself, since at this point I couldn't trust *his* sources. "Yes, of course you do, sir. Well, I'd better get on the phone and start kicking some."

"I suppose. And get a ruglayer into my room; the Wolf tore it up something fierce."

"Yes sir."

I didn't feel like going back to the room right now, and by her expression neither did Syl. "Want to take a walk, then maybe go for dinner?"

"As long as you'll be on the lookout. I don't know what that Wolf was up to, but he may not be the only one with that idea."

"Damn straight," I said, putting on my special glasses. They were a trial version of the CryWolf technology, using some of the more advanced circuitry currently available to make a detector which would, in theory, be just as good as my original clumsy gogglemounts, but looked just like one of those "light-adjusting" sets of sunglasses. I glanced back at Vic to offer him a stopgap solution in the form of one of the other gadgets I'd brought, but he was in the office behind the desk now, and I heard his Southern voice starting to rise, with the words *lawyer* and *sue* being audible.

We spent a couple hours wandering around on the beach, avoiding people in general. While the town was a pretty place, recent events and our forced residency were unfortunately starting to rob it of its charm. As dusk began to fall, we made our way back towards one of the restaurants. Remembering the layout of the town better now, we turned into a smaller alleyway that would take us to the next road.

In the growing shadows, I thought I saw someone coming down the alley ahead of us, and slowed to let him go around. Then I realized he or she was just standing there. "Hello?" I said to warn them someone was approaching, in case they had their back to us.

The figure didn't move or respond. As I got closer, I saw that it was all the same grayish color—a statue of some kind?

Sylvie gave a sudden gasp and stepped back; my reaction was to step forward, staring incredulously.

Gazing back at us, face frozen in an expression of terror, was Karl Weimar.

56

I poked at the thing several times. It was stone, all right, solid stone of a generally grayish cast—in the current light I couldn't do much to identify it. But the detail I could see was amazing. I glanced at Syl.

"It's not a statue," she said, confirming my gut intuition.

"Right," I said. Realizing I hadn't brought my cell phone with me, I headed up the alley to the nearest open store, which happened to be Marie's, the jewelry store we'd visited . . . was it only about a day ago?

"Hi," I said, walking towards the proprietor, "I was wondering if you . . ."

I'm not sure how I controlled voice or expression in the next few moments; perhaps a part of me already knew and was prepared. Because as I neared Marie, her image began to shimmer, glittering with a network of lines and sparks . . .

Without more than a slight pause I heard myself say " . . . would show us that lovely necklace in the third cabinet again?"

Marie smiled and headed for the cabinet in question. Syl stared at me for a split second, obviously wondering what the hell had gotten into me, but she knew I must have a reason, and followed Marie over. As she reached the third cabinet, Marie entered the effective range of the CryWolf camera over the door, and I turned and studied the image on the display behind her counter. I had to crane my neck to do it.

She and Syl both showed as perfectly normal on the monitor.

In that second the oddities I'd noticed all made sense, and I think it is a great accomplishment that I did not, in fact, scream out in horror. Instead, I turned and walked to the counter next to Syl. As Marie turned with the necklace in her hands, I said casually, "So . . . is the Sheriff one of you, too?"

She blinked. "I don't quite . . ."

I tapped the glasses. "These are CryWolf—experimental model."

Syl, realizing what I was saying, stepped back and slid her hand into her purse for her gun.

Marie stood, face utterly expressionless, for a moment, then closed her eyes and sighed. "How did you guess? You weren't wearing those last time."

"Since then one of your people tried to kill me, apparently thinking I was out hunting Wolves."

"Who would possibly be insane enough to . . . oh, I know. Must have been either Kheveriast or Mokildar." She shook her head. "Children are always fools."

The full implications finally seemed to have made their way to Sylvie's consciousness. "By the Earth, you can't mean . . . Jason, the whole town can't be Wolves!"

"Not every single family, no," I said, "but all the key people and a bunch more residents, is my guess. Right?"

Marie nodded.

"And you make sure it looks like everything's covered with CryWolf sensors, so no one ever gets an idea to start checking around otherwise. What I don't quite get is *why*."

Sheriff Baker's tired baritone spoke from behind us. "You don't get why? Mr. Genius Wood? *You* are the reason why."

"How . . . ?" I asked, then looked at Marie. "Ah. You can communicate with each other over some distance."

He glared at me, hands on his hips, and continued as though I hadn't spoken. "Ten thousand years, Wood. For ten thousand years I have walked the face of this planet, along with all my people, and never did we have anything really to fear from you. Oh, yes, if one of us was blatant, stupid, clumsy, and unfortunate, a silver weapon could end it for him or her, but all in all, that was just as well; if you have no respect for the potential danger of the cattle, you become fat and lazy, unworthy of being one of the great ones.

"And then you come along and invent a little toy." His hand lashed out, snatched the glasses from my face and pulverized them, "A *toy* that gets more of us killed off in three months than in my entire lifetime. That gets our race publicized so that we actually have to deal with people knowing—not guessing, but knowing—what walks among them."

"That," I indicated the crushed glasses, "will cost you about ten grand."

His expression became a snarl and his features rippled slightly.

"Unless you either want me to blow the gaff on your cozy little tourist village here, or want to assault me against your King's command, that is."

He seemed to be considering it through the bit about his village, but when I spoke of the King he instantly backed off, clearly frightened by the mere mention of Virigar. "N . . . no. You aren't intending to tell about us?"

"That depends on how you answer my question." I let my heartbeat slow down a bit. It looked like things might not end in a blaze of claws and gunfire. "Again, why the hell are all of you down here? Or is it just to give the words 'tourist trap' new meaning?"

He chuckled humorlessly. "The temptation is certainly there. But no, we don't kill anyone here. We can feed without killing, if we must, and if we control ourselves; and control is the complete and absolute law here. If we permitted killings, no matter how subtle, your law-enforcement people would eventually notice a change in the statistics and come to look." He gritted his teeth at my inquiring look, and finally forced himself to continue. "We are . . . we are *hiding* here."

I couldn't restrain a guffaw. The Wolves were running scared! "So you're living like the cattle now, hoping none of the bulls with silver horns catch up with you?"

He growled, a very inhuman sound coming from an apparently human throat. "For the moment . . . until we have decided how to properly deal with this new threat. So you didn't kill Jerry Mansfield?" he said, changing to his human guise's voice.

"Nope. Had no idea there were any Wolves around here until one of them tried to kill me earlier today. Now I understand your bit about denying he was a Wolf, though; you can't have any suspicion of Wolves being present at all."

"Mansfield was human," Baker said. "Someone

thought he was a Wolf, looks like, but I guarantee you he was human."

"The plot thickens," I commented. This was an interesting sidelight on the whole matter. "And since I didn't kill him, we still have a mystery on our hands. A real Wolf would have known he wasn't one. So Mansfield was killed by someone who wasn't Wolf and wasn't human either." Suddenly I remembered why we'd come here in the first place. "Hey, Sheriff, do you know a Wolf who goes by the human name Karl Weimar?"

He nodded. "That'd be young Kheveriast. What about him?"

"He tried to kill me earlier, assuming I'd been trying to hunt Wolves, but that's not the main thing. If you go down this alley at the side," I pointed, "you'll find a statue of him. Except I think it probably isn't really a statue."

Marie looked puzzled, but Baker's face was a study in dawning horror. "A . . . statue?"

For a moment I felt actually sympathetic towards Baker—but I remembered that despite his fighting to save his race, his speech had shown no remorse for his people's actions and had confirmed the usual Wolvish tendency to megalomania. "Gray stone, incredibly detailed."

He got a grip. "Mr. Wood, I have some calls to make. We will speak again. This business may concern both your people and mine."

"Maybe," I said. "Why would someone have thought Mansfield was a Wolf?"

"He worked for us," Baker answered after a moment. I blinked. "What?"

"I said, he worked for us. While we have a fairly good grip on this town, humans who move in, or who make additions to their houses, can't be controlled easily—and if they start installing their own sensors, none of our people dare get near the house. Jerry was . . . I suppose you'd call him a special agent. He would arrange for any active CryWolf sensors to become inactive. We'd use him to meet with agents who might be carrying their own gadgetry. Another reason we have to keep things low-profile here, obviously; if the Feds come in, they might well bring CryWolf-equipped cameras, goggles, and so on, and that would ruin it all."

I was utterly floored by this revelation. "What in the name of God could convince a human being to work for things like you?"

Baker grinned. It wasn't a comforting expression. "Your people are no angels, Wood. We can offer plenty to a wise human, especially when, as is now the case, you humans have something to offer us. And we generally play fair; after all, even your people don't butcher every cow—you keep some as breeding stock, some as working animals, and even a few as pets. If you weren't associated with Domingo, I have no doubt our King would have made you an offer to switch sides."

The very thought of someone—of a human being—working for these monsters, knowing what they were, was so repellent that I simply couldn't reply for a moment. Finally, I got my voice back.

"Okay, Baker. I won't blow your cover . . . for now. But I am not working with you any more. I will give you no help, no hints, nothing. So far whatever it is has hit either at you monsters, or at someone who was working hard to give up his humanity. As far as I'm concerned, that means they're doing the world a friggin' service."

Baker stepped forward again, glaring. "Wood, you'll assist if we say so, or I'll . . ."

"You'll what? Come on, tell me." I threw my own

sarcastic grin back in his face. "You can't do a god-damned thing to me, Baker, and you know it. I'm too well known to just disappear. If I get killed, your cover's blown for sure, and once the country realizes what you were up to, there won't be a safe community for you bastards anywhere on the planet. You'll have to go to ground in wilderness, away from all the comforts you've obviously come to like. Even if you somehow keep the Feds out of it, Verne Domingo will deal with you. And I don't think the King will stop him in that instance." I took Sylvie's arm and started to walk out.

"I still have an investigation ongoing, Wood," Baker said, with a cold intonation. "Leave town and I can have you brought right back here."

"Oh, I won't leave. Yet. But you finish this investigation, pin it on either the real crook, or one of your own people, I don't care which, and let me get out of this infested hellhole within the next week. Because I swear by God that if I have to hang around here any longer, I'll just phone the authorities anyway."

"You wouldn't!"

I whirled back, grabbed his collar and shoved him back against the counter. "The hell I wouldn't! Do you think I'm an idiot? That I can't do a little simple math? It's been less than a year since Morgantown, and here you are, in charge, hundreds of you furry bastards living like so many Addams-family rejects behind a coat of Brady Bunch paint. You didn't win any elections to get here—you whacked hundreds of people and took their places. The *only* reason I'm not blowing the whistle right now is that when your kind are cornered, you kill—and I don't want to be responsible for another bloodbath. I'll take your word—for the moment—that you're not killing any more. Maybe it's true. It had better be true from now on, believe you me." I let him go, turned back to Sylvie. "Let's go."

I ignored the crawling sensation between my shoulder blades and didn't look back as we left.

57

"Why the hell can't you keep your fifty thousand makeup things off the darn counter?!" I exploded as three bottles fell over.

"Probably for the same reason you can't put your stupid clothes away when you go to bed!" Syl snapped back. "Do you know how disgusting it is to leave your dirty clothes on the floor?"

I opened my mouth to fire back, saw the mingled anger and hurt in her eyes, and closed both eyes and mouth. "Jeez, I'm sorry, Syl. This thing's really getting to me."

She came over and put her arms around me. "Me too."

"Some honeymoon this is turning out to be."

Venice and Nokomis were still lovely places, but just how are you supposed to relax and enjoy your stay when you're aware that any of the nice people around you—on the beach, in the store, on the street—may be a soul-eating monstrosity just hiding out until such time as they can gain the upper hand on your own species? Baker had come through with the money for destroying my prototype, but without access to my homegrown lab and materials I wouldn't be able to duplicate the things. I was now carrying one of the commercial CryWolf goggles, but I didn't bother wearing it while out and about. I could do without drawing that much attention, and I really didn't want to know just how many Wolves were around me at any given time.

"The first part was fine. It's not your fault we've

found ourselves stuck in another strange circumstance."

I took a deep breath and tried to relax into her. There was no point in letting this drive me nuts. I'd given Baker a week, and it had only been two days. If I didn't get a grip, I'd be saying something I'd never be able to make up for by the time six days were past.

There was a knock on the door. Both Syl and I jumped, showing the state of our nerves. "Who is it?" I called back.

"Sheriff Baker sent me over, Mr. Wood. Might I come in?"

I went over to the recently repaired door, put on my goggles, and opened it, keeping the chain on as I studied the man standing there. He was a tall man, over my six foot one, with thick, wavy brown hair brushed back from a high forehead, piercing blue eyes, and sharp, patrician features. He was quite slender, though apparently fit, and his clothes were of impeccable cut—clearly upper class. I glanced back at Syl to make sure she didn't have a nasty feeling about the next few seconds, then nodded, taking off the CryWolf goggles and sliding the chain to the side. "Come on in. What's this about?" I asked.

"I have a . . . business proposition to make you, Mr. Wood," he said. He bowed to Sylvie. "Lady Sylvia Stake; I have heard of you. An honor."

As he was paying his respects, Syl was checking him out. His voice had a faint English accent, but not quite—perhaps Canadian influence? "A business proposition, Mr . . . ?"

"Carruthers, sir, Alexi Carruthers," he replied, shaking my hand firmly. "Yes. I would like to see if I can persuade you to reconsider your refusal to assist investigating the current string of unusual murders."

What had been a pair was now a string. "There have been more?"

Carruthers nodded, taking a seat when I indicated that he should. "Three, two Wolf and one Human."

"Was the human another of the Wolves' allies?" I asked.

"She was," Carruthers acknowledged. "This may be coincidence, however. Of necessity as many of the townspeople who could be have been recruited. It is not improbable for a killer to run into two collaborators."

I shook my head. "What's in it for me, Mr. Carruthers? So far, as I told Baker, this whatever-it-is seems to be perfectly happy killing Wolves and traitors to humanity. Since the Wolves perpetrated mass slaughter to move here, and don't show any sign of regretting it, I'm not particularly motivated to try to save them. I'm supposed to be on my honeymoon, not working."

Carruthers smiled faintly. "I suppose monetary recompense would be foolish?"

I snorted. "I may not be the richest man in the world, but I've got tons more money than I know what to do with."

"I told Baker that myself," Carruthers admitted, "but it was the simplest offer I could make. When he called me in, I warned him you would be difficult to deal with; you have many reasons not to wish any of us well."

I studied him. "Did you say 'us,' Mr. Carruthers?"

He smiled again. "Yes, I did."

"You're a Wolf?"

"I am."

The terrible, hollow feeling I'd had for a few moments after Karl Weimar had attacked us returned. The Wolves *had* found a way to hide themselves from the detectors. "Shit."

He looked momentarily confused, then laughed. "Ahhh, your clever little CryWolf devices! I must compliment you on that—an inspired piece of design. One that couldn't have been done effectively even a relatively few years ago."

"Useless now though," I said, trying to keep the bitterness out of my voice.

"Oh, far from it!" Carruthers assured me earnestly. "Really. Only a very, very select few of us can pass such devices with impunity. Only those of us who are truly Elder Wolves, and of course the King himself."

"Baker isn't an Elder?"

"Baker? Little Hastrikas?" Carruther's laugh filled the room with a rich baritone sound again. "Why, he's no more than eleven millennia—barely more than an infant, really, all things considered. No, no, Mr. Wood, there aren't more than a handful of the Great Elders left alive—I, of course, am one of them." For a moment, his eyes flickered, became soulless glowing yellow orbs. "Virigan, at your service."

I think both Syl and I gasped at that—in a way, that partial, instantaneous transformation was more macabre than the usual full-scale change. "So," I said, "you're saying that the CryWolf devices are still mostly reliable?"

"In the vast, vast majority of cases, indeed."

He seemed still rather relaxed and cheerful. "You don't appear particularly disturbed by this; if you don't mind my asking, why aren't you on the warpath along with the rest of your relatives?"

The smile faded; now Carruthers looked serious. "Mr. Wood, most of our people are children by our standards. Even the older ones, like Baker, have had easy times. They need to learn that sometimes the prey can turn on you, and how to survive such times. If they cannot, they do not deserve to live; other worlds are not nearly as forgiving as this one has been. We are the greatest and most powerful of all beings that have ever lived; only those who prove their worthiness again and again should have the right to even approach that potential. So has it ever been; if they wish a different course for our people, why," he smiled coldly, "all they need do is challenge the King for rulership. And win, of course."

"But enough about us, Mr. Wood; let's talk about you." Carruthers studied me for a moment. "I actually wanted to meet you quite some months ago, after you interfered with something I'd been working on for years." He raised an elegant eyebrow, waiting for me to guess.

I didn't have to think long; there was only one really likely candidate. "So you were one of the people behind the Project—the one in Vietnam, that had Tai Lee Xiang."

"Very good. I was in fact *the* person behind it all, and have been for several decades now."

I thought about that for a moment. "That would mean you were working on this stuff while the OSR was still active."

"Correct."

"Now, just what would a Werewolf want with a human genetic engineering project, Mr. Carruthers?"

He waved a finger in a "no, no" gesture. "Ah, ah, Mr. Wood, we are getting sidetracked again. Such questions should remain mysteries, the better to intrigue you. We are here to discuss your employment."

I smiled back with an easy laziness I didn't feel; I was in a room with one of the most lethal creatures on Earth, and knew all too well what it would do to me if circumstances changed. "No, *you* are here to discuss employing me. So far, I'm here to listen to whatever interesting facts you let slip and otherwise laugh at the very idea of helping you."

Carruthers gave a heavy sigh. "Yes, I rather thought so. Let me make you a more concrete proposal. Your interference in the Project cost us immensely. There are a number of people—human, my kind, and, well, *other*—who feel that you would make an ideal target as an example. The game of international intelligence, on this level, is not done in the standard way, since, if we are being honest, neither side admits of this level's existence. More grim and direct methods tend to be used in our realm of business. Your termination, despite certain allies who present formidable obstacles in this area, would serve as a clear warning to others who have begun to gain an annoying brashness in their intrusions.

"I am willing to offer you amnesty—we shall write off the cost of the operation with respect to you and your lovely wife. Since the King's decree protects you from my kind, this will essentially place you back at where you were before ever you were involved in such affairs; only mortal concerns to worry you."

I nodded, considering. I hadn't forgotten the possibility that the Project would take my interference amiss, but Carruthers had now made it a concrete threat, one that I couldn't afford to ignore, especially now that I had a wife and, potentially one day, a family of my own.

"What's your angle, Carruthers?"

He raised an eyebrow. "What do you mean?"

"I mean, you're a bright guy yourself. You have the Project for resources, plus gods only know what else. Why the hell do you want me in on this? What is it that keeps you and your own furry family from solving it?"

"A matter of symmetry, you might say," Carruthers

responded. "You ruined one project, now you present yourself in a perfect position to rectify another."

"Bullshit." I glanced at Syl, who nodded, glaring at our visitor. "Don't *even* try lying to me about stuff like that, Carruthers, or you can go sit on a silver spike and spin. Try again, the truth this time, or you can kiss any chance for a deal good-bye."

Carruthers' eyes narrowed, and for an instant the typical Wolf looked out, hungry, furious at being balked by this lesser creature; then the urbane mask was back. "As you will, Mr. Wood.

"Certain . . . features of this case are disquieting to my people. There are a few possible causes of the, um, particular condition of the corpses, but all of them imply a form of death which our people fear above all others. At least one of the possible causes would make us more, rather than less, vulnerable to this attacker than human beings, and in most cases the attacker will be growing stronger with each kill. None of my people want to be involved—not only is the death involved truly hideous, especially to a race that is by all rights immortal, but if the one explanation proves correct, those investigating would be potentially supplying our enemy with ever greater power. A human being will be at once somewhat less vulnerable and, if he fails, will not provide much of a boost to our adversary."

I snorted. "So you need an intelligent but dispensable agent who won't prove to be a battery for this bozo."

"Succinctly put."

"You're being awfully low on the details here. If you expect me to look into anything, you'd have to be a bit more forthcoming on them."

A nod acknowledged my point. "Indeed, but you have not yet agreed to the position, Mr. Wood. The more you learn, the more dangerous you could become to us, true?"

"True enough." I thought for a moment. "I'll make you a counter-offer, Mr. Carruthers. You will arrange the same immunity for *all* those associated with me—specifically, you give up on Tai Lee Xiang and all his relatives. If you have his wife or daughter still in your possession, or that of anyone you have influence over, you'll hand them back. Verne Domingo, myself, Sylvie, and to be blunt my whole damn hometown is off-limits to you and your gene-twiddled friends."

"Have you completely taken leave of your senses, Wood?" Carruthers stared at me. I couldn't completely blame him, I had upped the ante a bit, specifically in his own project's area.

"Hey, you're the one who came here. Take it or leave it. I'm not interested in just personal immunity—that's not enough to make it worth playing this game with you. I'll trust in Verne and Tai Lee to whip the crap out of any of your assassins that happen to wander through." I turned my back on him and got myself a ginger beer out of the fridge and congratulated myself that my hands shook hardly at all.

I turned back to face Carruthers' silent glare. I returned it with a raised eyebrow and sat back down.

Silence. None of us moved.

After what seemed an hour but was probably only a minute, Carruthers broke into a smile and spread his hands. "You have my measure, Mr. Wood. It is, indeed, that important to me. I accept your terms, with a single exception: Jeri Winthrope. While she is not, at present, high on our list of targets, she is connected to an organization which is in an adversarial position to us, and I will not agree to something which would potentially leave me bound to permit an enemy to strike at me without my own freedom to strike them as I saw fit."

I didn't like the exception, but I also knew what "organization" he had to be referring to, and whoever they were, they played their own brand of deadly hardball. A warning to the Jammer would suffice to make sure they kept their eyes open.

"Agreed."

"Excellent!" Carruthers stood to go.

"Whoa, there," I said. "I want you to swear to this agreement."

"Certainly," he began, but I held up my hand.

"In the name of the King himself."

His mouth tightened, then relaxed. "Yes, I suppose you would guess that one. So be it. I, Virigan, one of the Eldest Five, swear, by the name of our Father and King, the Final Devourer, Virigar, that from this day forth no forces under my control, or under the control of any I influence, involved with the Project or of our people, shall seek to harm, kill, interfere with, or otherwise inconvenience Jason Wood or any of the people associated with him as follows: V'ierna Dhomienkha, known as Verne Domingo; Tai Lee Xiang and any of his family; Sylvia Stake; and any and all residents of the community of Morgantown, New York, current or future, with the sole exception of Agent Jeri Winthrope and any that she recruits or imports to the area, aside from those already mentioned. In addition, I swear that if any of the family of the previously mentioned Tai Lee Xiang remain in the custody of any I control or influence, they will be returned to Tai Lee Xiang and will enjoy the same status of protection.

"In return, Jason Wood, you swear that you will undertake the investigation of these killings in Venice and environs, and will devote the same ingenuity and effort that you have to prior investigations, ignoring considerations of our races' differences in the pursuit of the perpetrator. Have I your word?"

"You have my word of honor, yes. I'll do the best I can."

Carruthers bowed. "Then it is agreed and sworn to. I would suggest you call the Sh'ekatha; he will be able to tell you many things about what you may be facing. In the meantime, I will be instructing my people to cooperate with you fully—including giving you information on ourselves and our enemies which we would otherwise never reveal. I shall not be available— I must return to my own duties elsewhere." He extended his hand, which I shook reflexively, a shiver going up my spine. "Good-bye, Mr. Wood. I doubt we shall meet again."

The door closed behind him. I looked at Sylvie. "Why do I have a feeling that despite having him over a barrel, I *still* got the short end of the stick in this one?

58

"You may have been tricked, Master Jason."

I closed my eyes for a moment. "Why, thank you, Morgan. Just what I needed to hear."

Sylvie and I had just finished filling Morgan in on the details; after I had called Verne and started to tell him the situation, he had cut me off, not wanting to discuss things by phone, and sent Morgan down by chartered jet. Another peculiarity of Verne's existence that I hadn't known until now was that he could not travel a great distance from home, or stay away for any length of time, without significant preparations. Therefore he had sent Morgan—his oldest living friend and retainer—to be his right arm.

"Would you mind at least filling that in?" Sylvie asked. "Exactly how we were tricked, I mean."

Morgan smiled slightly. "Perhaps 'tricked' is too harsh a word, but slightly misled, certainly. While it is, technically, true that there are several ways to produce the effects that you have described, only one seems to me and Master Verne at all likely—and even that one is so unlikely that only the very existence of these crimes would make us consider the possibility at all."

"I see." I said. "What you mean is that he made it look like the thing they were afraid of wasn't necessarily here, while in fact he was pretty darn sure that it was, right?"

"Essentially true, yes, sir. In our opinion, you are dealing with a *Maelkodan*."

I typed the word into my laptop and frowned. "That one does *not* come up in the little database I made a while ago, Morgan."

"Master Verne realizes this and sends his apologies, sir. The creatures were rare even before the disaster, and mostly not found on Earth in any case; it did not occur to him that any such could have survived until now."

I noted the word down. "And just what is a . . . Maelkodan?"

"As the Werewolf is the origin of several legends— that of the lycanthrope, several demons, and so on— the Maelkodan is the original source from which the legends of Medusa, the basilisk, the catoblepas, and so on have derived. They are monstrous creatures, intelligent and devious, of vast mystical potential.

"As were so many monsters, they were created by sorcerous experimentation. In the case of the Maelkodan, a misguided attempt to create a creature capable of hunting down Werewolves produced a monster with the requisite abilities, but with its own agenda. As nearly as Master Verne can determine, this was due either to a genuine mistake by the wizards doing the design, or possibly due to deliberate interference by someone—perhaps Virigar, perhaps one of the magicians themselves playing a deeper game. The Maelkodan was created from a combination of Werewolf, Human, and Teranahm souls and bodies."

"So," I said, "a group of powerful but possibly not very forward-thinking wizards went ahead and made this weird crossbreed. Um, what was that last species? Tera . . ."

"Teranahm," Morgan repeated. "The translation would be 'Great Dragon.'"

"Ooog." It wasn't the brightest-sounding rejoinder, but I wasn't able to think of appropriate words.

"Indeed, sir. The resulting creature lacked the fluid shapeshifting ability of the Wolf, but as both Wolf and Teranahm have this as an inherent ability, a Maelkodan nonetheless has three forms. The first is its true form, which from the fragmentary descriptions available would be something akin to a slender lizardlike body with a vaguely humanoid torso rising, centaurlike, in the front. It has Wolf-like claws and teeth, and the scales are excellent armor. Unlike the Werewolf, it is in fact not vulnerable to silver, but on the much brighter side is vulnerable to ordinary weapons, as a general rule, though if they become powerful enough their armor will withstand blows from swords and so on wielded by mortal strength. Master Verne and I are of the opinion that bullets will remain effective."

"Well, praise the Lord and pass the ammunition, will wonders never cease; a horror from beyond time that I really can just shoot dead." I said. "By the fact that the Wolves are scared of this thing, though, I guess it must have something to make up for the fact that it can be killed conventionally."

"Indeed, sir. Several." Morgan paused, knowing I liked to work things out myself if possible.

I considered what he'd said so far. "Okay. Given what you say it originated in the way of legends, it has a death gaze. If it looks at you, you die. I'd guess that you have to also be looking at it—not only is that what the legends say, but if it could just kill by looking around, the thing would be virtually impossible to beat by anyone, and I presume the things did get killed on occasion."

"Scoring pretty well so far, Wood," Baker said from the doorway, carrying a box of papers, presumably the records I needed.

"What I don't get is the different methodologies; why did Mansfield end up just plain dead and Karl playing statue?"

Baker shook his head. "Not different methods, Wood. Different kinds of beings are affected by the Mirrorkiller differently."

"Um, 'Mirrorkiller'?"

"It's what we call the things. For what it's worth, the damn things fulfilled their design purpose. They like hunting us. They just like hunting everything else, too."

"Quite so," Morgan said. "They were supposed to inherit some human behavioral traits, but instead apparently became mostly Wolfish in their outlook."

"Enough," I said, as I realized Baker was taking it personally as a snipe—which it may have been, but with Morgan's English-butler reserve there was no way to tell. "Three forms, you said. What are the others?"

"One is human," Baker said after a moment. "A secondary shape it can assume while hunting. The third shape is the shape of the last person it killed. So when first hatched, it's only got two forms until it succeeds at killing."

"Why does it just cause humans, for instance, to drop dead, and Wolves to turn to stone?"

"That has to do with the difference in the essential nature of human versus Wolf," Morgan answered. "Correct, Mr. Baker?"

"Yeah," Baker said. "Ya figured out our basic nature when ya made that gadget, right?"

I nodded. I thought I was starting to get the picture. "You're really energy matrices inhabiting a physical form. That's why you can perfectly duplicate a human being without becoming the human being."

"Right. Now, the Mirrorkiller, it eats the soul—the essential energy of any living thing. Being related to us, it's basically the same kind of thing."

"Now I understand. Since it was made using part of your essence, that's why your people can't just sense it, either—it can hide from you just as well as you can from us."

Baker grimaced. "Uh-huh. Now, when it gets you in its sights, it tries to eat your essence. But a human being, he's tied to that body. The body and the soul, they're just part of the same thing for you people. So it's got to rip the energy out of you, bit by bit, until the meat that's left falls over." Baker gave a shiver, a genuine sign of fear. "With us . . . it establishes, um, whattyacallit, a resonance, two similar patterns, and it damps part of ours out—negates part of the will to move, to fight. The resonance makes it take on the shape of the one it's killing."

"Thus 'Mirrorkiller.' "

"And then it moves to the target body, eating directly, leaving its own behind and taking over the shell."

I blinked. "So it's not really Karl's body out there carved in stone?"

"Not really, no. That's the mass which the Mirrorkiller was using beforehand. The next victim we found, well, that was Karl's body after the Mirrorkiller was done with it."

I had to admit, that was a pretty creepy picture. "But then Mansfield's body . . ."

"Well, of course that was the real body," Baker said. "The Mirrorkiller doesn't waste energy forcing its body to maintain a biological structure when it's moving to a new one. And it can't move into a human body the same way—it needs a soul connection to do the move, and it has to rip the soul out of a human first, rather than being able to move in via the resonance. It can use the resonance to paralyze the same way for a human, but that's the most it can manage."

"Okay, so it killed Mansfield. Then, as itself or Mansfield, it could –"

"No, not as Mansfield—where'd you get that idea?"

I looked at Baker. "You said its third form is the last person it . . . oh, I see, the usual Wolf attitude. We're not people. It only takes the form of people whose bodies it's taken over."

"Right."

"In the legends," I said, "basilisks could be killed with mirrors. Is this true?"

"As it so happens, yes," Morgan answered, consulting some notes. "The Maelkodan retain some tendencies of physical creatures; they must see their target with physical sight first, before their soulsense can engage. For them, the eyes are indeed the window to the soul. The mystical connection between sight and soul is exceedingly deep for them; therefore, when they are engaged in the hunt, seeing themselves in a mirror—in attack mode only, mind you—triggers an attack upon their own soul."

I nodded slowly. "I see . . . yes, that makes perfect

sense. The energy matrix is of course its own, and by trying to establish a suppressive phase shift, it's going to in essence cancel itself out."

Morgan blinked, as did Baker. "If you say so, sir."

"You emphasized 'in attack mode only,' Morgan. I suppose that means that we can't track down the Maelkodan by looking to see who might have no mirrors in their houses, or by lining the streets with reflective glass?"

Baker chuckled. "Sorry, nope. Only when it's chasing prey is it using the death-stare, focusing its own soul to attack. And they're all pretty well aware of the Perseus dodge, so it ain't easy to catch one off-guard." His tone became more serious. "And a Wolf don't have much chance of getting away with it. A human, he can catch a glimpse, get a jolt but maybe stumble on, break eye contact and keep going. One of us, once the lock starts . . . it's over."

"So there's two things you're more vulnerable to than us," I said, musing.

"Mr. Carruthers mentioned that these creatures gain in power as they kill," Sylvie said. "Can you clarify that, Mr. Baker? Do they have other abilities besides this death-gaze?"

"Ayup," Baker said dismally. "Humans ain't got much, for the most part, on the power scale. Oh, there's a few what have trained in certain disciplines whose souls burn more bright, but for the Mirrorkiller they're strictly potato chips—you gotta eat a whole bag to get much out of 'em. One Wolf, even one of the puppies around here, gives 'em a kick like fifty or sixty mortals. As they get more soul energy, they get stronger. More powerful energy matrix, in your terms—they can do a lot more with it. Physically they get more powerful, no doubt—by now, the bastard we're up against could probably toss a small car with effort. And at some point they'll be able to access the Draconic heritage those damn-fool wizards mixed in. That means magical effects. What with the pathetic magic ratio on Earth these days, at least we don't need to worry much about 'em casting spells, but inherent magical effects ain't out of the question. Poltergeist stuff, at least."

"Moving things by sheer will? Telekinesis?"

Morgan responded. "Yes, sir. Now, it's tied to the spiritual side, which means that it cannot directly affect people—of any sort—but other objects are fair game."

"What about the cosmic mind-woogie?" Sylvia asked.

"Beg pardon, Lady Sylvia?"

"I mean, both the Wolves and the vampires can mess with people's heads. How about these things?"

"Ah. Yes, well, they apparently have some small ability to do this, but it is more along the lines of standard hypnosis—anyone who is aware of what they are facing is really in no danger."

I noted that down, looked at the rather intimidating summary. "That about it?"

"Think so," Baker said.

"Okay. So let me summarize. The thing kills by mutual sight—even a glance is enough to lock down a Wolf, but a human has a chance to break eye contact if he's lucky, but a few seconds will finish anyone. It has three forms—one a lizardy centaur kind of thing, one a base human form—that's a preset, right? I mean, it's born able to turn into some specific human appearance?"

"Right."

"One base human form, and one form that changes with each kill of a Wolf or similar, um, energy-matrix being. So if it kills Joe Wolf, it can then be either its default form or Joe Wolf until it kills Jack Wolf, at which point it loses the option of looking like Joe, but gains the ability to look like Jack. Can these things kill each other?"

"Probably," Baker said. "They don't seem to hunt each other down much, though. There never were many of them, thank the King."

I nodded. "Okay, then we've got several possible investigative avenues for us. First, where'd the thing come from? Your people seem to keep fair contact with each other, at least for big important stuff, and I'd guess you'd have known if there were statues turning up before now. Besides that, I've been doing a search through police files across the country and even in other countries I've gotten access to, and there doesn't seem to be any pattern of a bunch of people being found dead without marks on them. So as a first guess, this thing just recently became active. How and why, and from where?

"Second, we follow the movements, as best we can, of the victims, see if we can come up with anything in common that might lead us to the killer's home. It's a damn shame about the statue trick; it doesn't give us much info on time of death, and that means that since the killer can take on the appearance of its last Wolf victim, sightings of the victim at any time during the day preceding the statue's discovery could actually have been the Maelkodan using the victim's shape.

"Third, we remember that the creature has to be living here somewhere. Probably as a human being. If that's so, it must be using its default form. So you want to look for people who have arrived here only recently and have been here since the first killing. Aside from myself and Sylvie, of course. "

"You I'll grant," Baker said. "But just out of sheer cussedness, why can't *she* be the one?"

I stared at him, speechless for a moment.

"Y'all gotta admit, the timing fits. And I hear tell she can sense us coming. That's impossible for a human. Nothing can find us except our own kind, and even that depends on how strong the other one is and how bad they want to hide. So just how can she sense us . . . unless she's either one of us, or a Mirrorkiller?" Baker's gun was out now, pointed straight at Sylvie . . . but his head was turned sideways, keeping him from looking at Syl's face.

"That would be extremely good evidence," Morgan said quickly, "were your statements entirely accurate. They are, however, not quite correct. It is true, sir, that there are very few things capable of sensing the Wolves, but as Master Jason's device demonstrates, it is not entirely impossible. In point of fact, there are a few examples in Master Verne's experience of human beings and others who had the true Sight—they were not seeing through the disguise, so much as sensing an outcome of events, watching the very flow of time in the short term. From my experience with Lady Sylvia, I am convinced that this is, in fact, how she senses your people."

Baker's gun hand wavered slightly. He was listening.

"And also," I said, "Syl's been living in Morgantown for years. No such killings ever took place there, and hell, during Virigar's visit there were so many Wolves around that I just can't imagine one of these Maelkodan things being able to restrain itself; instead of Verne killing Wolves in a warehouse, he would've gotten there to find a wonderful display gallery of statues and a Maelkodan so juiced up it'd be telekinesing city blocks for fun."

Slowly, Baker lowered the gun and raised his head cautiously. Looking at Syl, I saw what he did in her eyes; mild amusement, relief, and a trace of sympathy.

"Well, even a Mirrorkiller would've thought two or three times about trying that with the King nearby, but I guess y'all have a point." He sighed. "Damn, but it would've been a simple solution."

"The simple solutions rarely work out," I said, relaxing. "Now that we've got an idea of what we're up against, let's get to work finding the damn thing before it kills anyone else."

59

"Baker, what do you think about this?"

He looked up from his desk and took the sheet of paper from me. "Hmm. Ayup, I was wondering about that."

"Three disappearances in the same general time period. One of them from your department. Think maybe the Maelkodan might be responsible?"

He frowned. "Problem is . . . why the hell are these guys disappearing, but the others standing out in plain sight? It ain't like hiding just some of its victims is going to put us off the trail, the thing'd have to hide all of 'em. Or at least all the Wolf victims, anyways."

I nodded. "It's a puzzler, that. But I'm still putting these guys down as possible victims. Are these people all Wolves?"

He glanced at the names again. "Yep. All of 'em."

"I'll make that 'probable' victims, then. In this town you've made clear you people work together and talk to each other, and so they wouldn't go running off without a word to anyone . . . and I can't offhand think of easy accidental ways to kill you people off."

"S'trewth," he agreed.

"Any progress on movements?"

"Damn little," he growled, obviously frustrated. "Karl

Weimar, easy enough—we know he busted in on you, then left, talked with a couple others, then said he was heading back to talk to you people again. Timing makes it likely he got nailed at that point. Mansfield, well, he was all over town the last few days, bein' one of our contact men and all. Since he was killed at home, though, that don't tell us much. Same for the other victims—looks to me like the killer's picking vulnerable times and places, not waitin' to ambush a sucker who gets close."

"Which means we'll need to trace movements of people who might be the killer, rather than tracing the victims' movements."

He nodded. "O'course, without some decent suspects, that'll be a mite difficult. Can't run a trace on everyone."

"How about the correlation with recent arrivals?"

"Aside from you and your wife, you mean? Ain't looking very promising neither. If I give it about a month for new arrivals—assuming the thing decided to take a couple weeks to settle in an' decide how it wanted to start the killing—we've got about eight possibles. Problem is that so far it looks like at least half of 'em have ironclad alibis for Mansfield's murder, an' the rest might be a problem for some o' the others."

"Damn." It was starting to look like the creature might be hiding somewhere in its actual guise, not living among the regular citizens. While in theory that might make it easier to find because of the limitation of how many isolated, hidden areas there might be, in practice the thing could just pop out in its unknown "default" guise whenever it needed something, and since that default still wasn't known, no one would think twice about its appearance. Baker and I agreed that we might get somewhere by seeing if a stranger had been seen in the general area often enough—that is, if our monster was at all interested in living the civilized life, it had to be picking up its cokes and chips somewhere, and even if it varied the routine, after a few weeks it had to be repeating locations. If we were lucky, someone would remember that. If it wasn't into the comforts of the twentieth century, we might be in for a long, hard search.

"How about your end?"

I shrugged. "Depends on how the thing got here. So far we haven't found any probable entry times or points, but hell, we don't know if it slithered here under its own power, walked in as a human being, or got shipped here as a Ronco Peel-O-Matic in a little cardboard box."

"Maybe not, Wood, but ya are missing the point."

I was always open to suggestions. "And the point being . . . ?"

"Well, if'n we're right about this thing not bein' active until now, that means someone basically woke it up—either it just hatched, or someone found it trapped somewhere and let it out."

Maybe it was all the paper-pushing, but I didn't quite see what he meant. "So?"

He gave me a "stupid human" look. "So, big shot, there's damn few places you'd be able to have a Mirrorkiller—egg or suspended—hangin' around to be found. It'd have to be some place where the coverup job on the Old Civilization wasn't quite complete—real heavily defended vaults, places like that. Now, I ain't up on the geography of that time, but you got friends who are. I'd ask them."

I smacked my forehead. "Okay, thanks, I deserved that. Of course. I suppose the Greek legends came from one that was released in a similar fashion?"

Baker shrugged. "Probably. I don't know firsthand, but makes sense; seem to remember something of an alert on one of the things being on the loose 'bout two, three millennia back or so, but I was in Asia most o' that time. Ask your friends, they oughtta know."

I gave a tiny shiver. Just when I was half-forgetting what he was, something would happen to bring it home. Verne always had that otherworldly air about him, courtesy of the movie-vampire image which he happened to fit and his own immense dignity; Baker, on the other hand, was as down-to-business a Southern cop as you could imagine, and hearing that drawling voice casually mentioning a memory from before the time of Christ was still unnerving. "Okay, I'll get on it. Add in those disappearances and see if it gets anything new on the timing end."

"Will do."

60

"That few?"

Morgan nodded. "Ten is the largest number of reasonable sites that Master Verne can think of. You have been told the power involved, Master Jason. You must understand, the demonic forces did their very best—at the direction of their ruler—to eradicate every trace of the original civilization, and Atla'a Alandar apparently suffered a similar fate." He unrolled a set of maps and began to lay them out on the floor of our hotel room. "Seven of them are, of course, at the locations of the Seven Towers; these were the bulwarks of Atlantaea's defenses, and even in destruction may have continued to defend at least something in their immediate area from complete eradication."

"Odd," I said. "I'd have expected that such areas would have been the focus of specific clean-up efforts."

"They most likely were, sir. However, according to

Master Verne, the Towers' very nature made them difficult to completely destroy; even in destruction, it seems, they might have cloaked some material from detection."

I studied the maps and started marking off the locations on the globe. It was a bit of a jolt to notice that instead of all exotic, faraway places, one of them appeared to be somewhere in the vicinity of Cape Cod. The rest of the ten locales were scattered around the globe, ranging from somewhere out in the middle of the South Atlantic ocean to Germany.

"Now that you have this information, sir, do you have any idea what you will do with it?"

"Yep. That much I knew as soon as I asked. Obviously this Maelkodan thing wasn't mobile on its own before now, and I'll bet money that even immobile it wasn't anywhere with easy access." I was using my laptop to access my home machine and set up the search criteria, tapping in the commands and specs. "So someone just dug it up, or in the case of the ones in the ocean, maybe dredged it up."

I waited for that set of commands to be acknowledged, entered the next. "So what I'm doing is setting up a bunch of search parameters to locate, first, any expeditions or events that might have uncovered something unusual in the ten areas you've given me. In the case of deep-ocean sites, that'd have to be major scientific expeditions—no one goes down fifteen thousand feet in a casual dive, let me tell you. In land or shallow-water situations, there's more potential for casual digs and dives that might happen to turn up something that Man Was Not Meant to Know."

"I see," said Morgan. "And after that?"

"Then I tie this with law enforcement files."

"Why law enforcement, Jason?" Sylvie asked, looking over my shoulder.

"Think about the scenario. By far the most likely is this: Jane Doe finds something unusual—maybe it looks like an artifact, a fossil egg, whatever—on a dive or a dig. So the Maelkodan either wakes up right then, or it wakes up after she's brought the thing home or to the university or on board the ship. In any case, when it wakes up, what does it do? Barring some ridiculous coincidence involving its default human form looking just like one of the people present, it can't just slip out unnoticed, even assuming no one was looking when it woke up, hatched, whatever. Even if it *does* slip out, the finders are now missing part or all of their interesting find."

"Very clever, sir."

"Yes, I see, Jason. Either you'll have someone who disappeared, someone who got killed, or some item or artifact stolen or disappeared."

"Right. Now, if it was incredibly lucky, there might have been a Werewolf available when it popped out, and it then could have assumed a known form to the people there. But even so, that person would have had to leave the area and end up here—or rather, it would likely have said it was going to some particular locale but ended up coming here to lose possible pursuit. Either way, it's likely that someone would be looking for them by now unless the person in question was in the habit of just dropping out of sight for weeks at a time."

"How long do you think it will take to do this?"

"Now that I've put in the parameters? A few hours, maybe, depending on how much stuff there is that makes a close fit."

Morgan shook his head in amazement. "I still find myself shocked at the speed of such things, Master Jason. However, are you not making a bit of an assumption that what you are looking for is indeed online?"

"To an extent, certainly, but news services generally

carry most of the kind of thing I'm looking for. If we come up completely dry, we'll have to try something else, but let me give my machines a chance." I pulled out a deck of cards. "Anyone for a game?"

A couple hours later, I was glad we were playing for pennies. I'm not a complete putz at cards, but I'd forgotten that Morgan was probably older than the Sheriff. He was clearly trouncing both of us. "I should've suggested a game of Magic," I muttered as I shuffled and began to deal. "One-eyed jacks and the suicide king are wild."

"My geeky husband, you forget that you'd be the only one with a deck," Syl said, checking the cards as I dealt them.

"Couldn't lose then, could I?"

"Actually, Lady Sylvia, I happen to have a very nice red-black deck," Morgan said, causing Sylvia to boggle and me to chortle. "Although I confess to not going by tournament rules and hardly being up-to-date on my cards."

"No problem, Morgan, it's not like I'm a fanatic who has time to keep up—" my laptop played a small fanfare. "Oh, goody—I mean, oh, darn, I guess I'll have to sit this one out," I said, dropping my cards on the table.

The others dropped theirs, too and Morgan collected his small but significant winnings. I keyed in my go-ahead and data began to scroll across the screen.

"Anything?" Syl asked.

"Excavation in Chile . . . nope, nothing there . . . dredging . . . possible, but . . . digging for old Indian relics in New York, nothing promising there . . . well, well, what have we here?"

I highlighted the article and brought it up. "Doctor J. I. O'Connell of the University of Oxford Archaeology Department led a team of researchers in the past few months on a survey of supposed underwater ruins off the coast of Cuba and other Caribbean islands. Their purpose was to find an accessible site and see if they could uncover anything in these ruins which would verify their age and origin."

"Looks quite promising, Master Jason."

I grinned. "Yep. And the physical nearness is encouraging. I mean, if you're in Mongolia and are looking for some Wolves for lunch, I'd presume it'd be a lot easier to head for somewhere in China. But if you're in the Caribbean, you head for the good old USA." I keyed in a request for a search on more information on O'Connell, this recent expedition, where he might be presenting the results, and so on.

A few seconds later the results popped up. One carried the red flag signifying it was a law-enforcement file. "I'll be damned." I said. "Look at this."

Syl read aloud. "Missing Persons report: James I. O'Connell."

"I believe we have a winner," I said grimly.

"Even more so, sir," Morgan said, pointing to the bottom of the list.

From the screen, I read: "Underwater archaeology team hopes to present results at conference in Florida."

A double-click brought up the entire article, which was an interview with Dr. O'Connell and a few of his students. In it, O'Connell indicated that he hoped to present at least a preliminary review of the results at the UAR (Underwater Archaeological Researchers) local conference in Florida. " 'This is all very tentative,' O'Connell said with a grin, 'since we don't know our exact timetable yet, let alone if we're going to have any decent results to present. Still, I've given them tentative notification so they'll be ready.' " I read from the article. I looked up at the others. "Bingo. A few calls, and we'll know exactly how and when our little friend entered the country."

A quick Web search found the UAR page (I had to go back and specify, after encountering the acronym in use by things as diverse as a Mac networking program, a UK asset recovery agency, and Russian architects) and a listing of their event schedule. A chill went down my spine as I read:

"Local Archaeology Conference: September 22–25, Venice, Florida."

61

I listened to the ring tone. Again. Again.

"Hello?"

The London-accented voice was that of a young woman.

"Could I speak to Mandy Gennaro, please?" I said, making sure I was reading the right name.

"Speaking. Who is this?"

"Ms. Gennaro, my name is Jason Wood."

"Not the—"

"Yes, the," I said. I revised my estimate of how many people knew my name; given how much the Morgantown event had forced the revision of people's security systems, it might be that I was currently a household name in the civilized world. I wasn't sure what to think about that. "I'd like to ask you a few questions, if you have a few minutes."

"Hold on!" I heard footsteps hurry away, a clatter, then footsteps returning. "Sorry, had something on to cook. Is this about the Professor?"

"In part, certainly. I know the police have already gone over everything with you, so I'll try to make it quick."

"How are you involved, Mr. Wood?"

"It's rather complicated to explain. In a nutshell, I've gotten involved in an investigation here in the States which may be connected with Dr. O'Connell's disappearance in some way."

"Right, then. Go ahead."

I ran through a short list of questions, establishing that she knew O'Connell quite well, having had him as her advisor for the past three years, and that she had been his right-hand person on the expedition.

"So you were very familiar with the sites, then?"

She had a nice laugh. "No, no. I was in charge because I'd done underwater investigations before—in the Mediterranean, an old Greek merchantman. So I understood a lot more of the limitations and requirements than most of the students. You don't really grasp the dangers unless you've been down in the muck yourself, you see."

"Was all the equipment yours? The University's, I mean?"

"Oh, lordy no. 'Twas a joint project, you understand—your own National Geographic Society helped sponsor it, and we had a few others to help. Submersibles and so on, they aren't cheap, not even for a big university."

"I understand that Dr. O'Connell vanished at the airport."

She hesitated. "It did seem that way . . ."

It was an obvious opening. " . . . but?"

"Is this confidential?" she asked suddenly.

"Well, I'm not a lawyer or priest—I can't be protected under law against talking—but I won't say anything about this conversation that I don't have to legally to anyone not directly involved in the investigation I'm doing," I answered. "If you want to verify that I am who I say I am, I can give you some numbers to call to verify my bona fides."

"Oh, no, no. It's just that the issue's a bit touchy now, and the police are still being a bit hush-hush about it all," she answered. "Here it is. The night he disappeared, he left in a bit of a hurry—left some last-minute notes about how he wanted the materials handled and so on, but that he'd had a sudden personal emergency and had to leave immediately. Now, he got himself plane tickets out, right there at the airport, but he never actually left."

I nodded, then remembered she couldn't see it. "I get you. No one who knew him actually saw him from any point after . . . when?"

"Dinnertime. He went off to the lab to finish some notework on our finds, and since we were already getting ready to pull out, the rest of us were more into relaxing a bit."

"So if someone got to him on board your ship, they could've just left the notes and then used his card to buy the tickets."

"Right."

"Were the notes in his handwriting?"

I could almost hear a shrug in her tone. "Could've been. I wasn't studying them hard then. Since, well, they don't look quite right, but then if he was in a hurry and upset . . . anyway, the police will probably be able to say for sure."

"Anything else odd?"

Again, she hesitated. "Not at the time. But . . . well, we brought our finds to RLAHA when we arrived—"

" 'RLAHA'?"

"Sorry, the Research Laboratory for Archaeology and the History of Art." Mandy clarified. "And just the other day they found something very odd. We'd uncovered this thing—some of us think it was a sarcophagus, others that it was a vault box, others some kind of storage chest for holy relics—but whatever it was, it was big, had a lid, and seemed hollow. Anyway, RLAHA and our team start going over it so we can date it, open it properly and all, and what do we find? It's apparently already been opened—in the air."

"Dr. O'Connell wouldn't have done that on his own, maybe out of curiosity?"

Her voice was somewhat offended, somewhat tolerant of my ignorance (partial ignorance, actually—I thought I knew the answer, but it didn't hurt to ask). "Mr. Wood, no archaeologist worth his or her degree would even think of it. We're not playing Indiana Jones up here. Such an object is like a time capsule, but a very, very delicate one. Open it under the wrong conditions and you destroy more than half of what it can tell you."

"I understand. Was this sarcophagus, or whatever, one of the things you discussed at the UAR conference in Florida?"

There was a long pause. "I'm a bit confused, Mr. Wood. I wasn't at the UAR conference—Dr. O'Connell intended to go himself. He was going to confirm his travel plans with them either the night he disappeared or the next night, in fact. Naturally, that never happened . . ." Her voice trailed off, then came back, " . . . but it is a bit odd . . . I did get a letter a few days ago from Dr. Rodriguez of the UAR which was discussing some of our finds. I thought it a bit odd, but I hadn't really read it carefully yet."

"You didn't attend the UAR conference in Venice, Florida?" I repeated.

"No, I did not, Mr. Wood. Why?"

I looked down at the flyer in my hand, printed up from the UAR site. "Because, according to the UAR, not only were you there, you, not Dr. O'Connell, presented a quick but fascinating overview of what you had found," I answered. "Ms. Gennaro, would you do me a favor? Fax me a picture of yourself, so I can show it to some of the attendees?"

She was silent a moment, apparently still trying to absorb what I'd said. Then, "What . . . ? Yes, yes, of course. If someone's running around pretending to be me . . . well, I don't know what to think. Your number?"

I gave her my fax number—actually an e-fax number, one that would send the fax as an e-mail so I could retrieve it anywhere.

"Will there be anything else?"

"No, not at the moment. You've been immensely helpful, Ms. Gennaro."

"You're welcome. Could I trouble you to at least let me know what you find out?"

I hesitated. What the hell, I could certainly figure out a bowdlerized version which would be close enough for her to hear. "I certainly will."

I hung up the phone and turned to Morgan, Baker, and Sylvie, all of whom were waiting. "We have our smoking gun."

"The damn thing came to the conference?"

"Right here in this hotel," I said, enjoying Baker's expression. "And apparently wowed them with the presentation, too. It must've absconded with some of his notes and slides."

"Slides, yeah, but it wouldn't need the notes," Baker said, looking chagrined. "Assume it killed O'Connell, then it knew pretty much what O'Connell knew—about recent events, leastwise. Dunno just how extensive it is, but they sure steal enough to be able to get by. Probably just grabbed some rolls of film an' chose some good shots."

"And then, finding that the conference just happened

to be in Wolf City, it decided there was no reason at
all for it to move on."

"Ayup," Baker said dismally. "When's that girl going
to send her pic, so we can go around and trace her
movements?"

I grinned. "Receiving it now, but I'm willing to bet
half of what I own that not one person will recognize
her."

"What? Oh, damn. It booked it under her name
because its default human form is female, but no way
it looks like her, right?"

"Maybe close in the written essentials, but not close
enough to fool anyone, unless it's so lucky that it
oughtta be playing the lottery every day." A photo-
quality print came out of my little inkjet. "There you
go."

Mandy wasn't bad-looking—cute, mainly, with a fairly
round face, dark hair in a sort of pixieish cut, and a
reasonably trim body as you'd expect from someone
fit enough to do diving archaeological work. "There you
go, Baker."

"Nope, rather it was you. Remember, more contact
I have with the outside, more likely I run into some
paranoid who finds out what I am."

I sighed. "Fine, fine, look, you do the hotel staff
anyway, will you? I'll handle talking to the UAR
people."

"No need to bother," Syl's voice broke in.

Baker and I looked at her. "Why?"

"Tsk, tsk, Mr. Information Man. While you were
talking, I did a few searches under the members'
names, and looky what I found on Dr. Jesus Rodriguez'
web page."

On the screen was a large photo of a tall, slender,
dark-skinned girl of long hair and exotic beauty, pointing at a slide image showing a large stone object. The

caption read, "Mandy Gennaro showing some of the spectacular finds from the University of Oxford's Caribbean excavations."

Syl smiled at me smugly. "I think you get to keep everything, Jason."

62

I looked at the stony face and sighed. "Another one, I see."

"Fourth, or if we're right about the disappearances, seventh of us." Baker grimaced. "I swear, the thing's probably out there laughing."

I shrugged. "Maybe. We certainly aren't having luck catching it yet. The question is where the hell did it go after the convention? Plenty of people saw her there, but afterwards?"

Baker shook his head. "Nothing. We've been around with photos, checkin' the stores all through the area. Couple people saw her during the convention, but not afterwards."

I turned away from the statue of the late Deputy Arnaud and headed up the stairs to Baker's office. He shut the door behind us and followed. "So she went into hiding. But that's not a nondescript appearance; she's going to be noticed if she was looking like that."

"Ayup. But . . ." Baker's eyes narrowed; for a moment I almost thought I saw a yellow gleam. "Now there's an interesting possibility. Look here; it's hard to tell, but it looks to me, if we take best guesses, that we end up with a new statue around the time we get a new missing person's report. There's been a lot of events in the past couple weeks, so I dunno if we can say it's a real pattern, but . . . what if she's killin' people, takin' their place for a while, then shifting to someone else?

The people who been disappearin', she actually killed 'em days before. Then she hits someone else for a quick fix, uses them that day to scout out a new sucker, an' takes them. An' a few days later, it starts again."

I sucked in a breath. That theory made sense. "I see. Yeah, quite a bit. If that's so, then she's got to be either hiding the statues near the kill sites, or she's got herself a good storage spot for a bunch of statues . . ." I smacked my forehead. "Duh! She's not keeping the statues. She's pulverizing them." I gestured out the window, where you could occasionally get a glimpse of blue ocean. "Your *habeas corpii* are probably out there on the beach."

Baker looked like he wanted to kick himself as well. "Right, right, Wood. Shoulda thought of that. Ya must've hit it on the head. Damn."

"Around here, it's easy to get rid of something like that. Getting rid of a body like Mansfield's, that's harder. Unless this thing eats flesh too, and lots of it."

"Nope. They can eat—an' some do, overall, just like we do—but they ain't like us in that area. Me, I could've polished off Mansfield in eight or nine bites, bones an' all, but the Mirrorkillers don't do that."

"But then why the hell is it leaving any of the statues?"

Baker pursed his lips, thinking. "Well, I'm thinkin' it's like running a business. Location, location, location. Even at night, if you're out in the middle of town like she was with Weimar, it's gonna draw attention if someone sees ya lugging a statue down to wherever it is ya plan to do the rock-crushing. Sure, by now she can probably do it with her bare hands, but it's still gonna be noisy."

"Right," I said. "So the ones we find are just stopgaps—she takes the form like you said, uses it to find someone she can nail in a more private location and then replace them for a while. You people all work together, and once she killed a couple of you she'd know everything about who she could and couldn't talk to about what was going on—from your point of view, I mean. So I'd guess it wouldn't be hard for her, as one of you, to talk to the right people and get them into a convenient locale."

"Nope," Baker agreed. "We gotta be ready to cooperate with each other here, especially in shifting people around. The humans that work with us sometimes'll have to be in two places at once, so to speak, and it's our job to cooperate with 'em to that extent."

"Oh? Why do they have to do that?"

"People in any business that's got a lot o' contact with outsiders. Either the people doing the interaction have to be human, or we at least have to have humans who can do their jobs that we can swap places with. You have no idea how complicated this can get. So any of us can call on the others to help out—moving bodies, switching places, whatever."

I nodded my understanding. "So it would in fact be very easy for her, in the guise of her stopgap body, to get someone else to accompany her, or let her inside their house, or whatever."

"Ayup," he agreed.

"Then we've got her. Just make it so that people can't do it that easily—they have to coordinate it with you, or some other central group. Next time she tries it, *bang*, she's finished."

"Can't be done," he said heavily. "The masquerade can break with just one bad run o' luck, and my people've gotta be able to respond to an emergency right away. Besides, ya don't realize just how hard it is gettin' Wolves to work together this way if'n you ain't the King. They hate bein' shoved into coordinated slots,

an' it's takin' me just about everything I got to keep
this thing workin' as it is."

"Well, we've got a chance now, anyway. Look, she
can't be sure of exactly when the statues of her quick
kills are going to be found, so she's got to move fairly
quickly. So somewhere around the area should be the
place where she found her new longer-term host, so
to speak."

"And how does that help us?"

"I think there might be a way to test it. The
Maelkodan isn't vulnerable to silver. So if we can
check all the Wolves in the area, you just need to
find one that doesn't react. Wear a glove or something with a little silver on it and shake hands; anyone who doesn't get burned or whatever is your
monster."

Baker gave me a respectful look. "Y'know, that might
just work. I'll get my people on it right now . . . after
I give 'em a handshake m'self."

63

I put down the phone, sighed, and sank into one
of the chairs, toying with my just-finished duplicates
of my CryWolf glasses. One advantage of working for
the Wolves was that I wasn't actually restricted in
movements if I stayed on the case, so I'd ordered the
custom parts, then taken a day, flown up, and
assembled the things. At least now I could be subtle.
I put them on, adjusted the fit.

"Bad news?" Syl said, sympathetically.

"My bright idea was a bust. All we've got now is a
bunch of werewolves with itchy palms, and I don't
mean that they're looking for tips." I chewed my lower
lip idly. "Now, this could mean Baker's idea still works,

but she's going farther afield than we thought looking for her replacement."

"Why does she have to switch so often, though?"

"Remember her basic limitation, Syl. Every time she whacks a Wolf, she gets a brand-new face. She doesn't keep a record of the old ones in her matrix, so she can't just go back to where she was . . ."

I saw it then; it was, in its way, sheer genius. It wouldn't work forever, but certainly for longer than it had already gone. And I could confirm it so easily . . .

Picking up the phone, I called Baker and asked him a few questions, as though I was clarifying something. Then I hung up. Sylvie watched as I checked my gun once more. "What are you going to do?"

"The rest of my job. But I'll do it my way, not Carruthers' or Baker's way."

She nodded, serious. I started to say something else, as she began to put on her own gun, but stopped. She knew what I was going to do before I did it, there was no arguing with her when she decided what part she was going to play.

Besides, I needed her to play that part.

I went down to the lobby, where Vic glanced up. "Hey, Mr. Wood! Need anything?"

"Actually, yes, Vic. But it's kinda private . . . ?"

He nodded his understanding—certain business, after all, not being something you wanted to discuss in non-secured public areas. Even though it was late at night, there was always the possibility of an uninvolved traveller dropping by at the wrong moment. He hung a "back in 15 minutes" sign up and we went into one of the back rooms. "Okay, how can I help?"

I studied him. "First, let me congratulate you," I said, to his sparkling image in the glasses. "I almost didn't figure out how you were doing it, and without that, we'd never have caught you."

He froze for a moment, just as he had the night we checked in, then sighed. "God-damn. If you don't mind my asking, how'd you figure it?"

"Partly the timing of the killings, partly luck, and just a few little things that nagged at me," I said, making sure I was not blocked in and had at least two ways to run. "Baker's theory on what you were doing wasn't bad—and it was actually close, in some ways— but when we came up with nothing on that, I started thinking it was a complete bust. But then there had to be some explanation for the pattern. So I was thinking . . . why? If you're not moving from life to life, what's the point of the pattern of one person disappearing, one person being found?"

He nodded, sitting down on a crate some distance away. Apparently he really did want to hear the explanation. "Go on."

I was careful to avoid staring directly into his eyes; despite assurances that an alert human could probably break contact fast enough, I wasn't taking any more risks. "Then there was the whole Jerry Mansfield episode. It didn't quite fit with the others. Especially the silver dust bit.

"But it did make sense if I assumed someone got a little panicky. The Wolves certainly did. Mansfield was a quick and dirty attempt to get rid of me; it made it look like someone was out hunting Wolves, in the conventional way. Once I'd clearly weathered that threat—when Karl Weimar left my room with me still alive, in short—it was clear the quick impulse had failed. You knew who I was when I registered, and it flustered you. Here you were, still adjusting to the way this world works—and even with your ability to grab people's knowledge, I'll bet that still takes some getting used to, the changes in the world since you were last out and about—and along comes this guy with a reputation for dealing with Weird Shit. No warning. You knew you'd killed a fairly important guy already, the cops were looking for him, and if they'd gotten a whiff of the weird, well, who would they call? Jason Wood, of course.

"Naturally, you knew who and what everyone in the town was, and Mansfield made a perfect target—almost vital to the town's functioning, but wouldn't die in that all-too-telltale stony way. By the time the Wolves stopped panicking at my presence and the silver evidence, I'd be dead. Maybe. You didn't have that much to lose, since you planned on settling down here to eat anyway."

He hung his head. "I'm sorry about that. Really. But you're right, I just . . . what's your idiom? *Freaked*, that's it. After uncounted thousands of years, I was finally, finally *free*, and suddenly there you were."

"The first 'disappearance' was about due to be reported, anyway; Karl Weimar gave you the perfect chance to start confusing the trail," I continued. "Your first victim had been expected to be away for some time, so you'd had latitude. And you'd already gotten it figured out. Everyone knew you couldn't go back to the same form you had already had. And you couldn't take the form of human beings, only Wolves. So Victor Spangler, long-time resident, and well-known human collaborator, was a doubly safe identity.

"I didn't get all the keys to unravelling this puzzle until recently, or I might have caught on sooner. Certainly if I'd just been going by your movements en route here, Vic would have been high on the suspect list; you're in a fairly central location, you have contact with everyone, and so on.

"The key, of course, is the masquerade. The Wolves have to cooperate in order to keep the secret from being blown, and they *especially* have to do so with their human collaborators—the ones that sometimes have to be quickly moved around so as to be the interfaces with humans that might possibly be carting around CryWolf gadgets. These collaborators are of prime importance in all areas that have high contact with outsiders: convenience stores, gas stations, restaurants . . . and hotels."

He chuckled and nodded. "Right, right."

"I found out that the day the conference ended— that is, the day before I arrived—Vic had to go out and be counterman at one of the other hotels. Someone, of course, had to take his place here—a Wolf who had changed himself to look just like Vic! You, of course, noticed the substitution, and that was when the whole idea hit you. You immediately killed him and took his place, now having the guise of Vic the Human to work from. Now that you were 'in,' you could use that cooperative requirement to get other Wolves to take on Vic's form—on the excuse that you were needed elsewhere. That's why you had to destroy the other bodies, to hide the fact that otherwise there'd be quite a collection of Vic Spangler statues around. Once I had the idea, all I had to do was ask Baker if you were a collaborator—I said it as though I assumed you were a Wolf, he corrected me—and check a couple timing issues with your assumed ID."

He spread his hands. "You got me, all right. Had to kill the real Vic, too. So now what?"

I frowned. "Aye, there's the rub, as Hamlet put it. On paper, you're a murderer, or a dangerous animal, depending on who you ask. And I can't say I'm comfortable with the whole idea of what you are, or of letting you go after you killed off a harmless archaeologist. On the other hand, I also really hate being strung over a barrel by the Wolves. Their King's put me on reserve as a personal chew-toy for later, but they've basically bargained me to solve this problem in exchange for my friends being kept out of a bunch of other things. I wanted to see if there was a chance we can find a resolution for this that doesn't include my using this," I pushed my sport jacket aside and eased the gun out, "to turn you into a colander. And I'm also a bit of a conservationist, I suppose; killing off the entirety of a species doesn't sit well with me."

Vic sparkled; the shimmer intensified. It wasn't like a Werewolf's change, but more like watching clouds of sunshine-touched mist dissolve and then reform. The Maelkodan had taken her more natural, default-human form—and again I admired its tactical sense; if it wanted to play any sympathy cards, it knew perfectly well that a beautiful woman would have a better chance with me than even a nice cheerful hotel proprietor. "As I see it, the problem is that I need to eat."

"Not nearly as much as you have been," I pointed out. "They already told me just how much power you gain; by now you're getting quite a ways up there."

"And you believe everything they say?" she challenged.

It was my turn to chuckle. "Not at all. Unfortunately for you, Morgan was the source of confirmation on the information."

Her lips moved in a pout or a tightening; I couldn't be quite sure which without studying the eye area. "Ah. The one who feels like something from home. But, really, Mr. Wood, does it matter? Aside from poor Dr. O'Connell, who just happened to be the one present when I finally broke free and acted on my instincts, the only people I've killed have been either Wolves or their friends. Do you really care what I do to them?"

I acknowledged the point. "In truth, not really. I think the world's better off without them. But there's the issue of my own word versus theirs. I did promise to investigate this fully and track down the killer. Now, I could weasel *some* technicalities around, but I do have to solve the problem for which I'm hired, and saying 'Well, I did find the killer, but too bad, I'm not doing anything about it' really violates the spirit of the contract. The very *last* thing I want to do is encourage them to start playing technicality games with me."

She nodded. "I could just move on."

"And—be honest now, because if you lie about it and it comes out later, I will beyond any shadow of a doubt come after your ass—would you be able to keep from killing?"

For a long, long moment she paused.

Finally, "No. No, I could not. It is what I was created to do. I am a hunter. I hunt everything, especially the Wolves, but even your people. The hunt is part of my life. They made me that way. You would eventually hear of the deaths. And they would continue, so long as I live."

My heart pounded painfully against my chest. "Then let's at least settle it here."

"You have not called the Wolves?"

"No. I wanted to find out if there was a chance. And if not, at least deprive them of the pleasure."

She stood up, slowly, and shimmered again, holding her hands up in a "hold a moment" gesture. Rainbow-shimmering clouds formed, dissolved, coalesced, solidified.

Before me stood the Maelkodan.

The centauroid torso and head were just about my height; the body itself, perhaps three to four feet at the hip. It was twelve feet long, covered with iridescent scales in beautiful geometric patterns of green, black, red, silver, and gold. The legs, three-taloned affairs like a Jurassic Park raptor's (minus the one huge claw) moved smoothly, shifting back and forth nervously. The arms were edged, with wicked spikes at the elbows, and I could see the glitter of diamondlike teeth in the mouth. The head I couldn't focus on, without risking eye contact, but it seemed to be crested and fluted and spiked, as though wearing an elaborate helm.

It bowed low from the waist. "You risk your life and honor me. I shall cherish your soul."

"I don't intend to die."

"No more did any of the others." The eyes glowed suddenly, an iridescent flame that I glanced towards reflexively, eyes drawn by the sudden moving change.

It was like being hit by a mallet on the side of the head, combined with the utter fascination of every forbidden pleasure ever imagined. I knew—knew with absolute truth—that if I didn't look away, I would die, yet for a frozen instant of time I couldn't do it; I yearned to do nothing more than stare more deeply into those windows of horrid revelation.

But memory, duty, and the face of Sylvie warred against that lure, forced my eyes shut against the terrible siren call. Still, being blind is a bad combat situation, and I heard it starting forward.

Right on cue, Syl kicked open the door from the hotel. I went out the back way, as I'd intended all along. Sylvia's gunshots, unexpected as they were, convinced the Maelkodan to head out into the street with me, even though public locations were hardly where it wanted to be caught.

I sprinted out the door and down the alleyway. Behind me, I heard the swift scuttling of taloned feet; I whirled, keeping my eyes low, and snapped off two shots; the Maelkodan writhed sideways, behind a Dumpster, giving me back a lead and allowing me to round the corner ahead of it.

More gunshots, from Syl's Smith & Wesson, sounded out; I kept running, knowing I'd hear the creature on my tail in moments. It wouldn't try to charge Syl who was in the cover of the doorway and who was, I felt sure, firing with accuracy while her eyes were squeezed shut. Her Talent had many uses.

Skittering rhythm of claws on pavement behind me—and then a screeching of tires. I spun around, just in time to see one of the police cars slide to a halt right next to the Maelkodan. It flowed up and to the other side of the car, and I heard a suddenly-cut-off shriek. There was a metallic ripping sound, and I saw the passenger-side door fly out onto the street, followed by a statue that crumbled on impact with the pavement.

Then the whole car was hefted into the air.

I almost made eye contact again, goggling at the scene. The creature had its legs splayed wide and dug into the street, tail counterbalancing, performing a comic-book feat of strength with a wide grin on its fanged mouth. With an effort that sent it skidding backwards, tearing grooves through the blacktop, it hurled the cop car straight towards me.

I ran and dove aside at the last second; the impact was so close that it sounded like the crack of doom. *Jesus Christ, the thing was strong! Maybe as strong as Verne!*

As I rolled to my feet, I emptied the clip in its direction to slow it down and ran through another alleyway, slamming in another clip. I'd heard one squealing roar of pain—must have at least nicked the thing. I realized I'd been subconsciously underestimating the creature; our estimates of its capabilities had been based on it having killed three Wolves; by current estimate, that was off by at least a factor of two, maybe more if it had gotten lucky and caught a few others we hadn't noticed yet. I exited the alley, turned down the street. I was, naturally, cursing myself for having these ideas of fair play and justice when dealing with monstrosities from beyond time, and promising myself I'd change my ways if I could just live through this.

A shadow within the darkness was my only warning, as the Maelkodan dropped to the street fifty feet ahead of me, having apparently run and jumped along the tops of buildings to do so. However, in the landing it did pause slightly, perhaps enjoying the effect and the power, and I took full advantage to center my 10mm on the torso and fire three times.

The thing's eyes flared just as I did that, and I saw three sparks of light in line with my aim. In the streetlights, I could just barely make out three tiny objects, floating in the air scant feet from the thing. Telekinesis.

"I should have known, I should have known, you can *never* kill a monster with bullets, never, it's in the friggin' Monster Union Rules!" I heard myself half-wail as I turned and dashed inside the supermarket, which was mostly empty. The gunshots had drawn the attention of the proprietor, who had unlimbered a quite impressive-looking shotgun. He never had a chance to use it, however. With a roar like a jet engine going into overload, the Maelkodan demonstrated its newfound power by blowing the entire glass storefront inwards, blasting both of us off our feet, sending racks of candy, magazines, sunglasses, and other sundries tumbling end-over-end. I took advantage of the impetus to skid and roll down one of the aisles. Its shape and size would give me a slight edge in narrower spaces, although the convenience of customers of course dictated that the aisles weren't really narrow enough to restrict it.

"Let us prolong this no longer, Mr. Wood!" the

Maelkodan called, its voice oddly human; perhaps it, like the Wolves, could shift parts of itself while in motion. "I will still try to kill no innocent human during our hunt, but the more you resist, the more the chance that one such will get in the way!" It sounded sincere, and oddly enough I believed it. The creature was, perhaps, as soulless a killer in its own way as the Wolves, but even some Wolves seemed to take pleasure—perhaps honest pleasure, perhaps merely the pleasure of a properly played game, but pleasure nonetheless—in following through on a commitment. I had shown the Maelkodan more consideration than it might have expected; it was trying to live up to the standard I'd set.

"It's not in my nature to stand still and die," I shouted back, moving down another aisle. "Being honest, I doubt we'll get out of this store with both of us still moving."

"True enough," it said. I felt a wave of force ripple past me . . . and then the shelves, the whole aisle's worth of shelves and products, were moving, toppling towards me.

But I was close enough to my goal, slamming my way through the door and finding it was just large enough for my purpose.

There was a pause, one in which I recalled all too well a similar moment, waiting behind a door to see if the King of Wolves would take the bait or not.

I heard a genuine laugh from the Maelkodan, something like a steamkettle rattling. "The men's room? How clever." The door burst open. "But did you forget—"

"That you could turn off the killing mode and thus enter mirrored rooms safely?" I said from my position on the other side of the door. As it turned its startled, momentarily harmless gaze on me, I pressed the button. "I *counted* on it!"

There are commercial versions of that gadget, but I like making my own. The Dazzler detonated like a magnesium flare in that enclosed space, leaving a spotty afterimage on my eyes even through closed lids. I was diving back through the door even as I triggered it.

The Maelkodan shrieked; it felt like my ears had spikes being driven through them, and its tail gave a convulsive movement that whipped me fifteen feet across fallen cans and shelves. No telekinetic shield could have protected it from that blazing luminescence scarcely a foot and a half from its eyes. And as Morgan and Baker had both said . . . it had to be able to see its prey to use those eyes. It cursed and shouted in a language so ancient that only Verne and Kafan might have understood it.

For at least a few minutes, it was much less dangerous. But that trick had been meant as a last-ditch effort, we'd expected to kill it long before this. Once it recovered, I'd be meat. Even if it kept playing relatively fair, it was clearly going to wear me out, and then it would all be over. I picked myself up groggily, staring across at the scattered wreckage, candies, displays . . .

"Smarter . . . than I thought . . . Mr. Wood," it gasped, backing out of the bathroom clumsily. "Much smarter. I've been far too long without a decent opponent, and it shows, does it not?" It rubbed fiercely at its eyes. "Alas, my eyesight shall recover momentarily, and I am hardly harmless!"

Canned goods began floating into the air. I muttered another curse of my own; it was going to play Darth Vader, and I was no Luke Skywalker. I threw myself flat, ignoring the increase in bruises, and slid towards the front of the store as a hurricane of metal cylinders started streaking randomly around the enclosed space, ricocheting off of the remaining shelves, walls, support columns, an occasional one bouncing off the floor or me. I restrained the grunts and groans of pain—I didn't need to give it any help in targetting. Somehow I'd lost the CryWolf glasses, despite being better anchored. I was going to put in a hell of an expense account to Baker . . .

Lost my . . .

I somersaulted forward and moved into one of the remaining aisles, hunkering down. My gaze roved frantically, searching.

"Ah . . . there . . . starting to come back . . ." I heard it mutter. The cans stopped moving, and I could picture it standing there, listening. I knew I couldn't be noiseless, not in all this destruction. Despite my attempts, there were rustlings, cracklings, clanks of cans rolling. In the distance I heard sirens, but they wouldn't be here in time . . . assuming any Wolf was brave enough to enter the Maelkodan's range.

Clawed feet rattled through the supermarket stock, making a beeline for my aisle.

Where, dammit, where—ah-HA! I grabbed, then dove for the end of the aisle away from the creature—but my foot slipped on a can.

As I came down hard, jarring my chin so much that I bit my tongue and tasted blood, I thought to myself that at the least I'd managed to be convincing in that slippage; next time, perhaps, I might consider learning how to do it without hurting myself. Behind me, the Maelkodan scuttled at lightning speed. Taloned hands grasped me, and rolled me over, the sculpted head bending to deliver an unavoidable stare . . .

It had time for a single horrified "NO!!"

In a blaze of rainbow-clouded energy, the creature neutralized its own matrix, leaving a bending statue. With difficulty I wiggled free of the stony grip, and slowly hobbled away. Then I lowered my right hand, which had been pressed tight against my temple, and extended it towards the shaking, wide-eyed clerk who had just risen from the wrecked counter.

"I'll take these," I said, placing the mirrored sunglasses in front of him. "And most of your stock of Band-Aids."

64

Baker stood staring at the statue. "I can't believe it," he repeated for the fourth time. "You beat the thing."

"What you hired me for, isn't it?" I said, rather gratified by the reaction; it was nice to know that the Wolves were honest-to-God terrified of something and that it hadn't just been a matter of trying to make the human do their dirty work. "One Mirrorkiller, packaged for transport."

Baker finally got a hold of himself, and turned to face me. "So we're square up, then?"

"You make sure Carruthers understands that I carried through on the spirit as well as the letter of our agreement," I said. "No trouble from any of his people or yours, you won't have trouble from me. And two other things—one I just want to reinforce, since I warned you before, and one new one."

He looked at me suspiciously. "And those would be . . . ?"

"First, no more killings. I've got a good idea how many you had to do to take over here, and it's sickening, but we've gone into that. You just make damn sure no more people get killed—either natives or visitors—by your people, or under their orders."

Baker glowered at me. "We have to protect—"

"That isn't my problem." I cut him off with a cold glance. "You work your masquerade without killing people, at least until you're ready to take us all on, or you *will* be taking us all on. If you think someone's getting too close to your secret, you either figure a way to mislead them, or get ready to pull up stakes and move on. It's your call, but if you push me into blowing the whistle, I think you can bet that not one out of every ten of you will get out of Florida alive."

Baker spat on the ground, looking like he yearned to do something else to me, but we both knew I was off-limits. "Fine, fine. I got your message. What's the other thing?"

I pointed. "The statue. I want it carefully packed up and shipped to me."

Baker looked startled. "Oookay, if ya say so. I cain't say anyone in this here town's likely to want it for a decoration. I'll spring for that." We shook hands on the bargain, my skin only slightly crawling from the idea since at this point I was the one with the whip hand. "So, you know y'all are welcome to stay here for free— I know you were on your honeymoon, an' the beaches here are . . ."

I couldn't restrain a laugh. "Baker, it's a lovely town, but there's no way in hell we're staying here any longer. Right, Syl?" I said, as Sylvie finally crossed over the hastily erected yellow tape barrier and grabbed me in a hug that nearly cracked my sore ribs. "Ouch, watch it!"

"Sorry—I'm just sooo glad you're alive, Jason. I thought you would be, but you can never be sure." She glanced at Baker. "And he's right. We're out of here as soon as we can get packed." She looked up at me. "So, Romeo, wherefore art thou taking thy wife for the rest of the honeymoon?"

I winced at her mangled semi-Shakespeare, but smiled back. "Home to Morgantown, Syl. I think we've had enough adventure for now. Maybe we can go on another trip later."

She snuggled into me. "Sounds perfect to me."

65

"Oh, I had a king-sized attack of the shakes after it was all over," I admitted, leaning back in the comfortable, oversized recliner near Verne's fireplace and hugging Syl to me. "More than one. Cursing myself for giving it any chances at all, and so on."

"No, no, Jason. All in all, I think you did precisely the right thing," Verne said. "Perhaps it is merely that I am a relic myself, but I feel that there is such a thing as respecting one's opponent, and part of that respect is, in fact, giving him or her . . . or it . . . the chance to not be your enemy. It is evident that the Maelkodan shared that respect for you. It could have attempted to kill you much earlier, and even later in the combat there were tactics it might have used to kill you more efficiently. But just as you hadn't arranged for a multiple crossfire or something of similarly lethal nature, it did not attempt to use—how would you put it?—ah, *cheesy tricks* to finish the chase."

I chuckled, then sobered somewhat. "On that note, what do you think of this guy Carruthers' offer? Is he going to play fair on the deal, since I delivered the goods?"

"I would say without any shadow of a doubt, my friend—and I thank both your good fortune and good business sense for that bargain. Yes, he will abide by those terms; while some of the young Wolves may sneer at such commitments, a true Elder knows better than to even contemplate breaking a bargain sworn to in the King's name. And if Carruthers' name is truly

Virigan . . . well, then he is more than merely Elder; he is one of the only surviving Firstborn." He frowned, swirling his usual drink in its crystal glass. "I must admit, Jason, that I am as mystified—and concerned— with his outré interest in human genetic engineering as you. Such a thing would not, as far as I can tell, enhance the spiritual power or aspect of humanity— which is what they consume, as you know. Thus it cannot, at least directly, be concerned with improving their food supply. Indeed, tampering which interferes too much with certain aspects of humanity could actually damage humanity's usefulness to them, so Virigan must be interested in . . . something else."

I shrugged. "No hurry, I think. We'll keep looking— or rather, Jeri's outfit will, right?"

Jeri, still looking somewhat uptight at being in a meeting that so casually discussed burn-before-reading Secret material, nodded. "You can bet on it. Since we're not excluded from their hit list, unlike the rest of you, we also have no reason to hold back. I might note that when I gave my interim report on this incident, my boss did something I've never seen him do in all the years I've known him; give vent to an utterly spontaneous curse."

"Why?"

"It seems," Jeri answered, "that Mr. Carruthers was, in a way, sending us a message just by appearing to you in that guise. Obviously as a Wolf he could have chosen any shape he wanted. You see, Alexi Carruthers was, as far as we knew, killed off a number of years ago in a manner that remains classified. By showing us what he really is, he is basically telling Pantheon, and through Pantheon all of ISIS, that we're dealing with something much nastier than we'd yet suspected . . . and you can rest assured, we already suspected some seriously nasty things."

"Well, Miss Winthrope," Morgan said courteously, "I am sure I speak for us all when I say that you can count on our assistance if it could ever be of service."

I glanced at Syl with a raised eyebrow. She gave a secretive smile. Morgan did seem to like Jeri—how very strange, since I would never have thought she was his type. Whether Jeri had any interests outside of her job, of course, was something none of us would ever know unless she decided to tell us. "I have to give Ms. Gennaro a callback—it's been several days already. I'm just trying to decide what to tell her."

Kafan growled something, then sighed. "Twisty problem. Can't just tell her to stop poking around in those things—it's her job."

"Besides that, trying to shove her out might cause talk by itself, and certainly wouldn't keep someone else from going to the sites," I pointed out.

Verne nodded. "I am afraid, Jason, that you will simply have to use your own judgement. You and I are in essence safe—at least until that day when the King decides to try us again—but if she or her people learn too much, there will be more disappearances, regardless of whether they discover another monster or not. I would, in fact, judge it unlikely they will find anything of that magnitude again, but even a few more artifacts whose age they can accurately measure would be greatly troubling to certain people. The Demons cannot rework the face of a planet now, not with the changes wrought on Earth since those days, but the few of their agents who remain are more than strong enough to obliterate prying scientists."

"If it will help, I can always throw an international security umbrella over the work," Jeri offered.

"No!" Kafan snapped, jumping to his feet.

Jeri looked uncertainly at him, aware of his capabilities. "Why the panic?"

"Control yourself, Raiakafan," Verne said.

He closed his eyes, opened them again. "Because any such move would make it look like the governments are getting interested directly. The very last thing any of them want is for humanity, or its governments, really taking a deep look into these things. That's why you and your agency are all going to be dead sometime soon." He said the last line in the same way I might have said "I'll be ordering pizza for dinner tomorrow"— a casual statement of fact, impersonal but inarguable. "Your people ride the edge, and Carruthers' signal just means that he's marked you down as needing his attention, or that of some of the other surviving forces. If you start doing things officially, you could end up with them deciding that maybe the whole world's getting too close to the truth, and then they'd have to start a war or something."

"A nuclear war would definitely be interfering with my life," I pointed out, half-joking. I really didn't like considering this entire shadow war thing right now.

To my surprise, Kafan and Verne seemed to take the idea at least somewhat seriously. "You may have something of a point, jesting aside," Verne said. "Carruthers' own projects would be unlikely to survive an extreme sanction against the world order, and so he would have a vested interest in promoting maximum tolerance. Still, I agree with Kafan that unless there is no other choice, overt involvement of any intelligence agencies in such matters would be playing with fire."

"Hey, just offering," said Jeri. "And unless these Demon thingies *do* still have the power to reshape the world, don't be counting us out, Mr. Raiakafan Tai Lee Ularion Xiang. If someone does come gunning for us, you can bet they'll know they've been in a fight."

Kafan nodded to her, a mark of respect if not agreement.

I got up, leaving Syl on the recliner, and picked up the phone.

This time I had to contact her at the University, but she was available—preparing a paper on some of the finds.

"Mr. Wood!"

"Yes. Nice to speak to you again, Ms. Gennaro. Your information was invaluable."

Her voice was just slightly tense—she was trying to be relaxed, but not quite succeeding. "Please call me Mandy. So what exactly happened?"

"You can call me Jason, then. There was a series of murders happening in Florida . . ." I gave an expurgated version of events, leaving out things like werewolves, my bargain, and so on. " . . . And so I was finally able to kill it off. Some of this you might see on the news soon, even though there was a heavy lid clamped on it at first."

She was silent for a few moments. "So . . . you're saying that this 'Maelkodan' was inside that casket we brought aboard?"

"Yes," I answered. "And you were right, of course; Dr. O'Connell never left your ship. The Maelkodan killed him when it emerged. It, like the Wolves, gains a great deal of the knowledge of its victims, at least temporarily, so it was able to figure out a way to at least temporarily leave a false trail."

"How horrid." I could almost hear a little shiver in her voice. "If it weren't for the Morgantown material, I'd think this was insanity. But . . . when we opened the casket there were some odd traces that we didn't quite know what to make of. Any dating we do on the casket is of course questionable at this point, it having been out of controlled conditions when it was opened. We have a few other items from the same dig, however, so we are hopeful that we may be able to date it, at any rate—the results on the casket aren't reasonable."

I took a deep breath. "Mandy, I also have to give you a warning."

"A . . . warning, Mr. . . . Jason?"

"I can't—nor would I—try to tell you not to continue your line of research. However, I do have to caution you; you've heard the old expression 'Things Man Was Not Meant To Know,' of course?"

She gave an uncertain chuckle. "Um, yes . . . ?"

"I never gave much credence to that idea myself, but as it turns out, there are some things that . . . well, not to go into detail, but Things That Put Man Or Woman In Real Danger If They Know. Your research has just uncorked one nasty genie from a bottle; there are worse genies—some of them forces that just don't want certain things known. Think paranoid. Then think worse. I'm already in the soup, so to speak—there's no way for me to reduce my danger."

"And is there for me—aside from abandoning these sites, which I really cannot imagine doing?"

"I'm not sure. Legitimate archaeological work can't be stopped, after all, and even if you did stop on my vague say-so, someone else would surely try their hand."

She was quiet for a moment. "Is the danger in question other things like this Maelkodan, or are you more referring to just the fact of our knowing and publishing certain things?"

"The latter more than the former, although as we have both discovered, the former isn't to be discounted."

She thought for another few moments. "Mr. Wood, could you, personally, recognize these dangerous elements if you saw them?"

"I think so," I answered cautiously. In point of fact,

I could probably recognize most dangerous subjects, and with Verne and Raiakafan to back me up . . . "Yes, I could."

"Then perhaps this would at least minimize the risk; in view of this bizarre discovery, I could recommend to the Board that you be hired—if willing—as a consultant, who will examine finds for potential risks that lie outside of our normal expertise. In this way we would be able to pass material found at the sites in question to you for advice on how best to handle it, and you would be able to determine what time bombs—informational or actual—we may have unearthed."

I felt my interior tension ease some. Mandy Gennaro was clearly a smart cookie, and willing to listen. "That sounds excellent, Mandy. You can count on me. Obviously I'd try to reject as little as possible—and the final call would still be yours. I'll work on getting together a risk assessment methodology, so that you can make informed risk decisions."

"Right, then. I'll contact the Board immediately, in view of what happened to Dr. O'Connell. You have told the police about this?"

"I will be informing them shortly after I hang up with you. I felt you deserved to get the news first and directly."

"I truly appreciate that, Jason. Now let me get the ball rolling here; I'd like to be able to run all the discoveries past you pronto so that we can get publishing soon."

"By all means. Thank you, Mandy. Take care."

"Ta." She hung up.

"Smarter than many," Kafan said. "I guess she decided if she was going to trust you at all, she had to figure you knew what you were talking about."

"It is rude to eavesdrop, Kafan," Verne said mildly.

"You heard it too," Kafan retorted.

"Well, yes, but a gentleman doesn't admit to over-hearing things not meant for his own ears. I agree with your assessment; a woman of uncommon good sense. She recognized Jason as trustworthy, and thus no matter how outrageous the subject area, he was worth paying heed to."

"So you people think this will work?" I asked.

Verne gave a seesawing motion of his hand. "It is far better than nothing. She will still be running grave risks, but this approach may keep her and her people alive, or at least give them sufficient warning to know when they are, in fact, at risk of death or worse. And it is a far, far better thing that we have direct contact with those who may be uncovering traces of the past than that someone we know nothing of be doing the digging."

"Well then," Jeri said, getting up, "since that's pretty much taken care of, I'll be off to file a report and recommend that it be marked closed on our files."

"I shall show you out, Lady Jeri," Morgan said, and the two left.

"So, will you continue your honeymoon?" Verne asked.

We laughed. "Eventually, sure," I said. "Not that being home means it has to stop." I grinned lecherously at Syl, who poked me in one of my still very sore ribs. "Ow! In any case, there's lots for me to do here."

"And we can do it with less to fear, now," Syl said.

"Indeed. Again, Jason, I thank you. By good fortune and wise choices, you have lifted what was in truth a burden of worry and fear from us all."

I grinned and blushed. "Aw shucks, weren't nothin'."

"Do not sell yourself short, my friend."

I nodded, still smiling. "Okay, okay. You're welcome. I guess we're safe now. Well, except for the Demons."

"Perhaps even from them, at least for now," Verne said, lifting his glass. "As you deduced in that adventure which nearly killed me in my own home, the Project certainly must have connections of some sort to the remnants of those who caused the fall of Atlantaea originally. Given that, they will know that we are endeavoring to keep the number who know certain facts low, and, more importantly, that you, Lady Sylvia, and myself are explicitly reserved for Virigar's attention."

"Oh?" I said, skeptically. "Even if they do, so what? I mean, Virigar's the Big Bad Wolf, no doubt about it, but these guys obliterated cities, rewrote the surface of a planet to fit their own schemes—and didn't destroy it only because of some mystical connection that they wouldn't want to risk. What's to stop them from laughing in Virigar's face?"

Verne stared at me, then gave a faint, hollow laugh. "My friend, there is nothing I have seen in all my hundreds of thousands of years that I fear more than the Werewolf King. And I tell you, in all earnestness, that there is no being I have ever known—man or dragon, vampire or demon, ghost or living god—which would dare to laugh at him, if they knew what they faced. No, my friend, while the Great Demons might, under the right circumstances, disregard the Werewolf King's claims on someone, even they shall never do so lightly. I believe that if we continue to keep this knowledge limited, if we make any struggles against them a secret war, then they shall be willing to leave us alone when we move not against them; they do not want to borrow trouble they could easily avoid."

I stared at him for a while, realizing that he meant every word. I shrugged. "I don't know if I should consider this comforting or not. Okay, the big Demons will leave me alone, but any day now I could be a Wolf appetizer."

"Unlikely in the extreme, sir," Morgan said, returning. "Uncertainty and fear are part of his stock in trade. It will suit him far better to wait several years—and with the disruption to his people you have caused, he will have many better things to do with his time for many years. Both Master Verne and I are of the opinion that the Werewolf King will trouble us no more for quite some time to come."

I did relax at that. Something about Morgan's calm, English voice was infinitely reassuring. "In that case, I say we should celebrate."

"An excellent suggestion, sir!"

The party went on for a long time.